Arabic Sociolinguistics

Arabic Sociolinguistics

Topics in Diglossia, Gender, Identity, and Politics

Reem Bassiouney

Georgetown University Press
Washington, DC

First published in the United Kingdom by
Edinburgh University Press

Typeset in 11/13pt Ehrhardt
by Servis Filmsetting Ltd, Stockport, Cheshire, and
printed and bound in Great Britain by
CPI Antony Rowe Ltd, Chippenham, Wilts

Library of Congress Cataloging-in-Publication Data
Bassiouney, Reem.
Arabic sociolinguistics / Reem Bassiouney.
p. cm.
Includes bibliographical references and index.
ISBN 978-1-58901-573-9 (pbk. : alk. paper)
1. Sociolinguistics–Arab countries. 2. Language and culture–Arab countries. 3. Arabic language–Social aspects. 4. Arabic language–Dialects. I. Title.
P40.45.A65B37 2009
306.440917'4927–dc22
2009024873

∞ This book is printed on acid-free paper meeting the requirements of the American National Standard for Permanence in Paper for Printed Library Materials.

15 14 9 8 7 6 5 4 3 2

Contents

Acknowledgements

This work is the product of years of investigation in both sociolinguistics in general and Arabic sociolinguistics in particular. Two semesters of research-leave from the University of Utah and Georgetown University have helped me focus more on this book. I would like to thank both universities for this research period.

Professor Jean Aitchison has been and will remain a constant friend and a great scholar. I thank her for drawing my attention to Edinburgh University Press. Dr Mahmoud Hassan will also remain a teacher, a friend and a model of integrity. Thank you also to Professor Yasir Suleiman for suggesting the title *Arabic Sociolinguistics* instead of *Arabic and Society* and for being an inspiring scholar. I would like also to thank the two anonymous reviewers who read my proposal and made useful recommendations. Thank you to the reader of the manuscript, whose suggestions were very useful and insightful, and whose knowledge of the field is exemplary. I am very lucky to have such a reader. Needless to say any oversight is my responsibility.

I have benefited in one way or another from discussions and exchange of ideas, not necessarily about linguistics, with a lot of colleagues and friends. Among those, in alphabetical order, are: Ahmed Dallal, Marianna Di Paolo, Mushira Eid, Gail Grella, Clive Holes, Joe Metz, Carol Myers-Scotton, Karin Ryding, Keith Walters, Kees Versteegh and Malcah Yaeger-Dror.

There is nothing as satisfying as having students who are interested and engaged in the topics one teaches. My students in many ways helped me clarify my ideas in fruitful and stimulating class discussions. I thank them.

The team at Edinburgh University Press are a delight to work with. Nicola Ramsay and Sarah Edwards are both extremely dedicated and efficient. James Dale has been enthusiastic about the book, friendly, resourceful and efficient. Thanks also to Fiona Sewell my copy-editor for her diligent work.

Thanks to all my family, whose support and belief in me were my main incentive always, especially my parents Nour El-Hoda and Ahmed Refaat. It becomes clearer over time that without moral support from people who care, the journey is aimless.

This book is dedicated to Mark Muehlhaeusler.

Charts, maps and tables

Abbreviations

LANGUAGES AND VARIETIES

CA	Classical Arabic
CB	Christian Baghdadi Arabic
ECA	Egyptian Colloquial Arabic
ESA	Educated Spoken Arabic
ICA	Iraqi Colloquial Arabic
LCA	Lebanese Colloquial Arabic
MB	Muslim Baghdadi Arabic
MSA	Modern Standard Arabic
SA	Standard Arabic
SCA	Saudi Colloquial Arabic
SYCA	Syrian Colloquial Arabic
TCA	Tunisian Colloquial Arabic

OTHER ABBREVIATIONS AND SYMBOLS

acc	accusative
adj	adjective
adv	adverb
asp	aspect
conj	conjugation
CP	projection of a complementiser
def	definite
dem	demonstrative
det	definite article
EL	embedded language
f	feminine

fut	future tense
gen	genitive
H	high, highly valued
Imperf	imperfect tense
indef	indefinite
ind	indicative
juss	jussive
L	low, lowly valued
loc adv	locative adverb
m	masculine
ML	matrix language
n	noun
neg	negative marker
nom	nominative
NP	noun phrase
par	particle
part	participle
pass	passive
perf	perfect tense
pl	plural
poss par	possessive particle
pp	prepositional phrase
pr	pronoun
prep	preposition
pres	present tense
rel	relative pronoun
sub	subjunctive
sg	singular
v	verb
voc	vocative
1	first person
2	second person
3	third person

Conventions used in this book

TRANSCRIPTION

This book uses the following symbols shown in Table 1 to transcribe examples and other linguistic data. The table illustrates the pronunciation of the letters of the Arabic alphabet in Modern Standard Arabic.

Table 1 Pronounciation of the letters of the Arabic alphabet in Modern Standard Arabic

ا	*ʔ / a / a:*	ذ	*ð*	ظ	*ẓ*	ن	*m*
ب	*b*	ر	*r*	ع	*ʕ*	ه	*h*
ت	*t*	ز	*z*	غ	*ġ*	و	*w / u / u:*
ث	*θ*	س	*s*	ف	*ʃ*	ي	*y / i/ i:*
ج	*j /g* *	ش	*ʃ*	ق	*q*		
ح	*ḥ*	ص	*ṣ*	ك	*k*	ـة	*-a*
خ	*x*	ض	*ḍ*	ل	*l*	ء	*ʔ*
د	*d*	ط	*ṭ*	م	*m*		

Note: *In Egypt, *g* is accepted as the MSA pronunciation of the letter ج in addition to *j*.

This study uses a broad kind of transcription. However, it should be noted that the data used in this book is mainly spoken data. Thus there is considerable variation within that data. For instance, the same word could be pronounced by the same speaker first with a long vowel and then with a short one in the same stretch of discourse. It is important for sociolinguists to capture the performance of speakers, rather than the idealised way in which words and phonemes are 'supposed' to be pronounced. Thus, the aim of transcribing the data is not to idealise but to render actual pronunciation.

Within the examples, a forward slash denotes a short pause, while two slashes denote a long pause.

GLOSSES

For the benefit of students and researchers who are not necessarily specialised in Arabic, or in all dialects of Arabic, most examples are glossed, except those in which the structure is not highlighted.

In the glosses, whenever verb forms are fully analysed, the gloss follows the translation for verbs in the perfect (which has a suffix conjugation in Arabic), whereas the gloss precedes the translation for the imperfect (which has a prefix conjugation), while the mood marking of the verb – if present – is glossed in its natural location at the end of the verb unit.

However, the glossing of examples is related to the context of the example, and is not always detailed. If the example is intended to demonstrate how individuals switch between two varieties, or languages, and if this demonstration concentrates on specific morpho-syntactic variables (such as demonstratives, negation, tense, aspect, mood marking and case marking) then the glossing is detailed as in the example below from Chapter 2:

(76)	*ka:na*	*l-gahdu̲*	*mustanfara̲n̲*	*fi*	*muwa:gahati̲*	*muʃkila:ti̲*
	To be-3msg-perf	det-effort-nom	exerted-acc	in	facing-gen	problems-gen
	l-ams					
	det-yesterday					

'All efforts were exerted to face the problems of the past.'

If, on the other hand, the example is used to demonstrate an argument which is more related to content, then the glossing is more basic, as in the following example from Chapter 4:

(56) *ya rabb/ daʕwa min ʔalb ʕumru ma faqad il- ʔamal wala il-ʔima:n bi:k'*
Voc God/ prayer from heart never neg lost the hope nor the-faith in-you
'Oh God. This is a prayer from a heart that never lost hope or belief in you.'

Thus, the glossing is not consistent but changes with the change in the nature of the analysis of the data. However, all abbreviations and symbols are listed above.

Now note this last example, from Chapter 4:

(58) لقد دخلت هذه الدار وهي مجرد جدران..كانوا لا يوافقون على زواج أبيكم مني..و كنت وحيدة ابوى..و لم اكن فلاحة..فزرعتهما أشجاراً و خضروات..و قال جدكم لأبيكم كيف تتزوج بنت أرملة لا عائلة لها؟

laqad	*daxaltu*	*ha:ða*	*ad-da:r*	*wa*	*hiya*	*mugarrad*	*gudra:n/*
Already	enter-1sg-perf	this	the-house	and	she	only	walls

ka:nu:	*la:*	*yuwa:fiqu:n*	*ʕala*	*zawa:g*	*ʔabi:kum*	*minni:/*
be-3mpl-perf	neg	3mpl-agree	on	marriage	father-yours	from-me

wa	*kuntu*	*waḥi:dat*	*ʔabawayyi/*
and	be-1sg-perf	lonely	parents-mine

wa	*lam*	*ʔakun*	*falla:ḥa/*	*fazaraʕtuhuma:*	*ʔaʃga:ran*	*wa*	*xuḍrawa:t*
and	neg	1sg-be	peasant/	plant-1sg-they	trees-acc	and	vegetables

wa	*qa:la*	*gaddukum*	*li-ʔabi:kum/*	*kayfa*
and	say-3msg-perf	grandfather-your-pl	to-father-your-pl	how

tatazawwag	*bint*	*ʔarmala*	*la:*	*ʕa:ʔila laha:/*
2msg-marry	girl	widow	neg	family to-her

'I had come to your grandfather's house when it was just walls. They did not approve my marriage to your father. I was an only child and I was no peasant then. Since then, I have planted trees and vegetables. Your grandfather then asked your father how he can marry a mere widow with no family.'

This example is, in fact, from a novel written in Egypt about Egyptians. I transcribe it as an Egyptian would read it; with the g rather than the j.

PERSONAL NAMES, TITLES AND TOPONYMS

This book employs the transliteration scheme of the Library of Congress to transcribe names and titles. This facilitates the search for these materials in Library catalogues, where the same conventions are used (Table 2).

Table 2 Transliteration scheme of the Library of Congress

ا	ā	ذ	dh	ظ	ẓ	ن	m
ب	b	ر	r	ع	ʿ	ه	h
ت	t	ز	z	غ	gh	و	w / ū
ث	th	س	s	ف	f	ي	y / ī
ج	j	ش	sh	ق	q		
ح	ḥ	ص	ṣ	ك	k	ة	-ah
خ	kh	ض	ḍ	ل	l	ء	ʾ
د	d	ط	ṭ	م	m	ى	-á

Place-names, or proper names of prominent persons for whom there is a common equivalent in English, are excepted from this rule; hence, I refer to

Jamāl ʻAbd al-Nāṣir as ʻNasser', and to al-Quds as ʻJerusalem'. Lesser historical figures, however, are given in full transliteration, in order to preserve the original form of the name, e.g. Salāmah Mūsá.

CITING AT ONE REMOVE

I don't give bibiliographic details of sources I mention as cited in another work, e.g. for Silverstein (1998) cited in Woolard (2004), I give source details for Woolard but not for Silverstein.

Introduction

The earth speaks Arabic.

Egyptian catchphrase

This Egyptian catchphrase has always intrigued me. Of course it shows the amount of pride Egyptians and perhaps all Arabs take in their language. But what I find fascinating is the word 'Arabic'. What does 'Arabic' here refer to? Is it the Standard Arabic used in newspapers? The Classical Arabic of the Qur'an? The colloquial Arabic of Egypt?[1] Or is it the Gulf Arabic of Saudi Arabia? For the layperson, there is only one language called 'Arabic'. For the linguist, there are at least three different varieties of Arabic in each Arab country, and some linguists even claim that there are at least five different levels of Arabic in each country, not counting the different dialects of each country.

This is the first problem that one encounters in analysing this catchphrase. The other problem that one encounters is why, if 'Arabic' is the inherent language of the earth, are Arabs so keen on teaching their children foreign languages. Why is it that in North Africa French is still a crucial instrumental language? And why is it that at the time that all Arabs are defending their language as the main source of pride and identity they are also mastering English and French? The answers to all these questions are not clear cut. Language's symbolic nature has always been important in any community and/or nation. Before proceeding with what this book discusses, I would like to refer to specific incidents that the reader may find interesting and that in general terms show the importance of Arabic sociolinguistics and the relationship between language and society.

Years ago, when I was still working in the UK, I was asked by an organisation to become a simultaneous translator in a forum that discusses security issues in Iraq. The forum had Iraqis from different sects and factions. There were Shiites, Sunnis, Kurds and Christians, as well as British politicians. I started translating from Arabic to English. The Iraqis would usually express themselves in Arabic, whether Standard, Iraqi or both, and I would simultaneously translate what had been said into English. While I was interpreting, a female politician started speaking in a language that I did not recognise. I was then at a loss, thinking that perhaps she was speaking a dialect of Iraqi that I was not familiar with. I stopped translating and waited until she finished. Once she had finished, a colleague of hers started translating what she had said into Iraqi Arabic. After he did that, I then translated his Iraqi Arabic into English. It took me minutes to realise that she was a female Kurdish politician and her colleague who was translating for her was also Kurdish. During the break, which I was very glad to have, the female Kurdish politician approached me in a friendly manner and started addressing me in Iraqi Arabic. For an outsider it may seem impractical and a waste of time that she should speak Kurdish first to an audience that was mostly not Kurd, and then her colleague should have to translate, and then I have to translate. For a sociolinguist, this is perhaps expected. I asked her why she had not spoken 'Arabic' since she was so fluent, and she said confidently that she was Kurdish and by speaking Kurdish, she was making a political statement.

Her statement was indeed appealing, and it alludes to the power and symbolic significance of language choice. The relations between language and politics, and language and identity, are worth investigating. This is exactly what I do in Chapters 2 and 5 of this book.

Later, still while I was working in the UK, I came across a young Moroccan woman working in the Foreign Office. She was a second-generation Moroccan, and I was happy to discover that her parents were keen on teaching her 'Arabic' and that she spoke 'Arabic' fluently. And indeed she did – except that she spoke Moroccan Arabic. We decided to meet for lunch, and she started complaining to me in Moroccan Arabic about her Moroccan husband, who did not understand her. Apart from knowing the general topic of discussion, I did not understand much of what she said, nor did she understand my Egyptian Colloquial Arabic (ECA), nor even my attempts at speaking Modern Standard Arabic (MSA). We basically, after five minutes, reached a deadlock. It was clear that we both had to switch to English to understand each other. It was also clear that the Moroccan woman was exposed to neither ECA nor MSA. She was fluent only in Moroccan Arabic. Had the woman been exposed to ECA or any other dialect and not specifically MSA via the media, TV and satellite channels, our communication would have been much easier. The dialects are sometimes mutually unintelligible, and while educated speakers have developed sets of strategies for communicating across dialect boundaries that include using resources from MSA, someone who knows only a dialect of spoken Arabic will be likely not to understand an educated speaker of another dialect or be able to make herself or himself understood, especially if one of the speakers comes from North Africa and the other does not. Speakers of ECA have an advantage, but only if their interlocutor has watched a lot of television in a country that broadcasts programmes from Egypt. Thus, after this incident

I could understand the fear that Arabs have of losing their grip on MSA and thus losing their concept of the nation. This will again be discussed in detail in Chapters 1 and 5, although there are many implications of this story that merit more investigation, especially the role of vernaculars in inter-dialectal communication and not just that of MSA.

A third event that left its impact on me was when I was invited to give a lecture at Cairo University about language choice and code-switching. Egypt, like any other country in the world, has more than one dialect spoken within it, the most prestigious one being the Cairene dialect for Egyptians. After I finished the lecture, a male student came to me to congratulate me on giving a very good lecture. He was speaking to me in perfect Cairene Arabic. We started a conversation, and he then told me that he comes from upper Egypt (*al-ṣaʕi:d*), which has a distinct dialect/dialects characteristically different from Cairene Arabic phonologically, semantically and even morpho-syntactically. I then asked him how he spoke Cairene Arabic so fluently, and he seemed a bit embarrassed and said to me 'I speak Cairene Arabic to you. I can never speak it to my mother. If I speak Cairene Arabic to my mother, she will call me a sissy and possibly kill me!' Knowing how powerful upper-Egyptian women are reputed to be, I feared he might be right. Note that speakers of non-standard language varieties are expected or even compelled to master prestige varieties. In Egypt, for a person from upper Egypt this would be Cairene. However, the survival of an upper-Egyptian dialect amidst all the pressure from a highly centralised Egypt for all Egyptians to speak Cairene Arabic is indeed worth investigating. The survival of a dialect which may be less prestigious but which carries its own 'covert prestige' (cf. Trudgill 1974) will be discussed in detail in Chapter 3 of this book.

I recall that throughout my childhood in Egypt I was fascinated and confused by the way women were addressed. We were living in the second floor of an eight-storey building. Our first-floor female neighbour, who was a middle-aged woman with a husband and four children, was always addressed by the caretaker as '*ḥagga laila*', 'Laila who had made the pilgrimage', thus her first name was always used with the title '*ḥagga*'. Our third-floor neighbour, on the other hand, was always referred to as '*ʕummi sa:miḥ*', 'mother of sa:miḥ', and never by her first name. The reason why one neighbour maintained her first name although she still had sons and another lost it is still beyond me. But it also shows that the linguistic situation of the Arab world, especially that pertaining to women, is complicated, as will be made clear in Chapter 4.

ARABIC SOCIOLINGUISTICS

My book is called *Arabic Sociolinguistics*. Therefore, in this section I will explain what sociolinguistics is and why Arabic is important. I will start with the latter.

Arabic is the sole or joint official or national language of twenty-three countries, ranging from Morocco in the north to Sudan in the south and from Mauritania to Yemen. Native speakers of Arabic total about 300 million. Arabic has always been important to western linguists. However, Arabic variationist sociolinguistics flourished after Ferguson's article about diglossia in 1959. In this article, he drew the distinction between the standard language and the different vernaculars of each Arab country. In subsequent years, Arabic variationist sociolinguistics research has tended to concentrate on relating variation in language use to demographic factors like education, age and sex/gender, and more recently on issues related to language and identity and its ethnic and nationalistic manifestations (cf. Suleiman 2003: 1).[2]

In addition, Holes (2004: 8) states that 'the earliest definite textual evidence we have for the existence of a distinct language identifiable as Arabic is an inscription on a tombstone found at Nemara in the Syrian desert. This has been dated to AD 328 – recent by the standards of Semitic languages.' He also suggests that a spoken language may have existed before that.

In the next paragraphs I will define the term sociolinguistics and the main themes that sociolinguists are concerned with as well as the tasks of sociolinguists. I will briefly touch on the problems of terminology in the field. After that I will highlight the contents of this book as well as the limitations of this work. The last section is devoted to the organisation of the book.

There are two kinds of linguistic analysts: those concerned with universals and what languages have in common, and those who look for differences between individuals in relation to a community of speakers. The former are theoretical linguists and the latter are sociolinguists (Shuy 2003). According to Gumperz and Hymes (1972) theoretical linguists analyse linguistic competence while sociolinguists analyse communicative competence. Communicative competence is defined by Gumperz as the ability of the individual to 'select from the totality of grammatically correct expressions available to him, forms which appropriately reflect the social norms governing behaviour in specific encounters' (1972: 205).

Sociolinguistics, according to Crystal (1987: 412), is 'the study of the interaction between language and the structures and functioning of society'. The field of sociolinguistics has developed vastly within the last fifty years (cf. Paulston and Tucker 2003). Now the field 'examines in depth more minute aspects of language in social context' (Shuy 2003: 5).

According to Hymes (2003: 30), 'diversity of speech has been singled out as the hallmark of sociolinguistics'. Sociolinguistics entails relations other than social and grammatical structures that can be studied qualitatively. Sociolinguists all agree that no normal person and no normal community is limited to a single way of speaking, nor to unchanging monotony that would preclude indication of respect, insolence, mock seriousness, humour, role distance etc.

In studying language in society and the ways in which linguistic resources and access to them are unequally distributed, sociolinguists give evidence of how patterns of linguistic variation reflect and contrast social differences. In studying responses language users have to instances of language use, they demonstrate the reality and power of affective, cognitive and behavioural language attitudes. In analysing how language users create links between language varieties and users, institutions, or contexts, they uncover language ideologies that create social realities. These are only some of the things that sociolinguists are concerned with. The list is indeed very long.

THE DEVELOPMENT OF SOCIOLINGUISTICS AS A FIELD OF STUDY

Sociolinguistics is in fact a recent field of study, as was said earlier. This may be because, as Labov puts it, it is a field that depended to a large extent on the development of technology. According to Labov nothing could be achieved until the field developed a clearer way of presenting phonological structure, which required the development of tape recorders, spectrograms, sampling procedures, and computers to process large quantities of data (in Shuy 2003: 5). However, such a claim is only true for variationist sociolinguists, not the many who have studied language policy, code-switching and language ideology. The interest in the differences in ways people speak is very old, and Arabic linguistics as a field may be traced back to Khalīl ibn Aḥmad (d. between 776 and 791), if not before (cf. Bohas et al. 2006). Khalīl ibn Aḥmad was an Arab philologist who compiled the first Arabic dictionary and is credited with the formulation of the rules of Arabic prosody.

In fact, at the beginning of the twentieth century, there was a great interest in dialectology (see Chapter 5). Linguists of the colonising powers started becoming interested in the dialects and the linguistic situations of the colonised countries. Because of the existence of colonies for countries like France, the UK, the Netherlands and Portugal, linguists started describing multilingual situations, language contact and creolisation (cf. Whiteley 1969; Houis 1971). However, until 1961, the term 'sociolinguistics' was not listed in the *Webster new international dictionary* (Shuy 2003).

Issues of terminology are not entirely resolved even now (cf. Shuy 2003). How do we define a community? What is a social class? What is the difference between code-switching and borrowing? Or even questions related purely to Arabic, like: what is educated spoken Arabic? Is there a pure Standard Arabic? These are not easy questions to answer.

To give an example of such problems of defining terms, the variationist linguist Labov objected to the term 'sociolinguistics' as early as 1965. Until 1965 there was no name agreed upon to define the field; should it be called linguistics, since this is indeed a way of examining language? Or should it be called language and culture, sociology of language, or language and behaviour?[3]

In spite of the imprecision of sociolinguistic terms in general, as a field of study it has yielded insights into the way people use language that are unprecedented in their significance, as will become clear in this book. It is sociolinguistics that has helped us understand each other more as well as acknowledge differences and similarities between us and others – whoever this 'us' is and 'others' are.

AIMS OF THE BOOK

This book provides an up-to-date account of major themes in Arabic sociolinguistics. It discusses trends in research on diglossia, code-switching, gendered discourse, language variation and change, and language policies in relation to Arabic. In doing so, it introduces and evaluates the various theoretical approaches, and illustrates the usefulness and the limitations of these approaches with empirical data. Note that a significant number of the theoretical approaches introduced are based on or inspired by western, especially Anglo-American work, on sociolinguistics. The reasons for this will be discussed in detail in the next section. The book aims to show how sociolinguistic theories can be applied to Arabic, and conversely, what the study of Arabic can contribute to our understanding of the function of language in society.

This book addresses both students and researchers of Arabic and linguistics. The book will not require any knowledge of Arabic, nor will it focus narrowly on a single Arabic dialect, or a single group of Arabic dialects; instead, it summarises the present state of research on Arabic in its various forms. The book, also, does not require knowledge of sociolinguistics or linguistics, though knowledge of both is of course an asset in reading this work.

There are inevitably crucial topics that cannot be covered in this book but that definitely need to be addressed. Thus, pidginisation and creolisation, though mentioned in passing in this book, deserve a book by themselves, although studies in the topic are still developing (cf. Versteegh 2001). Also, with the large number of Arab immigrants in different parts of the Arab world, one has to acknowledge the unique and interesting status of Arabic in the diaspora (cf. Rouchdy 1992). Finally, Arabic as a minority language in different parts of the world is again a topic of interest and has been discussed by Versteegh (2001) and Owens (2007).

One problem that I encountered in writing this book is dividing it into chapters. This has sometimes been done forcibly, since language variation and change are related to gender, and gender is related to politics, while politics is related to diglossia, and diglossia is related to code-switching. Since there has to be a division somewhere, I have had to divide the book into different chapters.

ORGANISATION OF THE BOOK

The framing of the book is crucial though not symbolic in itself. Each chapter starts with a discussion of classic work conducted on the west and then moves on to the Arab world. This is not because I believe that work conducted on the Arab world is subordinate to work conducted on the west but because of other reasons. First, a great number of works published in the western world about the Arab world adopt the classic theories that I discuss, even though these theories were applied first in the west. This is not wrong in any way as long as theories are modified and adjusted to explain the situation in the Arab world. Second, the aim of the book is to help scholars and students to begin thinking about how and why matters of language in the Arab world are not always like matters of language in the west. This cannot be done unless I shed light on the essential theories of western linguists. Lastly, as a matter of practicality, since the book does not assume prior knowledge of linguistics or Arabic, as was said earlier, although knowledge of both is an asset, it is necessary to familiarise the reader with the groundbreaking research in the west before discussing the Arab world.

The book is divided into five chapters. The first chapter presents a bird's-eye view of the linguistic status quo of the Arab world. This is achieved by introducing the reader first to the diglossic situation in the Arab world and its implications, then to the different approaches to the grouping of dialects in the Arab world.

The second chapter examines diglossic switching and code-switching as a single phenomenon. In this chapter I give an overview of theories of code-switching that concentrate on assigning structural constraints on switching, thus answering the question of how switching occurs, and theories that examine the motivations for switching – why people switch. The chapter refers to studies done by a number of linguists as well as two studies conducted by myself.

In Chapter 3, I highlight three crucial theories in examining variation: the social class theory, the social networks theory and the third wave approach to variation studies. I first shed light on methods used in quantitative variation research and problems related to them. Then I concentrate on specific variables that trigger language variation and change, and finally I discuss diglossia and levelling.

In Chapter 4, I concentrate on gender, starting with different theories that examine the relation between gender and language, as well as gender universals and postulates about gender in general and gender in the Arab world in particular. I also examine the speech of educated women in Egypt in this chapter and how they at times challenge the gender universals.

The final chapter deals with the relation between language policies and politics in the Arab world. I examine some case studies and the political/historical factors that influence language policy, as well as the relation between language policies and language ideologies. The status of Arabic and foreign languages in the education system of countries in the Arab world is highlighted. Linguistic rights are also discussed.

What I try to do throughout is to provide empirical data from my own research, in addition to data from other studies, to help explain the phenomena discussed. Thus there is in most chapters a section on data analysis.

When discussing Arabic sociolinguistics, Owens mentions that studies may still lack the feel of a coherent entity, and his explanation for this is as follows: 'Arabic covers sociolinguistic landscapes whose only coherency at times appears to be the almost accidental fact that the language used in each part happens to be Arabic' (Owens 2001: 463).

Indeed, writing a book about Arabic sociolinguistics is a challenging task. Arabic sociolinguistics has proven to be a vast field and one that has not yet been completely discovered. It is therefore unavoidable that there has to be a selection and focus on particular issues, topics and studies and not others.

NOTES

1. The phrase is spoken in colloquial Egyptian Arabic. Still, it is not clear Egyptians mean colloquial Egyptian by 'Arabic'.
2. It is worth mentioning that there is still a large amount of work done on issues of language policy and planning, descriptions of linguistic situations in various countries, Arabisation, debates about the proper role of second or foreign languages, and corpus planning, especially technical vocabulary. These issues will be discussed in Chapter 5.
3. It is noteworthy, however, that Labov's objections to the term at the time were of a different nature. He did not want a hyphenated label for what he did; in other words, he did not want to be marginalised by a label in just the way that sociolinguists has been for some time, especially in the USA.

CHAPTER 1

Diglossia and dialect groups in the Arab world

> Mustafa is still Mustafa. He did not change. He still has two tongues in his mouth, two hearts in his chest. A tongue that speaks for him and a tongue that speaks against him. A heart that speaks for him and a heart that speaks against him. When he speaks sincerely his words are in colloquial. A colloquial that was the only variety he knew and used in narration before. But once he starts speaking what they dictate to him, then he speaks in the language of books, and his words become comic!
>
> Muhra, Mustafa's ex-wife, in *Qismat al-ghuramāʾ* ('The debtor's share') by Yūsuf al-Qaʿīd (2004)

This extract from the novel *Qismat al-ghuramāʾ* ('The debtor's share') reflects the tension and ambivalent feelings Egyptians have towards both Modern Standard Arabic (MSA) and Egyptian Colloquial Arabic (ECA). Perhaps it also reflects the tension that exists in all Arab countries, where people speak one language variety at home and learn a different one in school, write in one language and express their feelings in another, memorise poetry in one language and sing songs in another. Whether doing this is practical or not is a moot point. However, as a linguist, one knows that most linguists would agree that whenever one has more than one language or variety at one's disposal, it is indeed a good thing. Muhra, Mustafa's ex-wife, summarises the dilemma of the Arab world neatly when she says that Mustafa still has 'two tongues in his mouth, two hearts in his chest'. What this means exactly is that Mustafa, like all Egyptians and all Arabs, lives in a diglossic community. Diglossia is what I would like to discuss in the first part of this chapter.

This chapter is divided into two parts: the first part deals with issues relating to the vertical (diglossia) and the second deals with issues related to the horizontal (national varieties/groups of dialects). However, note that the focus in this chapter is the linguistic facts. I do not examine, in this chapter, the complex ways language attitude and exposure to other varieties might influence inter-dialectal comprehensibility or inter-dialectal conversation.[1] In section 1.1 I discuss the concept of diglossia as analysed by Charles Ferguson and others and the developments that have occurred in the evolution of this concept until the present day. I will also differentiate between MSA and Classical Arabic (CA) (sections 1.1.1–1.1.3). In section 1.2 I discuss the growing realisation by a number of linguists that the 'standard' variety is not necessarily the same as the 'prestige' variety in Arab speech communities. Finally I give concrete examples of different dialects in the Arab world and compare and contrast them in real contexts (sections 1.2.1–1.2.2).

1.1 DIGLOSSIA

1.1.1 An overview of the study of diglossia

The twenty-three countries in which Arabic is an official language have been described as diglossic speech communities, i.e. communities in which two varieties of a single language exist side by side. The official language is usually MSA[2] but there is usually at least one prestigious vernacular that is spoken in each country.

1.1.1.1 Ferguson's contribution to the study of diglossia

The following is Ferguson's definition of diglossia:

> Diglossia is a relatively stable language situation in which, in addition to the primary dialects of the language (which may include a standard or regional standards), there is a very divergent, highly codified (often grammatically more complex) superposed variety, the vehicle of a large and respected body of written literature, either of an earlier period or in another speech community, which is learned largely by formal education and is used for most written and formal spoken purposes but is not used by any sector of the community for ordinary conversation. (Ferguson 1972 [1959]: 345)

According to Ferguson, diglossia is a different situation from one where there are merely different dialects within a speech community. In diglossic communities there is a highly valued H (high) variety which is learned in schools and is not used for ordinary conversations. That is to say, no one speaks the H variety natively. The L (low) variety is the one used in conversations.[3] Most importantly, Ferguson claims that the crucial test for diglossia is that the language varieties in question must be functionally allocated within the community concerned (Fasold 1995: 35). Ferguson stresses that both H and L have to be in 'complimentary distribution functionally' (Boussofara-Omar 2006a: 630). According to him, diglossia is a relatively stable phenomenon. Ferguson implies that if a society is changing and diglossia is beginning to fade away this will have specific signs: mixing between the forms of H and L, and thus an overlap between the functions of H and L (Ferguson 1972 [1959]: 356).[4]

Ferguson proceeds by exemplifying situations in which only H is appropriate and others in which only L is appropriate (1972 [1959]: 236). According to him, the following are situations in which H is appropriate:

1. Sermon in church or mosque
2. Speech in parliament, political speech
3. Personal letters
4. University lecture
5. News broadcast
6. Newspaper editorial, news story, caption on picture
7. Poetry

He also gives situations in which L is the 'only' variety used:

1. Instructions to servants, waiters, workmen and clerks
2. Conversation with family, friends and colleagues
3. Radio soap opera
4. Caption on political cartoon
5. Folk literature

Ferguson's definition has been criticised and discussed extensively even by Ferguson himself (Ferguson 1996 [1991]), although it is only fair at that stage to note that he was describing a general linguistic situation; he did not set out to describe Arabic diglossia as language standardisation. He was describing diglossia cross-linguistically as it relates to issues of standardisation. He, as he acknowledged, was giving an idealised picture of the situation. Questions that arose from his definition of diglossia are summarised below.

How far apart or how close together should the H and L be for a language situation to be called 'diglossia'? This question was posed by Fasold (1995: 50ff.), who claimed that there are no absolute measures that could specify the distance between H and L in a diglossic community. Britto (1986: 10–12, 321) considered the same question and argued that H and L must be 'optimally' distant, as in Arabic, but not 'super-optimally', as with Spanish and Guaraní, or 'sub-optimally', as with formal–informal styles in English.[5]

Is there only one H? Ferguson spoke only about a distinction between H and L, without distinguishing the two different kinds of H such as exist in the Arab world, where there is a distinction between CA and MSA, although one has to note that this distinction is a western invention and does not correspond to any Arabic term, as will be clear in this chapter. However, CA is the religious language of the Qur'an and is rarely used except in reciting the Qur'an, or quoting older classical texts, while MSA could be used in a public speech, for example. Ryding, in her book *A reference grammar of Modern Standard Arabic* (2005:7), mentions that both MSA and CA are referred to as '*al-luġa al-fuṣha:*' (lit. 'the language of the eloquent'), 'the standard language'. This, in a sense, creates a shared past and present. She argues that there are few structural inconsistencies between MSA and CA. The main differences between both are stylistic and lexical rather than grammatical. However, she posits that the journalistic style of MSA has more flexible word order, coinage of neologisms and loan translations from western languages. For example, journalistic-style MSA uses the *iḍa:fa* construction (genitive 'of construction') to create neologisms for compound words or complex concepts. Bateson (1967: 84) posits that there are three kinds of changes between MSA and CA. MSA is characterised by having a simpler syntactic structure, by being different in lexicon because of modern technology, and by being stylistically different due to translations from other languages and the influence of bilingualism. However, these differences were not taken into account by Ferguson.

What happens in countries where more than one language is in everyday use, such as in Tunisia, where some people are also fluent in French? In such countries the term 'diglossia' is too narrow for the type of situation which exists.

How much switching can there be between H and L? Ferguson considered only to a very limited extent the fact that there can be switching between both varieties (H and L) in the same stretch of discourse. Again, this is because he did not set out to reflect the realistic situation in Arab countries but rather to give an idealised picture of diglossia. A number of more recent studies have examined switching between H and L in Arabic, some of which will be mentioned in Chapter 2.

Furthermore, Ferguson did not really discuss the sociolinguistic significance of the competing varieties. He did not propose that social factors may have a part to play in the negotiation of choice of variety in a diglossic community in specific sets of circumstances. This may be because, as he said himself, social factors of this kind were not in fashion at the time the paper was written. They were not considered 'true science' (1996 [1991]: 60). Instead, Ferguson placed much emphasis on the 'external situation' in determining language choice. He claimed that in certain set situations H is appropriate, while in others L is appropriate, without taking account of the possible significance of the individual in negotiating (or deliberately subverting) 'socially agreed' patterns of language choice (and ultimately changing them). Having reviewed these recent reformulations and revisions to his general theory, let us now briefly review the contributions Ferguson made to the study of Arabic diglossia.

Ferguson drew the attention of linguists to the existence of two language varieties in the Arab world, and the fact that people have different attitudes towards these two varieties, although the term 'diglossie' had been used earlier by the French dialectologist William Marçais with specific reference to Arabic

(Fasold 1995: 34). The following is an anecdote narrated by Ferguson (1990: 44). Ferguson says that he was once discussing with some Arab scholars a way of teaching foreigners Arabic – whether it is more useful to teach them MSA or one of the vernaculars used in the Arab world, like ECA, for example. One distinguished scholar said immediately that there was no need to teach them any kind of Arabic except MSA. The professor then claimed that he himself only used 'the correct kind of Arabic' (meaning MSA). Then the phone rang, and the distinguished scholar went to answer the phone. Ferguson said that he heard the man saying '*flonki*' [6](= 'How are you (f sg)?' in Baghdadi and many eastern Arabic dialects). When the man came back, Ferguson could not help commenting 'You said you never use a kind of dialect Arabic.' 'No, I never do', said the man. 'You know, there was a phone call a couple of minutes ago and I heard you say the word *flonki*.' The man nodded. 'Is that not a kind of dialect?' Ferguson asked. The scholar's reply was, 'Oh, I was just speaking to my wife.'

This story neatly highlights the discrepancy between people's perceptions of their language use and their actual language use. Note also that the professor thought it acceptable to use dialect with his wife (a person who is close and familiar) and that this fact did not invalidate his statement that he 'never used dialect'. This example shows one role played by the vernacular in the Arab world, which is that of signalling a relationship of intimacy. Gumperz (1976) discusses the role of code-switching as a means of creating solidarity (see Chapter 2).[7]

Despite all the subsequent criticism of Ferguson's theory, his proposal that there are two poles, an H and an L, is still valid, although they both formally and functionally overlap, perhaps more than Ferguson suspected or was ready to admit.[8] Mejdell (1999: 226) posits that the H–L division still has validity. After Ferguson's article, linguists tried to refine his concept by proposing intermediate levels, but still these intermediate levels cannot be understood unless one presupposes the existence of two 'poles', H and L. It may be that 'pure H' or 'pure L' does not occur very often, and that there are usually elements of both varieties in any stretch of normal speech, but still one has to consider a hypothetical pure H or L in order to presuppose that there are elements that occur from one or the other in a stretch of discourse. Ferguson himself did, in fact, recognise the existence of intermediate levels, but insisted that they cannot be described except within the framework of H and L:

> I recognised the existence of intermediate forms and mentioned them briefly in the article, but I felt then and still feel that in the diglossia case the analyst finds two poles in terms of which the intermediate varieties can be described, there is no third pole. (1996 [1991]: 59)

Ferguson certainly spurred linguists to examine diglossia, but he did not provide any definite answers to a great number of questions. As Walters (2003: 103) puts it,

> Our understanding of these phenomena [i.e. sociolinguistic phenomenona] would be far less nuanced than it is today had Fergie not taught us to look at Arabic as he did, looking past the norm and deviation paradigm that too often still characterises discussions of Arabic and all diglossic languages. In so doing, he encouraged us to examine with care specific varieties and specific sets of linguistic practices as ways of better understanding the sociolinguistic processes found across speech communities that at first glance might appear quite disparate.

Note also that Fishman (1967) in line with Ferguson identified specific domains to define diglossia. For example, speech events can fall under different domains, like a baseball conversation and an electrical engineering lecture. The major domains he identifies are family, friendship, religion, education and employment (see also Myers-Scotton 2006). He also claims that these speech events are speech-community specific.

Let us now examine models of diglossia which sought to refine and improve on Ferguson's ideas.

1.1.2 Theories that explain diglossia in terms of levels

After Ferguson's 1959 article on diglossia, Blanc (1960), Badawi (1973) and Meiseles (1980) thought proposing intermediate levels between H and L would give a more accurate description of the situation in the Arab world. Thus, they recognised that people shift between H and L, especially when speaking, but often they do not shift the whole way, resulting in levels which are neither fully H nor fully L. Blanc, basing his analysis on a tape recording of cross-dialectal conversation, distinguished between five varieties (1960: 85): classical, modified classical, semi-literary or elevated colloquial, koineised colloquial, and plain colloquial. Meiseles (1980) distinguished between four varieties: literary Arabic or standard Arabic, oral literary Arabic, educated spoken Arabic and plain vernacular. Badawi, on the other hand, proposed that there are five different varieties: *fuṣḥa: al-tura:θ* 'heritage classical', *fuṣḥa: al-ʕaṣr* 'contemporary classical', *ʕa:mmiyyat al-muθaqqafi:n* 'colloquial of the cultured', *ʕa:mmiyyat al-mutanawwiri:n* 'colloquial of the basically educated', and *ʕa:mmiyyat al-ʔummiyi:n* 'colloquial of the illiterates'. Badawi based his study on the output of the Egyptian media. His classification is both more crucial and more problematic than the other two, because his labelling of varieties implies both a stylistic and a social hierarchy.

Badawi tries to explain which levels of the spoken language are typical of which types of speaker and which type of situation in Egypt.

1. *fuṣḥa: al-tura:θ* 'heritage classical': This is the CA of the Arab literary heritage and the Qur'an. It represents the prescriptive Arabic grammar as taught at traditional institutions like Al-Azhar University (Egypt's

oldest university). It is a written language, but is heard in its spoken form on religious programmes on TV.

2. *fuṣḥa: al-ʕaṣr* 'contemporary classical': This is what I, as well as western-trained linguists, call MSA, which is a modification and simplification of CA created for the need of the modern age. It is used in news bulletins, for example. It is usually read aloud from texts and, if the speaker is highly skilled, may also be used in the commentary to the text.
3. *ʕa:mmiyyat al-muθaqqafi:n* 'colloquial of the cultured': This is a colloquial influenced by MSA which may be used for serious discussion, but is not normally written. It is used by 'cultured' (i.e. well-educated) people on television. It is also often the language used in formal teaching in Egyptian universities, and it is becoming the means of educating students and discussing with them different topics. In other words, it is becoming the medium of instruction in Egyptian classrooms.
4. *ʕa:mmiyyat al-mutanawwiri:n* 'colloquial of the basically educated': This is the everyday language that people educated to a basic level (but not university level) use with family and friends, and may occur on TV in a discussion of sport or fashion and other 'non-intellectual' topics. Cultured and well-educated people also use it when talking in a relaxed fashion about non-serious topics.
5. *ʕa:mmiyyat al-ʔummiyi:n* 'colloquial of the illiterates': This is the form of colloquial which is characterised by the absence of influence from MSA. On TV, it occurs only in the mouths of certain characters in soap operas, children's shows and comic situations.[9]

Badawi explains that almost everyone has more than one of these levels at their disposal; people often shift between them in the same conversation (1973: 93). Illiterates and the less well-educated, however, may find it difficult to shift as much, since they control only one or two levels with confidence. It is noteworthy that, when he defines different levels, Badawi uses sociolinguistic factors like education. Using education as a criterion can be considered a problem in his description. It is not clear whether the colloquial levels are built on socioeconomic variables like education or are just 'stylistic registers', or whether they can be both. It is worth mentioning here that Blanc (1960: 151) acknowledges the existence of 'gradual transitions between the various registers', while Badawi (1973: 95) says that these five levels do not have clear, permanent boundaries between one another, but rather fade into one another like the colours in a rainbow. Therefore instead of five, one could theoretically propose an infinite number of levels. Even in the three levels which Badawi defines as 'colloquial', there are no variants which are exclusively allocated to any one of the three. It is always a question of 'more or less', with no clear dividing lines between the levels.

Before I conclude this section, I will shed light on a different concept from that of levels, but one which is related still to diglossia, as well as the different dialects/varieties in the Arab world: the concept of Educated Spoken Arabic (ESA).

1.1.3 The idea of Educated Spoken Arabic

Mitchell claims that 'vernacular Arabic (meaning dialectal/colloquial Arabic) is never plain or unmixed but constantly subject to the influences of modern times' (1986: 9). According to him, ESA[10] is not a separate variety but is 'created' and 'maintained' by the interaction between the written language and the vernacular.[11] He gives the following reasons for the existence of ESA. First, in the modern world, educated men and women tend to converse on topics beyond the scope of a given regional vernacular. Second, educated people want to 'share and commune' with other Arabs of similar educational background. They want to promote forms that are required to meet the pressures of modernisation, urbanisation, industrialisation, mass education and internationalism (1986: 8). Therefore, Arabs need a shared means of communication, and this is inevitably influenced by what they all have in common: a knowledge of the structure and vocabulary of MSA. This does not mean, however, that they switch to 'oral MSA', but that they switch to a form of language which contains shared vernacular elements as well as MSA. I want to clarify that understanding regional/national dialects is tied to daily life to a great extent, and not academic/professional life; hence, speakers may not have ready vocabulary for discussing technological, learned subjects.

The idea of a shared ESA is important because it is concerned not just with the way people from the immediate community communicate, but with the way different Arabs from different communities communicate across community boundaries. Compare the following similar definition of ESA (from Meiseles):

> It is the current informal language used among educated Arabs, fulfilling in general their daily language needs. It is also the main means of Arabic interdialectal communication, one of its most important trends being its intercomprehensibility among speakers of different vernaculars, arising mainly from the speaker's incentive to share a common language with his interlocutor or interlocutors. (1980: 126)

Mitchell also tries to describe some general structural rules of this shared ESA. For example, in MSA dual number is marked throughout: in demonstratives, verbs, nouns, pronouns and adjectives. In ESA, according to Mitchell, it is marked only in the nouns and adjectives. Negation in MSA is expressed by the particles *lam*, *lan*, *la:* and *ma:*. These are replaced in ESA by other forms used in colloquial varieties with some differences between the regions.

The idea of ESA acknowledges the possibility of switching between the vernacular and MSA without assuming anything about intermediate styles. In that sense it is more inclusive and promising as a heuristic device than the concept of levels. Moreover, ESA tries to account for how Arabs from different countries manage to communicate together, rather than focusing on Arabs in a specific country. The idea that different Arabs from different communities modify their language when they speak together is worthy of attention since it is presumably a rule-governed, not a random, process.

However, the idea of ESA poses a number of questions about the nature of the synchronic relationship between MSA and the different vernaculars. First, the term 'educated Arabs' seems vague. Is an educated Arab a merely functionally literate one or a 'cultured' one? Second, if it is still difficult for linguists to agree about the different levels used even in a single community, how much more difficult could it be to try to describe what the rules are for inter-communal communication? In my view, one has to try to describe the situation in specific countries first. Merely claiming that ESA exists does not help in applying the concept to the language situation in a particular country, since Mitchell did not manage to give a comprehensive description of how ESA works: that is, of exactly what people do when they switch between MSA and their vernacular. Parkinson (2003) also argued that although ESA is supposed to be rule-governed, there are no clear rules that describe it. He claims that "Educated spoken Arabic may not actually be anything" (2003: 29). The following is Nielsen's criticism of ESA:

> ESA is a mixed variety which is very badly codified . . . apart from very few studies (for example Eid 1982), no research has established what kind of rules actually govern this mixing, nor do we know whether or not such rules are subject to generalisations. This is not to say that native speakers do not know how to mix; but we have no reliable information establishing that the mixing is not a phenomenon heavily influenced, say, by personal or regional factors. (1996: 225)

Part of the issue with ESA is the descriptive versus prescriptive notion of 'rule'. One has to be able to describe the linguistic situation thoroughly and meticulously before starting to specify a set of practices in a specific community or communities. One also needs to know whether there are discourse functions of ESA which govern its occurrence, and whether these functions differ from country to country.

In the next sections I concentrate on national varieties. However, before I list the groups of dialects or varieties in the Arab world, I want to clarify the distinction between a prestige variety and a standard one.

1.2 DIALECTS/VARIETIES IN THE ARAB WORLD

1.2.1 The concept of prestige as different from that of standard

There has been a growing realisation since the mid-1980s that variation in Arabic speech is not merely (or even mainly) a question of H interference in L. According to Ibrahim (1986: 115), 'the identification of H as both the standard and the prestigious variety at one and the same time has led to problems of interpreting data and findings from Arabic sociolinguistic research'. This identification is the result of applying western research to the Arab world, without noting the different linguistic situation. In research in western speech communities, researchers have generally been able to assume that the standardised variety of a language, the one that has undergone the conscious process of standardisation, is also the variety accorded the most overt prestige.

Many studies have shown that for most speakers, there is a prestige variety of L, the identity of which depends on many geographical, political and social factors within each country, and which may in certain circumstances influence speech. In Egypt, for non-Cairenes, it is the prestige variety of Egyptian Arabic Cairene; for Jordanian women from Bedouin or rural backgrounds, on the other hand, it may be the urban dialects of the big cities (Abdel-Jawad 1986: 58).

In a diachronic study conducted by Palva (1982), materials from Arabic dialects spoken, recorded and collected since 1914 in the Levant, Yemen, Egypt and Iraq were compared. Palva examined the occurrence of phonological, morphological and lexical items in the dialects over a period of time. He found that certain dialectal variants gradually become more dominant than the 'standard' variants. For example, the glottal realisation *ʔ* of the historical *q*, which is a phonological feature of several vernaculars in the area, became widespread and dominant rather than the MSA *q* (1982: 22–4). Holes (1983a, 1983b) discusses the influence of MSA on two Bahraini dialects from a phonological and lexical viewpoint. Amongst other observations, he shows that the degree of influence of MSA on the speech of educated Bahrainis is dependent on the social status of the speakers. The socially prestigious Sunni speakers are not influenced much by the standard, while the speech of the low-status Shiite speakers is relatively more influenced by the standard (1983a: 448).

Abu-Haidar (1991), in her study of the Muslim and the Christian dialects of Baghdad, posits that:

> Apart from MSA (the H variety for all Baghdadis), CB speakers [Christian Baghdadi] use their own dialect as a L variety in informal situations at home and with in-group members, while they use MB [Muslim Baghdadi] as another H variety in more formal situations with non-Christians. (1991: 92)

It has been realised that MSA is not the only source of linguistic prestige and that in virtually every Arab speech community that has been examined, there is a dominant L which exerts influence on the other lower-status Ls in that country or in the surrounding region. The reasons for its influence are various, but principal among them are factors like the socioeconomic dominance of the city over the countryside (e.g. Cairo) or the influence of a ruling political group (e.g. the royal families of the Gulf). The dialects of these entities become a symbol of their power and exercise a potent influence over those who come into contact with them or have to interact with speakers of these dialects. This sociolinguistic variation between different varieties will be discussed in detail in Chapter 3.

In the next section I introduce the five different groups of dialects that exist in the Arab world, in addition to both MSA and CA. I also discuss different approaches of classifying dialects in the Arab world.

1.2.2 Groups of dialects in the Arab world

1.2.2.1 Bedouin and sedentary dialects

There is more than one choice of approach to classifying dialects. One can use a synchronic approach classification, which is made by measuring and selecting salient linguistic variables for each dialect or group of dialects (Palva 2006: 604). This is the classification that will be adopted in section 1.2.2.2. On the other hand, one can also use a sociological, anthropological and historical approach which takes into consideration the division between Bedouin and sedentary dialects in the Arab world (Palva 2006: 605). The division in terms of Bedouin and sedentary reflects the historical settlements in the area as well as the language shift and change that have been taking place. Sedentary dialects could be further divided into rural and urban.

Cities in the Arab world do not necessarily speak an urban dialect. In fact in a number of cities in the Arab world speakers speak a Bedouin dialect, and in other cities the Bedouin dialect is more prestigious than the sedentary one (see Chapter 3).

Bedouin and sedentary dialects can be distinguished mainly by comparing and contrasting the realisation of phonological variables in both. However, morpho-syntactic variables as well as lexical ones are also significant. The realisation of the MSA phonological variable *q* as *g* has been a major criterion in distinguishing between Bedouin and sedentary dialects. According to Palva, 'Bedouin dialects have retained more morpho-phonemic categories than the sedentary dialects' (2006: 606). An example of this is the use of the indefinite marker in (*tanwi:n*) as in *kita:bin* (book) as opposed to the sedentary realisation *kita:b* (cf. Palva 2006: 605 for detailed examples of differences between Bedouin and sedentary dialects, and Versteegh 2001 for a historical discussion of dialects).

1.2.2.2 Regional dialects

Versteegh (2001: 145) distinguishes between five groups of regional dialects in the Arab world:[12]

1. Dialects of the Arabian peninsula, which are spoken in Saudi Arabia and the Gulf area
2. Mesopotamian dialects, which are spoken in Iraq
3. Syro-Lebanese dialects, which are spoken in Lebanon and Syria
4. Egyptian dialects, spoken in Egypt
5. Maghreb dialects, spoken in North Africa

Versteegh himself thinks that the division can at times be arbitrary and depends largely on geographical factors (2001: 145). There are, however, a number of similarities among all the dialects that differentiate them from MSA and CA. These similarities have led to a great deal of speculation about the emergence of dialects in the whole Arab world (cf. Holes 2004: Versteegh 2001).

In all the five groups of dialects, the MSA glottal stop disappears. For example, the MSA *raʔs* 'head' is in Syrian, north African and Egyptian Arabic *ra:s* (cf. Versteegh 2001: 107). Likewise the genitive case in the possessive construction is replaced by an analytical possessive construction. Thus *qalam al-walad*, (lit. 'pen def-boy') 'the boy's pen' is in Egyptian Arabic *il-ʔalam bita:ʕ il-walad* (lit. 'pen poss par def-boy'). In Levantine it will be *il-ʔalam tabaʕ il-walad* (lit. 'pen poss par def-boy'), and in dialects of the Arabian Peninsula it will be *il-ʔalam ḥagg il-walad* (lit. 'pen poss par def-boy'). Note that the

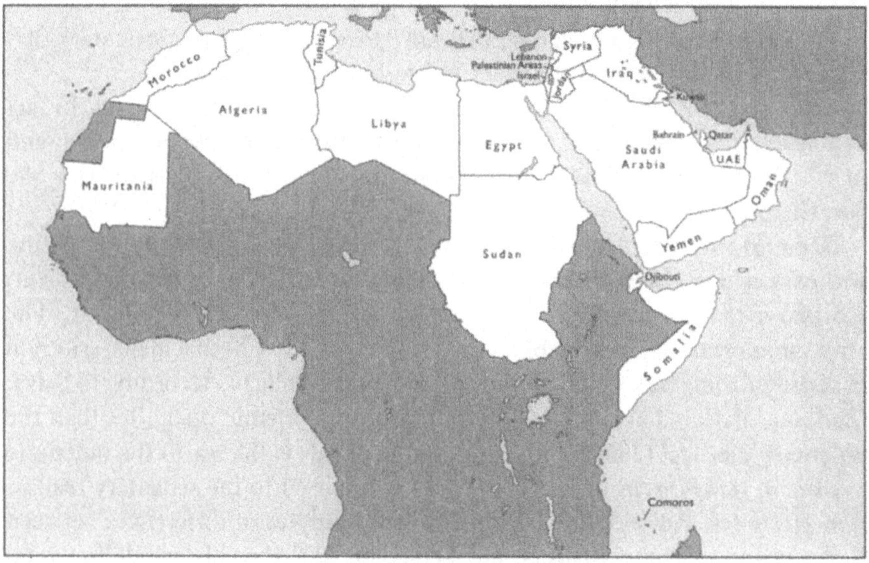

Map 1.1 The Arab world

possessive particle is different in the three examples of the dialects given above. Additionally, the MSA future aspectual marker *sa-/sawfa* is replaced in all the dialects by a different marker. In Syrian Arabic it is *raḥ(a)- laḥ(a)-*, in Egyptian Arabic it is *ḥa-*, in Moroccan Arabic it is *ġa-*, in Iraqi Arabic it is *raḥ*, and in Yemeni Arabic it is *ʔa* (Versteegh 2001: 108). Versteegh (2001: 98) comments on the range of variability across regional dialects by positing that, 'It is fair to say that the linguistic distance between the dialects is as large as that between the Germanic languages and the Romance languages, including Romanian, if not larger.' To some extent this postulation is exaggerated. However, it still alludes to the extent of differences between dialects.

Perhaps because of these differences between dialects, Arab governments are in general still keen on promoting Standard Arabic (SA) as their official language rather than the various vernaculars; this promotion of SA as the official language will be examined in detail in Chapter 5.

I want to illustrate some differences between the different vernaculars for countries in the Arab world by giving a detailed concrete example. I will choose five vernaculars that belong to the five groups discussed above. The vernaculars chosen are: Tunisian Colloquial Arabic (TCA), part of the North African group of dialects; ECA, part of the Egyptian group of dialects; Lebanese Colloquial Arabic (LCA), part of the Levantine group of dialects; Iraqi Colloquial Arabic (ICA), part of the Mesopotamian Arabic group; and finally Saudi Colloquial Arabic (SCA), part of the Gulf Arabic dialect group.

Note that I choose one dialect within Egypt, Cairene Arabic, and one dialect within Lebanon, the dialect of Beirut and so on and so forth. Thus, the examples do not represent the whole spectrum of dialects within each country but only give an example of the kind of differences that exist between different national vernaculars.

However, before starting to compare and contrast the differences, one first has to show the MSA counterpart.[13]

(1) **English**
'I love reading a lot. When I went to the library I only found this old book. I wanted to read a book about the history of women in France.'

(2) **MSA**

ʔana	*ʔuḥibbu*	*l-qira:ʔa*	*kaθi:ran/*	*ʕindama*	*ðahabtu*	*ʔila*	*l-mak-taba/*
I	1sg-love-ind	the-reading	a lot/	when	went-1sg	to	the-library/

lam	*ʔajid*	*siwa*	*ha:ða:*	*l-kita:b*	*al-qadi:m/*	*wa*	*kuntu*	*ʔuri:du*
neg	1sg-find	except	this	the-book	the-old/	and	was-1sg	1sg-want-ind

ʔan	*ʔaqraʔa*	*kita:ban*	*ʕan*	*tari:x*	*al-marʔa*	*fi*	*fara:nsa/*
that	1sg-read-sub	book-acc	about	history	the-woman	in	France

(3) **TCA**

ʔana	*n-ḥibb*	*il-qra:ya barʃa/*	*waqtalli*	*mʃi:t*	*l il-maktba/*
I	asp-1sg love	the-reading a lot/	When	walked-1sg	to-the-library

ma-lqi:ti-ʃ	*illa*	*ha l-kta:b*	*l-qdi:m/*	*u*	*kunt*	*nḥibb*
neg-1sg-find-neg	except	this-the-book	the-old/	and	was-1sg	1sg-love

naqra	*kta:b*	*ʕala*	*tari:x*	*l-mra*	*fi*	*fra:nsa/*
1sg-read	book	about	history	the-woman	in	France

(4) **ECA**

ʔana	*ba-ḥibb*	*il-ʔira:ya*	*ʔawi/*	*lamma*	*ruḥt*	*il-maktaba/*
I	asp-1sg love	the-reading	a lot/	When	went-1sg	the-library

ma-laʔit-ʃ	*ʔilla*	*l-kita:b*	*il-ʔadi:m*	*da/*	*wa na*	*kunt*	*ʕa:yiz*
neg-1sg-find-neg	except	the-book	the-old	this/	and I	was-1sg	sg-part

ʔaʔra	*kita:b*	*ʕan*	*tari:x*	*il-sitt*	*fi*	*faransa/*
1sg-read	book	about	history	the-woman	in	France

(5) **LCA**

ʔana	*b-ḥibb*	*il-ʔire:ya*	*kti:r/*	*lamma*	*reḥit*	*ʕ-al-maktebe/*
I	asp-1sg love	the-reading	a lot/	When	went-1sg	to-the-library

ma lʔe:t	*ʔilla*	*hal-i-kete:b*	*li-ʔedi:m/*	*wi*	*ken*	*beddi*
neg-1sg-find	except	this-the-book	the-old/	and	was-1sg	1sg-want

ʔeʔra	*kete:b*	*ʕan*	*tari:x*	*l-mara*	*b-fre:nse/*
1sg-read	book	about	history	the-woman	in France

(6) **ICA**

ʔa:ni	*ḥibb*	*il-iqra:ya*	*kulli:ʃ/*	*lamman*	*riḥit*	*l il-maktaba/*
I	1sg love	the-reading	a lot/	When	went-1sg	to the-library

ma lige:t	*ġe:r*	*haðe l-ikta:b*	*il-ʕati:g/*	*u*	*tʃinit*	*ari:d*
neg-1sg-find	except	this-the-book	the-old/	and	was-1sg	1sg-want

ʔaqra	*kta:b*	*ʕan*	*tari:x*	*al-marʔa*	*b-fransa/*
1sg-read	book	about	history	the-woman	in France

(7) **SCA**

ʔana	*ḥibb*	*il-gra:ya*	*kθi:r/*	*ḥi:n*	*reḥt*	*l-mekteba/*
I	1sg love	the-reading	a lot/	When	went-1sg	the-library
ma lge:t	*ġe:r*	*haða l-kta:b*	*il-gedi:m/*	*wa*	*kint*	*abġa*
neg-1sg-find	except	this-the-book	the-old/	and	was-1sg	1sg-aim-(want)
ʔagra	*kta:b*	*ʕan*	*tari:x*	*il-mara*	*fi*	*fransa/*
1sg-read	book	about	history	the-woman	in	France

I would like to mention that 'Arabic' – meaning CA, MSA and the different varieties – is a Semitic language, and therefore built on a root and pattern system. The root is 'a series of typically three consonants, always occurring in a fixed sequence that has lexical identity' (McCarus 2007: 240). For example, the root *k-t-b* means to write; writing and so on and so forth. The word *maktaba*, which ocurs in the examples and means 'library', is derived from this root. Pattern is defined by McCarus (2007: 240) as 'a fixed framework of consonants and vowels that likewise has lexical meaning'. McCarus gives the example of the pattern *mafʕal*, which denotes a noun of place. Although the root can change, the *ma-* and the vowel *a* before the consonant are obligatory. An example of this pattern is *maktab*, derived from the root *k-t-b* discussed above, and meaning 'office'. *Maktaba* also follows this pattern. This is worth mentioning because it will show the similarities and differences between the dialects and also explain why it is sometimes easy and at other times difficult to comprehend the different dialects for different natives of Arabic.

Now I will compare and contrast each clause in detail.

(8)	pr 1sg 'I'	v 1sg imperf-ind 'to like'	det-n 'reading'	adv 'a lot'
MSA	*ʔana*	*ʔuḥibbu*	*l-qira:ʔa*	*kaθi:ran*
TCA	*ʔana*	*n-ḥibb*	*il-qra:ya*	*barʃa*
ECA	*ʔana*	*ba- ḥibb*	*il-ʔira:ya*	*ʔawi*
LCA	*ʔana*	*b-ḥibb*	*il-ʔire:ya*	*kti:r*
ICA	*ʔa:ni*	*ḥibb*	*il-iqra:ya*	*kulli:ʃ*
SCA	*ʔana*	*ḥibb*	*il-gra:ya*	*kθi:r*

In this clause, the personal pronoun in four varieties is the same; the exception is in ICA, in which it is phonologically different. The verb is lexically the same but phonologically different in some varieties. Note that an aspectual maker *b-* that denotes the present tense in ECA and LCA is not used in all varieties. This is a morpho-syntactic difference that differentiates ECA and LCA from other varieties. The phonological realisation of the definite article and noun 'to read' is also different in all five varieties. The MSA *q* of *l-qira:ʔa* is realised as a *q* only in TCA and ICA, and is realised as *g* in SCA and as a glottal stop in ECA and LCA. Meanwhile, the adverb 'a lot' is in fact lexically different in MSA, TCA, ECA, and ICA. In LCA and SCA it is phonologically different from its MSA counterpart.

(9)	adv	v 1sg perf	prep	det-n
	'when'	'to go'	'to'	'the library'
MSA	*ʕindama*	*ðahabtu*	*ʔila*	*l-maktaba*
TCA	*waqtalli*	*mʃi:t*	*l*	*il-maktba*
ECA	*lamma*	*ruḥt*		*il-maktaba*
LCA	*lamma*	*reḥit*	*ʕ-*	*al-maktebe*
ICA	*lamman*	*riḥit*	*l*	*il-maktaba*
SCA	*ḥi:n*	*reḥt*		*l-mekteba*

This second clause is telling in terms of varieties. The adverb 'when' is lexically different in most varieties. The problem of the different usage of prepositions between varieties is very clear. The preposition 'to' is realised differently in four varieties. TCA and ICA use the same preposition in that example. In fact, ECA and SCA do not use a preposition at all, while each of the other varieties uses a different one from MSA. Also the verb 'to go' is lexically different in all varieties from MSA. It is also phonologically different in all varieties. Once more, phonological differences are prominent in the realisation of the noun 'library' with the definite article.

(10)	neg	v 1sg	-neg	part.	dem	det-n	det-adj	dem
	'not'	'to find'		'but'	'this'	'book'	'old'	'this'
MSA	*lam*	*ʔajid*		*siwa*	*ha:ða*	*l-kita:b*	*al-qadi:m*	
TCA	*ma-*	*lqi:-ti-*	*ʃ*	*illa*	*ha*	*l-kta:b*	*l-qdi:m*	
ECA	*ma-*	*laʔi-t-*	*ʃ*	*ʔilla*		*l-kita:b*	*il-ʔadi:m*	*da*
LCA	*ma*	*lʔe:-t*		*ʔilla*	*ha-*	*l-ikete:b*	*li-ʔedi:m*	
ICA	*ma*	*lige:-t*		*ġe:r*	*haðe*	*l-ikta:b*	*il-ʕati:g*	
SCA	*ma*	*lge:-t*		*ġe:r*	*haða*	*l-kta:b*	*il-gedi:m*	

The verb 'to find' *ʔajid* is realised as the jussive first person singular, with no mood marking (0-suffix), of the imperfect of *wajada*. The use of the jussive here is mandatory after the negative particle *lam*. The person is marked by the prefix *ʔa*. The varieties/dialects, on the other hand, invariably use derivations from the root *l-q-y* (to find) in the first person singular perfect form, rather than the imperfect form as MSA does. In the perfect form the person is marked by the suffix *-t*. Thus, MSA uses a different aspect/tense for the verb from all the dialects. MSA uses the imperfect, while all the varieties use the perfect.

Negation is also realised differently in most of the varieties; the discontinuous morphemes *ma-...-ʃ* occur only in TCA and ECA. Most of the other dialects use *ma-* only. The MSA demonstrative *ha:ða:* is phonologically different in all the five vernaculars. In fact ECA is structurally different from all other varieties in that the demonstrative occurs after rather than before the noun it modifies. The adjective 'old' is phonologically different in three varieties and the *q* is realised as a *q* only in MSA and TCA. In ICA it is also lexically different.

(11)	conj 'and'	pr 1sg 'I'	v 1sg perf 'to be'	v 1sg imperf-ind 'to want/ like'	par
MSA	*wa*		*kuntu*	*ʔuri:du*	*ʔan*
TCA	*u*		*kunt*	*nḥibb*	
ECA	*wa*	*na*	*kunt*	*ʕa:yiz* [pres part]	
LCA	*wi*		*ken*	*beddi*	
ICA	*u*		*tʃinit*	*ari:d*	
SCA	*wa*		*kint*	*abġa*	

Again, most of the differences among the six varieties are phonological, but there are still lexical and morphological differences in the realisation of the verb 'to want'. In ECA, it is a participle rather than a tensed imperfect verb as is the case with the other dialects. In fact, it is a different lexical item in five varieties and only ICA shares the same lexical item with MSA, but there are still phonological differences between the two. Note that MSA alone requires a complementiser with this verb.

(12)	v1sg imperf -sub 'to read'	n indef -acc 'book'	prep 'about'	n det-n 'history of women'	prep 'in'	n def 'France'
MSA	*ʔaqraʔa*	*kita:ban*	*ʕan*	*tari:x al-marʔa*	*fi*	*fara:nsa*
TCA	*naqra*	*kta:b*	*ʕala*	*tari:x l-mra*	*fi*	*fra:nsa*
ECA	*ʔaʔra*	*kita:b*	*ʕan*	*tari:x il-sitt*	*fi*	*faransa*
LCA	*ʔeʔra*	*kete:b*	*ʕan*	*tari:x l-mara*	*b-*	*fre:nse*
ICA	*ʔaqra*	*kta:b*	*ʕan*	*tari:x al-marʔa*	*b-*	*fransa*
SCA	*ʔagra*	*kta:b*	*ʕan*	*tari:x il-mara*	*fi*	*fransa*

The variation in prepositions is indeed apparent again in this clause. The preposition 'in' is realised differently in different dialects. ECA has a lexically different item for 'woman' from the other four varieties. There are morphological differences between TCA realisation of the first person and all the other varieties. Phonological differences are still apparent.

It is noteworthy, however, that in some cases the lexical differences are not very difficult to reconcile. Thus for the verb 'to want', ECA uses *ʕa:yiz*, TCA uses *nḥibb* and SCA uses *abġa*. In MSA the verb *ʔahabba* means 'to love'. The

MSA *baġa:* means 'to aim at', or 'to want'. Thus although four varieties use a different lexical item for the verb 'to want', all the lexical items are related in meaning via knowledge of MSA. This indeed poses the question of whether, with no knowledge of MSA at all and with knowledge of only one dialect, the one a person speaks natively, it would still be possible for people from Tunisia to understand, for example, people from Egypt or the Gulf.

Using the same example, I want to show the differences between two Germanic languages: German and Dutch.

(13) **German**
Ich lese sehr gerne. Als ich in zur Bibliothek ging, fand ich nur dieses alte Buch, obwohl ich ein Buch über die Geschichte der Frau in Frankreich hatte lesen wollen.

(14) **Dutch**
Ik hou heel erg van lezen. Toen ik naar de bibliotheek ging, vond ik slechts dit oude boek, hoewel ik een boek over vrouwengeschiedenis in Frankrijk had willen lezen.

As one can see from this example, even without knowledge of German or Dutch, the differences are similar to differences between the different vernaculars examined above. The examples make one wonder about the differences between different languages and different varieties and whether terms like 'language' and 'variety' are not political terms rather than linguistic ones.

In this section I wanted to give examples of the different groups of varieties in the Arab world. The question of whether people switch between their variety and MSA will be dealt with in more detail in the next chapter.

1.3 CONCLUSION

To conclude I would like to clarify that, first, Arabs perceive all the varieties discussed above as 'Arabic'. Second, all the varieties above came from countries in which 'Arabic', meaning SA is the sole official language. The complexity of the situation arises from the fact that native speakers of Arabic do not distinguish between MSA and CA. For them there is only one SA, as was said earlier. In addition, they also use the term 'Arabic' to refer to the standard language and the colloquials of different countries, the national varieties. In these matters native speakers and linguists can disagree. Left to their own devices, linguists could claim each of the national varieties as a separate, distinct language. Speakers of Arabic are aware of a larger entity that somehow unites them: SA. The H variety of diglossia, SA, provides educated individuals with some of the tools they need to understand other varieties.

NOTES

1. Examples of diglossic switching are given not in this chapter but in the next one.
2. It is important to mention at that stage that native speakers and constitutions in Arab countries do not specify what 'Arabic' refers to, but it is usually MSA. Native speakers also do not make a distinction between MSA and CA. For them there is only one kind of Standard Arabic, which is called '*fuṣha:*'.
3. Note that this H and L labelling reflects, first, language attitudes among users and, second, the superposed nature of the H. Likewise, it is worth mentioning that sociolinguists may feel discomfort with these labels, since clear covert prestige attaches so strongly to the L and since the L has sometimes been the target of attempts in Egypt and Lebanon, among others, to be considered the national variety. This issue of territorial nationalism as opposed to pan-Arabism will be dealt with in detail in Chapter 5.
4. Fishman (2002) defines diglossia slightly differently from Ferguson. For Fishman, a diglossic situation is one in which the roles of both varieties are kept separate; there are clear group boundaries between both languages or varieties. The access to the H variety or language is usually restricted to an outsider. He gives the example of pre-World War I European elites who spoke French or another H language or variety, while the masses spoke a different and not necessarily related language or variety. In his definition the H variety or language is a spoken standard, while in Arabic it is not the spoken variety of any country.
5. The question of how different the two varieties should be was perhaps not the main issue for Ferguson, who was more interested in the conditions which could give rise to diglossia in the first place.
6. The word means literally 'what is your colour?'.
7. Gumperz is mentioned here, although he did not discuss diglossia in the Arab world, because his concepts of the discourse functions of code-switching will be applied to diglossic switching in Chapter 2, and diglossic switching and code-switching will be studied within the same framework.
8. I assume that the overlap between H and L existed even at the time when Ferguson wrote his article (1959), since Arabic, as any other language, is dynamic rather than static and unchanging. Walters (1996a), posits that the linguistic situation in the Arab world has always been in a state of change.
9. In Egyptian soap operas almost all characters, even the educated ones, speak in ECA. Only in defined situations, like that of a lawyer in a courtroom, would a speaker use MSA or switch to any of the levels mentioned by Badawi. This has been the case since the beginning of the soap opera market in Egypt in the 1960s.
10. The idea of ESA started to take shape with the Leeds project in 1976, which 'comprises unscripted, unprepared conversations and discussions based on a wide range of interpersonal relationships' (El-Hassan 1977: 120; see also Mejdell 2006 for a full discussion of ESA). Note also that the data concentrated on educated speakers in Egypt and the Levant specifically.
11. The H variety and MSA are in many ways associated with writing and the written language, including the reading aloud of written texts.
12. The words 'dialects' and 'varieties' will be used interchangeably throughout this chapter.
13. The MSA example does not always include case and mood endings; it is, rather, the way it would have been spoken by a native speaker, and I am interested in the oral performance of this utterance.

CHAPTER 2

Code-switching

> Language duality is not a problem but an innate ability. It is an accurate reflection of a duality that exists in all of us, a duality between our mundane daily life and our spiritual one.
>
> Najīb Maḥfūẓ, Nobel Prize winner for literature 1988, in a letter to Luwīs ʿAwaḍ

Although he is referring here to the duality between ECA and MSA – what Ferguson calls diglossia – Maḥfūẓ touches upon one of the main functions of language choice. He does not think that duality or bilingualism in general is an impairment.[1] In fact, it is an enriching ability that all humans possess and that enables them to express themselves differently and express their diverse needs. He echoes what Myers-Scotton discusses in her book *Social motivations for code switching* (1993). She refers to code-switching as part of the 'communicative competence' of a speaker, which is the competence that individuals acquire from their community and which enables them to communicate effectively with other members of their community. This will be discussed in detail below. Note that Maḥfūẓ does not limit 'language duality' to a diglossic community or a bilingual one. In this chapter I will discuss code choice and code-switching, whether this code is a variety or a language. After an introduction and discussion of terminology (sections 2.1–2.3), the chapter falls into two main parts. The first part (section 2.4) will examine structural constraints on classic code-switching; switching between different languages, when one of the languages is a variety of Arabic (2.4.1), and diglossic switching as a subcategory of code-switching (2.4.2). I discuss structural constraints on code-switching by examining different theories that can be applied to Arabic. I then provide a case study from my work on structural constraints on diglossic switching as part of code-switching (2.4.2.1). The second part (section 2.5) explains the social motivations and discourse functions of switching in relation to Arabic. The first subsection will concentrate on classic code-switching (2.5.1) and the second subsection will deal with diglossic switching (2.5.2). Again at the end of this section I provide a case study of motivations for diglossic switching from my own work (2.5.2.1).

2.1 INTRODUCTION

Code-switching until very recently has been looked down upon for different reasons, in both the Arab world and the western world. In fact, in the Arab world switching between Arabic and a foreign language has been called by one Arab writer, according to Suleiman (2004: 227), 'linguistic prostitution'. It can also be considered a form of 'colonial penetration'. Before the classic article by Blom and Gumperz (1972) on code-switching between dialects of Norwegian in Hemnesberget (a Norwegian fishing town), code-switching was considered part of the performance of the imperfect bilingual who could not carry on a conversation in one language in different situations (Myers-Scotton 1993: 47).

When bilinguals are asked why they switch codes, they usually claim that they do so to fill in lexical gaps, i.e. they do not know a specific word in one of their languages so they use the word from the other one. They may also claim that they do not have a certain word to express their feelings in one of the codes they have mastered, so they have to switch. But this is not always true, because bilinguals can switch between a word from one code and an equivalent from another with exactly the same meaning. And when they switch consistently, they usually do so for a specific purpose (Romaine 1995: 169). If we approach code-switching as a discourse-related phenomenon, then we have to assume that it has sociolinguistic motivations. These motivations cannot be understood in terms of syntactic constraints only, although syntactic constraints are still crucial in that they govern where switching might take place.

The term 'code-switching' can be very broad or very narrow, as are all terms in sociolinguistics. It is noteworthy, however, that what Myers-Scotton calls code-switching does not apply just to switching between different languages, but also to switching between varieties of the same language. Therefore, according to her theory, diglossic switching is a kind of code-switching.[2] She argues that 'varieties is a cover term for selections at all linguistic levels so that choices between varieties include, for example, choices of one language rather than another, one dialect over another, one style or register over another, and one form of a directive or refusal over another' (Myers-Scotton 1998b: 18). Arguing from a similar perspective, Gumperz defines code-switching as 'the juxtaposition within the same speech exchange of passages of speech belonging to two different grammatical systems or subsystems' (1982a: 59). He also does not restrict code-switching to switching between different languages. Because of its greater flexibility, I think that Myers-Scotton's and Gumperz's definitions are more adaptable than other definitions. It is more precise to use the term 'code' rather than the terms 'language' or 'variety'. However, there is still a problem of terminology that needs to be addressed in the next section.

2.2 PROBLEM OF TERMINOLOGY: CODE-SWITCHING AND CODE-MIXING

According to Mazraani (1997: 8–9), there is a difference between code-switching and code-mixing. Code-switching usually has a discourse function, and is defined as a phenomenon where 'sections in one code are followed by sections in another one in the same conversation'. She adds that code-switching affects most linguistic levels, syntactic, morphological, phonological and lexical. Code-mixing, on the other hand, is defined as 'the mixing of different varieties within a single utterance or even within a single word'. Code-mixing, according to her, does not have to affect all linguistic levels.

Although Mazraani's distinction may be useful within her framework, I think her definitions are still on the vague side. She does not provide a clear definition of the terms 'sections' and 'utterance'. One cannot be sure what the borderline is for a section or an utterance. However, other linguists like Myers-Scotton (1997: 24) do not distinguish between code-switching and code-mixing and regard this distinction as creating 'unnecessary confusion'. Myers-Scotton states that:

> A number of researchers associated with Braj Kachru [. . .], but also some others, prefer to label as 'code-mixing' alternations which are intrasentential, although it is not entirely clear whether this applies to all intrasentential CS (code-switching). While I grant that intrasentential CS puts different psycholinguistic 'stresses' on the language-production system from intersentential (code switching) CS (a valid reason to differentiate the two), the two types of CS may have similar socio-psychological motivations. For this reason, I prefer 'CS' as a cover term; the two types can be differentiated by the labels 'intersentential' and 'intrasentential' when structural constraints are considered. (1993: 1)

Intersentential code-switching is switching across sentences, while intrasentential code-switching is switching that takes place within a sentence. I think that it would be difficult if not impossible to consider code-switching and code-mixing two separate processes. The definition of code-switching by different linguists renders the term very inclusive and general (see the definition of Gumperz above and that of Myers-Scotton 1993: 1). Therefore, I will stick to the term 'code-switching' to cover also what Mazraani calls code-mixing.

2.3 CODE-SWITCHING AND DIGLOSSIA

Diglossia can, in my opinion, be studied within the framework of code-switching, since switching can occur not only between different languages, but also between different varieties of the same language, as mentioned above. So rather than use the term 'diglossic switching' to refer to switching between MSA and the different vernaculars, one can use the term 'code-switching' for that purpose.[3] As Mejdell posits, code-switching 'should be understood in a broad context to encompass both varieties and different languages, (Mejdell 2006: 418)

2.4 THE STUDY OF CONSTRAINTS ON CODE-SWITCHING IN RELATION TO THE ARAB WORLD

2.4.1 Structural constraints on classic code-switching

In this section, I will concentrate on three theories that propose constraints on code-switching, with special reference to Myers-Scotton's model of a matrix language (ML). I will also provide examples of switching that involves different Arabic dialects. Linguists concentrating on the Arab world have tended to focus on the syntactic constraints on code-switching rather than the motivations for switching. Also, switching between North African dialects and European languages has been studied extensively, as will become clear below.

Although Gumperz (1982a) argues that code-switching is not a random process, but that it depends more on stylistic and metaphorical factors than on grammatical restrictions, some linguists (Sankoff and Poplack 1981; DiSciullo et al. 1986; Myers-Scotton 1997) have proposed that there must be grammatical constraints on any kind of code-switching. The question is, are these constraints universal? Do they apply to all language pairs? If we believe in the idea of universal grammar, then we might expect universal grammar to impose constraints on code-switching. I will examine the following theories introduced by linguists to identify structural constraints on code-switching:

1. the two constraints theory
2. the government principle
3. the model of matrix and embedded language.

I will then try to explain each theory and the problems associated with it in relation to Arabic and other languages.

2.4.1.1 The two constraints theory

This theory was one of the first attempts to identify syntactic constraints on code-switching. Sankoff and Poplack (1981) proposed that there are two factors important in code-switching: the free morpheme constraint and the equivalence constraint. The free morpheme constraint predicts that there cannot be a code-switch between a bound morpheme and a lexical form unless the lexical form is phonologically integrated into the language of the bound morpheme. They appeal in their analysis to data from Spanish/English code-switching.[4] This constraint would predict that *flipeando*, meaning 'flipping', is a possible form (1981: 5). In this example, *-eando* is the Spanish progressive suffix. The lexical English form (*flip*) is integral as it stands, in the phonology of Spanish. But the form **runeando* 'running' is not possible, because the lexical form *run* has not been integrated into the phonology of Spanish. As a result, it cannot take the Spanish progressive suffix *-eando*.

The equivalence constraint theory states that code-switching tends to occur at points where the juxtaposition of elements from the two languages does not violate a syntactic rule of either language. It will occur at points where the surface structure of the two languages is the same. Sankoff and Poplack (1981: 34–5) applied this theory to Spanish, and they found that Spanish/English code-switching may occur between determiners and nouns, but not between nouns and adjectives in the noun phrase. Thus, it would be unacceptable to say (Lipski 1977: 252):

(1) **his favorito spot*
'his favourite spot'

This example cannot occur because it would violate the surface structure rules of Spanish. In Spanish the adjective must come after the noun, whereas in English it comes before.

Moreover, Sankoff and Poplack predict possible sites for switches for pairs of languages which differ in basic word order, for example, SOV (subject–object–verb) and SVO (subject–verb–object) languages. In such cases they predict that there will be no switches between V (verb) and O (object). For example, in Panjabi/English code-switching, there should be no switches between verb and object, since Panjabi is an SOV language, while English is an SVO language.

Sankoff and Poplack admit, however, that sometimes switching of this type can occur where there is no structural equivalence between the languages. But if this happens it is always accompanied by omissions, repetitions etc. Note the following example from German/English code-switching (Clyne 1987: 753). The verb constituents are repeated several times.

(2) *Das ist ein Foto, gemacht an der beach, can be kann be, kann sein in Mount Martha.*
'This is a photo taken on the beach, could be in Mount Martha.'

According to Clyne, the switch to English may have been triggered by the use of the English noun *beach*. In German, unlike English, a verb governed by an auxiliary is sentence final; the auxiliary has to be separated from the main verb in declarative clauses, i.e. *es kann in Mount Martha sein*. In this example, there is violation of the equivalence constraint.

The two constraints theory can be applied very neatly to code-switching between Spanish and English, because both languages have, more or less, the same word order, and both have the same government categories, i.e. noun, verb, definite article, adjective etc. However, it turns out that it is difficult to apply the same theory to two languages that do not share the same categories, for example, the pidgin Tok Pisin and English (Romaine 1995: 129). It is in fact hard to assign grammatical categories to a language like Tok Pisin (verb, article, negative marker etc.). Moreover, Berk-Seligson (1986: 328) found that in Hebrew/Spanish code-switching, many ungrammatical sequences, like the omission of the definite or indefinite article, occur because the indefinite article does not exist as a grammatical category in Hebrew. Besides, this theory relies on linear order and adjacency (surface structure of the sentence) and not on hierarchical order as in the theory of government, for example (Romaine 1995: 129).[5]

As for studies that involve a variety of Arabic, Nait M'barek and Sankoff (1988) studied Moroccan Arabic/French code-switching. They posit that French declarative sentences have the word order subject–verb, whereas Arabic allows for both SV and VS. This leads to recurrent violation of the equivalence constraint.

(3)	*l'époque*	*où*	*les*	*Arabes*	*weṣl-u*	*ḥetta*	*l' andalousie*
	det-time	when	det	Arab-pl	arrive-3pl-perf	to	det-Andalusia

'at the time when the Arabs reached Andalusia' (1988: 145)

This acceptable example can be explained according to the two constraints theory, since it follows a linear left-to-right switch under equivalent word order from a French subject NP *les Arabes* 'the Arabs' to an Arabic verb *weṣlu* 'they arrived'. This is not true for the next example, in which the word order verb–subject is not found in French declarative sentences.

(4)	*ʕamor-hum*	*jawa-k*	*les*	*plats*	*que*	*tu*	*fais*	*içi*
	never-pr3pl	come-pr2msg-perf	det	dishes	rel	pr2sg	make	here

'the dishes that you prepare here never have the taste . . .' (1988: 145)

Additionally, in French, nouns inserted with French definite articles challenge the equivalence constraint. Nait M'barek and Sankoff also apply the borrowing versus switching distinction to Moroccan Arabic/French data. They argue that the notion of 'insertion' must be introduced to account for the frequent use of NP constituents with French article + French noun in an otherwise Arabic context.

Bentahila and Davies (1983: 321), when discussing French and Moroccan Arabic switching, also examine the two constraints theory in their data. They suggest refinement of some other constraints like subcategorisation rules, combining grammatical structures with French lexicon etc. One of the problems that they find with the equivalence constraint is that it would predict that the order of adjective and noun has to satisfy the rules of both languages for a switch to be possible. In Arabic adjectives follow nouns, while in French they can either follow or precede the noun. According to the equivalence constraint, we expect a switch only in positions when the French adjective follows the noun. However, Bentahila and Davies find acceptable examples in which this is not the case. The following example is a case in point (1983: 319):

(5)	*kayn*	*un*	*autre*	*muʃkil*
	to be-3msg-perf	indef	another	problem
	'There is another problem.'			

2.4.1.2 The government principle

DiSciullo et al. (1986) postulate that code-switching is universally constrained by the government relation holding between sentence constituents. On the basis of data from Hindi/English code-switching, French/Italian code-switching and English/Spanish code-switching, they found that it is possible for speakers to switch codes between verbs and subjects but not between verbs and objects. Therefore, they tried to identify the constraints that lead to this distribution pattern of switches. They define government in the following way: X governs Y if the first node dominating X also dominates Y, where X is a major category N (noun), V (verb), A (adjective), P (preposition). They argue that 'if X has language index q and if it governs Y, Y must have language index q also' (1986: 5). Their main claim is that within a maximal projection no switch is allowed, i.e. within a verb phrase or a noun phrase, for example, no switching is allowed. According to them, code-switching occurs only between elements that are not related by government. This would explain why there are no switches between a verb and an object in their data, since a verb governs the object.

The idea of government is more promising than that of the equivalence constraint, because it can account for switching between languages with different word orders and different distributions of categories. It also assumes that switching depends on hierarchical structure rather than linear structure, and can thus take account of a wider range of languages. However, this theory still has its limitations and cannot really be applied universally, at least for the time being.

According to the government constraint theory, there can be a switch between a subject and a verb, but not within a prepositional phrase, or between a verb and an object (Romaine 1995: 137). In the following example, quoted from Romaine (1995: 138), of Panjabi/English code-switching, an English noun is governed by a Panjabi postposition. This configuration is not allowed according to the government principle.

(6) *Family de nal*
'In the family'

In this example, there is a switch within the preposition phrase, which is a maximal projection. DiSciullo et al. (1986) would have predicted that there could be no switch in this case, as the noun and the preposition should have the same language index. Sankoff et al. (1990), in a quantitative study of Tamil/English code-switching, found that it is precisely in object position that switches occur. This finding again violates the government theory, although Sankoff et al. then dismiss these cases as borrowings. I do not, however, think it is acceptable to resort to explaining counter-examples as 'borrowing' whenever one encounters a problem in one's hypothesis about code-switching, since borrowing and code-switching may simply be different labels for what often seem to be identical processes (although perhaps different in terms of the size of the chunks of language to which they are applied). I do not think explaining exceptions as 'borrowings' solves the problem. I agree with Myers-Scotton that 'borrowing' and 'code-switching' are related processes and should be accommodated within one model (1997: 163).

Bentahila and Davies (1983) also found that French and Arabic switching happens within the verb phrase (between the verb and the object). This should not be possible under the government principle of DiSciullo et al. According to Boumans (1998), there are recurrent counter-examples, such as switches between determiners and nouns or between complementisers and complement clauses, found in data with Arabic and a European language.

Other studies that concentrate on constraints on code-switching between a variety of Arabic and another language include Belazi et al. (1994) study of Tunisian Arabic, which found that usually in switching between Tunisian Arabic and French, French nouns are inserted together with the French definite article, like *l'anémie*. This is also the case in Moroccan and Algerian Arabic (cf. Boumans 1998). The following is an example from the data of Belazi et al.

(7) *c'est le fer qui donne... lli yi-ḥa:rib l'anémie*
It is det-m iron rel gives... rel 3msg-fight det-anaemia
'it's iron that gives . . . that fights anaemia' (1994: 226; Tunisian Arabic/French)

In this example, French nouns have a French definite article and Arabic nouns have Arabic definite articles. This is not always the case, though.

Another enlightening study, which examines code-switching between Iraqi Arabic and English among university students in Mosul, is the one by Sallo (1994). He reports that he encountered in his data cases of collocations with English head nouns and Arabic modifier adjectives where the adjective shows gender agreement with the Arabic equivalent of the noun. Note the following examples (1994: 124):

(8) *as-sensitivity* *ʕaliya*
det-sensitivity high-f
'The sensitivity is high.'

In this example the Arabic word *ʕaliya* for 'high' is in fact feminine. This is almost assuredly because the Arabic word for 'sensitivity', *ḥasa:siyya,* is feminine.

(9) *at-temperature* *munxafiḍa*
det-temperature low-f
'The temperature is low.'

Again in this example the Arabic word for 'temperature', *daraja*, is feminine. Thus, the Arabic word for 'low', *munxafiḍa,* agrees with it in gender and is also feminine.

The following example flouts the government constraint theory as explained by DiSciullo et al. (1986), since there can be a switch even within governed constituents. Note that in Iraqi Arabic possessive constructions are expressed with *ma:l.*

(10) *ar-result* *ma:lti* *taku:n* *negative*
det-result poss-f-pr1sg 3fsg-be negative
'My result will be negative.'

We have the feminine form of the possessive particle *ma:l* + the pronoun suffix of the first person singular. The verb is inflected for the feminine singular: it is *taku:n* rather than masculine y*aku:n*. The Arabic noun for 'result' would have been in this case *nati:ja*, which is a feminine noun.

In the reverse case, the modifying English adjective is not inflected according to Arabic agreement rules as in the last example above. Note the use of the singular form of the count noun following numerals 11–99 in the following example (Sallo 1994: 120):

(11) *na:xud xamasta:ʃ* *rat*
1pl-take fifteen rat
'We will take 15 rats.'

It is obvious that the underlying structure in these last examples is Iraqi Arabic rather than English. In the next section I will discuss the concept of an underlying structure or 'matrix language', as Myers-Scotton calls it, in detail.

2.4.1.3 Myers-Scotton's model of a matrix language

A third theory that attempts to identify constraints on the process of code-switching is the hypothesis that there is normally a base language during the process of switching.

Myers-Scotton's view (1998b: 19–21) is that human beings are equipped with an innate language faculty that enables them to assess linguistic choices. Code-switching as defined by her (1998a: 296) is a phenomenon that allows morphemes from two or more codes in the same projection of a complementiser (CP), which is a more precise term than a sentence. A CP refers to a subordinate clause (see also Roberts 1997: 34–5). For example, in the sentence 'I think that he will come', the CP is 'that he will come'. This idea will become clearer later when examples are analysed.

According to Myers-Scotton, when two languages are brought together by a bilingual, there is a dominant language at work.[6] Thus, one language should be assigned the status of what she terms 'a matrix language'. The matrix language (ML) supplies the grammatical frame of constituents, while morphemes are supplied by both languages. That is to say, in code-switching, content morphemes from another language — the embedded language (EL) – may appear in this grammatical frame, as well as ML system and content morphemes. Myers-Scotton's hypothesis is that there is always an ML in bilingual communities, and there is always only one ML at a time. Thus, one has first to recognise the ML, then analyse a structure, and maybe later assign discourse functions to it. According to her, there is an affinity between structural analysis and discourse functions. Both have to be analysed, and both are relevant.

An ML is defined by 'system morphemes'. There are two kinds of morphemes, based on the lexical feature of plus or minus 'thematic roles'. Content morphemes assign or receive thematic roles, like 'agent', 'experiencer', 'beneficiary' etc. This category includes nouns, descriptive adjectives and most verb stems. System morphemes, on the other hand, cannot assign or receive thematic roles. This category includes inflections, determiners, possessive adjectives and intensifier adverbs. Thus, an ML supplies system morphemes which are syntactically relevant. The EL supplies only content morphemes. Myers-Scotton's hypothesis is that 'languages can sustain structural incursion and remain robust, but the taking in of alien inflections and function words is often a step leading to language attrition and language death' (1998a: 289). That is to say, she argues that as long as the system morphemes, like inflections for example, come from the ML, then the language is in no danger.

Once the inflections, and other system morphemes, come from more than one language, there is no one ML any more and this may lead to language change and language death.

The following example, quoted from Myers-Scotton (1997: 78), will show how the ML theory works in practice.

(12) (*leo*) [*si-ku-come na books z-angu*]
'(Today) I didn't come with my books' (Swahili/English code-switching)

This sentence, according to Myers-Scotton, shows not only intrasentential code-switching (code-switching within a sentence), but also intra-word code-switching (code-switching within a word). I will now explain the example in more detail:

si-ku-come	*na books z-angu*
	(prepositional phrase)
one word (which is a verbal phrase)	*na*, preposition
the verbal phrase is:	*books*, noun, English
an ML + EL consituent	*z- angu*, possessive pronoun
si pronoun, first person singular	
ku, tense marker denoting the past, and denoting negation	
come, verb, English	

Note that in this example, the system morphemes (pronouns, tense markers, negative markers and prepositions) are all in Swahili, while the content morphemes (verbs and nouns) are in English. Therefore, the ML is Swahili, while English is the EL.

Myers-Scotton also introduced the idea of *islands* in relation to code-switching, which still falls under the ML model (1998a: 297). There are two kinds of islands, ML islands and EL islands.[7] Islands are generally maximal projections within a CP, for example a noun phrase or a prepositional phrase. ML islands are maximal projections within a CP with all the morphemes from the matrix language. These are quite expected, since one might anticipate finding both system morphemes and content morphemes from the ML in a CP. However, EL islands are more complicated, since they are maximal projections that occur within a CP, and are in the EL rather than the ML. In other words, a hierarchical phrase from the EL is inserted into the ML.

In a study that concentrates on the syntactic constraints on code-switching and applies the ML hypothesis to Moroccan Arabic/Dutch code-switching, Boumans (1998) finds cases which are difficult to explain under the ML hypothesis and even more so under the other two theories discussed above. He gives examples like the following (1998: 83):

(13)	*beʕḍ*	*l-xeṭr-at*	*ka-ne-lqa-h*	*f*	*mensa*	*teḥt*	*ʕend-na*
	some	det-time-pl	asp-l-find-pr3msg	in	student restaurant	below	at-1pl

'Sometimes I find it [a periodical] in the student restaurant below.'

In this example both Moroccan Arabic and Dutch grammar would assign a definite article to *mensa* because the student restaurant in this example is identifiable by the interlocutors, but there is no article. Thus the NP is neither Dutch nor Arabic in structure.

When applying the ML hypothesis to Moroccan Arabic and French, Lahlou (1991) had to explain some of his examples as EL islands. Note the following example of EL islands:

(14)	*Je*	*devais*	*faire*	*pilote*	*f*	*l'armée*	*de*	*l' air*
	I	would	do	pilot	in	det-force	of	det-air

'I was going to become a pilot in the air force.'
(Lahlou 1991: 254; Moroccan Arabic/French)

In this example, the determiner and the French noun *l'armée* can be considered an island.

Note also the following example from Bentahila and Davies (1983):

(15)	*Dak*	*la*	*chemise*
	Dem	det-f	shirt

'That shirt.' (Bentahila and Davies 1983: 317; Moroccan Arabic/French)

Again, the determiner and French noun can be considered an island.

A good example in which the ML is Arabic, although the researcher did not apply the ML hypothesis, is the one given by Rouchdy (1992):

(16)	*huwwa*	*la*	*yu-sammok*	*wa*	*la*	*yu-darnik*	*wa*	*la*	*yu-ðar*	*awit*
	He	neg	3msg-smoke	and	neg	3msg-drink	and	neg	3msg-appear	out

'He doesn't smoke and doesn't drink and doesn't go out at night.'
(Rouchdy 1992: 48; Lebanese or Palestinian Arabic/English)

The morpho-phonological structure of the English words is, in fact, Arabic. For example, *yu-sammok* originates from the English verb ('to smoke') but is inflected for tense, gender and number in Arabic. The same is true for *yu-darnik* which originates from the English verb ('to drink'). Thus the system morphemes are from Arabic.

A final study that applies the ML model is the one conducted by Ziamari

(2007), in which she examines the conversations of students in two French schools in Morocco. Ziamari argues that the ML for the students examined is Moroccan Arabic and the EL is French and/or English. She gives examples in which French and English verbs adopt Moroccan Arabic morphology. Note the following examples (2007: 280–1):

(17) *yetabli*
3msg- établir
'He will establish.'

In this example the imperfect French verb is inflected for person, number and gender according to Moroccan Arabic morphological rules.

(18) *Laykiti-na*
Like-2fsg-perf-pr1pl
'You liked us.'

In this example the English verb ('to like') is again inflected for person, number and gender according to Moroccan Arabic morphological rules.

In general, I think the ML model is the most promising of them all, for a number of reasons. First, it does not rely on a specific theory of grammar such as government and binding theory. This means that the ML hypothesis is not affected no matter which theory of grammatical structure is adopted. This, in fact, is an essential point since syntacticians have been improving on government and binding theory (see Chomsky 1993). The ML theory in its basic framework does not rely on specific languages which happen to be quite similar, like Spanish and English, for example, but is capable of being used with languages which are quintessentially different in their content morphemes and system morphemes, like Arabic and English. More importantly, Myers-Scotton does not claim that code-switching should be studied with reference to structural constraints only. In fact, she emphasises the intertwined role of the discourse and structural aspects of code-switching. She tries, in an unprecedented manner, to formulate a theory that can explain both the discourse function of code-switching and the structural constraints on code-switching. She suggests that by positing an ML, linguists can then start addressing the question more clearly of why people switch between languages, since the ML will be the basis of their hypothesis. Linguists can question why the EL and the ML are used when they are used and how both affect discourse.

Recently Myers-Scotton has refined the ML model to make it account for more cases of code-switching. She proposed a 4-M model.

According to Myers-Scotton (2004a: 109), the 4-M model is based on the notion that when there is code-switching between two languages, both languages should follow the 'morpheme order principle', which posits that the structure of the ML is always the preferred structure. This is because languages 'participating in code switching do not have equal roles' (2004a: 110). There are four kinds of morphemes and not just two as posited earlier in the ML model. The four are listed below:

1. *Content morphemes*: These have been discussed above. They are usually viewed as heads of the maximal projection in which they occur, and they give and receive thematic roles. Nouns and verbs fall into this category.
2. *Early system morphemes*: These are called early system morphemes because they occur at an earlier level in language production and are in fact accessed at the same abstract level as content morphemes. Early system morphemes rely on their heads (content morphemes) for information about their forms. They add semantic/pragmatic information to their heads. For example, English determiners add specificity to their heads, and plural markers also add specific information to their head.
3. *Bridges (late system morphemes)*: Bridges are late system morphemes and do not occur at the same abstract level as early system morphemes. However, they are still dependent on their heads, since they signal information between elements. They too receive information about their form within the immediate maximal projection in which they occur. Note, however, that they only connect content morphemes to each other, without specific reference to the semantics of these morphemes. Possession or association fall into this category. Thus the English preposition 'of' fits this category.
4. *Outsider late system morphemes*: These are different from all the morphemes above because their form depends on information outside their maximal projection. Even though their form depends on information that comes from governing verbs or prepositions, they function across maximal projections. Case markers, affixes to nouns, and markers on verbs that refer to the subject of the verb (which is not the same maximal projection as the verb itself) all fit into this category (2004a: 111). These morphemes are crucial in determining the ML.

It is difficult to understand how the 4-M model works without concrete examples. In section 2.4.2.1 I apply the 4-M model to my data.

In the next section, as was said before, I consider diglossic switching as part of code-switching and shed light on some of the studies that try to assign constraints on diglossic switching as part of code-switching.

2.4.2 Structural constraints on diglossic switching

In the 1980s, some researchers started to turn their attention to specifying how speakers combine elements from the H and L systems to make 'mixed' forms at the word or phrase level. The focus was usually more on the 'form' of language rather than the motivations for switching. For example, Eid (1988), in a study of diglossic switching unprecedented in its detail, attempted an analysis of the syntactic constraints on diglossic switching between ECA and MSA. Her study examined switching in four syntactic constructions: relative clauses, subordinate clauses, tense plus verb constructions (proclitic plus verb construction, e.g. *ḥa*, *b-* prefixes), and negative plus verb constructions (1988: 54). She concluded that the process of switching between ECA and MSA is governed by rules that depend on the sentence position of the element that can be switched, the type of syntactic element involved at the switch, and the direction (ECA→MSA, MSA→ECA) of the switch. El Hassan (1980) also studied the demonstrative system in ESA, in particular the frequency of occurrence of standard and vernacular forms of demonstratives (MSA forms and different vernacular forms) in various types of cross-dialectal communication (between Arabs from different countries, Jordanians and non-Jordanians, Egyptians and non-Egyptians etc.).

Linguists who concentrated on structural constraints on diglossic switching include Boussofara-Omar (1999, 2003, 2006b), Bassiouney (2003a, 2006) and Mejdell (1999, 2006). Boussofara-Omar used political speeches in Tunisia as the basis of her study, and analysed her data in the light of Myers-Scotton's ML model and 4-M model to explain switching between MSA and TCA. Her data comprised seventeen public political speeches by the former president of Tunisia, Habib Bourguiba, delivered between the years 1956 and 1968. The recordings were approximately fourteen hours. Mejdell's study is based on two public seminars held in Egypt. The first was on problems of higher education in Egypt and took place at the American University in Cairo. The second one was a literary seminar, discussed a newly published collection of short stories, and was held at the premises of a political leftist party in Cairo. The recording of both seminars lasted for two hours. Mejdell examines the possible positions and constraints on switching between ECA and MSA. Both studies will be referred to and exemplified in the next section.

2.4.2.1 Application of the ML model and the 4-M model to MSA/ECA switching: a case study

In the following paragraphs I would like to shed light on the results of a study in which both the ML model and the 4-M model were applied to switching between MSA and ECA in different kinds of Egyptian monologues. The data consisted of thirty hours of mosque sermons, university lectures and political speeches. For the sake of clarity MSA will be bold, ECA will be in italics and morphemes that belong to both MSA and ECA, the ones I call 'neutral morphemes', will be in non-italic. I will use the expression 'mixed forms' to refer to code-switches which occur between a system morpheme and a content morpheme and which take place in the same projection of a complementiser. For example, in

(19) *al-qaḍiyya* *di* **muhimma** **giddan**
det-issue dem-f-sg important very
'This issue is very important.'

al-qaḍiyya di is a mixed form, since the MSA content and system morphemes in *al-qaḍiyya* 'the issue' are followed by a system morpheme in ECA *di* 'this', and they both occur in the same projection of the complementiser, *al-qaḍiyya di muhimma giddan* 'This issue is very important.'

The data suggests that although at first glance it seems that the ML in the Egyptian community is ECA while the EL is MSA, Myers-Scotton's idea of an ML does not explain thoroughly what goes on in the Egyptian community. The 4-M model can save some of the problematic examples discussed below. However, the 4-M model yields different results from the ML model. The 4-M model can only explain examples that do not fit the ML model by assuming that the ML is in fact MSA rather than ECA. Nevertheless, Myers-Scotton's theory of 'a composite ML' has more validity in any attempt at explaining the situation in the Egyptian community, and perhaps other communities in the Arab world, as will be clear below.

In the data there are examples of mixed forms consisting of:

1. a negative marker in one code and a verb in another
2. a demonstrative marker in one code and a noun in another
3. an aspectual marker (the *b*-prefix) in one code and a verb in another.[8]

Negative markers, demonstratives and aspectual markers are all system morphemes, as was said before. They do not assign thematic roles. All the mixed forms that occur in the data can be analysed as follows:

ECA negative marker + MSA verbs
ECA demonstrative marker + MSA nouns
ECA aspectual marker (*b*-prefix) + MSA verbs.

There are no examples of the following:

MSA negative marker + ECA verbs

(20) *lam* *yiru:ḥ*
MSA (neg) ECA (3msg-go)
'He did not go.'

MSA demonstrative marker + ECA nouns

(21) *ha:ʔula:ʔi* *r-rigga:la*
MSA (dem-m-pl) ECA (n-m-pl)
'these men'

MSA verbal marker (e.g. *sawfa*, *sa-*) + ECA verbs

(22) *sa-* *yiru:ḥu*
MSA (fut.) ECA (3pl-go)
'They will go.'

At first glance, one may claim that if the three markers, which are system morphemes, are realised in ECA, then, according to the ML hypothesis, the ML tends to be ECA, and the EL is MSA. The basis of switching is an ECA syntactic frame-structure, into which MSA lexical elements are inserted.

One can even find examples in my data to support this view. Note the following:

Negative markers:

(23) *il-ʔi:ma:n* *miʃ* *ka:fi:*
det-belief neg enough
'Belief by itself is not enough.'

System morphemes:
il definite article ECA
miʃ negative marker ECA

Content morphemes:
ʔi:ma:n noun ('belief') MSA
ka:fi: adjective ('enough') MSA

In this example one finds a clear-cut case of one ML at work. The negative marker and the definite article, which are considered by Myers-Scotton as system morphemes, are in ECA, while the content morphemes which assign thematic roles, like nouns and adjectives, are in MSA. Therefore the ML in this example is ECA while the EL is MSA. ECA provides the frame-structure for the sentence, while the speaker fills in the lexical slots with MSA items.

Demonstratives:

(24) *il-ʕaqli* *da* **ma:dda**
det-mind dem-m-sg substance
'This mind is a substance.'

System morphemes:
il definite article ECA
da demonstrative marker ECA

Content morphemes:
ʕaqli noun ('mind') MSA
ma:dda noun ('substance') neutral[9]

Again in this example the morphemes that do not assign thematic (theta) roles, like the demonstratives and the definite article, are in ECA, while the morphemes that assign theta roles, like nouns, are in MSA. This is another example of the ML being ECA and the EL, being MSA.

The b-prefix:

(25) *illi bi-taqaʕ* *ʕala* *ḥo:ḍ* *il-***baḥr** **il-mutawassiṭ**
rel asp-3fsg-fall prep basin/base det-sea det-Mediterranean
'that lie on the Mediterranean'

System morphemes:
illi relative marker ECA
bi- aspectual marker ECA
ʕala preposition neutral
il definite article

il is a definite article. It is not clear whether the vowel preceding the article is the case ending of the preceding word, or the ECA realisation of the definite article. The definite article in this example can be considered both ECA and MSA.

Content morphemes:
taqaʕ verb ('fall') MSA
ḥo:ḍ noun ('basin', 'base') ECA
baḥr noun ('sea') neutral
mutawassiṭ adjective ('middle') neutral in that case because used in a collocation

The system morphemes in this example, like the aspectual marker *b-*, occur in ECA rather than MSA, while the content morphemes like nouns, verbs and adjectives are from both codes, ECA and MSA. But note also that in this example some system morphemes are difficult to classify as belonging to one code rather than another.

Apparently then (judging from the above examples), one may conclude that the ML in the Egyptian community is ECA, and the EL is MSA. But this neat distinction between system morphemes and content morphemes does not always seem to work. A number of examples in the data pose problems for the ML hypothesis, and although, as was said earlier, the 4-M model can explain some of them, it can only explain them by assuming that the ML is in fact MSA. I think these examples suggest that the situation in the Egyptian community is more complicated. Therefore one may have to abandon the idea of an ML in favour of a more sophisticated framework that can explain more precisely what takes place in the Egyptian community.

Let us consider the following example that poses problems for the ML hypothesis:

(26)	*ka:n*	*fi:*	*ʔittifa:qat*	*bi-tunaffað*
	To be-3msg-perf	loc-adv	agreements	asp-fsg-pass-implement
	'Agreements were being implemented.'			

System morphemes:
bi- aspectual marker ECA
the *u-a* theme in the verb *tunaffað* denotes the MSA passive form of the verb (discontinuous passive morpheme)

Content morphemes:
ka:n verb ('to be') neutral
fi: dummy verb ('there is') ECA
ʔittifa:qa:t noun ('agreements') MSA
tunaffað verb ('to be implemented') MSA

If one accepts the ML-EL hypothesis, then in this example it is difficult to decide what the ML is. As the aspectual marker on the verb is in ECA, one might expect the other ML features to be ECA also, as was the case in the previous examples. In this example one cannot claim that there is only one ML at work. But in fact, there is a discontinuous system morpheme taken from MSA, and one system morpheme taken from ECA. The speaker uses the *b*-prefix, which is an ECA element. However, he applies the discontinuous passive morpheme *u-a* to a verb to passivise it, which is a quintessentially MSA system morpheme. This 'internal' form of the passive is not available for him in ECA, in the sense that it cannot be applied to verbs which are exclusively part of the ECA lexicon. Such verbs passivise in ECA by the prefixing of *it-* to the suffix stem and *yit-* (*tit-* for feminine) to the prefix stem (Holes 2004). Here are the ECA and MSA counterparts of this example:

(27) **ECA counterpart**

ka:n	*fi:*	*ʔittifaʔa:t*	*bi-titnaffiz*
To be-3msg -perf	loc-adv	agreements	asp-fsg-pass-implement

'Agreements were being implemented.'

(28) **MSA counterpart**

ka:nat	***huna:ka***	***ʔittifa:qa:t***	***tunaffað***
To be-3fsg -perf.	adv-existence	agreements	fsg- pass-implement

'Agreements were being implemented.'

Existence is expressed in ECA by a morpheme which is historically a locative adverb *fi:* (in it), which has no morpho-semantic analogue in MSA. In MSA existence is expressed by *yu:jad* (a passive verb, 'is found') or *huna:k* (an adverb, 'there'). The example below illustrates this:

(29)

yu:jad	***rajulun***	***fi***	***al-bayti***
msg-pass is found	man-nom	prep	det-house

This means that there should be no possibility of switching between the two systems to express existence – the two systems do not overlap at this point of morpho-syntactic structure. In the example the ECA form has been selected. Similarly, as far as the verb (being implemented) is concerned, the passive form is expressed in MSA by structures that have no morpho-semantic analogue in ECA. Here the MSA form has been selected. (Just as there should be no switching possible between *fi:* and *yu:jad* or *huna:k*, so there should be none possible between *tunaffað* and *titnaffiz*.)

If this is the case, one cannot say that in a sentence like that quoted as example (26) above, the ML is ECA. The speaker obviously knows specific morpho-syntactic forms of both ECA and MSA, and uses them in this example. The example is also particularly interesting because it has intra-word code-switching: in the same word we have an aspectual morpheme from ECA and a passive morpheme from MSA. In this example we have system morphemes from two different codes in the same projection of a complementiser, more specifically within the single-word verb.

The 4-M model can save this example. If we divide morphemes into four types then the ML of this example will in fact be MSA. The two system morphemes can be classified differently: *bi*, the aspectual ECA marker, can be considered an early system morpheme, since it adds aspect to its head, which is the verb. Thus it adds information to its head. As an early system morpheme it relies on its head, a content morpheme for its form. On the other hand, the *u-a* theme in the verb *tunaffað*, which denotes the MSA passive form of the verb (discontinuous passive morpheme), can be considered an outsider late system morpheme. This is because its form is dependent on information outside its head. This information is supplied by the noun *ʔittifa:qat* (agreements). In that case, the ML of this clause is in fact, MSA rather than ECA.

The following examples will pose problems for the ML and yield different results with the 4-M model:

(30) *ha:ða* *k*-kala:m *laysa* *ka:fiyan*
dem-m-sg det-talk neg enough-acc
'This kind of thing is not enough.'

System morphemes:
ha:ða demonstrative MSA
k assimilated definite article ECA
laysa negative marker MSA
-an case marker MSA

Content morphemes:
kala:m noun ('talk') neutral
ka:fi: adjective ('enough') MSA

(31) **ECA counterpart**
ik-kala:m *da* *miʃ* *kifa:ya*
det-talk dem-sg-m neg enough
'This kind of thing is not enough.'

(32) **MSA counterpart**
ha:ða *al-kala:m* *laysa* *ka:fiyan*
dem-sg-m det-talk neg enough-acc
'This kind of thing is not enough.'

In this example there are system morphemes from both codes. The MSA demonstrative, case marker and negative markers are used, but also the ECA definite article. Therefore, this example poses problems for the ML hypothesis, but again the 4-M model can save this example. According to the 4-M model the ECA definite article *k* is an early system morpheme, since it adds specificity to its head; it adds information that is semantic in nature to its head. Similarly, it depends on its head for its form. Additionally, the structure of the clause is MSA, since in ECA the demonstrative usually follows the noun rather than precedes it as is the case in this example. According to the uniform structure principle, the ML has to provide the structure of the morphemes in the clause. Since this is the case, then we can consider the ML to be MSA in this example as well.

(33) *yurfaʕ* *ʕanhu* *t-takli:f* *da*
msg-pass-lift prep-pr3msg det-responsibility dem-m-sg
'And this responsibility is lifted off his back.'

System morphemes:
u-a passive morpheme MSA
ʕan- preposition ('from') neutral
-hu third person pronoun MSA
t- definite article MSA or ECA
da demonstrative ECA

Content morphemes:
yurfaʕ verb ('raised') MSA
takli:f noun ('responsibility') neutral

(34) **ECA counterpart**
wi yitrafaʕ *ʕannu* *t-takli:f* *da*
And msg-pass-lift prep-pr3msg det-responsibility dem-m-sg
'And this responsibility is lifted off his back.'

(35) **MSA counterpart**
yurfaʕ *ʕanhu* *ha:ða* *t-takli:f*
msg-pass-lift prep-pr3msg dem-m-sg det-responsibility
'And this responsibility is lifted off his back.'

The speaker uses MSA content morphemes. He also uses MSA system morphemes, except for the ECA demonstrative. Therefore there are system morphemes from both codes, MSA and ECA. Again in this example it is difficult to claim that ECA is the ML while MSA is the EL. Moreover, as with the previous examples, there are system morphemes that are difficult to categorise as ECA or MSA. The definite article is a case in point. The 4-M model would predict that the ML in this example is MSA. The passive MSA morpheme *u-a* is an outsider late system morpheme; its form depends on information outside its head, the verb. Also the MSA third person pronoun is considered an outsider late system morpheme since it refers to information outside its maximal projection. It refers to the person whom this responsibility is lifted off. The definite article, which is considered an early morpheme as explained in the earlier examples, can be either MSA or ECA. The ECA demonstrative *da* is also considered an early system morpheme, as explained before.

2.4.2.1.1 Examples that pose problems for the 4-M model

(36)

il-mawḍu:ʕ *da*	ka:n	*ʕuriḍ*	ʕala	l-muʔtamar
det-issue dem-m-sg	to be-3msg -perf	msg-pass present	prep	det-conference

il-isla:mi
det-Islamic
'This issue was presented to the Islamic Conference.'

System morphemes:
il definite article ECA
da demonstrative ECA
u-i discontinuous passive morpheme MSA
ʕala preposition ('at, on') neutral
l definite article probably MSA, but I am not sure.
il definite article; again, the vowel of the article may in fact belong to the word
preceding it (MSA), or to the article, in which case the article is ECA

Content morphemes:
mawḍu:ʕ noun ('issue') neutral
ka:n verb ('to be') neutral
ʕuriḍ verb ('to be presented') MSA
muʔtamar noun (conference) by itself neutral, but the preceding article can make it ECA or MSA
isla:mi adjective (Islamic) neutral

(37) **ECA counterpart**

il-mawḍu:ʕ da	*ʔitʕarad̩*	*ʕala*	*l-muʔtamar*	*il-isla:mi*
det-issue dem-m-sg	msg-pass-perf present	prep	det-conference	det-Islamic

'This issue was presented to the Islamic Conference.'

(38) **MSA counterpart**

ha:ða	*al-mawḍu:ʕ*	*ka:n*	*qad*	*ʕuriḍ*	*ʕala*	*l-muʔtamar*
dem-m-sg	det-issue	3msg-to be-perf	*qad*	msg-pass-present	to	det-conference

al-isla:mi
det-Islamic
'This issue was presented to the Islamic Conference.'

In this last example the speaker uses an ECA system morpheme, the demonstrative *da*, as well as an MSA system morpheme, the discontinuous s-stem passive morpheme *u-i*, in the same CP. Even with content morphemes, one encounters the problem that several items are shared by both codes.

The 4-M model will consider the MSA discontinuous passive morpheme *u-i* to be the only outsider late system morpheme, which will yield the ML as MSA. However, there is a problem for the ML because in a pure MSA structure, one has to add the morpheme *qad* to the structure of the clause. Thus one may claim that this example violates the uniform structure principle.

(39)

yaʕni	*b-yibʔa*	*fi:h*	ḥima:ya	fi:	***haðihi***	***l-mana:ṭiq/***
msg-means	asp-3msg-become	prep	protection	prep	dem-f-sg	det-areas

'That is to say, there was protection in these places.'

System morphemes:
b-prefix ECA aspectual marker
fi preposition ECA or MSA
haðihi demonstrative MSA
l definite article MSA

Content morphemes:
yaʕni verb ('to mean') neutral
yibʔa verb ('to become') ECA
fi:h dummy verb ('there is') ECA
ḥima:ya noun ('protection') neutral
mana:ṭiq noun MSA

(40) **ECA counterpart**

yaʕni	*b-yibʔa*	*fi:h*	*ḥima:ya*	*fi*	*l-mana:ṭiʔ*	*di/*
msg-means	asp-3msg-become	prep	protection	prep	det-areas	dem-f-sg

'That is to say, there was protection in these places.'

(41) **MSA counterpart**

ha:ða	***yaʕni***	***ʔanna***	***huna:ka***	***ḥima:ya***	***fi:***	***haðihi***	***l-mana:ṭiq/***
dem-m-sg	msg-means	that	adv	protection	prep	dem-f-sg	det-areas

'That is to say, there was protection in these places.'

In this example the content morphemes that occur are from both codes. This is expected under the ML hypothesis. The problem is that the system morphemes that occur are also from both codes. The *b*-prefix is an ECA system morpheme and it occurs this time with an ECA verb *yibʔa* ('to become'), but the demonstrative, which is also a system morpheme, is in

MSA. There are system morphemes from more than one code in the same projection of a complementiser. Besides, as with the example in (30), there are system morphemes that are difficult to classify as MSA or ECA, like the preposition *fi*.

According to the 4-M model the system morphemes that occur, excluding the preposition which is used in both varieties, are all early system morphemes. The ECA aspecual marker *b-* is lexically related to its head, the verb, and it also denotes meaning to its head. The MSA demonstrative is another early system morpheme, because again it adds meaning to its head; the noun *mana:ṭiq* ('places') is also dependent in its form (the feminine singular) on this head. The MSA definite article *l* is also an early system morpheme since it denotes meaning to its head. There is no clear ML in this example.

Now note the following example:

(42) *ḥarakit il-ḥaya:h* *ma-tantaẓim-ʃi* *ʔilla bi:ha*
Cycle det-life neg 3fsg-organise-neg except with-pr3fsg
'Life does not function without it.'

(43) **ECA counterpart**

ḥarakit	*il-ḥaya:h*	*ma-tibʔa:-ʃ*	*munaẓẓama*	*ʔilla*	*bi:ha*
Cycle	det-life	neg-3fsg-become-neg	organised	except	with-pr3fsg

(44) **MSA counterpart**

ḥarakat	*al-ḥaya:h*	*la tantaẓimu*	*siwa*	*biha*
Cycle	det-life	neg 3fsg-organise-ind	except	with-pr3fsg

The negation in this example is in ECA, but the verb is in MSA; although there is no mood marking, the vowel pattern is that of MSA. What is of interest here is that the ECA counterpart of this example will in fact yield a different structure. Thus according to the 4-M model the structure of this sentence is an MSA one. Since the negation here refers to *ḥarakit il-ḥaya:h*, and it is not directly related to its immediate head *tantaẓim*, then one can consider it an ECA outsider late system morpheme. In this example, there is a clear composite of two MLs: MSA and ECA.

It is worth mentioning that Boussofara-Omar (2003: 40), when analysing data in the light of the 4-M model, found some similar problematic examples of switching between MSA and TCA. The following example is one of them.

(45) *ma-sa-ta-qif-ʃ*
neg-fut-3fsg-cease-neg
'It will not cease to be.'

The TCA counterpart would be

(46) *Mu:ʃ be:ʃ te:qif*
neg-fut 3fsg-cease
'It will not cease to be.'

The MSA counterpart would be:

(47) *Lan taqifa*
fut-neg 3fsg-cease-sub
'It will not cease to be.'

The problem in this example arises from the fact that there are system morphemes from TCA and MSA in the same CP. The future marker *sa* is in MSA and can be considered an early system morpheme since it adds information to its head, while the negative marker *ma-ʃ* is TCA and can also be considered an early system morpheme since it also adds information to its head, the verb. However, the tense person morpheme *ta* is MSA, and can be considered an outsider late system morpheme since it depends on information from outside its head, the verb; it derives its information from the subject. Boussofara claims that the ML in this example is TCA while the EL is MSA. But she admits that this is difficult to explain according to both the ML and the 4-M models.

Note that the structure of an ECA negative marker combined by an MSA future marker and an MSA verb does not occur in my data. This seems to be a structure that occurs in Tunisia but not in Egypt. Thus the following example is a possible structure in Egypt:

(48) *ma-tagif-ʃ*
neg-3fsg-stop-neg
'It will not cease to be.'

However, the following combination is awkward and perhaps not possible for an Egyptian speaker:[10]

(49) *ma-sa-ta-qif-ʃ*
neg-fut-3fsg-stop-neg
'It will not cease to be.'

ECA negation does not permit a future marker from MSA. This is evidence that intrasentential code-switching between MSA and different colloquials is dependent on the community being studied to a great extent, and to the exposure of this community to MSA as well as the means of this exposure: whether it is in schools, clubs, televisions or the political arena.

These examples resist interpretation within the framework of diglossia, and challenge ideas about syntactic constraints on code-switching. First, as was said before, most linguists studying diglossia have not explained cases of switching of this sort, and have tended to study ECA and MSA variables separately. Although Mitchell (1986: 9) acknowledges the existence of a code that he calls 'ESA' (see Chapter 1 above), he does not explain the rules and patterns that govern it. There have been few practical attempts to study the use of these variables in actual data (cf. Boussofara-Omar 2003, 2006b; Mejdell 2006). The two constraints theory (Sankoff and Poplack 1981) and the government principle (DiSciullo et al. 1986) fall short of explaining the above examples. For example, both would predict that there would be no switching between an aspectual marker like the *b*-prefix and a verb.[11] They would predict that both have to be in the same code, which is not the case in many examples in my data. More importantly, the ML hypothesis cannot really explain this phenomenon. The ML hypothesis predicts that all system morphemes will be in the ML, and here we see examples of system morphemes from two different codes being used together in the same word and not just in the same clause or CP. The 4-M model would in fact yield opposite results. It would predict that MSA may be the ML for most of the examples.

It is only fair to say that Myers-Scotton did not set off to explain diglossia and that most of the linguists analysing constraints on code-switching were more interested in switching between different languages: bilingual switching rather than diglossic switching. However, if linguists argue that both diglossic switching and code-switching should be studied within the same framework, since the definitions of code-switching given at the beginning of this chapter render code-switching an inclusive rather than an exclusive term, then one would expect theories of code-switching to explain diglossic switching as well. The data above makes it clear that although theories of code-switching can help explain diglossic switching, the situation in diglossic communities is different in many ways and more complicated in others. This does not imply that one should abandon the inclusive definition of code-switching, but rather that within this inclusive definition, one can find a way of explaining the peculiarities of the diglossic situation. I propose that there are two MLs at work here: ECA and MSA. I make this proposition for the following reasons.

First, one might expect that the basis of switching in these monologues would be an ECA syntactic substructure, into which MSA lexical elements would be inserted. This is generally true in the case of the three variables chosen for analysis, but some examples proved to be more problematic, even with the 4-M model. The idea of a single frame-structure (an ML) falls short of explaining the last examples (26, 30, 33, 36, 39) for a number of reasons. First, the ML hypothesis is based on the idea that there is always only one ML at a time. As was stated before, Myers-Scotton's main hypothesis is that 'languages can sustain structural incursion and remain robust, but the taking in of alien inflections and function words is often a step leading to language attrition and language death' (1998a: 289). That is to say, once there is more than one ML at a time, then this is often an indicator of language death; for example, the taking of inflections and function words from a code other than the ML is a step towards language attrition and death. As was shown in all the examples above, sometimes there seems to be more than one ML at work. Although the theory of ML is indeed valid in certain cases, it does not seem to give a clear-cut picture of what goes on in this diglossic community.

Second, as was said earlier, the ML model claims to account for classic code-switching and not necessarily diglossic switching, although it has been applied to diglossic switching (cf. Boussofara-Omar 2003, 2006). What makes the model difficult to apply is the fact that in some examples it is difficult to decide whether a certain morpheme belongs to ECA or MSA. The MSA definite article is *(v)l*, where *v* stands for a vowel that has no value of its own, the vowel quality of the article (*a*, *i*, *u*) changing according to its position and function in the sentence. The ECA article is *(i)l-*. It is therefore sometimes difficult to classify actual examples of usage (*il-*) as MSA or ECA. In addition, some prepositions (which are system morphemes) are shared by both codes. (Note also that it is sometimes difficult to decide what a system morpheme is, since, for example, some prepositions can also assign thematic roles. But this problem cannot be dealt with here.)

ECA and MSA are different codes but with a lot of shared content and system morphemes, and it is almost impossible at times to say whether a certain morpheme belongs to ECA or to MSA. Thus, it is not easy to come up with one ML, since it is sometimes difficult to decide which code is being used in the first place. I argue that the existence of two codes that are partially overlapping and partially distinct, as in Arabic, may cause problems for both the ML and the 4-M model.

Unlike other theories, such as the two constraints theory (Sankoff and Poplack 1981), the ML model seems to work better with languages/codes that are typologically different, i.e. codes with different morpheme systems, like Arabic and English, or Turkish and French, than it does with closely related languages, like German and Dutch, or two codes from the same language, like ECA and MSA.

The idea of islands, discussed earlier, seems to permit the occurrence of system morphemes from the EL, under the condition that these system morphemes occur with content morphemes from the EL as well in a maximal projection (NP, PP etc.) that is still governed by the CP. This condition limits the occurrence of islands. For instance, in example (26), one cannot claim that there is an EL island and that there is only one ML at work, which is ECA, since in the verb *bi-tunaffað* there is switching within a maximal projection, and thus this example cannot be explained by the idea of islands, at least not as it is currently formulated. There are system morphemes from both codes within this word, as discussed above. In example (30), one can consider *laysa ka:fiyan* an EL island since it is a maximal projection, but *ha:ða k-kala:m* will still pose the same problem of two MLs at work within one maximal projection, since there are system morphemes from two different codes in the same NP. Example (39) may be explained under the idea of islands: one may claim that *haðihi l-mana:ṭiq* is an EL island and the ML is ECA. However, as was said earlier, this example still poses problems for the 4-M model. In addition, one cannot use the idea of islands in order to explain examples (33) or (36), because in both there is switching between two different codes within a maximal projection. Therefore there is only one example that can be explained by using the idea of islands, and all the rest of the examples still pose the same problem of having more than one ML, or having a completely different ML according to the 4-M model. The idea of islands falls short in explaining these examples because it does not take into account mixed forms. Similarly, as was said earlier, while the ML fails to explain the problematic examples, the 4-M model can explain most of them. However, the 4-M model would predict that in the problematic examples the ML is in fact MSA.

2.4.2.1.2 A predictable composite

Myers-Scotton (1998a) has proposed another idea to explain some cases of code-switching. This is the idea of a so-called composite ML (1998a: 299). She posits that when there is a change in progress in a bilingual community, the ML is a composite, based on structures from both codes, but moving towards the new ML. Eventually the change in progress is completed, and a language shift follows, with the new code playing the role of an ML. Myers-Scotton (1998a: 310–12) supports her hypothesis by giving evidence from other linguistic studies on code-switching, like the study of Bolonyai (1996).

Bolonyai gives an example of a young Hungarian girl who lives in the USA with her parents, and how her ML changes from Hungarian to a composite of Hungarian and English, and finally the new ML becomes English. The following example demonstrates the use of a composite ML.

(50) *Mom, en meg-find-t-am a ket quarters-t*
Mom 1sg perf-find-past-1sg det two quarters-acc
'Mom, I found two quarters.' (Bolonyai 1996: 12)

Although Hungarian is a pro-drop language, the girl uses an overt subject (*en*, 1 sg). This is an example of convergence to English. The verb, which is a content morpheme, is English (*find*), but the tense marker, which is a system morpheme, is in Hungarian. The word *quarters-t* is an English word with an English system morpheme (*s*), and a Hungarian system morpheme (*t*), which is a Hungarian case marker. There are different system morphemes from two different codes in the same projection of a complementiser, in fact, and even in the same word. Therefore the ML is a composite. In this example, a composite ML is leading to language change, because eventually English will become the ML.

Now let us consider again example (30) from my data, repeated here as example (51), in which the ML is a composite.

(51) *ha:ða k-kala:m laysa ka:fiyan*
'This kind of thing is not enough.'

In this example the ML is a composite of both ECA and MSA, since there are system morphemes from both codes. The idea of a composite ML can help us explain what is going on in the Egyptian speech community. The problem with this hypothesis is that one cannot just claim that there is change in progress in Egypt, whether language shift or language death. The situation of the Hungarian girl in the USA is different from that of Egyptians in Egypt.

There is, however, something similar in all the Egyptian monologues analysed: the speakers are all educated, and have thus been exposed to MSA. They are all over 40; that is to say, their exposure to MSA has been over quite a long time. I think there are certain system morphemes from both MSA and ECA which they have internalised. But again, it is quite difficult to say that these speakers have an ECA substructure only (an ECA ML). The ECA substructure may be dominant but they still make use of certain MSA system morphemes. Their ML is not just ECA (although it verges on it); it is a composite. The fact that their ML is a composite does not necessarily mean that one code is changing or dying, and it does not mean that one code will take the place of another. Children are exposed to MSA from their first year in school in Egypt. MSA is, in other words, part of the average educated Egyptian's everyday existence[12]. This systematic exposure to MSA is perhaps different from one country to another in the Arab world, with the result that there are different possible forms for each community, as was clear in example (45), discussed above, from Boussofara-Omar's Tunisian data. Therefore language policies in the Arab world have an input in shaping and modifying structural constraints on code-switching (see Chapter 5).

Myers-Scotton later (2004a: 116) says, about composite code-switching, that 'little systematic analysis of this type of CS (code switching) exists to date'. In the next paragraphs I would like to show some forms that do and do not occur in relation to my data and other data as well. These forms are predictable in the sense that they tend to occur frequently and regularly when speakers switch between MSA and ECA. Thus one can posit that structural constraints on diglossic switching in Egypt can be explained in the light of a predictable composite in which system morphemes occur from both codes: MSA and ECA.

An MSA salient system morpheme that occurs frequently in a composite ML structure is the MSA discontinuous passive morpheme. This morpheme is considered a system morpheme. As was clear from the examples above, the speakers analysed used the MSA passive form rather than the ECA one; see examples (26, 33, 36). In fact this was prevalent in my data.

However, Boussofara-Omar (2006b), when discussing diglossic switching between MSA and TCA, analysed a number of examples in which the passive is realised in MSA.

(52) *Haðaya* *yuðkar* *fa yuʃkar*
dem 3msg-imperf-pass-mention so 3msg-imperf-pass-thank
'This should be mentioned and thanked for.'

Boussofara-Omar, however, posits that in Tunisia, MSA verb stems inflected with MSA tense affixes tend to occur in frozen expressions, as in the example above (2006b: 71). This could mean that with regard to the realisation of the MSA passive Egypt is indeed different from Tunisia. This may also be related to language policies in both countries, as was said earlier and will be discussed in Chapter 5. One can only make tentative predictions at this stage but it is indeed a phenomenon worth more investigation.

ECA salient features that occur frequently in my data include the ECA aspectual marker *b-* with MSA verbs. This aspectual marker occurs even with pure MSA verbs. Mejdell (2006: 389) also noted this in her study and posits that although 'its representation in script violates orthography, [and] its phonetic value is distinct', it still appears even when speakers attempt hard to stick to MSA. She gives the following example in which the *b*-prefix is affixed to an MSA verb (2006: 352):

(53) *b-yataga:waz-ha*
asp-3msg-overcome-pr3fsg
'He overcomes it.'

The verb is realised in MSA. The ECA counterpart would be *yitga:wiz*.

Additionally, the following are the predictable structures discussed earlier that can be deduced from my data: a negative marker in ECA and a verb in MSA are a possible combination, while a negative marker in MSA and a verb in ECA do not occur together. The same is true for demonstratives: a demonstrative in ECA and a noun in MSA are possible, but the opposite does not occur.

One needs more data to reach definite conclusions about the structural patterns that occur in diglossic switching, and definitely more studies are needed that concentrate on structural constraints on diglossic switching in the Arab world.

Next, I would like to discuss studies that concentrate on motivations for and discourse functions of code-switching and diglossic switching.

2.5 MOTIVATIONS FOR CODE-SWITCHING

2.5.1 Motivations and discourse functions of classic code-switching

Before Gumperz (1976), Weinreich (1953: 73) claimed that people switch because of the environment around them and because of a certain speech event or situation. For example, a university lecturer is likely to use a formal code when he delivers a lecture because of the environment surrounding him, i.e. because he is in a lecture room, and he is discussing a non-personal topic. He is expected by the audience to speak in a formal code. If after the lecture, while he is walking home, a student asks him about a more personal subject, then the situation is different. He may take the student aside and speak in a different code (a less formal one).[13] Thus, according to Weinreich, the nature of the speech event (here 'talking about personal matters') triggers the switch that occurs. On this view, switching depends on the topic first and then the participants. These two factors together create a speech event. However, according to this view, participants do not exercise choice, but it is the speech event which determines everything. Gumperz questions these assumptions.

According to Gumperz (1982a: 61), the speaker is not just a pawn controlled by the situation. In fact the opposite is true: it is the speaker who manipulates the situation. That is to say, the speaker, rather than the speech event, is the prime mover in code-switching: 'Rather than claiming that speakers use language in response to a fixed predetermined set of prescriptions, it seems more reasonable to assume that they build on their own and their audience's abstract understanding of situational norms, to communicate metaphoric information about how they intend their words to be understood.' Thus, the individual plays the key, creative role in code-switching.

Gumperz's importance, in our understanding of code-switching, also arises from the fact that he treats code-switching as a phenomenon worthy of analysis and study in its own right. He introduced the distinction between situational and metaphorical code-switching (Blom and Gumperz 1972). Situational code-switching is motivated by factors external to the participants, like setting, topic or change in social situation (as in Weinreich above). Metaphorical code-switching, on the other hand, is motivated by the individuals themselves, and is related to the individuals' perception of and presentation of themselves in relation to the external factors, like setting, topic or social situation. For example, Blom and Gumperz (1972: 434) point out that if students in the Norwegian fishing village of Hemnesberget choose to use the standard dialect (after using the non-standard one), it may be not only because the topic has changed, but also because the use of the standard signals the students' shared group membership as intellectuals. Thus, the students as individuals take account of the fact that all the participants in an interaction (their audience) share the same well-educated background, and use that group's dialect. In this example, using one code rather than another has a discourse function of identifying the speaker with a specific social group.

Additionally Gumperz later (1982a: 95) discusses for the first time the 'we' and 'they' dichotomy. There are two different codes used by speakers generally: the 'we' code and the 'they' code. The socially inclusive 'we' code is associated with home and family bonds, while the socially distanced 'they' code is associated with public interactions.

Gumperz (1982a: 75–84) identified the following functions for code-switching. According to him, people typically switch for the following purposes:

1. quotations[14]
2. to specify the addressee as the recipient of the message
3. reiterations and interjections
4. to qualify a message
5. to differentiate between what is personal and what is general.

Romaine (1995: 161–2) summarises Gumperz's functions, and also claims that switching can serve the following purposes:

6. as sentence fillers
7. to clarify or emphasise a point
8. to shift to a new topic
9. to mark the type of discourse
10. to specify a social arena.

Safi (1992: 75), examining the speech of male and female Saudi students in the USA, uses Gumperz's model of functions of code-switching to analyse her data. Her data comprised two hours of tape recording. The speakers were enrolled in undergraduate and graduate courses. She had one female informant who was 28 years old and two male informants who were 19 and 33 years old. All informants had been in the USA for at least a year. She found that students switch from English to Saudi colloquial Arabic when they aim at arousing religious or spiritual feelings, as in the following examples:

(54) *They had a beautiful mubxara.*
'They had a beautiful incense burner.'

(55) *They used a big piece of towb-i-kaʕba for decoration.*
'They used a big piece of the black dress of the kaʕba.'

In fact these switches refer to referents that have no exact equivalent in English, and the English equivalents do not carry the affective load that the Arabic ones would for Saudis or Muslims more generally. Safi also noted that

SCA is usually used as sentence fillers, as Gumperz predicts. Sentence fillers in SCA include words like *yaʕni* 'it means' and *zayn* 'good'. English sentence fillers include 'OK'.

In a similar vein, Wernberg-Moller (1999: 238) analysed the speech of eight Moroccans living in Edinburgh.[15] Wernberg-Moller was interested mainly in first-generation immigrants ranging in age from 34 to 49. This first generation had lived there between 17 and 22 years. They usually had very little education and were manual workers. Her data was gathered in 1994 and the interviewers spoke Moroccan Arabic to the informants. The study gives an illustration of situational code-switching: an informant is describing in English a book that she read, which possibly, although it is not clear, was also written in English. While she is doing so, another informant, her mother, enters the room and interrupts. The first speaker gets distracted and starts speaking to her mother in Arabic.

(56) SA: *it's based on a girl it's like it goes through different. . .it's like. . .y'know it goes through in stages like y'know you've got a seed time, harvest time. . .em. . .*
ZA: *qulha b-lʕarabiyya!*
'Tell her in Arabic!'
SA: *manʕraffi kayff nqulha b-lʕarabiyya and those times y'know are sort of like. . ..it's like a circle y'know how things change.*
'I do not know how to tell her in Arabic, and those times you know are sort of like. . .it's like a circle you know how things change.'

When the first speaker turns her attention back to the interviewers, she switches back to English. When she speaks to her mother, she speaks in Arabic.

Wernberg-Moller (1999) even compares this study to the one done by Gumperz in Norway, noting that the Moroccan community in Edinburgh is different from the community in Norway. The former is not a well-established community yet. Its members use different languages for different activities. Thus, Arabic is used in religious activities and at home, for example, while English is used outside the house. In fact, excessive English at home is viewed with disapproval by the Moroccan immigrant community.

Note the following example, in which the speaker compares and contrasts how old people are cared for in Britain and the Arab world (Wernberg-Moller 1999: 245):

(57) *Wledha, bnetha, awledha,. . .katimʃi l- nursing home. . .katimʃi l- . . .lhosbitar. He look after it. . .ḥḥna ʕandna ʕayb!. . .ḥḥna ʕandna ʕayb!. . .makaynʃ. . .kayn sbita. . .lima fḥal lima lmra li ma-ʕandha-ʃ oo rrajl li ma-ʕandu-ʃ ḥata ʃi li yqablu kayimʃi l-sbitar, huma yqablu θat tmma Hata ymut.*

'Her son, her daughter, she goes to a nursing home. She goes to hospital where they take care of her [look after her]. We think that is a bad thing, (with us bad)[16] we think that is a bad thing[17] (with us bad) we don't have it! (it isn't there)[18]. . .there are hospitals. . .when, for example, when the woman who doesn't have anything or the man who doesn't have even someone (something) to look after him, he goes to the hospital (and) they look after (him) there until he dies.'

According to Wernerg-Moller this represents an example of metaphorical code-switching since there is no change in setting at all. Hospital is referred to twice, once as *hosbitar* (a wrong pronunciation of the English word) and once as *isbitar*. The English use is to refer to establishments in Britain and the Moroccan Arabic use is to refer to hospitals in Morocco. Also the 'we' and 'they' dichotomy is of use here. The speaker contrasts 'our' way of life and 'their' way of life. The British way of life is not looked upon favourably.

Another discourse function of code-switching mentioned by Wernberg-Moller is that of authority and factuality. English is associated with these, as in the example below (1999: 254):

(58) AA: *hedi, hedi [this is, this is] important taʕarafha*
'This is important that you know it.'

Note also that Arabic is used when speaking about something personal and English is used when trying to be objective, as in the example below:

(59) AA: *a rasi! a rasi! you need just somebody to cure you!*
'Oh my head! Oh my head! You just need someone to cure you.'

Note that the postulation that English is associated with factuality and authority is too general to make and needs more data to prove. In addition, in Wernberg-Moller's study the informants were aware that the recording would be used for linguistic research. They in fact 'viewed the recording as an excellent means by which the researcher could learn more about their language and dialect in particular' (1999: 254). This could have posed a methodological problem for the research since the code used may have been a reaction to the knowledge of the participants that they were being recorded by a linguist. Such problems are difficult to deal with and will be discussed in Chapter 3.

In a different vein, Goffman (1981) discusses the individual as a speaker who plays different roles and who uses language to mark the new role she or he plays. Each person plays different roles with different people in different situations. This is what Goffman calls 'a change in footing', i.e. a change in the frame of an event. By 'frame' he means it is a change in the way speakers perceive each other and perceive the situation. It is noteworthy, however, that when Goffman speaks about change in footing he refers not just to the bilingual, but to the monolingual who uses different codes in different situations. According to Romaine (1995), code-switching is merely 'changing of hats', which all speakers engage in all the time. People spontaneously manipulate their language for their own needs, changing their attitude and style continuously.[19]

To sum up, Gumperz and others have emphasised the controlling role of the speaker, and listed speaker-initiated factors in code-switching. Although there have been few criticisms of Gumperz's model, it still has its limitations.

In general, functional approaches to social phenomena necessarily represent incomplete taxonomies, and we could even expect them to, because in contrast to formal taxonomies, which begin with an assumption of comprehensiveness and exclusivity of categories, functional taxonomies begin with the assumption that new functions may be uncovered and are generally expected to be. Likewise, most would assume that a switch can simultaneously serve multiple purposes.

Gumperz's division of code-switching into two kinds, situational and metaphorical, is in practice not always easy to make, and it presupposes that there are different motivations for each type of code-switching. Myers-Scotton (1993: 55) questions the viability of this division, and claims that there are a number of similarities between situational and metaphorical code-switching, to the extent that they should be accounted for in one theory of code-switching. Auer and Di Luzio (1984: 91) also think that this distinction should be replaced by a continuum. One has to admit that even Gumperz himself moves away from this distinction (1982a) and emphasises the role of metaphorical rather than situational code-switching. In *Discourse strategies* (1982a: 59), the title of the chapter on code-switching is 'Conversational code-switching', rather than 'metaphorical' or 'situational' code-switching. The point of emphasis in his theory is the individual in relation to codes. Gumperz gave credit to the individual in code-switching in an unprecedented manner. According to him, code-switching is a creative act with the individual playing the major role. However, Myers-Scotton (1993: 59–60) finds problems with this idea. According to her, placing a great deal of emphasis on the individual's creative role in code-switching may make one lose sight of the general nature of the process, since, in her view, code-switching is a rule-governed phenomenon and should be studied as such. She argues that Gumperz views each interaction between people in its own right: 'One must believe in the possibility of generalising across interactions in order to build explanatory theories, I argue. It is not at all clear that Gumperz has this belief' (1993: 59). She also argues that this emphasis on the individual may 'promote individualised ad hoc explanations' for code-switching (1993: 62).[20]

Another point which Myers-Scotton objects to is that Gumperz and others give lists of functions of code-switching. These lists are useful in explaining why people switch in a certain community, but they fall short of explaining and organising motivations for code-switching in a 'coherent theoretical framework' (1993: 63). There is a distinction between the rhetorical significance of code-switching, which highlights functions of switching, and the interactional significance of switching, which highlights motivations for switching. One needs a theory that can explain code-switching as a universal phenomenon and not as a phenomenon peculiar to one speech community rather than another. Also, these lists can never be exhaustive, because they are linked to communities and how they vary.

In short, what seem to be lacking in Gumperz's analysis are more abstract tools or ideas that can account for what goes on in code-switching. His analysis as well as that of his successors is too descriptive, to the extent that one cannot make generalisations. What is needed is a theory that explains the functions of code-switching at a level of abstraction that applies in both bilingual and monolingual societies, i.e. a universal theory.

Now, I will examine three theories that attempt to explain code-switching without recourse to lists of its discourse functions or motivations. I will concentrate on the third theory, as it is the most valid one in my opinion. These three theories are the accommodation theory propounded by Giles et al. (1987), the social arena theory of Scotton and Ury (1977), and finally the markedness theory of Myers-Scotton (1993).

Howard Giles et al. (1987) use what they term 'accommodation theory' to explain the social motivations for code-switching among other interaction phenomena. They claim that in social interactions speakers desire their listener's social approval and modify their speech in the direction of the listener's code to get this approval. This is called 'convergence' or 'accommodation'. In some circumstances, however, the speaker may want to differentiate herself or himself from the listener. She or he will do this by emphasising the difference between them through choice of code. This is called 'speech divergence'. Heller (1982: 108–18), in a study carried out in Montreal, gave an example of divergence. She showed that some people in the bilingual city of Montreal found it problematic to communicate with other fellow citizens because they, the other fellow citizens, refuse to code-switch from one language to another (English and French). They do this for political, national or cultural reasons. Thus, refusing to switch can serve an individual's purposes just as much as switching. It can convey a negative feeling or attitude towards a rival group, and it is one of the strategies used in maintaining and reinforcing boundaries between groups.

A second model was that proposed by Scotton and Ury (1977), who use the idea of the 'social arena'. According to them, there are three universal social arenas which affect code choice: identity, power and transaction. A speaker switches to different codes to define the interaction taking place in terms of a certain social arena or to keep it undefined. The first universal social arena is identity: a speaker switches according to the identity of the person she or he is speaking to, and according to her or his own identity as well. The second social arena is power: code-switching also depends on the power that one has over others, or the power that others have over one. The third social arena is transaction: code-switching depends on the situation, and on the purpose of the speech act. A speaker may not be sure about the social arena: she or he may not be sure about the status of the other person, for example. In that case she or he uses a code which will help keep the interaction undefined. Myers-Scotton (1986: 408) gives the example of a brother and a sister in western Kenya who were conversing in the brother's shop. The sister wanted to have special treatment from her brother, so she used their shared mother tongue. He, on the other hand, replied in Swahili to show her that he was treating her as a customer in his store. The sister chose to emphasise her identity as a 'sister' rather than her identity as a customer in her brother's shop. She used code choice to do so. He, on the other hand, did not accept the identity that she assigned herself. I think to some extent one can say that the sister expected to have power over the brother, and, therefore, to receive special treatment, a better price, a better cut of meat etc. In the end his power as shop keeper prevailed over her power as his sister. The brother and sister also did not agree on the kind of transaction taking place. The brother wanted the situation to be that of a customer and a shop owner, while the sister did not want that. The brother refused to act within the social arena the sister assigned to him and chose another one instead.

Myers-Scotton (1993) proposes a third theory which tries to explain code-switching as a universal, rule-governed phenomenon. She contends that the fact that people switch from one code to another or from one language to another does not necessarily mean that this switching has a social motivation. Code-switching in itself does not have to denote any effect, nor does it necessarily have any discourse function. Code-switching can be used as the unmarked variety of certain communities (as the normal linguistic behaviour). It can be used with no particular social motivation behind it; although for an outsider on this community it does carry a social message, for an insider it is the norm. Labov (1971: 462) gives an example of switching with no social motivation in mind, in which a young African American boy switched between two different codes: Black English Vernacular and Standard English. The boy was describing a game of skelly (a New York street game). Labov found the following:

1. Switching sites are often difficult to limit, since many items are shared by both systems: the Vernacular and the Standard.
2. The speaker switches between both systems at least sixteen times without an apparent motivation in the same stretch of discourse.

Labov therefore considers it unproductive to regard this as code-switching.

Romaine, however (1995: 171), posits that this can be considered code-switching since this kind of switching does not just occur in the USA, but in other places as well. She contends that this case of code-switching is similar to the one examined by Gumperz for Delhi, between Panjabi and Hindi (1982a: 85). Gumperz suggests that the two codes appear indistinguishable phonetically and almost identical in syntax and lexicon as a result of convergence and borrowing.

Myers-Scotton also argues that whether code-switching has a discourse function or a social motivation depends on both the speaker and the audience. Both are aware of what is conventionally expected from them in a community. This idea of mutual agreement concerning the expectations of audience and speaker is what differentiates marked from unmarked choices. Myers-Scotton explains what she means by markedness by proposing that 'what community norms would predict is unmarked, what is not predicted is marked' (1998b: 5). In other words, switching is governed by tacit social conventions.

Myers-Scotton goes further, by proposing that an ability to switch is implied in the communicative competence which all individuals possess (1998b: 6). She compares this communicative competence to the grammatical competence of a language. In her theory, switching is not just a performance process, but a rule-governed competence which native speakers learn. In other words, all cognitively developmentally normal humans have the ability to learn how the community/communities they are part of evaluate switches, whether style shifts, dialect switches, diglossic switches or bilingual code-switching, and likewise, they possess the ability to learn to perform/practise/use such switches for a range of interactional purposes.

First, Myers-Scotton differentiates between using code-switching with no motivation in mind, as the unmarked choice, and using it with a specific motivation in mind, as the marked choice. Where the phenomenon of switching is unmarked, actual switches are more frequent, and the phenomenon more predictable (one can predict that it will happen, but not how many times or where, i.e. it is predictably unpredictable).

In the following example, the speakers switch between English and Swahili. English is the marked choice in this case. Therefore switching to English has a specific discourse function, as will become clear below (Scotton and Ury 1977: 16–17). A passenger on a bus to Nairobi and a bus conductor enter into an interaction. The conductor asks the passenger where he is going, to determine his fare. English (the marked choice) is underlined, and the rest of the interaction is in the unmarked choice (Swahili).

(60) *Passenger:* *Nataka kwenda posta.*
'I want to go to the post office.'
Conductor: *Kutoka hapa mpaka posta nauli ni senti hamsini.*
'From here to the post office, the fare is 50 cents.'
(Passenger gives the conductor a shilling, from which he should get 50 cents in change.)

Conductor: *Ngojea change yako.*
'Wait for your change.'
(The passenger says nothing until some minutes have passed and the bus is nearing the post office where the passenger plans to get off.)
Passenger: *Nattaka change yangu.*
'I want my change.'
Conductor: *change utapa, Bwana.*
'You'll get your change.'
Passenger: *I am nearing my destination.*
Conductor: *Do you think I could run away with your change?.*

The passenger switches to English when the conversation has thus far been in Swahili to renegotiate the interaction. Minimally the conductor knows that some extra information has been implicated; it necessarily shows the passenger's level of education. The content of the message also carries a Grician implicature, which the code-switch underlines. The conductor then replies in English, showing his level of education and thus asserting his own position as equal to the passenger. English here is used as the marked variety. As such, it has a discourse function: it is used to express authority as well as anger.

A similar example is reported by Suleiman (2004: 9), in which he describes his trip to Israel as a British Palestinian. He was expected to speak Arabic to the Israeli soldiers and policemen, whether Jewish or Druze, at checkpoints, since his passport indicated that he was of Palestinian origin. He in fact did not use Arabic, although his name and origin all prove he is Palestinian. Yet he decided to answer their questions only in English even when the questions were asked in Arabic. By doing so, he was refusing to acknowledge any bonds of solidarity or even understanding between him and them. Further, using Arabic would have put the soldiers in a privileged power position over him as a Palestinian. He was basically making it clear that they were on an equal footing. He appealed to the British part of his identity, which gave him more power over the soldiers. It could also be that he spoke English specifically to have power over the soldiers because his English was much better than theirs. In this case they were not on equal footing; thanks to his British passport and mastery of English, he was clearly in a more powerful position interactionally.

As noted earlier, however, the fact that someone switches between two different codes does not necessarily mean that she or he wants to convey a certain feeling or assert her or his role. In the following example (Myers-Scotton 1993: 123–4), two school teachers who are native speakers of Shona, a South African language, are conversing about the relative progress of their students. English elements are underlined (according to Myers-Scotton's model of ML, the ML in this example is Shona).

(61) *Teacher: Manje zvakafanana kana nekuti uri kuita grade one manje saka vana vazhinji vechisikana ku-primary vanogona sitereki. Vanokasika ku-absorb zvinhu. But as time goes on vana kuenda ku-grade five, six, seven, form one vanonoka kuita catch up mu-ma-lessons. But once they catch up they go ahead.*
'Now, for example, it is the same when you are in grade one now so that many of the girls understand much better. They hurry to absorb things. But as time goes on, children go to grade five, six, seven, and form one boys are late to catch up with lessons. But once they catch up they go ahead.'

Code-switching between Shona and English is frequent, unpredictable and normal for the speakers in this kind of interaction. That is, it is predictable that there will be switches between Shona and English. The audience or addressee expects it as well. It does not denote any specific discourse function. For these speakers, code-switching is the normal, unmarked choice. But note that this type of switching only occurs in certain communities between people who perceive one another as peers in some way. Hence it may communicate an important message at a more abstract level. However, it is the overall pattern of switching rather than the individual switches that are meaningful.

In my English-language school, we started at the age of four to be taught MSA and English simultaneously. The following song was very common among girls at the age of eight when playing together.

(62) *One day wana wana wana ma:ʃi*
I saw a beautiful girl
ʔulti laha saba:ḥ il-xe:r
ʔa:lit li sabaḥ innu:r
ʔulti liha I love you
ʔa:lit li very much.'
'One day while I was walking (lit. 'and I walking'. 'And I' is repeated three times)
I saw a beautiful girl
I told her 'good morning' (lit. 'morning of blessing').
She answered 'good morning' (lit. 'morning of light').
I said 'I love you'.
She said 'very much'.

It is quite obvious that the reason why schoolgirls in an English-language school in Egypt switch between English and ECA in this song is simply because they have access to both. They form a community of bilinguals within their school borders. They are in fact expected to switch between both. The song does not have a symbolic effect on any of the participants within the borders of the community. Outside that border it does signal out the speakers as coming from an English-language school rather than a government school or a French one.

All people, according to Myers-Scotton, are equipped with the competence to assess linguistic choices. All people have a 'predisposition' (1998b: 6) to see linguistic choices as marked or unmarked. There is perhaps an extra message in a linguistic choice which is sociopsychological in nature. All speakers have a markedness evaluator, to measure the markedness of an utterance, and crucially they learn the local community's ways of assessing markedness. They have the ability to understand that marked choices will be received differently from unmarked choices. For speakers to have this competence, they have to be exposed to the use of unmarked and marked choices. Just as exposure to grammatical structures makes people competent in a language, so exposure to marked and unmarked choices makes them competent in making and understanding linguistic choices. There is always a link between the use of a linguistic code and its effect in a certain situation, and this is part of learning a language.

The speaker has the competence to assess all code choices as more or less unmarked or marked for the exchange type in which they occur. It is claimed that this communicative competence is both universal, in the sense that all people possess it, and particular, because it is developed in relation to a certain community. That is to say, this competence is acquired through social experience in interactions in a particular community.

Within this framework, speakers as individuals make choices from their linguistic repertoire to achieve certain goals which are of significance to them. They act rationally because they have a set of choices and they presumably make the best choice. By 'the best choice', I mean the choice that will benefit the speaker most given the audience and the circumstances surrounding the speech event, and that involves the least effort on the speaker's part. That is to say, a speaker must calculate the costs and rewards of one choice over another (Myers-Scotton 1993: 110). 'Costs' refer to the quantity of words the speaker uses and the stylistic devices, and 'rewards' refer to the intentional as well as referential meaning she or he conveys to the listener (see also Grice's 1975 maxims and the relevance theory of Sperber and Wilson 1986). The speaker makes a choice that minimises costs and maximises rewards. Thus, speakers choose one code over another because of the rewards they expect from that choice, relative to its costs. So the role of the speaker is emphasised. But note also that the choice made by the speaker is connected to the audience's expectations. The speaker wants to leave an effect on the audience, and thus maximise her or his own rewards: the audience has certain expectations from the speaker, and whether these expectations are met or not determines whether the choice the speaker has made is marked or not. That is to say, if the code used is expected by the audience, then the speaker is using an unmarked choice, and does not necessarily want to leave a particular effect on that audience. If, on the other hand, the speaker uses a code which is not expected by the audience then she or he is making a marked choice for the purpose of leaving an impact on the audience.

Another point I want to mention about Myers-Scotton's theory is that she recalls the fact that speakers negotiate different identities all the time, and she claims that this is a major factor in code-switching, 'A major motivation for variety in linguistic choices in a given community is the possibility of social identity negotiations' (1993: 111).

Speakers negotiate mainly in order to reach an agreement about the mode of the interaction. They make choices either to emphasise their position, or to convey their own views.

Myers-Scotton lists five different maxims to help us understand the choice that people make in code-switching (1998b: 25): the unmarked choice maxim, the marked choice maxim, the exploratory choice maxim, the deference maxim and the virtuosity maxim. Although I agree that the idea of maxims that Myers-Scotton proposes is indeed more accurate and thorough than just assigning discourse functions to certain codes, the maxims seem to be more than is needed in an analysis for code-switching, since they could all fall under the umbrella of marked and unmarked choices. Myers-Scotton, for example, posits that the deference maxim and the virtuosity maxim 'complement the unmarked choice maxim' (1993: 148). I think one can concentrate on both the marked and unmarked choices by emphasising the role of both speaker and audience, and by doing this, one is still generating a more general theoretical framework. Nevertheless, I think her theory deserves attention because of the factors mentioned above.

A related concept to markedness is that of indexicality, which is discussed in detail by Woolard (2004). Woolard explains marked choices in terms of indexes. Indexicality is a relation of associations through which utterances are understood. For example, if a specific code or form of language presupposes a 'certain social context, then use of that form may create the perception of such context where it did not exist before' (Woolard 2004: 88). If a code is associated with the authority of courtrooms and this code is then used in a different context, it will denote authority. The language of the speaker would then be considered an authoritative language (Silverstein 1996: 267).

To conclude this section, I would like to say that it was quite surprising to find a large number of studies done on constraints of code-switching in relation to Arabic and few studies done on the social motivations of code-switching. More studies are needed that concentrate on motivations and on different parts of the Arab world and not just among North Africans.

There are still a number of studies that examined the discourse functions of diglossic switching as part of code-switching. These are what I will examine below.

2.5.2 Motivations and discourse functions of diglossic switching

A number of other studies have attempted to explain the motivations of switching between the H and L varieties in Arabic-speaking societies. These studies have concentrated less on form and more on motivations for switching. I will mention briefly some of these studies.

Abu-Melhim's (1991) application of the accommodation theory tries to explain communication across Arabic dialects, arguing (1991: 248) that the idea that Arabic speakers of different dialects rely on MSA when they converse together is not accurate. He studies five conversations, each lasting for half an hour, involving a Jordanian couple and an Egyptian couple. The subjects chose their own topics. The Jordanians were from Irbid and the Egyptians from Cairo. Thus, according to him, they spoke urban dialects. Abu-Melhim demonstrates that speakers employ a variety of accommodation strategies when conversing with each other, and that these strategies include not just switching from their regional dialect to MSA but also switching from their regional dialect to another dialect; for example, from Jordanian to ECA, and even from their dialect to English (1991: 249). For instance, he posits that Jordanians switch to English to emphasise or clarify a statement (1991: 242), while they may switch to MSA when quoting someone or again to emphasise a statement. Switching from Jordanian Arabic to Egyptian is used by Jordanians to accommodate to the dominant prestigious variety (Egyptian Arabic) and thus to facilitate conversation (1991: 237).

There have also been a number of studies that have attempted to explain switching between ECA and MSA in Egypt, whether in written or oral performance. Abdel-Malek conducted research on the influence of diglossia in the novels of Yūsuf al-Sibāʿī. He found (1972: 141) that the development of the genre 'novel' in Arabic literature in the early twentieth century resulted in considerable tension between H and L, and in response to that tension a new linguistic style (developed by Yūsuf al-Sibāʿī) appeared in Arabic prose literature. Abdel-Malek's idea of a mixed written style is similar to the idea of ESA, although he specifies no clear rules to define this style.

Holes (1993) examined the relation between language form and function in Nasser's political speeches. Holes detects that there can be an element of conscious choice in using one variety rather than another. In general, 'Speakers are free to move up and down it [the stylistic spectrum] in accordance with what they perceive to be the moment-by-moment requirements for appropriate language use' (1993: 15). He stresses the role of the speaker by claiming that speakers always have 'intentions' and 'strategies', and these two factors influence their language choice (1993: 13–45) at both the micro and macro levels. In a similar vein, Mazraani (1997) examines language variation in relation to three political figures in Egypt, Libya and Iraq and how these three political leaders use language variation as a 'rhetorical strategy' (1997: 25).

Mejdell (1996) examines stylistic variations in spoken Arabic with reference to recordings of the prolific Egyptian novelist Naguib Mahfouz (Najīb Maḥfūẓ), quoted at the beginning of this chapter, talking about his life, and tries to explain the kinds of processes that motivate stylistic choices by matching certain discourse functions with the use of one variety rather than another. She comes to the same conclusion suggested by Holes (1993): that people often switch from MSA to ECA when giving examples, explaining, rephrasing or commenting on a previous statement in MSA. She also alludes to the fact that code choice is related to the way one perceives oneself as well as to the way one perceives others. In a later article (1999), she studies the interaction between MSA and ECA in the spoken performance of Egyptian academics and writers 'in settings where community norms require a mode of speaking that is more formal' (1999: 228). She suggests that code choice should be examined in relation to the speaker's change of role vis-à-vis her or his audience (1999: 231). Mejdell concludes that she considers 'the access to both varieties [MSA and ECA], with the wide span of cultural and social connotations attached to them, a rich stylistic resource for speakers to use creatively' (1999: 227; see also Mejdell 2006).

Note that there is no determinism here: speakers can choose how they speak (though within socially prescribed limits). This refers to the point we discussed earlier which was made by Myers-Scotton (1993) that speakers are free to choose but their choices will be interpreted within local understandings of markedness. Rosenbaum (2000) studies the occurrence of a mixed style MSA and ECA in texts written by Egyptians, a phenomenon which seems to be gaining in popularity. Rosenbaum thinks that a mixed written style, involving clear shifts between H (MSA) and L (ECA), breaks the 'rules, old and new, of writing in Arabic, but does not encounter any serious opposition in Egyptian culture, probably because Egyptian readers have been accustomed to seeing ECA forms in print already for decades' (2000: 82). However, I think the situation in Egypt as well as in other parts of the Arab world is more complex than this and there are still intellectuals who object to the use of dialect in literature. This will be discussed in detail in Chapter 5, but to give an example, Mahfouz (Najīb Maḥfūẓ) himself refused to use any dialect in his writing, even in dialogues.

One can see from all the above studies that linguists have moved forward since Ferguson's article on diglossia and have acknowledged and tried to explain the diglossic switching that takes place in the Arab world. In the next section I will examine empirical data from Egypt.

2.5.2.1 The relationship between code choice and speaker's role in Egyptian political discourse: a case study

In the following study I will examine the relation between code choice and choice of role by the speaker. I argue that in political speeches in general there is a direct relation between change of role and change of code. This relation, though examined here in a modern political speech, is not a new phenomenon.

The speaker will usually choose a linguistic code in order to convey her or his aim. In my data, this means essentially whether she or he chooses to do so using ECA or MSA. However, there are some types of 'moves' a speaker may make, for rhetorical purposes, in relation to the audience, and some ways of expressing her or his intention, which appear to be particularly significant for what they tell us about how she or he perceives her or his role in relation to them. These 'moves' are often signalled by specific types of syntactic or phonological choices. For example, the use of exclamations rather than declaratives may indicate a change in the speaker's role vis-à-vis the audience. The choice of the first, second or third persons of the verb can also be significant: for example, in developing an argument, if the speaker starts by using verbs in the first person and then shifts to verbs in the third person, his or her doing so may be a sign of a change in his/her role vis-à-vis both the message and the audience. Syntactic processes like negation, deixis and the expression of verbal aspect require the speaker to make code choices between ECA and MSA (as we have seen), and these choices, quite apparent from the actual message, send signals as to the role she or he is adopting in relation to the audience.

After examining my political data I found that there is a direct relationship between change of role and change of code. This gives evidence for the claims of Gumperz and Goffman.

The speech analysed here was delivered on Labour Day 1999. The speaker is the Egyptian president, Hosni Mubarak, and the audience consists of government ministers and government employees from all classes of society. In this speech the president gives the Egyptians an account of the achievements of the year, as well as problems that still need to be tackled. The speaker switches from MSA to ECA and back twice in the speech. The speech is, therefore, divisible into four parts.

2.5.2.1.1 Part one of the speech

Speaker's role:

Mubarak starts his speech by outlining the political agenda of the past year, the country's achievements and aspirations. He assigns himself his basic 'default' role, that of a head of state giving an account of what he did throughout the year. By doing so, he creates a formal relation with the audience of governor–governed. For example, he states the importance of an increase in exports and a decrease in imports. He also mentions the fact that it is important for the economy of Egypt not to be dependent on fluctuations of price in a small number of raw materials like petrol. Consider the following example from part one (analysed examples will be glossed below).

(63) *θa:niyan/iṣla:ḥu l-xalali fil-mi:za:ni t-tuga:ri/ ʕan ṭari:qi ziya:dati ṣ-ṣa:ḍira:t wa tarʃi:di l-ʔistira:d/ fa qaḍiyyatu ṣ-ṣa:dira:ti l-miṣriyya qaḍ iyyatun maṣi:riyyah/ yagib ʕan taʃġala ʔihtima:ma kullu l-fiʔa:t/ allati tataḥammalu ga:niban min ʕibʔ/ wa masʔu:liyyati l-inta:gi fi maṣr/ wa kullu l-muʔassasa:ti allati taʕmalu min ʔagli sala:mati l-iqtiṣa:di l-maṣ ri/ wa nuqṭati l-badʔi ṣ-ṣaḥi:ḥ fi taqdi:ri/ hiya ʔan taku:na huna:ka siya:satun wa:ḍiḥa/ hadafuha tawsi:ʕa qa:ʕidat wa nawwʕiyyati ṣ-ṣa:ḍ ira:ti l-miṣriyya ḥatta la: taku:na ʕurdatan li-taqalluba:tin kabi:ratin murtabiṭatin bi-ʔasʕa:ri ʕadadin qali:lin min al-silaʕi kal-bitro:l*
'Secondly, redressing the deficit in the trade balance, by increasing exports and controlling imports. This is because the issue of Egyptian exports is a crucial issue that has to occupy the minds of everyone who is involved in Egyptian production. This issue should also occupy the mind of all establishments that work for the security of the Egyptian economy. The true starting point in my estimation is to have a clear policy that aims at increasing the scale and quality of Egyptian exports, so that it is not susceptible to great fluctuations, related to the price of a few raw materials like petrol.'

Code choice:
The code used here is pure MSA in which even case and mood endings are respected. Usually, as was said earlier, speakers drop case and mood endings even when speaking MSA. However, the president is in fact reading and this makes it easier to use case and mood endings. The reason for this choice of code seems connected to the role the speaker is playing in this part of the speech.

There are no verbs in the first person at all. In fact, there is a high degree of depersonalising nominalization (underlined), which adds to the 'objectivity' of the message. For example:

(64)

θa:niyan/	*iṣla:ḥu*	*l-xalali*	*fil-mi:za:ni*	*t-tuga:ri/*	*ʕan*
Secondly	redressing-nom	det-deficit-gen	in-det-balance-gen	det-trade	by

ṭari:qi	*ziya:dati*	*ṣ-ṣa:ḍira:t*	*wa*	*tarʃi:di*	*l-ʔistira:d*
way-gen	increasing-gen	det-exports	and	controlling-gen	det-imports

'Secondly, redressing the deficit in the trade balance, by increasing exports and controlling imports.'

Had the speaker chosen to do so, these nouns could have been replaced by verbs like *nuṣliḥ* (v1pl 'we redress'), *nuraʃʃid* (v1pl 'we control') etc. These verbs would be realised as first person plural and not singular, and the air of objectivity and professionalism that prevails in this part might have been partly lost by the use of inclusive first person verbs.

Mubarak also uses several highly marked MSA features:

1. He uses *ʔiʕra:b* (mood and case endings) in many instances.

Consider the following example, and note the case and mood marking, underlined:

(65)

fa	*qaḍiyyatu*	*ṣ-ṣa:dira:ti*	*l-miṣriyya*	*qaḍiyyatun*	*maṣi: riyyah/*
Thus	issue-nom	det-exports-gen	det-Egyptian	issue-nom	crucial

yagib	*ʕan*	*taʃġala*	*ʔihtima:ma*	*kullu*	*l-fiʔa:t/*
must	that	3fsg-occupy-sub	interest-acc	all-nom	det-people

allati	*tataḥammalu*	*ga:niban*	*min*	*ʕibʔ/*
rel	3fsg-carry-ind	part-acc	from	burden

wa	*masʔu:liyyati*	*l-inta:gi*	*fi*	*maṣr*
and	responsibility-gen	det-production-gen	in	Egypt

'This is because the issue of Egyptian exports is a crucial issue that has to occupy the minds of everyone who is involved in Egyptian production.'

2. He also uses MSA relative pronouns (underlined).

(66)

wa	*kullu*	*l-muʔassasa:ti*	*allati*	*taʕmalu*
and	all-nom	det-institutions-gen	rel	work-ind

min	*ʔagli*	*sala:mati*	*l-iqtiṣa:di*	*l-maṣri/*
for	sake-gen	safety-gen	det-economics-gen	det-Egyptian

'This issue should also occupy the mind of all establishments that work for the security of the Egyptian economy.'

3. He uses MSA negative structures (underlined).

(67)

ḥatta	*la:*	*taku:na*	*ʕurdatan*	*li-taqalluba: tin*	*kabi:ratin*
So that	neg	3fsg-become-sub	susceptible-acc	to fluctuations-gen	big-gen

'So that it is not susceptible to great fluctuations.'

He also uses highly marked MSA phraseology and vocabulary, e.g.

(68)

ḥatta	*la:*	*taku:na*	*ʕurdatan*	*li-taqalluba:tin*	*kabi:ratin*
So that	neg	3fsg-become-sub	susceptible-acc	to fluctuations-gen	big-gen

'So that it is not susceptible to great fluctuations.'

In this example, there is only one verb marked for mood and a number of case marked nouns and adjectives, which again renders the sentence saliently MSA rather than ECA.

Phonologically, this whole section of his speech conforms to MSA, rather than Egyptian norms. Thus, he consistently uses MSA phonemes like *q*, instead of the ECA glottal stop, in cases where theoretically either *q* or *ʔ* could have occurred, e.g. *taqdi:ri* rather than *taʔdi:ri*

2.5.2.1.2 Part two of the speech

Now let us consider the role of Mubarak in part two of the same speech, which occurs immediately after part one. In this part the code changes from MSA to ECA. The change is sudden and quite drastic. This drastic change in the code level from MSA to ECA corresponds to an equally radical change of role on the part of the speaker, vis-à-vis the audience and the way he mediates his message.

Speaker's role:

Here, Mubarak narrates a story to support his abstract argument about the trade balance. In narrating the story, he also changes his role vis-à-vis the audience to that of a 'good old friend', or a 'fellow Egyptian'. He takes it for granted that the audience will understand what he is talking about. The audience here is treated like someone who was born, like him, in the countryside, and who, like him, used to make kites out of paper and pieces of string as a child. This was a common activity for poor boys who had no choice but to make their own kites. The kites he and his audience used to make as children are now being imported from Brazil. He goes on to make a similar point, this time about the importation of ice-cream cups and spoons. These concrete examples are given to make his point, that something needs to be done about the increase of imports into Egypt, clear in a code all will not only understand but also identify with. Here he is nowhere near as formal as in part one of the speech; he seems more like a concerned friend chatting with his audience over the garden fence, and part of the way he conveys this is through the use of the language of everyday life.

(69) *da ʔana marra ʔana kunt/ fi ʃarm iʃ-ʃe:x/ ʕarfi:n iṭ-ṭayyara:t illi kunna b-niʕmilha fil-fallaḥi:n di/ il-waraʔ di/ wi-nilzaʔha bi-bu:ṣ wi kuryit duba:ra wi nṭayyarha/ gaybinha mil-barazi:l/ ṭabʕan da mablaġ ha:yif/ bi-yʔul lak wi da mablaġ/ ʔana ba-ḍrab masal/ ʃaryinha mil-barazi:l (applause)*

il/ il maḥall illi b-yibi:ʕ ʔays kre:m bi-yaftaxir/ il-ʔays kre:m min barra/ ik-kubbaya gayya min barra l-maʕlaʔa gayya min barra/ ya farḥiti/ ṭabb ma ʕandina maṣa:niʕ

'I was in Sharm El Sheikh the other day. Do you know these kites we used to make in the countryside, the ones made from paper, the ones we used to fix with reed and a piece of string and then we would let them fly? They

import these kites from Brazil. Of course this is a trivial amount of money. Then someone comes and tells you, "is this an amount worth bothering about?" I am just giving an example. They buy them from Brazil! (applause)
The shop that sells ice cream is very proud to say that the ice cream is from abroad, the cups are from abroad, and the spoons are from abroad. How wonderful! Come on! Don't we have factories?'

It is noteworthy that there is no change in topic between parts one and two. Mubarak is explaining the same thing: that it is important for Egypt to have a stable economy and to reduce imports and increase exports. The difference in approach is not in the subject matter, but rather in the way he chooses to tackle it, that is, in the 'ideation' triggered by a change in his role and approach, and not by a change in topic. In the first part of his speech, on the other hand, he took a 'presidential' look at economic problems. In the second, he alludes to everyday experiences and observations he shares with the audience. The difference between parts one and two is the difference between abstract and concrete, and the shift in code choice permits him to demonstrate this difference and to reach people's intellect as well as emotions.

Code choice:
Before I analyse the choice of code in this part, I would like to refer to Milroy's work, which is significant for this part and which will be discussed in detail in the next chapter. Milroy, in her book *Language and social networks* (1987: 10), indicates the relationship between heavy usage of vernacular speech and the internal structure of the group using that speech. She also indicates that people, whether educated or uneducated, exploit dialect as a means of projecting their local identity and emphasising it (see chapter 3).

Now consider the following typical examples of Mubarak's use of ECA:

(70)

ṭabʕan	*da*	*mablaġ*	*ha:yif/*	*bi-yʔul*	*lak*	*wi*	*da*	*mablaġ*
Of course	dem	amount	trivial	asp-3msg-say	to-pr2msg	and	dem	amount

Of course this is a trivial amount of money. Then someone comes and tells you "is this an amount worth bothering about?"

(71)

ṭabb ma	*ʕandina*	*maṣa:niʕ*
OK	prep-have-pr1pl	factories

'Come on! Don't we have factories?'

The use of the underlined expression 'someone comes and tells you' and the use of the word *ṭabb* are typical features of ECA, but in fact the whole passage is in ECA. Furthermore, Mubarak refers to a very special thing that children (he and his audience in earlier years) used to do in the countryside, which is making kites out of paper and pieces of strings. As a consequence, the verbs are in the first person singular, first person plural and second person plural: *ʔana kunt*, *ʕarfi:n* ('I was', 'do you know'). Moreover, Mubarak starts with a question rather than a proposition to involve the audience and remind them of their shared past:

(72) *ʕarfi:n* *iṭ-ṭayyara:t* *illi kunna* *b-niʕmilha*
2pl-know det-plans rel to be-2pl-perf asp-2pl-do-pr3fsg
fil-fallaḥi:n *di*
in det-countryside dem
'Do you know these kites we used to make in the countryside?'

There is also a quintessentially ECA exclamation used here ironically. It does not have a counterpart in MSA and is usually used by Egyptians in personal conversations to signal irony or sarcasm.

(73) *ya farḥiti*
Oh happiness-pr1sg
'How wonderful!' (lit. 'oh my happiness')

It may seem surprising that this expression is used by an Arab head of state, but it seems less surprising if one takes account of the fact that the president is now playing a different role, a role which no doubt appeals very much to his audience. The degree of the audience's empathy is indicated by a big burst of applause. The applause suggests that the audience approves of his change of role, and appreciates his popular mode of addressing them. The tone of voice of the speaker also changes in this part to a much more conversational one. One can even hear a trace of a countryside accent in this part. Obviously, the speaker uses ECA rather than MSA phonology. For example, he uses Egyptian *ʔ* rather than MSA *q* in *waraʔ* 'paper', *nilzaʔ* 'fix, stick', *yiʔu:l* 'says', *maʕlaʔa* 'spoon' (compare this with the use of *q* in part one of his speech).

2.5.2.1.3 Part three of the speech

Speaker's role:

The basic role of head of state giving an account of past achievements and future plans returns in part three, and the code is again MSA. In part three, as in part one, Mubarak again constructs an abstract economic argument, this time part-historical. Egypt is personified as an abstract entity, competing with other countries, and obtaining the respect of financial organisations. This was achieved only very recently, and Mubarak (by implication) played a role in this achievement:

(74) *wa ḥatta l-ʔams al-qari:b lam yakun fi wusʕi miṣr/ lam yakun fi wusʕi miṣr/ wa ʔukarrir/ ʔan tufakkira fil-ġadi l-baʕi:di ʔaw il-qari:b/ ka:na l-gahdu*

mustanfaran fi muwa:gahati muʃkila:ti l-ams/ muḥa:ṣaran fi ʔiṭa:ri rudu:di ʔafʕa:l/ aw ḥulu:lin waqtiyya mutafarriqa/ wa fi ha:ða l-mana:x/ lam yakun mumkinan ʔabadan/ ʔan nufakkira/ ʔan tufakkira miṣru fi d-duxu:l ʔila ʕaṣri l-maʃru:ʕa:ti l-kubra/ ʔilla baʕda ʔiʕa:dati taʃyi:di binya:tiha l-asa:siyya/ wa ziya:dati qudrati muʔassasa:tiha l-muxtalifa/ fi tanfiði l-maʃru:ʕa:ti d-daxma wa rtifa:ʕ naṣi:biha min al-istiθma:ra:ti l-kabi:ra/ baʕda ʔan ʔaṣbaḥat nuqṭata gaðbin lil-ʔistiθma:ra:t il-ʕa:lamiyya/ taḥẓa b-θiqati l-muʔassasa:ti l-ma:liyya k-kubra/
'And until very recently Egypt could not, I repeat, Egypt could not think of the far or near future. All efforts were exerted to face the problems of the past. And all efforts were limited to various temporary solutions and reactions. In this environment, it was not possible for us, for Egypt to think about entering an era of big projects, except after rebuilding its main base, increasing the ability of its different institutions to implement big projects, and increasing its share of great investments. All of this after Egypt became attractive for international investment that had the confidence of great financial institutions.'

Code choice:
The speaker here, as in part one, uses highly marked MSA features. These include

MSA phraseology (underlined):

(75)	*wa*	*ḥatta*	*l-ʔams*	*al-qari:b*	*lam*	*yakun*	*fi*	*wusʕi*	*miṣr*
	And	until	det-yesterday	det-near	neg	3msg-to be-juss	in	power-gen	Egypt

'And until very recently Egypt could not,'

Case marking (underlined):

(76)	*ka:na*	*l-gahdu*	*mustanfaran*	*fi*	*muwa:gahati*	*muʃkila:ti*
	To be-3msg-perf	det-effort-nom	exerted-acc	in	facing-gen	problems-gen
						l-ams
						det-yesterday

'All efforts were exerted to face the problems of the past.'

and negative and demonstrative features:

(77)	*lam*	*yakun*	*fi*	*wusʕi*	*miṣr*
	neg	3msg-to be-juss	in	capacity-gen	Egypt

'Egypt could not'

(78)

wa	*fi*	*ha:ða*	*l-mana:x/*	*lam yakun*	*mumkinan*	*ʔabadan/*
And	in	dem	det-climate	neg 3msg-to be-juss	possible-acc	ever

ʔan	*nufakkira/*	*ʔan*	*tufakkira*	*miṣru*	*fi*	*d-duxu:l*
that	1pl-think-sub	that	3fsg-think-sub	Egypt-nom	in	det-entering

ʔila	*ʕaṣri*	*l-maʃru:ʕa:ti*	*l-kubra*
to	age-gen	det-projects-gen	det-big

'In this environment, it was not possible for us, for Egypt to think about entering an era of big projects'

The speaker also goes back to using a highly nominalised style:

(79)

ʔilla	*baʕda*	*ʔiʕa:dati*	*taʃyi:di*	*binya:tiha*	*l-asa:siyya*
Except	after	repeating-gen	building-gen	base-gen-pr3fsg	det-main

'except after rebuilding its main base'

(80)

wa	*ziya:dati*	*qudrati*	*muʔassasa:tiha*	*l-muxtalifa*
and	increasing-gen	ability-gen	institutions-gen-pr3fsg	det-different

'increasing the ability of its different institutions'

In both these latter cases the speaker could have used verbs rather than the noun phrases. He also uses MSA rather than ECA phonology. For example, again he uses the MSA *q* instead of the glottal stop in *qari:b* 'near' and *qudra* 'ability'.

2.5.2.1.4 Part four of the speech

Speaker's role:

Here the role of the 'good old friend' returns, and the code is again ECA. This part occurs immediately after part three. Mubarak narrates the history of a shared Egyptian crisis that Egyptians managed to overcome because of their good luck and hard work, and because God was on their side. He again appeals to the past he shares with the audience, but this time he does not remind them of their childhood. He rather reminds them of the crisis the country went through, a crisis which was felt by him 'as an Egyptian', as well as by them. When there is victory at the end for them all, it is a victory that he as a fellow Egyptian shares with them. Egypt had been losing its economic reputation, internationally. As president, he had no choice but to borrow money from abroad. He did, and the problem was solved. He (as well as all Egyptians) managed to return all the money borrowed.

(81) *ʔintum ʕarfi:n ir-ra:gil il-mustaθmir lama ka:n yi:gi hine/ ʔana kunt ba-ʃu:f/ ʕa:wiz yiḍrab tilifo:n ʕalaʃa:n yisʔal ʕala miʕa:d walla ḥa:ga/*

yiʔu:m ya:xud baʕḍu wi yisa:fir min hina/ ya ʔimma l-ʔubruṣ ya ʔimma lil-yuna:n/ yitkallim wi yirgaʕ/ wi baʕde:n wa:ḥid ʔalha li/ ʔana ʕalaʃa:n kulli ma ʔaʕu:z qiṭaʕ ġiya:r ḥa-ru:ḥ ʔasa:fir ʔubruṣ walla l-yuna:n/ ah ma-fi:-ʃfayda maʕa:kum/ ʔalha li kida bi-ṣara:ḥa/ ʔulna baʔa nistilif mil-xa:rig/ ʔahu l-mukawwina:t il-xa:rigiyya wi ʔamrina li-lla:h/
wi rabbina la buddi ḥa-yifrigha/ ʔistalafna/ wi miʃi:na/ wi baʕde:n ya xwanna rabbina faragha/ wi ʃilna xamsa wi ʕiʃri:n milya:r min id-diyu:n illi ʕali:na wi rigiʕna ṭabiʕiyyi:n//
(applause)
fa rabbina dayman maʕa maṣr/
(big applause)
Audience: yiḥmi:k ya rayyis
'You know, when an investor used to come to Egypt, I could see that if he wanted to make a phone call to ask about an appointment or something of that sort, he had to go to Cyprus or Greece to make a phone call and then come back. And then some one told me, "Do I have to travel to Greece or Cyprus whenever I need spare parts? Oh, there is no hope for you." He told me so quite frankly. So we said, "Let's borrow money from abroad, get those materials from abroad for heaven's sake! God will surely make it better." We borrowed money. We progressed. Then, brothers, God did make it better, and we paid back 25 billion pounds of debt. We are back as we were before, with no debts.
(applause)
So God is always with Egypt.'
(applause)
Audience: 'May God protect you, Mr President.'

The story has a happy ending, and the audience shows its pleasure by spontaneously shouting 'May God protect you, Mr President.' Note that Mubarak does not claim that getting rid of Egypt's debts is just his doing. It is not even just the people's doing; it is also God's doing. God 'is always' with Egypt. Again the topic is essentially the same as in part three: the lack of economic planning in Egypt. Mubarak emphasises once more the fact that Egypt has achieved a lot in a short period, but this time he puts this fact across to his audience with everyday examples, and very concrete ones, like the difficulties people had in making a phone call and obtaining spare parts. This story could have been narrated in MSA, but much of its vividness would have been lost, especially for an Egyptian audience with whom he shares ECA.

Code choice:
Mubarak in this part of his speech uses ECA. He starts with the introductory phrase:

(82) *ʔintum ʕarfi:n*
pr2mpl part-know
'You know'

People in Egypt usually start telling an anecdote with this phrase. Mubarak uses a similar tactic in part two. In this part, he also uses a story to speak about his achievements, and those of Egyptians. As in any normal ECA story, he uses ECA conjunctions and other linking phrases: the ECA inchoative verb *yiʔu:m* (3msg-to embark on) to introduce a new episode, for example, and *wi baʕde:n* 'and then'. He employs dialogue to make the story more vivid to the audience:

(83) *wi baʕde:n wa:ḥid ʔalha li/ ʔana ʕalaʃa:n*
And then one say-perf-3msg -pr3fsg to-pr1sg I because
kulli ma ʔaʕu:z qiṭaʕ ġiya:r ḥa-ru:ḥ ʔasa:fir
Whenever 1sg-part-need parts spare fut-1sg-go 1sg-travel
ʔubruṣ walla l-yuna:n/ ah ma-fi:-ʃ fayda maʕa:kum/
Cyprus or det-Greece yes neg-adv-neg benefit with-pr2mpl
ʔalha li kida bi-ṣara:ḥa
say-3msg-perf-pr3fsg to-pr1sg like this with honesty
'And then some one told me, "Do I have to travel to Greece or Cyprus whenever I need spare parts? Oh, there is no hope for you." He told me so quite frankly.'

Egypt's problem is posed and 'we' (the speaker and the audience) have to deal with it. Mubarak does not claim that he dealt with it himself, but that 'we' did it, and 'we' decided. This use of the inclusive first person plural is strongly associated with the use of colloquial.

(84) *ʔistalafna/ wi miʃi:na/*
Borrow-1pl-perf and walk-1pl-perf
wi baʕde:n ya xwanna rabbina faragha/
and then voc brothers-pr1pl God make better-perf-3msg-pr3fsg
'We borrowed money. We progressed. Then, brothers, God did make it better.'

This is a good example of the 'we' and 'they' dichotomy that Gumperz (1982a: 95) mentions. He uses first and second person pronouns with ECA and third person pronouns with MSA. Mubarak uses ECA and the inclusive first person plural to create solidarity with his audience.

(85) *ʔulna* *baʔa* *nistilif* *mil-xa:rig/* *ʔahu* *l-mukawwina:t*
1pl say-perf then 1pl-borrow from-det-abroad that is det-material
il-xa:rigiyya *wi* *ʔamrina* *li-lla:h/* *wi* *rabbina*
det-abroad and destiny-pr1pl to det-God and God
la buddi *ḥa-yifrigha/* *ʔistalafna/* *wi* *miʃi:na/*
must fut-3msg-make better-pr3fsg borrow-1pl-perf and 1pl-walk-perf
wi *baʕde:n* *ya* *xwanna* *rabbina* *faragha/*
and then voc brothers God make better-3msg-perf-pr3fsg
wi *ʃilna* *xamsa* *wi* *ʕiʃri:n* *milya:r* *min*
and 1pl-remove-perf five and twenty billion from
id-diyu:n *illi* *ʕali:na* *wi* *rigiʕna* *ṭabiʕiyyin//*
det-debts rel on-pr1pl and 1pl return-perf normal

'So we said, "Let's borrow money from abroad, get those materials from abroad for heaven's sake! God will surely make it better." We borrowed money. We progressed. Then, brothers, God did make it better, and we paid back 25 billion pounds of debt. We are back as we were before, with no debts.'

The verbs in this part of the speech are mostly in the first person singular or plural, *ʔulna*, *nistilif*, 'we said', 'we borrowed' etc. Mubarak also uses a host of other ECA linguistic features, like the relative marker *illi*, and negative structures like *ma. . .ʃ* in *ma-fi:-ʃ fayda*, 'you are hopeless'. Phonologically, this section of the speech is entirely in accordance with ECA norms, the only exception being the imported MSA word *mustaθmir* 'investor'. The *θ* could have become *s* as in ECA pronunciation, but the word itself has no other equivalent in ECA.

2.5.2.1.5 General pattern of the speech

In this speech the speaker adopts a particular strategy of code-switching. He states abstract facts in MSA, and then explains these facts in ECA with concrete, personalised examples, changing his role in the process. This strategy of moving back and forth from MSA to ECA is the basic feature of the 'design' of this speech. Table 2.1 summarises the discussion above.

As was said earlier, this phenomenon of switching between ECA and MSA, which corresponds to a change in role on the part of the speaker, is not a new phenomenon. To support my data I would like to refer to an older political speech by Nasser, the late president of Egypt.

Nasser (1918–70; Prime Minister 1954; president 1956–70) was an excellent manipulator of language. He was known for using ECA in his speeches (see Holes 1993). In using ECA, Nasser demonstrated to his audience that he was

Table 2.1 Relation between code choice and speaker's role

Kind of monologue	Speaker's public identity	Role adopted by speaker	Role given to audience	Speaker's code
Pt one	President of Egypt	President	Citizens	MSA
Pt two	President of Egypt	Good old friend	Old friends/ fellow Egyptians	ECA
Pt three	President of Egypt	President	Citizens	MSA
Pt four	President of Egypt	Good old friend	Old friends/ fellow Egyptians	ECA

one of them, by speaking as they spoke in their daily life. He also made himself comprehensible for those who knew little MSA.

On 26 October 1954, the year of his becoming president, and in one of Alexandria's oldest areas, Manshīyah, Nasser delivered a speech to all Egyptians: students, peasants, workers and politicians. While he was delivering the speech, a man stood up and tried to assassinate him by shooting a gun at him. This was all on air in front of all the audience, and broadcast to all the people listening to the radio at that time. Not surprisingly, it became a very famous incident in Egyptian history. The would-be assassin was arrested instantly, but Nasser refused to move and decided to speak to the people. Indeed, his speech then took another line. He had nearly lost his life. This is enough to explain his feelings at that moment. He must have been frustrated and shocked if not terrified. He asked the people to listen to him and not to panic or move. He told them that they had to be aware of the fact that, if Nasser died, they were all Nasser. What is quite surprising is that he spoke in MSA.

(86) *ʔayyuha l-muwa:ṭini:n ʔiða: ma:ta gama:l ʕabd in-na:ṣir fa ʔana ʔalʔa:n ʔamu:t wa ʔana muṭmaʔinn/ fa kullakum gama:l ʕabd in-na:ṣir (multi. 3) tuda:fiʕu:n ʕan il-ʕizza wa tuda:fiʕu:n ʕan il-ḥurriyya wa tuda:fiʕu:n ʕan ik-kara:ma. . . ʔayyuha ir-riga:l si:ru: ʕala barakat illa:h*
'Citizens, if Gamal Abdel Nasser dies, he will die happily because you are all Gamal Abdel Nasser (3 times). You all fight for freedom and dignity. Men, move, with God's blessing.'

These words still resonate in Egypt among the fans of Nasser. He spontaneously, in the heat of the moment, spoke in MSA, repeating sentences and words, in a moving voice, probably because he was excited and shocked. It seems MSA is used in danger, when one is shocked or furious, at least for the president. Nasser was then changing his role. He was no more the friend or peer. He was now giving himself a more subtle status. He was a symbol, an idea, and this idea was inherent in all Egyptians. Anyone could be him, and anyone could play his role. He was not trying to identify with them; rather he was trying to express his anger and defiance. Even if they killed him, he would still live in every Egyptian. When challenging all those who wanted to get rid of him, he used MSA. MSA also granted him authority: he used the voice of the tradition, religious and historical, and the power of his office. This is another example of the direct relation between change of role and code choice.

To conclude this section, it is obvious that there is a clear tendency in political speeches for speakers to change their code as and when they change their role. Given that the point of much political speech-making is to persuade, it is unsurprising that there is such a large amount of switching between ECA and MSA. Persuasion often involves role change. The question remains whether the relationship between change of role and code-switching is limited to political speeches, or whether it is a general phenomenon, as some linguists have claimed (Goffman 1981; Romaine 1995).[21] There is also a general pattern in the way both MSA and ECA are used in the political speech analysed. The older speech by Nasser helps support the claim that the relation between change of role and code change is an old one. Note that in Egypt as a diglossic community, it is the speaker rather than the situation that influences language choice, although the role of the situation cannot be denied; but in a hierarchical order the speaker comes first.

2.6 CONCLUSION

In this chapter I have discussed both structural constraints and social motivations of code-switching in relation to Arabic. For the sake of clarity I divided the chapter into two main parts, one (section 2.4) about constraints on both code-switching and diglossic switching as a subcategory of code-switching, and one (section 2.5) about motivations and discourse functions of code-switching and diglossic switching. There were also two empirical case studies from my own research presented in this chapter.

I would like to conclude this chapter by highlighting two important facts.

1. Diglossia can be studied within the framework of code-switching. Applying theories of code-switching to diglossia can clarify and refine our understanding of diglossia in the Arab world in general. When exploring motivations and discourse functions of both classic code-switching and diglossic switching, it is apparent that research on code-switching can indeed shed more light on diglossia and can be applied successfully to data in which there is switching between two varieties of Arabic, when one of the two is MSA. However, when applying structural constraints theories and models of code-switching to

diglossic switching, it becomes clear that the theories and models that work with different languages do not necessarily work in a diglossic community. Diglossia is more complex than bilingualism. In addition, structural constraints on diglossic switching must consider one diglossic community at a time before making any generalisations, given the difference in exposure to MSA between Arab communities, and the difference in internalised MSA structures that have been acquired in each community.

2. The second point worth mentioning is that the amount of work done on diglossic switching as part of code-switching is small compared to work done on classic code-switching. There is still a great deal of work needed to comprehend fully or even predict the phenomenon of diglossic switching.

After examining diglossia and code-switching, it is time to study in more detail language variation in the Arab world and the reasons that trigger both variation and change.

NOTES

1. Mahfouz (Najīb Maḥfūẓ) was vague in his statement, and did not limit duality to diglossia, although perhaps diglossia was what he was describing. It is difficult to know what he had in mind exactly.
2. Diglossic switching will be dealt with later in this chapter, but for the sake of clarity, I want to mention that this switching is usually between the H and L varieties. It is usually between MSA and one of the dialects, like Tunisian (cf. Boussofara-Omar 2006a), or Egyptian (cf. Mejdell 2006 and Bassiouney 2006), or any other dialect from the dialect group discussed in Chapter 1.
3. There may still be particularities of diglossic switching that are due to the specifics of diglossia seen as a case of prolonged intimate contact between two varieties of what is perceived as a single language.
4. Data on code-switching usually comes from oral performance rather than written.
5. This fact in itself is not enough to reject a theory.
6. It is noteworthy, however, that Mejdell (2006: 391) differentiates between a dominant variety and an ML. According to Mejdell, a dominant variety will characterise the speech of all speakers, while an ML can be any variety or language they master depending on the situation. It is not necessarily a prevalent variety all the time.
7. Myers-Scotton's use of islands is distinct in some ways from its general use in syntax literature.
8. These possible structures are exemplified below.
9. The term 'neutral' refers to morphemes that can occur in both MSA and ECA.
10. I neither came across this form in my data nor found it in other data from Egypt such as that of Holes (1995), Mazraani (1997) and Mejdell (2006).
11. Mejdell (2006) also found numerous cases in which a *b*-prefix is inserted with an MSA verb.

12. This may be changing now in Egypt as well, since it has become more prestigious to learn English than MSA. This will be discussed in detail in Chapter 5.
13. Reality is more complex. Many will shift their code in bilingual lectures, and even in monolingual lectures, lecturers may shift their style from formal to informal and the opposite.
14. Note that code-switched quotations are often not reporting the language of the actual utterance, but in using code-switching demarcate the quotation from the surrounding talk.
15. Wernberg-Moller did not state the number of hours of her interviews.
16. See note 17.
17. The word 'bad' here may be translated better as 'shame'. Thus what the speaker wants to say is 'we would be ashamed' rather than 'we think it is a bad thing'.
18. This sentence is better translated as 'it is not like that there' or 'we do not have anything like that there'.
19. Following Gumperz, a number of linguists began to examine switching as a phenomenon with sociological linguistic relevance (see Gardener-Chloros 1985, 1991; Heller 1988; Thakerar et al. 1982). Auer and Di Luzio (1984) examined code-switching among the children of Italian guest workers in Germany. Clyne (1982) examined European immigrants' languages in contact with English in Australia, and Appel and Muysken (1987) examined language contact and code-switching.
20. The difference between Gumperz and Myers-Scotton is to some extent a case in point, illustrating more formal versus more functional approaches in terms of what each thinks is necessary for progress in the field.
21. It could be that the relationship differs from one community to another. This needs more studies that compare and contrast different Arab communities or even Arab and non-Arab communities.

CHAPTER 3

Language variation and change

> There are differences between me and the children in the area. These differences make me feel inferior although some of them are as miserable as I am . . . They say about me, 'he is from the countryside. He comes from the place of hunger and murderers . . . he does not know how to speak Arabic! All villagers are ill this year. They have the hunger disease'.
>
> From the autobiographical novel *al-Khubz al-ḥāfī* ('For bread alone') by the Moroccan writer Muḥammad Shukrī (2000)

The protagonist in the passage above moves from a village to a city. In the village he spoke a dialect of Berber, but now in the city his native language is looked down upon and is associated with poverty and death. If he does not speak Arabic, he will be forever ostracised from this new community. In the novel he does indeed learn to speak Arabic. Because he moves from one place to another and thus breaks his social ties to the village, and because of the negative associations of his native language, he has to give it up in favour of Moroccan Arabic. The change that he undertakes reflects not only on him personally, but also on both his old community and his new one.[1] The association of a particular dialect with economic power and another with poverty is an important factor that will be clear in the study by Holes in Bahrain (1986), discussed in this chapter in section 3.4.2.

In this chapter I will examine variation and change in the Arab world and the different factors that trigger such change. But before doing so, I will first introduce the subfield of language variation and change, which is essential in any sociolinguistic study.

3.1 INTRODUCTION

William Labov is often considered to have initiated a new perspective in the study of language. He posited that language in general is not static, but is as dynamic as society itself. Although this postulation in itself is not necessarily new, Labov's contribution is that he showed that the dynamic aspect of language can be quantified. For him language is always moving, changing, in accordance with the interaction between different parts of society and the way society is organised and is being developed (cf. Guy et al. 1996). Labov was interested in examining linguistic variation and change in different communities. He wanted to know the direction of the change and the reasons behind it. It is also worth noting that, unlike earlier students of language change who assumed that it is invisible and difficult to study except after it has taken place, Labov contended that diachronic change grows out of synchronic variation. Thus, if we want to understand diachronic change, we must analyse variation at any given time. In this chapter I first highlight the main concepts that Labov concentrated on (section 3.2.1). I then move on to the idea of social networks as developed by Milroy (section 3.2.2). I also briefly refer to what is called the 'third wave' of variation studies, as discussed by Eckert (section 3.2.3). Then I briefly shed light on the methods used to study language variation and change in relation to the western world as well as the Arab world (section 3.3). There are specific extra-linguistic variables that influence language variation and the process of change. Some of these variables are examined in section 3.4 in relation to studies done on the Arab world and with reference to studies done on other parts of the world. One variable which perhaps does not play a major role in the studies done by Labov and others outside the Arab world is diglossia. Therefore, section 3.5 is devoted to diglossia and its outcome, levelling. My main aim is to provide the framework for future studies and to give a sometimes theoretical, sometimes empirical background of work done on variation and change. Before proceeding to do so, I would like first to clarify some sociolinguistic terms that will recur whenever one discusses language variation and change.

A sociolinguistic variable, according to Milroy (1987: 10), is 'a linguistic element (phonological usually, in practice) which co-varies not only with other linguistic elements, but also with a number of extra-linguistic independent variables such as social class, age, sex, ethnic group, or contextual style'. This concept was in fact developed by Labov. Walters adds that 'empirical studies of sociolinguistic variation in the Arab world have, like quantitative studies in the west, generally been studies of phonological variation' (1996a: 184). What this means is that usually linguists interested in variation will be interested in phonological variables, such as vowels and consonants, although there are still studies that include lexical, grammatical or morphological variables.[2] Traditionally the target of a linguistic study has been a speech community. There has been more than one definition of a speech community. Labov (1966: 125) contends that it is an entity that is 'united by a common evaluation of the same variables which differentiate the speakers'. However, Trudgill (1974: 33) alludes to the difficulty of assigning individuals to abstract groups. Milroy (1987: 14) posits that a community constitutes 'cohesive groups to which people have a clear consciousness of belonging'. These groups have a strong territorial basis and a common locality to the extent that they might fear moving outside their area. Milroy thus emphasises the geographical component of a speech community. This will be very significant when studying the Arab world.

Labov likewise assumes that individuals usually belong to a specific social class. 'People can be ordered with respect to the rest of society by quantifiable characteristics such as income, education, occupation, residence, or life-style' (Milroy 1987: 13). For example, a clergyman is perceived as being of higher status than a plumber, although in some countries the plumber may actually earn more than the clergyman. That is to say, Labov, following American sociologists, assumes that society is organised into social classes, hierarchically arranged.

Meanwhile, the question of how to observe language change is definitely worth asking. Usually irregularities in the usage of a variable may provide evidence of linguistic change in progress (Guy et al. 1996). Thus, if a phonological variable such as the *q* in Arabic is used irregularly by a specific community, this may be a sign of a change in progress. Labov (1972a: 163) contends that the best way to observe change is to observe two or more successive generations of speakers. These generations have to have comparable social characteristics, 'which will represent stages in the evolution of the same speech community'. He also posits that there are two directions for change. There is a change from below, which is the 'generalization of all forms to all members of the subgroup' (1972a: 178). It is also a change that is below the level of consciousness and generally moves from the lower social classes to the higher ones without the latter's awareness. Stigmatisation, which is the association of a variable with a lower social class or a social group not highly regarded, can also initiate change from above, which indicates a correction of a variable towards the model of the highest-status group. A change from above is a conscious choice and often involves inconsistent borrowing from outside the group. In section 3.2 I will analyse in more detail Labov's and Milroy's classic works in sociolinguistic variation and change.

3.2 LANGUAGE VARIATION AND CHANGE

3.2.1 Social class approach

Labov also took the initiative in moulding and emphasising the relation between language variation and even change and the social stratum of a specific group. In 1961, he began his research into the role of social patterns in linguistic change on the island of Martha's Vineyard, off the coast of Massachusetts. The island had the advantage of being a self-contained unit, separated from the mainland by three miles of ocean. Yet still it had enough social and geographical complexity to make studying it worthwhile for any linguist (1972a). Labov conducted his study by interviewing a large number of speakers drawn from various social groups on the island. He interviewed a range of people representing various sociodemographic groups; he had both sexes and different age groups represented. Instead of eliciting single lexical items from one speaker by means of a formal questionnaire, Labov based his analysis on the conversational speech of his many informants, supplemented by data from reading passages and word lists. He researched a great deal of background information about the island. For example, one important change which may have influenced language is that the island had first been dependent on fishing for its income but in the 1960s was already becoming dependent on tourism from the mainland. Today tourism is the major industry. This kind of economic and historical change is very similar to the change that took place in the 1970s in Gulf countries and will be referred to frequently in this book, since it also reflects on language.

Labov examined in detail the location and ethnic origin of typical Vineyarders' families. He also examined other communities living on the island, and was very interested in the attitude of Vineyarders towards their community. This method used by Labov sets a standard in the study of variation and change, as will become clear in section 3.3.

Labov analysed the use of the diphthongs *ay* and *aw* as in 'mice' and 'mouse', and was in fact able to observe linguistic change in progress in relation to these two. He noted that a movement was taking place away from the standard New England realisations of the vowels, towards a centralised pronunciation of the second element of the diphthongs associated with conservative and characteristically Vineyard speakers. The heaviest users of the centralised diphthongs were young men who wanted to identify themselves as Vineyarders, who rejected the values of the mainland and resented the interference of wealthy summer visitors in the traditional island way of life. It was clear that there was a change taking place, and a change that was not towards Standard English and that was initiated not by older speakers but by young ones. What is interesting, according to Milroy (1987), is that this use of diphthongs was independent of education. Some college-educated young men who had returned to the island were the heaviest users of the vernacular diphthongs.

A methodologically more rigorous study, according to Milroy (1987), was the one Labov conducted in New York City. The study used 340 informants selected by means of a random sample,[3] which suggests that the sample was truly representative of the speech of all Lower-Eastside New Yorkers. He also sampled a range of different styles from the formal to the quintessentially casual. His method this time was acquiring recordings of conversations, both formal and casual. There was always a stranger asking the questions. Then sometimes there would be someone entering the room to get the participants more involved. This newcomer might start narrating some personal experience, for example. Labov also asked his informants to read long passages of prose, and he followed that with a word list of single lexical items and sets of minimal pairs, such as 'god' and 'guard', which many New Yorkers pronounce the same.[4]

Labov mainly examined phonological variables such as the *r* sound and how it was realised differently in his target community. He was interested in whether a speaker pronounced or deleted the consonant *r* in final or post-vocalic pre-consonantal position, as in 'car' and 'cart'. His concern was post-vocalic *r* in two contexts: syllable/word–final, and followed by a consonant. He found that all New York speakers of all statuses agree that pronunciation of post-vocalic *r* is prestigious. Southern British English speakers behave in opposite fashion by stigmatising this pronunciation, because they in fact represent a different speech community with different rules. Another example is the dropping of *h*, which is stigmatised in Southern British English but is irrelevant in New York, Belfast or Glasgow (see Trudgill 1974).

In this section I have defined what a social class is according to Labov. However, a number of linguists find problems with the concept of class (e.g. Trudgill 1974; Milroy 1987). Trudgill, for example, points out the difficulties that arise in trying to assign individuals to abstract groups such as an upper class or a lower class etc. Milroy also asks 'why people continue to speak low-status vernaculars and, even more interestingly, how they manage to maintain vernacular norms, when the social gains in adopting a form of speech closer to the standard are apparently considerable' (1987: 8).

Because of the fact that specific variables which are not necessarily associated with a powerful or a richer group persist in a society, Milroy decided to use a different sort of framework when examining language change and variation. She uses the concept of social networks.

3.2.2 Social networks approach

Milroy's classic work on Belfast was based on the concept of social networks; this concept not only complements Labov's work based on social class, but also stands by itself as sometimes the main and only explanation of language variation and change. Milroy conducted her fieldwork for the study of Belfast working-class speech in 1975–6 in three well-defined communities: 'Ballymacarrett', 'the Hammer' and 'the Clonard'. She immediately noticed the problems associated with the presence of the tape recorder, the use of reading word lists and the nature of interviews. Milroy discovered a big methodological obstacle, different from the observer's paradox (discussed below), which is the fact that a linguist analysing a specific community is indeed a stranger, and as such his or her access to the real linguistic situation is limited, no matter how hard he or she tries. Thus, she introduced herself to the three communities as a friend of a friend. She called her relation to the members of the three communities that of a 'second order network contact' (1987: 44). She was also a woman fieldworker, which meant that people were less suspicious and aggressive towards her than they would probably have been to a male fieldworker in Belfast at that time. Since she was not only a woman but also alone, she did not present any threat. Both facts triggered good faith and trust on the part of community members. She was thus both an insider and an outsider. She was an insider who could be trusted, but still an outsider who could ask certain questions and inquire about different facts in the community. By recording her informants, she hoped to get a clearer picture of community life as well as samples of language in interaction that were closer to the way the speakers normally spoke than Labov was able to capture for the Lower East Side.

Because of the limitations of the concept of social class, Milroy and Gordon highlighted the concept of social networks. Their definition of networks is as follows: 'An individual's social network is the aggregate of relationships contracted with others, a boundless web of ties which reaches out through social and geographical space linking many individuals, sometimes remotely' (2003: 118). The researchers admitted later that no canonically correct procedure for analysing social networks can be identified (2003: 118). Networks can be described in relation to density and multiplexity. A dense network is one in which a large number of people are linked to each other in ties of kinship, occupation, specific voluntary group membership etc. For example, in certain areas there are youth gangs who spend a long time together and belong to the same club and neighbourhood (2003: 121). A network can also be multiplex in that the same person, for example, is connected to another as a co-employee, neighbour, kin etc – that is, in several ways. Both density and multiplexity are efficient indicators of pressure to adopt the norm of a community. They act as 'norm enforcement mechanisms' (Milroy 1987: 50). For example, an older woman in 'Ballymacarrett' placed a low value on her relationship with neighbours and seemed to reject the local team value. Thus, she had weak networks within the community and her behaviour was unlike that of someone with closer ties to the community. It is easy to maintain one's vernacular in close-knit communities in spite of cultural pressure. However, when networks are weakened then language change is often triggered. Social networks can also interact with other variables such as gender (see also Aitchison 2001).

3.2.3 Third wave approach to variation studies: community of practice

Eckert (2005) introduced a more recent approach to the study of variation and change and called it the 'third wave' of variation studies. According to this approach, variation should not be studied as a reflection of an individual's social place, but as a 'source' for the 'construction of social meaning' (Eckert 2005: 1). A key factor in this new approach is the concept of a community of practice, defined by Eckert (2005: 16) as:

> An aggregate of people who come together on a regular basis to engage in some enterprise. A family, a linguistics class, a garage, band, roommates, a sports team, even a small village. In the course of their engagement, the community of practice develops ways of doing things – practices. And these practices involve the construction of a shared orientation to the world around them – a tacit definition of themselves in relation to each other, and in relation to other communities of practice.

Thus, instead of examining the relation between individuals and abstract categories defined by the researcher, such as class, gender, ethnicity, one has to examine the constructed relation between an individual and a larger imagined community, which is mainly his or her community of practice. According to this approach the individual usually uses variables to build an identity and to select a community of practice. Eckert supports her argument by work done by anthropologists such as Ochs (1991), who claims that linguistic choices do not mark the social categories of individuals directly but rather reflect attitudes, activities and ways of life that are associated with particular categories. Rather than placing people into categories – gender categories, class categories, age categories and so on and so forth – linguists should try to understand how the construction of identity is part and parcel of the construction of social meaning. As Eckert puts it, linguists should question 'how do variables mean?' (2002: 4); that is to say, linguists should ask themselves 'how linguistic variants acquire the social meaning that is locally relevant to speakers' (Clark 2008: 267). This approach to variation and change is yet to be tested in the Arab world.

In section 3.3 I summarise the methodologies used to measure variation and change. Since measuring variation and change is crucial in assessing the situation in any community, methodology is the key factor in a valid analysis of any kind. I also give an overview of methodological tools used by linguists in analysing language variation and change, especially in the Arab world.

3.3 METHODOLOGY

The methodologies used by both Labov and Milroy in collecting data served as a template for other studies in both the Arab world and the western one. Before discussing this issue further, I would like to refer to the main methodological problem recognised first by Labov and eventually by all those who came after him. Labov (1972a: 207) stated that the main aim of a linguist working on language variation is to find out how people talk when they are not 'systematically observed'. To do that linguists depend on data that can only be obtained by systematic observation. This situation creates what he terms the 'observer's paradox'. To overcome this paradox, one can supplement formal interviews with other data, or seek to change the structure of the interview situation one way or another, that is, to manipulate the context in some way – for example by asking people to discuss childhood experiences or relate affectively charged events. However, the problem persists until the present day and there is no thorough and efficient way of eliminating it all together.

Problems of collecting data for measuring variation and change have been discussed by Milroy. According to Milroy (1987), using word lists or eliciting single lexical items is not sufficient to permit us to note the regularity and direction of language change, nor is the interview a reliable method by itself. If the interview is held by a stranger with an isolated speaker, it will be difficult for the linguist to have access to the real vernacular of that speaker. By its nature the interview's format is not likely to illicit the speaker's vernacular or most unguarded speech. Gumperz (1982a) tried to deal with this problem by having family members present during the interview to make it less formal, or by asking about something personal and getting his informants involved in narrating a personal experience.

One way of trying to collect data that is more natural and presents unguarded speech is to use both insiders and outsiders as interviewers, as Labov did when he studied what was then termed 'Black English Vernacular' (1972b). He focused on the speech of adolescents up to the age of sixteen and used African American fieldworkers, insiders and outsiders. He also used peer-group recordings of his informants together and alone. He recorded them in real-life situations such as eating, drinking and card playing.

Collecting background information is really the first step in variation research. This is what Labov did with his study of Martha's Vineyard. This is also what Milroy did in her study of Belfast, and what Gumperz did in his study of the Norwegian village of Hemnes (Gumperz and Hymes 1972).

Linguists studying the Arab world have used mainly the same methods as Labov and Milroy. In fact, Milroy's method of collecting data was used in Haeri's study of sociolinguistic variation in Cairo (Haeri 1997). Haeri also was a female working alone, and as an Iranian, she shared the religion of her informants, Islam. Therefore, it was easy for her to be both an insider and an outsider in various ways. She was then able to study phonological variation in the speech of men and women in Cairo in relation to class. She used the sociolinguistic interview in addition to radio and TV programmes for children and adults, as well as a word list reading. She analysed the speech of eighty-seven speakers (fifty women and thirty-seven men) and limited her study to traditional urban and modern or industrial urban groups in Cairo. To overcome the observer's paradox, she not only used the social network approach, but also tried to speak about personal things with her informants, such as childhood games, school days, family, falling in love and local customs.[5]

In Holes' study of Shiite and Sunni speakers in Bahrain (1984, 1986), he analysed tape-recorded conversations of eighty-seven speakers. He divided his group according to education, literacy and illiteracy, age group, and social networks. To help overcome the observer's paradox, he explained to his informants that his interest was to gather information about social customs rather than to gather speech for analysis, a common practice among linguists. He started recording people in different settings; at home, in the workplace and in the market. He was then able to measure variation. He also collected sociodemographic background information on the community being analysed and the individuals being interviewed before conducting his study. Khan (1997), in his study of Karaitis Jews, used the interview as the main method for collecting data. He interviewed older members who then spoke the dialect fluently. See Al-Wer (1999), discussed in section 3.4.1, for a similar methodology.

Daher (1999), in his study of variation in Damascene Arabic, was aware that the presence of the tape recorder makes it difficult to elicit spontaneous speech. This is because the tape recorder makes informants more careful about their speech; educated speakers are more likely to use MSA more often than they usually would. Daher tried to overcome this problem by using an interviewer who was familiar with the culture, had the trust of the informants and was a member of the speech community. The interviewer was also a member of the large social network. Most of the informants were either friends, family members or co-workers, which as noted above influences the degree of representativeness of the data. Daher also chose a cosy setting for the interviews, usually the home of the informants, when other family members were present. Then he began the interview by asking about personal experiences, memorable stories, hobbies, school and television in Syrian society – unthreatening topics. He found that stories based on lasting memories worked well in reflecting the real vernacular used by the informants. He recorded long narratives of informants' stories about a journey on foot from Beirut to Damascus, a marriage and an accident. In analysing the data, he also decided to ignore the first five minutes of the interview.

Jabeur (1987), in his sociolinguistic study of Rades, decided first to gather information about the history of the place, the reasons for the increasing population, internal rural migration, and the phenomenon of increasing residential mobility. He conducted a study of the sociodemographic characteristics of Rades. He studied the language of twelve women, and to overcome the observer's paradox he adopted, in collecting his data, the social network approach, which is based, as stated earlier, on the idea that people behave differently in a group, influenced by their network. Jabeur introduced himself as a friend of a friend. Thus he depended on existing relations within a community rather than creating new relationships. He used the interview by recording information in places where people usually met to drink tea, and since they were network members, this would have reduced the effect of observation.[6]

Before examining independent social factors that influence language variation and change, I would like to note that most of the linguists dealing with the issue of variation, especially those dealing with it in the Arab world, build their work on the concept of quantitative studies. Quantitative studies aim to examine the correlation between linguistic variation and other variables, in particular social class (Coates 1993: 61). One uses quantitative methods to seek to uncover statistical relationships between independent variables such as age, sex, sect, social class, place of origin or level of education, and dependent variables such as the relative use of specific linguistic variants that together make up a linguistic variable.[7]

3.4 SOCIOLINGUISTIC VARIABLES

I will now examine some of the extra-linguistic variables that influence change and variation, and that have been studied by linguists examining the Arab world. Independent variables analysed below include ethnicity, religion, urbanisation and social class (sections 3.4.1–3.4.4). Gender will be examined in Chapter 4. It is noteworthy, however, that dividing the triggers of language variation and change into independent variables is not an easy task and is at times arbitrary. The variables studied overlap and interact with each other. Their definitions also overlap in most cases. For example, in a study that concentrates on women, urbanisation and ethnicity, such as Al-Wer's study in Jordan (1999) discussed below, it is difficult to examine the study from the perspective of one specific variable. Also, across the Arab world sectarian differences are often linked to issues of social class and ethnicity in complex ways. Thus the division of variables is flexible and serves only as a guide in our understanding of variation and change.

intersectionality

3.4.1 Ethnicity

Ethnicity is a crucial variable in a great number of places in the world at large, and in parts of the Arab world in particular. However, it is a variable that is crucial when present but not as crucial in places or communities that are not ethnically diverse, although these are now few and far between. In the next paragraphs I will explain how ethnicity in the Arab world may differ from ethnicity in the west and how linguists dealing with the Arab world define ethnicity. The definition of ethnicity is flexible, as in some cases it could include differences built on nationalities or religious affiliation and in other cases it could be built on skin colour.

According to Davies and Bentahila (2006: 58), ethnicity is 'an analytical concept used to describe the bonds which lead certain people to identify themselves as a group'. This bond could be an ancestral lineage. Fishman (1977: 17) describes this bond as a paternity bond, and posits that 'Ethnicity is, in part, but at its core, experienced as an inherited constellation acquired from one's parents as they acquired it from theirs, and so on back further and further, ad infinitum'. As Edwards (1985: 10) argues, the ethnic group's boundary 'can be sustained by shared objective characteristics (language, religion, etc.) or more subjective contributions to a sense of "groupness", or by some combination of both'.

Note that according to Fishman this bond can be lost and is not inherent, that is, one can acquire or lose an ethnicity.

However, in my opinion losing or acquiring an ethnicity is difficult if not impossible. Ethnicity is different from identity in the sense that identity is related to the individual and his or her projection of himself or herself (see the definition of identity in Chapters 2 and 5), while ethnicity is something one is born with. Thus changing one's identity or appealing to different parts of one's identity is easier than changing one's ethnicity.

Davies and Bentahila (2006: 59) also argue that both ethnicity and nationalism can be considered 'as points on a continuum'. Degrees of self-awareness, organisation, mobilisation or ideologisation can all be factors that distinguish nationalism and ethnicity (cf. Connor 1978; Edwards 1985; Fasold 1995; Paulston 1994).

The definition of ethnicity by Fishman relies on patrimony and ancestral lineage. However, Owens (2001: 434), when discussing ethnicity in the Arab world, posits that ethnicity is 'Any of a number of social parameters by which, non-national social groupings are distinguished, including religion, shared history, skin colour, kinship, lineage and place of origin. The relevant criterion or criteria defining ethnicity may differ from place to place.' Owens includes religion in the definition of ethnicity, which may imply that in Iraq Sunnis and Shiites can be considered two ethnic groups, and in Egypt Copts and Muslims can also be considered two ethnic groups. Such a proposition would be politically charged and may not reflect the way in which people perceive themselves. For example, most Egyptians tend to perceive themselves, whether they are Copts or Muslims, as descendants of the Ancient Egyptians, and tacitly feel different from other Arabs because of their Ancient Egyptian history[8] (see also the views of Salāmah Mūsá, discussed in Chapter 5). However, Kurds in Iraq may be considered an ethnically different group because historically they were part of a specific entity with the same ancestors and a shared history (Davies and Bentahila 2006), although they are mostly Sunni Muslims.

I prefer to retain Fishman's definition of ethnicity rather than Owens' more flexible one, simply because religion is a more complicated and historical intertwined factor than it seems. Thus I will consider Palestinians (both Muslims and Christians) as one ethnic group and Jordanians (both Muslims and Christians) as another ethnic group. Although Palestinians and Jordanians may have much in common, they both perceive themselves and each other as different, although they may still share the same religion. They perceive themselves as coming from different lineage and different ancestors. This is when the line distinguishing nationality from ethnicity is blurred. The importance of family bonds and paternal ancestors is a salient feature in the Arab world. Arabs from different countries define themselves according to the tribe they belong to, the family they belong to and finally the country they belong to. Omani men, for example, until recently needed permission to marry a foreign woman (a non-Omani one). I have attempted above to clarify what ethnicity refers to in this book, and how it is different from religion and other extra-linguistic factors.

In multi-ethnic communities language variation and change are very apparent and significant. In the past century the Arab world has been in a state of flux for different reasons, some of them political and some economic. We definitely need more studies that examine variation between different ethnic communities in the Arab world.

A country that has been analysed exhaustively by linguists is Jordan. Although a small country with a small population (6 million), Jordan has one of the most interesting situations in the Arab world with two nationalities living together, sometimes as friends and sometimes as enemies: the Palestinians and the Jordanians. In fact, the present-day situation is even more interesting, with the king, Abd-Allah, being of Jordanian origin and Queen Rania being of Palestinian origin. Whether this will eventually influence language variation and change in Jordan is still to be seen.

It is worth mentioning, though, that Jordan itself was formed after World War I by Britain. Again note that Palestinians and Jordanians are not precisely two ethnic groups but rather two political entities, but they perceive themselves and each other as different, as was said earlier. This is a case when politics meddles with linguistics. There will be numerous cases of this meddling in Chapter 5. Given that the Arab world is loaded with political changes and foreign political interference, this is not surprising. Before explaining the linguistic situation in Jordan, I first want to give an overview of the history of Jordan.

3.4.1.1 Jordanians versus Palestinians

3.4.1.1.1 History of Jordan

Jordan lies between Israel to the west, Syria to the north, Iraq to the east and Saudi Arabia to the south. Jordan as we know it now was created by Britain after World War I. Britain seized what was then referred to as Transjordan from the Turks after the war, separated it from the Palestinian mandate, and placed it under the rule of ʿAbd Allāh ibn Ḥusayn in 1921. In 1946 Britain abolished the mandate and Jordan gained independence.

Al-Wer (1999: 38) posits that historical events have determined the 'demographic and socio-political constitution of Jordan'. The 1948 war resulted in the displacement of half a million Palestinians, most of whom fled to Jordan as refugees. This war also led to the incorporation of the West Bank into the Jordanian kingdom, thus changing the western borders of the country. The population of Jordan then rose from half a million to 1.4 million. In May 1967 King Hussein of Jordan signed a defence pact with Egypt against Israel (Mansfield 2003: 273). After the 1967 war, another 250,000 Palestinians sought refuge in Jordan. The war also resulted in the loss by Jordan of East Jerusalem and the West Bank. After the defeat of the 1967 Arab–Israeli war, frustrated Palestinian guerrilla forces took over sections of Jordan and open warfare broke out between the Palestinian Liberation Organisation (PLO) and government forces in 1970. Syria intervened then but Hussein's army defeated the Palestinians. The Jordanians drove out the Syrians and 12,000 Iraqi troops who had been in the country since the 1967 war. Despite protests from Arab countries, Hussein, by mid-1971, crushed Palestinian strength in Jordan and shifted the problem to Lebanon, where many of the guerrillas had fled. This indeed created tension between both groups for a long time. In July 1989, Jordan renounced its sovereignty over the West Bank. In so doing, it emphasised that there are two separate national entities, a Palestinian one and a Jordanian one.

Nowadays, within Jordan, the legal status of Palestinians is equal to that of Jordanians. Both groups are considered citizens of Jordan (Al-Wer 1999). In fact, some Palestinians claim that of all countries in the Arab world, the only one that treats them as equal to its natives is Jordan. Jordan also has the largest community of Palestinians in the Arab world. It is noteworthy that not all Palestinians who settled in Jordan were war refugees. Some bourgeois families settled there early on. Palestinians were, in fact, better trained to open their own business and also to work in the public sector because of education and experience they brought with them when they came to Jordan. They started early on in Jordan to take a leading economic, academic and even political role.

The linguistic situation in Jordan is as follows. There is an urban Palestinian dialect, a rural Palestinian dialect, and Bedouin and rural Jordanian dialects (Cleveland 1963). To illustrate the difference between these dialects, note the realisation of the phonological variable *q* in all these dialects:

urban Palestinian dialect: [*ʔ*] (glottal stop)
rural Palestinian dialect: [*k*] (voiceless stop)
Bedouin and rural Jordanian: [*g*] (voiced stop) (cf. Abdel-Jawad 1986).

According to Suleiman (2004), after the bloody confrontation between Palestinians and Jordanians in 1970, Palestinian male students at university started using the *g* variable as opposed to the glottal stop of their urban dialect or the *k* of their rural one. They started accommodating to Jordanian Bedouin men. Suleiman recalls how his Palestinian male friends, especially the rural Palestinian students, started to use *g* with the soldiers who operated the checkpoints between the town centre and the university (2004: 115). At that point the Jordanian dialect was not only the more prestigious one but also the safest one to use at a time when the Jordanian government was using force in dealing with Palestinians. Thus, although the Palestinian urban dialect was associated with urbanism, finesse, wealth and modernism, for Jordanians, the change seemed to be towards the local dialect of Jordanian Bedouins.[9]

After the reconciliation between Jordanians and Palestinians, the Palestinian urban dialect was still a symbol of modernity and education, but Jordanians, especially men, did not accommodate to it. Abdel-Jawad (1986) claimed that this refusal had to do with feelings of local identity, pride in origin, and solidarity. In fact, although Abdel-Jawad does not spell it out in these terms, it has to do mainly with social networks. Jordanian tribes have dense and multiplex social networks. Abdel-Jawad, for example, noted that each tribe had a clubhouse in which members meet to discuss different matters. Thus it is not surprising that Jordanians, whether rural or Bedouin, kept their *g*. Linguists do not agree on the present status of *q* in Jordan. In the past twenty years or so, the tendency has been for female Jordanians and female Palestinians to use the glottal stop, the variant associated with Palestinians. This had to do with the fact that Jordanian women aspire to the modernity and finesse of Palestinians (cf. Abdel-Jawad 1986; Al-Wer 1999). Male Jordanians retain the *g*, but it is not clear what male Palestinians use. However, the linguistic differences between both groups may have decreased immensely lately. Note that Suleiman disagrees on the analysis based on gender distinction (2004: 115).

Al-Wer (1999) has postulated that in Jordan nowadays there is a new dialect in the making that is the result of contact between indigenous Jordanian varieties and urban Palestinian varieties. This new dialect is different from any other variety in the region. Her empirical research was carried out on 116 women, all of indigenous Jordanian origin. Some of the phonological variables investigated are the following realisations:

q as *g* or *ʔ*, as in *ga:l* or *ʔa:l* 'he said'
θ as *θ* or *t*, as in *θa:ni* and *ta:ni* 'again'
ẓ as ẓ or ḍ , as in *ẓall* and *ḍall* 'he remained'
j as *dj* or *j*, as in *dja:r* and *ja:r* 'neighbour' (1999: 39).

Her data indicates that the interdental variables *θ* and ẓ exhibit the largest amount of variation in the direction of the stop variants. She found that there is a degree of maintenance of the local variant [*g*], even among women. The glottal stop is scarcely used by her informants. She contends that the reason for this usage is that the realisation of *q* as *g* or *ʔ* is used to stereotype speakers as belonging to one or another ethnic group or sex. It is such a salient feature that speakers are aware of its implications. Thus, she says that 'speakers, regardless of their sex, reflect various identities in their linguistic behaviour' (1999: 54).

Al-Wer likewise argues that this new dialect, which is in the formation stages, involves particular patterns of variation involving a combination of the variables *g*, *t*, *d* and *j*. This dialect is different from any other in the region and thus cannot be classified as Levantine or otherwise. Therefore, although among older speakers dialects can be identified as either Jordanian or Palestinian, the same is not true for the speech of the younger generation, in which language plays a role in decreasing regional differences and constructing a new dialect, and thus potentially a new identity. Language here is used to increase localised and marked features as well as being a symbol of a new identity in which ethnic differences are less significant (Al-Wer 2002: 45).

In a later study (2007), Al-Wer analyses further the new dialect in the making in Amman. She argues that Amman had no specific dialect because basically until recently it had no stable inhabitants. Now 39 per cent of the inhabitants of Jordan live in Amman. Her data comprises 25 hours of recorded interviews across three generations of both Jordanians and Palestinians in Amman. The variables she examines include the vowel quality of the *a:* when preceded by *r* and the use of the glottal stop and *g* variables discussed above in detail. Al-Wer posits that the quality of the vowel preceding *r* is different in the Palestinian dialect of Nablus and the Jordanian one of Sult. The Palestinian dialect is more back, with lip rounding and pharyngeal constrictions (2007: 69). She concludes that the differences between the Jordanians and Palestinians are reduced now to the minimum, with Palestinians accommodating to the pronunciation of Jordanians with regard to this variable. What Al-Wer notices in her study in general is, again, the neutralisation of the differences between both groups in the younger generation. Note that according to Abdel-Jawad and Al-Wer the linguistic situation in Jordan is very different from that in Syria, where Palestinians have a socially inferior status to Syrians and thus are expected to accommodate thoroughly to the Syrian dialect. This is despite the fact that there are approximately 450 thousand Palestinian refugees in Syria. One cannot measure the truth of this postulation except with quantitative empirical data.

In this section I have concentrated on Jordan as a multi-ethnic community. As I said earlier, while it is easy to project a different facet of one's identity at different stages of one's life, it is difficult to change one's ethnicity. For example, in the case of Palestinians in Jordan, although they are integrating to a great extent with the Jordanians at different levels, they still perceive themselves as Palestinians and not Jordanians.

Another point worth mentioning here is that tribes form communities of practice. Individuals choose to belong to their tribe because this provides them with social strength and status. A clubhouse exclusive to tribe members is a community of practice.

However, more studies are needed about language variation in other multi-ethnic communities. For example, a study that examined the dialect of Palestinians in Egypt or Syria and how it is changing, or not changing, would be well worth its salt. The Gulf, since the 1970s, has also attracted people of different ethnic origins. More studies done on the Gulf and pidgin Arabic are also necessary.

3.4.2 Religion

3.4.2.1 Religion in the Arab world

The religious landscape of the Arab world is an extremely complex one. It is common knowledge that Islam, Christianity and Judaism are represented among the populations of the region. At the same time, these religions themselves are divided into different sects.

Thus, Muslims may be divided into Sunnis and Shiites. The former group is largely coherent theologically (if not in actual practice); the latter group in turn falls into various subgroups, such as the 'Twelvers' (after the number of consecutive imams in their theological system), Ismailis, Ibadis and Zaydis. In addition, there are historical offshoots of (Shiite) Islam, such as the Druze, the Alevis and Bahais.

Christianity, likewise, falls roughly into three large groups: Orthodox churches, Catholics and Uniate churches, as well as Protestants, with some additional offshoots that belong to none of these categories, such as the Mandeans. Many of these churches are also national churches in the sense that they are linked with a particular territory, and in the sense that they employ a particular language in their liturgy. Hence, there is the Coptic Orthodox Church (which uses Coptic and Arabic in its liturgy), the Greek Orthodox (Greek and Arabic), the Armenian Orthodox Church (Armenian), etc.[10] Finally, there are distinct subgroups within Judaism, too, such as the Karaites, and offshoots, such as the Samaritans.

With all this variation, it is difficult to generalise about religious groups, as their presence or absence in the various parts of the Arab world are largely the result of historical circumstance. Thus, the Arabian peninsula has no native Christians to speak of, whereas Egypt, Iraq, Syria, Jordan, Israel-Palestine and above all Lebanon all have sizeable Christian communities. Of these, the Copts are found almost exclusively in Egypt, where they form the national church, while the Maronites are restricted mostly to Lebanon (that is, if we ignore expatriate communities elsewhere). The once thriving Jewish communities of Egypt and Iraq have all but disappeared, but in Morocco and Tunisia, small communities remain.

These communities, groups and subgroups often live side by side within the same national entity, but they may at times enter into fierce competition among themselves; an example of this is the ongoing contention among the Christian denominations for space and rights within the Church of the Holy Sepulchre in Jerusalem, which has turned violent at times. The Shiite–Sunni conflicts in Lebanon and Iraq are cases in point. It is clear, then, that religious identities in the Arab world are multi-layered, as they relate not only to an abstract religion, but also to a distinct group or community within that religious group, or even to a 'national' or ethnic group, as is the case with the Armenians in Egypt or Lebanon.

Lebanon, as an Arab country, used to contain the largest number of Christians. In 1975, on the eve of the Lebanese civil war (1975–90), Christians constituted 55 per cent of the population of Lebanon, most of which adhered to the Maronite Church. This has dropped to 40 per cent (2,200,000) in recent years, as has the percentage of Christians throughout the Arab world. As for Syria, while in 1960 Christians formed approximately 15 per cent of the population (about 1.2 million), they are estimated to constitute only 10 per cent now, due to immigration and to lower birth rates among Christians than among their Muslim counterparts. In Jordan, Christians constitute 7 per cent of the population (400,000). In the Palestinian territories of the West Bank and Gaza Strip there are about 90,000 Palestinian Christians. There are also 190,000 Palestinian Christians living in Israel and about 400,000 Palestinian Christians living in the diaspora. Egypt's population is estimated at 80 million, among which at least 7–9 percent are Christian Copts. In North Africa, there are very small communities of Christians, who mainly belong to the Roman Catholic church and who live in Tunisia, Algeria and Morocco.

Jews, on the other hand, who formed a significant minority in the Arab world, were forced to leave or migrated after the formation of Israel in 1948. The small communities that remain in the Arab world range from about 10 in Bahrain to 7,000 in Morocco and 1,000 in Tunisia.

It is worth mentioning that Muslims in the Arab world make up less than one quarter of the world's Muslims in general – estimated at around 1.4 billion. They are mainly Sunnis with a substantial Shiite minority. In fact, Shiites comprise 65 per cent of the population of Iraq, and approximately 75 per cent of the population of Bahrain. Countries such as Lebanon, Yemen and Kuwait have substantial Shiite groups. Saudi Arabia also has a Shiite minority in its eastern province of al-Aḥasāʾ, and the southern province city Najrān harbours a minority of Ismailis.

3.4.2.2 Religion as an independent variable

Like other social variables, religion does not stand in isolation but is connected to other categories, and in the Arab world specifically, it is also closely connected to the political system of each country. Religion is important in terms of language variation and change only in the sense that it can create a close-knit community whose members feel for one reason or another that they are united by it.[11] I think political factors are essential in a great number of communities in the Arab world and may be intertwined with religion in most cases. Al-Wer (2002: 45) discusses why pressures towards regional levelling[12] will not make the dialects of Beirut, Damascus, Jerusalem and Amman identical. The reason she gives is that the countries of the Levant are separate political entities with different political and social attitudes. Whether this attitude is that of members of these communities or of the political regime of these communities is not clear.

It is worth mentioning, however, that in the Arab world, unlike the west, religion is usually not seen as a matter of individual choice, but as a matter of family and group affiliation; one is born a Muslim, a Jew or a Christian, and that fact becomes almost similar to one's ethnicity. As was established earlier, it is almost impossible to change one's ethnicity, because it is dependent on how you perceive yourself and how others perceive you, not just as an individual but as part of a community. The same is true for religion. This kind of attachment to religion is perhaps different among highly educated westerners. It is not only that changing one's religion is perceived as a serious misdemeanour, but also that the convert is seen as rejecting the existing social order, tradition and family obligations. Even the rituals and appearance of religion are more prominent in the Arab world, where it is common for a Muslim man to go to the mosque regularly and for a Muslim woman to wear a headscarf, and also for a Christian man or woman to go to church regularly and to wear a cross.

Studies that have concentrated on religion as a variable in the Arab world include Holes' study of Bahrain (1984, 1986), in which he highlights some very significant factors in language change and variation in this country. He first stresses the relation between language variation, change and identity. He states that there is a difference between the concept of identity in European and American society and the concept of identity in Bahrain specifically. That is because while the former is defined by characteristics such as age, education, occupation etc., the latter is foundationally defined by sectarian differences. These differences are basically between the Shiite Baharnas and the Sunni Arabs. These sectarian differences are also reflected in language. The Baharnas are monolingual, Arabic-speaking Shiites who form the oldest population of Bahrain, and they are traditionally rural. The Arab Sunnis are descendants of the Bedouin tribes which began immigrating to Bahrain in the late eighteenth century, and they form the majority of the urban population. Importantly, the ruling family in Bahrain is from the Sunnis. Thus, power, prestige and financial control are associated with the Sunni Arabs. This will in fact have a great impact on the direction of language change in this region. As was said earlier, religion is deeply intertwined with politics in the Arab world. This is reflected in the direction of language change and variation.

Before discussing this further, I would first like to show some of the phonological differences between the Baharna Shiite dialect and the Arab Sunni dialect. As usual, we will also include the realisation of the phonological variable in MSA. The variables studied are *j* and *q*.

j
MSA: *j*
Shiites: *j*
Sunnis: *y*

q
MSA: *q*
Shiites: *q*
Sunnis: *g*

Holes found that the Shiite Baharna dialect is changing with regard to these variables in the direction of the Sunni Arab dialect even when the Sunni Arab dialect does not conform to MSA. This finding in itself is important, because it draws attention to the fact that change is not always in the direction of MSA. In fact if the prestige dialect, in this case the Arab dialect, deviates from MSA, the change can be away from MSA towards the prestige dialect. Even though more and more people are exposed to MSA for longer and longer periods of time and in more and more contexts, it is not the case that the dialects are necessarily becoming more like MSA.

The change that has been taking place in the dialect of the Shiite Baharnas, according to Holes, reflects a change in their social identity, because of changes in employment opportunities and increase in social contact between both sects. Holes calls this phenomenon a 'conspiracy of convergence' (1986: 34). For example, the variant *q*, which was used by the Shiite Baharnas, is now associated with peasants and thus, not surprisingly, ignorance, while the variant *g*, which is used in other parts of the Arab world such as Kuwait, Saudi Arabia and Qatar, is associated with wealth and sophistication (Holes 2005: 57). Holes provides evidence that there is a change in progress in the direction of *g* taking place among Shiite Baharnas.

The Shiite Baharnas living in the town of Muḥarraq were originally craftsmen specialising in sail-making. With the changes that took place in the Gulf in the 1970s because of oil and the collapse of Beirut as the centre of commerce, it became important for the Baharna Shiites politically and economically to change their dialect towards that of the Sunni Arabs. The Shiite Baharnas were suddenly in contact with Arabs much more, whether in the market or in public places, and had to accommodate to them, since the Arabs were politically and economically superior (Holes 2005: 60). There were also campaigns to eradicate illiteracy in both groups, which may have helped in the convergence process. Holes alludes to the lack of linguistic security on the part of the Baharna Shiites, which also has to do with weakening in the social network ties within this sect. He gives the example of Shiite Baharnas in the village of Muḥarraq who started working in the international airport, and since then have been spending their time with Arab Sunni co-workers and are not interested any more in going to their local mosque. Note also that the dialect used in the media – in television soap operas, songs, speech bubbles in newspaper cartoons – is the one used by the Sunni Arabs (Holes 2005: 57).

While in this study the linguistic distinction is between Sunnis and Shiites, the real situation is more nuanced and factors like political and economic power are in play here. Also, the weakening of social ties within the community, due to historical changes that have taken place in the region in the past two decades, is important in shaping language change (see also Holes 2006a, 2006b).

Third wave variation studies, though not used to explain variation in Bahrain, can be applied neatly to describe the linguistic situation in Bahrain. The linguistic variation in the speech of Baharnas is the result of the way they perceive their community of practice. The Baharnas have changed their community of practice. They do not meet as a community in the mosques any more, for example. In addition, their use of Arab linguistic variables is the result of the way they perceive their identity. Their social identity is changing and the Arab variables they use are acquiring different meanings and connotations.

In another study that concentrated on religion, Abu–Haidar (1991) examined the differences between the Muslim (MB) and Christian (CB) Arabic of Baghdad. Her study is different from a great number of studies on language variation since it does not depend only on phonological variables but also examines syntactic and semantic ones, which are more difficult to observe. Her study predicts a change in progress towards the Muslim dialect, but for different reasons from the ones given by Holes. What her study has in common with Holes is the fact that the dialect which is changing, CB, is in fact the older dialect but is moving towards a newer one, in this case MB.

Abu-Haidar states that there were one million Christians in Iraq at the time of her data collection. There were in fact villages in the north of the country where the population was entirely Christian. Baghdad, on the other hand, had around 100 churches – the largest concentration of churches in the whole country. She goes on to explain the history and tradition of the Christians in Iraq. The indigenous Christian group, the Jacobites, traditionally live in northern villages as well as in central cities such as Baghdad and Basra. Their church was founded in the sixth century and follows the belief that there is only one nature of the divine in the person of Christ; thus the church is regarded as heretical by both the Roman Catholic and Greek Orthodox churches. However, there are also some Armenian Orthodox, Greek Orthodox, Greek Catholics and Protestants in Iraq, although their percentage is very low compared to the Jacobites. The Christians of Baghdad are a well-established community. Their dialect is a sedentary variety of Arabic which evolved from the Arabic vernacular of medieval Iraq. In that sense it is different from the Muslim dialect of Baghdad, which is more recent and of Bedouin origin (Jastrow 1978: 318). In fact, some districts in Baghdad remained completely Christian, at least until the time of the US invasion of Iraq in 2003. Christians are usually clustered around churches.

In Baghdad, speakers of MB and CB, like everyone across the Arab world, share MSA as a high variety. MB is the low variety for Muslim Baghdadis, but as the language of the more powerful, richer community, it also serves as a second dialect for Christian Baghdadis. For Christians it is not used at home and not spoken among group members, but it is used in formal, less spontaneous situations. Therefore, one can think of CB speakers as triglossic speakers, who use three varieties of Arabic in different situations that differ in their formality. Abu-Haidar gives an example from her childhood. In her primary school in Baghdad in the early 1950s, the conversation between the teachers, who were all Christian women at the time, and the pupils was often in CB, but when the teacher referred to the text or assumed a more serious tone, even with a Christian child, she would use MB. Interestingly, MSA was not the only variety used as the medium of instruction in schools. The following are examples that show the difference between MSA, MB and CB (Abu-Haidar 1991: 144):

(1) MSA: *laqad samiʕa annaka huna:*
laqad hear-3msg-perf that-pr2msg here
'He heard you were here.'
MB: *Semaʕ enta hna:*
hear-3msg-perf you here
CB: *ken samaʕ anta ho:na*
ken hear-3msg-perf you here

(2) MSA: *al-kalbu kabi:run*
det-dog-nom big-nom
'The dog is big.'
MB: *tʃaleb tʃabi:r*
Dog big
CB: *l-kaleb agbi:ġ ya:nu*
Det-dog big

It is noteworthy, however, that Abu-Haidar recognises that even within CB, there is still variation between one group of speakers and another, and even within the repertoire of the same speaker. For example, there is a high level of phonological variation within CB. She stresses that this variation is not related to social variables such as gender or generation. She gives the example of an elderly woman who gave both *tma:m* and *tama:m* for 'complete' or 'whole'. A man from a younger group of informants provided the two variants *nha:ġ* and *nahaġ* for 'day', while Blanc (1964: 146) gives '*nha:ġ*' as the CB equivalent for day.

Abu-Haidar contends that CB is changing and that its existence is being threatened from several directions. The reasons for these changes are, first, the accommodation process. Most CB salient features are adjusted towards MB during CB/non-CB interaction. Some sociolinguists, like Dorian (1973) and Trudgill (1983, 1986), argue that long-term adjustment can sometimes result in complete reduction and/or loss of certain salient stigmatised features, that is, language change. To support her claim, Abu-Haidar mentions the fact that Blanc (1964) found that some overtly stigmatised features, such as dental *t* for interdental *ṯ*-, were optional among speakers he interviewed.[13] Such irregularity can itself be an indicator of language change in progress, as was mentioned before by Labov. Additionally, some of Abu-Haidar's older informants thought that CB features serve as overt markers of one's Christian identity, and that many young people do not want to retain them in their speech. Most of her young informants saw the postpositional copula and particle *ken* as redundant.

Abu-Haidar posits that, 'The most immediate danger to CB which could lead to dialect death, similar to the fate Dorian (1981) predicted for Scottish Gaelic, is due to social, rather than to linguistic factors' (1991: 150). She explains that the main threat for CB is the fact that CB speakers have recently been scattered all over the world. Since the 1960s many have settled in non-Arab-speaking communities. Although first-generation CB emigrants tend to preserve their variety, it is difficult to predict whether they can maintain it. In fact, there is a strong likelihood that they cannot. Furthermore, even if they do, it will undergo changes in its various locations.

It is apparent that once more it is weak network ties that may encourage language change. Yet, although the situations in Iraq and Bahrain are similar in the sense that it is the group that is losing its strong social ties that leads the change, the situations in the two countries differ historically, politically and economically. Christian Baghdadis are losing their ties because of immigration rather than economic changes and movement within the country associated with the distribution of wealth and power, as is the case in Bahrain.

Khan (1997) studied the Arabic dialect of the Karaite Jews in the Iraqi town Ḥīt on the Euphrates, 150 km west of Baghdad. Khan, like Holes and Abu-Haidar, provides historical background about the community he studied and their present status. Unlike the other two researchers, though, Khan did not try to examine language change in progress, but rather to describe the dialect and record it. The Karaites are a Jewish sect that broke away from mainstream Judaism in the Middle Ages: the movement began in Iran and Iraq in the eighth century and spread to Palestine, Egypt, North Africa, Spain, Asia Minor and Eastern Europe. Early urban settlement of Ḥīt can be traced back to the tenth century. The Karaite Jewish community there was one of the most important in the Middle East, and known for its scholarly tradition. However, by 1951 the community had declined to twenty families, who then emigrated to Israel and settled on the same street in Beersheba. The dialect is characterised by some particular syntactic, phonological and lexical features. For example, the consonant *h* is dropped in the third person pronominal suffixes immediately after other consonants, as in *gibtim* 'I brought them' as opposed to *gibthim, or ma:lim* 'belonging to them' as opposed to *ma:lhim.* It is still retained sometimes, as in *minhim* 'from them' (1997: 69). Khan claims that the dialect still maintains some variables of the Qəltu dialect that was spoken in the old urban settlement of Ḥīt. Although the community is a direct descendant of medieval urban settlements, it still maintains Bedouin features today and shows almost no interference from other Arabic dialects. However, some Hebrew words have entered the dialect because speakers were bilingual in Arabic and Hebrew. Although Khan did not mention it, it seems that the reason why this dialect maintained itself even after the families immigrated to Israel is related to the density and multiplexity of their ties.

The question still remains as to what extent religion as a variable is significant in the Arab world. We certainly know that as with other variables, one cannot speak about the 'Arab world' as one entity. The situation is different from one country to another and even from one community to another in the same country.

Tomiche (1968: 1178–80) tried to distinguish the Jewish dialect spoken by the Jewish community of Alexandria and Cairo until the 1960s from other dialects. He states that the Jewish dialect was characterised by the absence of emphatics and the use of *n-* and *n-u* for first person singular and plural imperfect. According to Miller (2004), this claim was refuted by Blanc (1974), who prefers to call this dialect a non-standard Cairene Arabic which is shared by other groups. For example, the *n* is one of the North African features as well as a feature of other areas of Egypt, namely the western delta and the western oases (Behnstedt and Woidich 1985–8). In fact, coming from Alexandria myself, I know that the use of *n-* and *n-. . .-u* for first person singular is a characteristic of Alexandrian Arabic and not just limited to a specific religion.

Other studies that concentrate on religion include studies on Bethlehem in Palestine by Spolsky et al. (2000), in which they indicate that Christian speakers, both women and men, tend to use more urban features, like the glottal stop, than do Muslim speakers, who tend to use MSA *q*. Blanc's 1953 study of the Northern Palestinian Arabic dialect used by Druze remains a classic, one-of-a-kind study, mainly because there are very few if any studies that concentrated on linguistic variation in the speech of Druze (cf. Walters 2006a for other references).

Miller (2004) explains religion as a variable by positing that in most Arab cities religious minorities used to live in certain areas and thus developed different linguistic models, as in Baghdad and Fes. Different religious communities kept their vernaculars for centuries and did not acquire the dialect of the Muslim community. This was due to a degree of segregation, but also to the fact that the Muslim urban Arabic dialects were not associated with power, because political power was in the hands of foreign rulers up to the beginning of the twentieth century. Only recently has there been any change. An additional cause is the demographic changes that have taken place in different parts of the Arab world.

Miller states that there has been some linguistic variation between different religious groups but mainly at the lexical level, for religious terms and the like. She also thinks that the belief that there are still religiously segregated areas is open to question, and the situation may not be as clear cut as was thought before. This postulation by Miller has to be tested. There are still religious segregated areas in Lebanon and Iraq, for example, but to what extent this influences language variation beyond the lexical level needs more study.

One can conclude from the above discussion that religion by itself is not enough to explain variation or to initiate change. Religion is only one factor in shaping and moulding linguistic variation and change. Blanc (1964) claims that religious linguistic differences are not dominant in Arab cities. They are in fact the result of political changes and demographic changes related to the sedentarisation and urbanisation of former Bedouin groups as well as ethno-regional differences (Miller 2004: 189).[14] This postulation may not be true for all the Arab world, though.

3.4.3 Urbanisation

Miller posits that 'urbanization has been one of the greatest social changes of the last century in Arab countries' (2004: 177). The population of most Arab countries was mainly rural until the mid-twentieth century (Miller 2007: 2). To illustrate this, note that the creation of Nouakchott, the capital of Mauritania, took place in 1957. It was created mainly for political and administrative reasons. In 1962 the population of the city was 5,807, and by 2005 it had risen to 743,511 (cf. Taine-Cheikh 2007). The same rapid growth occurred in the second half of the twentieth century in Casa Blanca, the capital of Morocco (cf. Hachimi 2007). This rapid growth in the urban populations has a number of linguistic ramifications.

Miller (2004) claims that the process of Arabisation in general started in urban centres. Sometimes in cases of inter-dialectal contact, speakers who use features close to MSA may drop them and acquire non-MSA urban/regional features. An example of this behaviour occurs in the variety of Arabic spoken by Shiites in Bahrain, as discussed above (cf. Holes 1984). The question of how a prestige urban dialect develops is very difficult to answer, since we do not have sufficient data. Holes posits that it depends on the communities' political importance, not just their size (1995: 285). Note the cases of Egypt and Syria, in which the migrant population came from rural neighbouring areas speaking sedentary rural dialects, and accommodated to the main urban dialects, Cairene and Damascene respectively, which are considered the prestige variety of the national dialect. Bedouin dialects have not had any significant influence on the dialects of these centres. One can also add that the ruling family in Egypt (before the revolution) did not speak a Bedouin dialect, as was the case in Jordan or Iraq, for example. Even after the presidency was in place in Egypt, the president did not speak Bedouin. Thus political power also has a role in language change, and not just urbanisation.[15]

Urbanisation also means interaction, language contact and a greater degree of homogeneity. In fact, there is a difference between the degree of homogeneity in Damascus and Cairo. Miller (1997) posits that the degree of homogeneity in Cairo is greater than in Damascus. Children born in Cairo to migrants from rural areas shift to Cairene Arabic almost automatically (see also Lentin 1981). When there is interaction between different groups and one group's variety is stigmatised, change towards the non-stigmatised variety will take place. The following example will clarify this point: Woidich (1994) mentions that the Cairene dialect of today is a mixed dialect formed in the second half of the nineteenth century, when many people from the countryside moved to Cairo. A number of features became stigmatised as a result of being associated with low-prestige rural dialects. According to Versteegh (2001), this process of stigmatisation led to the disappearance of rural forms and the emergence of new forms, as for example the loss of pausal *ima:la* (palatalization) in Cairene Arabic. Versteegh (1993: 70) also describes the influence of Cairene Arabic in the delta[16]. He mentions the example of the isoglosses of the realisation of *q* and *j*. In Cairene the letter *q* is pronounced as *ʔ* and the *j* is pronounced as *g*; in the Delta *q* is pronounced as *g* and *j* as *j*. Versteegh postulates that there is a 'formidable clustering of isoglosses' in Egypt. Many Egyptians will admit modifying their dialect once they come into contact with the speech of the capital, and with time they may give up their original speech habits.

In fact, sound change in a community such as that in Cairo will be of a different nature from sound change in an isolated community, like Oman, for example. This may be because Cairo is in a state of flux – because of its geographical position, because of the waves of immigrants from all over Egypt, and simply because of the sheer number of people who live there, estimated at about 20 million now. In contrast, Oman has been geographically isolated for a long time, and its population is small. Trudgill (1974) claims that isolated communities – of the sort found in Oman – are more resistant to change.

Thus, while the differences between Cairene Arabic, the delta dialects of Egypt and the Bedouin dialect of Egypt are clearly demarcated and registered, the differences between rural and urban communities within Oman are likely to be much more difficult to study.

Holes (1996–2006) conducted a study of the sedentary and Bedouin dialects of Oman.[17] As was established, one can classify Arabic dialects into Bedouin and sedentary. In the Levant, sedentary dialects can be divided into urban and rural. Meanwhile, the Bedouin dialects are also changing and Bedouins are moving towards an urban setting, as has been the case throughout history. Bedouins are giving up their nomadic existence, although they may still call themselves 'Bedouins' (1996: 34).

Although there are differences between Bedouin and sedentary dialects in the northern part of the Arab world, this is not the case in Oman, where there is relative similarity between Bedouin and sedentary dialects. This is related to the social, geographic and economic structure of the two areas. In fact, until the early 1970s, Oman, a country which is the size of France, had only 10 km of paved road. Geographically, Oman is cut off from the rest of Arabia by deserts and mountains rising to 10,000 feet. As late as the 1970s, non-Omani visitors were rare and the population was almost illiterate. The tribal structure of society helped preserve archaic features in both the Bedouin and sedentary dialects. Each of the tribes had similar dress, dwelling, social organisations and customs. This, of course, has changed now because of a huge wave of immigration to Oman and a modernisation policy that must have affected language. The main change that has taken place in Oman in the past thirty or so years is urbanisation. I am sure this urbanisation has affected language in irrevocable ways.

According to Miller (2004), old urban centres with a declining urban elite and population are going through a great wave of language change now. In North African cities such as Fes, Tangier, Rabat and even Tunis, the old urban vernaculars are restricted to older women (Caubet 1998; Dendane 1994; Iraqui-Sinaceur 1998; Jabeur 1996; Messaoudi 2001, 2002; Trabelsi 1988). It is worth mentioning, however, that this fact in itself is not surprising. Older women are most likely to retain and use features associated with older prestigious urban varieties, given the constraints placed on their lives, along with changes related to urbanisation. Note also that, in general, sedentary urban dialects are often perceived as more effeminate than rural Bedouin ones, especially at the phonological level. In Egypt, for example, upper-Egyptian migrants regard Cairene Arabic as more soft and effeminate than their own upper-Egyptian dialects. Some male workers consciously keep realising *q* as *g* rather than *ʔ* (Miller 1997). This situation seems very similar to the one in Jordan discussed above.

I would like to conclude this section with a study that concentrated on the city of Tripoli in Libya (Pereira 2007). The people of Libya, like those of a number of other countries in the Arab world, led a nomadic life to a large extent until independence in 1951 and the discovery of oil in 1955. Since then, there have been large waves of urban migration into big cities such as Tripoli and Benghazi. Libya is now considered one of the most highly urbanised countries in Africa and the Arab world. The population of Libya is 6 million, 85.8 per cent of whom live in urban centres. In 1954 there were only 25.1 per cent who lived in urban centres. The population of Tripoli specifically increased between 1964 and 1995 by 450 per cent (Fontaine 2004). The Tripoli dialect started as a Bedouin-type dialect but has changed over time due to internal and external immigration. Between 1954 and 1973 there were 187,000 foreigners in Libya, half of them settling in Tripoli. The main immigrants came from neighbouring Egypt, but there were also some from Syria, Lebanon and Tunisia. Because of the complex nature of Tripoli, its dialect is a hybrid; it has maintained features from Bedouin dialects, Egyptian colloquial Arabic, MSA and even Italian (Pereira 2007: 91).

Pereira's data is not described clearly. He compiled it between November 2002 and February 2005 in Tripoli and enhanced it with recordings he made with two 25-year-old Tripolitans in Genoa in 2003 (2007: 77). Pereira examines morpho-syntactic as well as phonological and lexical characteristics of the dialect of Tripoli. Bedouin morpho-syntactic features include the dual number for nouns, which is formed by suffixing *-e:n* to nouns, as in *walde:n* 'parents' and *yome:n* 'two days' (Pereira 2007: 87). In addition, the dialect of Tripoli 'makes a gender distinction in the second person singular of the verb inflection for prefixal and suffixal conjugations', as in the following examples: (2007: 85)

(3) *kle:t* 2msg *kle:ti* 2fsg (to eat)
tji:b 2msg *tji:bi* 2fsg (to bring)
di:r 2msg *di:ri* 2fsg (to do)

Phonological characteristics include the MSA *q* variable which is also realised as a voiced *g* (2007: 84). ECA borrowing includes words such as *kuwayyis* 'good', *fi* 'there is', *bi-yithayaʔli*, 'I think, in my opinion' (2007: 90).

What is noteworthy, however, is that the dialect of Tripoli, unlike that of Cairo for example, is not the most prestigious dialect in Libya. According to Pereira (2007: 92) everyone in Libya is proud of his or her own dialect. The president of Libya is, in fact, of rural Bedouin origin and those who hold political and economic power in Libya are also of Bedouin origin.

3.4.4 Social class

Class, as a variable and not in isolation, can be useful. In an effective study of Philadelphia vernacular, Kroch (1996) managed to define a specific community as belonging to the upper class. He first claimed that there are well-defined geographical boundaries and ethnic boundaries that determine contemporary urban dialects. For example, the Philadelphia vernacular was confined to the local metropolitan area and did not extend to the countryside beyond Philadelphia suburbs. Thus, it was not spoken by the African American residents of the city.[18] Ethnic and geographic factors are as important in studying different communities in the Arab world, as was shown above.

Kroch's study compared the vowel pronunciation of upper- and middle-class Philadelphians. The speech of the upper class was called 'main line', 'chestnut hill' and 'lockjaw'. Membership in the upper class was limited to families who meet its financial, ethnic and religious standards. The upper class was based on inherited wealth, and ethnicity, since it was white and 'Anglo-Saxon'. Since the Civil War its religion had been Episcopalian. It constituted a generation that grew up before World War II. Its members were privileged and isolated, and the men usually worked as managers or lawyers or owned large business enterprises. They had large households with domestic staff, such as a butler, servants etc. The women did not work outside the home, but were engaged in civic and charitable work. Men and women belonged to sexually segregated social clubs where membership was limited to that class. They also all received invitations to the yearly assembly ball. Kroch found that vowel pronunciation cannot be the source of the distinctiveness of upper-class speech. There were no important differences between upper- and middle-class pronunciations of vowels. The properties that distinguished upper-class speech were not phonemic but prosodic and lexical. Upper-class speech was characterised by a drawling and laryngealised voice quality and frequent use of intensifying modifiers for both men and women.

I refer to this study because I think similar studies in the Arab world are greatly needed. Also, this study defines social class in relation to ethnicity and religion. This may be needed when analysing parts of the Arab world. A study that examines the language of the ruling class in different Arab countries like Saudi Arabia and Kuwait would be useful, and a study that concentrates on the speech of upper-class Egyptians would also be worthwhile. Some of the work that examined class as a variable includes Haeri's study of the phonological change of urban middle-class women in Cairo who had a stable urban vernacular (1996a). One of the phonological variables she concentrated on is palatalisation. She found that variables associated with upper-middle-class women tend to become prestigious norms associated with refinement (see Chapter 4, section 4.7.2).

Unfortunately there are few studies that concentrate on class. According to Owens (2001), social class as an independent variable is not as effective as other variables, like education and ethnicity. The reason for this is that researchers still lack the economic and social data that can help them define social class. Linguists still know very little about how class status is defined in the Arab world, especially for the old elites. There is also the problem of access. How can linguists who do not belong to an elite class in the Arab world themselves have access to the upper elite classes, for example? The upper class in the Arab world can keep social scientists out of their lives in a way the middle and lower class cannot. As was said earlier, in countries such as Jordan, Iraq and Saudi Arabia, tribal affiliation and family ties are more dominant than social class (Holes 2007). Nevertheless, there is still room for new studies that deal with language variation and change, especially in relation to class.

3.4.5 Other factors

Other factors that are significant in the study of language variation and change include sociodemographic variables such as age and education, and external factors such as political upheavals and civil wars. Miller (2004) claims that more studies are needed that concentrate on young speakers of Arabic in different communities, since youth speakers constitute the majority of Arabs. There have been very few studies on this group. I agree with Miller on that point. According to Eckert (2005: 4), in the USA it is, in fact, adolescents that lead other age groups in sound change and in the use of 'vernacular variants' more generally. I would predict that this is the case in a large number of communities in the Arab world as well, but studies that examine this are needed. Further, countries that have gone through civil wars or upheavals such as Lebanon are worth studying, since they are likely to be undergoing language change. There have been some studies on Sanʿāʾ (Watson 2003, 2007) and Algiers (Boucherit 1986, 2002). Still, more studies are needed about Beirut or Baghdad, for example.

One study that concentrates on Beirut is the one conducted by Germanos (2007) in which she examines not a phonological variable but greetings in Beirut. Germanos depends in her study on observations in public places, shops, kiosks, fast food outlets, business areas and medical centres. Unlike other cities discussed above, such as Tripoli, Casa Blanca and Nouakchott, Beirut is not growing. In fact, since the beginning of the civil war in 1975 the city's population has not increased. When the war broke out the city was divided into two parts: East Beirut for Christians, and West Beirut where Muslims lived. During the first years of the war 110,000 Muslims and 75,000 Christians left Beirut. Still today the line between East and West Beirut is 'very much alive' in the minds of its inhabitants. This division is not just a territorial one, but a 'human and economic' one (Germanos 2007: 150). The Muslim greeting *as-sala:mu ʕalaykum* 'peace be upon you' is restricted to specific areas such as Sabra and Nweyri. The French form of greeting, *Bonjour*, is never used in these areas, and the same is true for the English form *hi*. Christians seem to prefer the French *bonjour*, while Shiites prefer *as-sala:mu ʕalaykum*. Forms such as *marhaba* 'welcome' are more neutral.

According to Miller (2004), the widespread increase of education in the Arab world has resulted in the use of a written form of Arabic by more and more speakers. This gives more exposure to MSA and a wider range of changes, perhaps sometimes in the direction of MSA. However, although education is an important variable discussed by most linguists studying variation in the Arab world, there is no study that concentrates on education as a main variable. There are some, however, that focus on the role of diglossia in language change. Walters (2003) posits that diglossia represents a case of long and stable language contact between two varieties. This is indeed a defining feature of diglossia as characterized by Ferguson. This means that any type of change must be related to the nature of the contact and degree of similarities or differences between the varieties involved, namely MSA and the vernacular. Walters contends that increased access to literacy and MSA has given rise to an intermediate variety based on the grammar of the dialect but with a large mixture of MSA vocabulary. However, it is only fair to say that Walters makes it clear that linguists are better off thinking about practices of switching rather than focussing on an intermediate variety. Likewise, we need to distinguish inter-dialectal and intra-dialectal interactions.

Haeri (1991), for example, contends that a variable such as *q* is a diglossic variable. This is indeed true, since one cannot study the glottal stop or the *g* sound without referring to the standard realisation, the *q*. In these senses, language variation in the Arab world is different from that in the west. In addition, because of the increase of inter-dialectal communication in the Arab world due to satellite channels and immigration, it is necessary to study levelling in relation to language change. Therefore, I would like to discuss levelling in relation to diglossia and change in the Arab world.

3.5 LEVELLING

Levelling, like a number of linguistic terms, can be sloppy and hard to define. The definitions that follow may overlap with some of the concepts already discussed or to be discussed in the next chapters, such as accommodation (discussed in Chapter 2). In the Arabic-speaking world, levelling occurs in inter-dialectal communication between people from different countries, and it is also closely related to the diglossic situation. Here are some definitions of levelling by different linguists, with examples.

Levelling is defined by Blanc (1960: 62) as a process that occurs in 'inter-dialectal contact', meaning contact between dialects of different countries in the Arab world rather than dialects within the same country. According to Blanc, levelling refers to the influence of standard Arabic on different dialects. In such contacts, speakers may replace some features from their dialect with others from a different dialect that carries more prestige. This different dialect is not necessarily that of the listener. Blanc quotes the example of villagers in central Palestine who may try to use the dialect of Jerusalem, or that of non-Muslim Baghdadis who may try to move towards features of Muslim Baghdadi. Note that levelling does not necessarily mean that speakers will abandon their dialect in favour of another one. They may, for example, choose features which are more 'urban' and abandon features which are more 'rural' and therefore more difficult for the urban listener to understand. Thus, levelling as defined by Blanc is not just accommodation to a different dialect, but rather a process of unselecting local and rural features in favour of others which are easier to understand because they are more common. In the following paragraphs, I will first explain the process of levelling more thoroughly, and then proceed to examine the relation between levelling and language change.

According to Holes (1995: 39), while levelling is only the 'elimination of very localised dialectal features in favour of more regionally general ones', standardisation (or classicisation, as it is called by Blanc) is the elimination of local features in favour of standard ones. This use of standard or classical features is not just to facilitate conversation, but goes beyond that level. However, it is noteworthy that this distinction is not always maintained. Sometimes the term 'levelling' is used to refer to both to levelling as defined here and to standardisation or classicisation.

Versteegh (2001: 65) defines levelling as a general process in which the differences between the different varieties of speakers that make a speech community have almost disappeared. This new variety, which is the result of levelling, is different from all the specific existing varieties of the speakers. He also uses the term 'koineisation' as synonymous with levelling. Versteegh posits that the process of koineisation or levelling is in most cases connected with situations in which groups of speakers were thrown together by accident. Therefore, the process is in his opinion usually an unplanned one. However, he mentions one case where levelling was a planned process, namely that involving settlers in the new polders of North Holland that were reclaimed in the first half of the twentieth century (1993: 65).

According to Holes (1995: 294), levelling can affect all linguistic levels: semantic, syntactic, phonological etc. He gives the example of a recorded conversation between educated Arabs from the Gulf, Baghdad, Cairo and Jerusalem. He examines how these people express the existential 'there', as in: 'There are people'. For these dialects there are at least three dialectal ways of expressing existential 'there':

(4) Gulf: */hast/*, */aku/*
Baghdad: */aku/*
Cairo: */fi:/*
Jerusalem: */fi:/*

In this case */fi:/* is the feature likely to be used by all of the speakers since it has no clear associations with any particular area, and represents the nearest thing to a dialectal common meeting point for this specific group. Speakers in a 'heterogeneous group tend to level their speech in the direction of a pan-Arab dialectal form', even if it means in this case that the Iraqis will have to resort to using a form that they do not have in their dialect. It is still a form that is not uncommon to them.

3.5.1 Diglossia and levelling

The position of MSA is strong and it is difficult for any vernacular to replace it (Versteegh 2001: 71). MSA is in most Arabic-speaking countries the only official and national language in the constitution. This situation may be different from levelling in other communities in which there is no language or variety with a special status. Versteegh contends that as a result of this special status of MSA, inter-Arabic conversation in dialect will not converge in the direction of a regional dialectal variety but tend to exhibit an increasing use of MSA features against inter-dialectal conversations. That is to say, levelling will not eventually lead to the disappearance of MSA in favour of any vernacular. Holes (1995: 294) posits that levelling is a reaction to the dialectal differences between speakers whose aim is to emphasise shared elements and eliminate local ones. In addition, interaction between dialects both economically and socially also encourages the use of levelling (cf. Versteegh 2001).

For example, Gibson (2002) mentions the fact that increased mobility and education influence language in Tunisia. He claims that during the twentieth century non-standard dialects have become closer to the standard variety in many languages, including English, because of the spread of television, radio and other mass media. He tries to examine whether the same is true in the Arabic-speaking world, with reference to ongoing phonological and morphological changes in Tunisian Arabic. He admits that although there is a great influence from MSA on the vocabulary of Arabic dialects, including the Tunisian one, the same may not be true for phonology and morphology. Thus, he examines the assumption that because of the prestige of MSA, as well as the spread of education and mass media, change is towards MSA. He studies four Tunisian variables, including the increased use of *q* instead of *g* which is used in Bedouin dialects. But one should bear in mind that the realisation of this variable is shared between the urban dialect of Tunis and MSA. Another variable examined is the treatment of the final vowel in defective verbs. Gibson concludes that the direction of many of the changes is towards the modern-day dialect of Tunis (2002: 28). In fact, in the case of the conjugation of defective verbs changes are moving away from MSA-like forms. This may still be related to the spread of mass media, since media makes use not just of MSA but of different varieties, especially urban ones.

3.5.2 Levelling and language change

Versteegh (2001: 103) gives the example of the Arab armies in the past to illustrate the relation between levelling and language change. They consisted of a mixture of different tribes, so as a result the existing differences between pre-Islamic dialects were levelled out. He posits that the new dialects in the conquered territories must have been the result of independent local evolution. Continuing on this historical line, he explains cases of levelling within the same dialect (2001: 149). He contends that, in the Arabian peninsula, the 'nomadic–sedentary dichotomy does not function in the same way as outside'. This is because many tribes have settled members with whom there is frequent interaction both economically and socially. Therefore, all dialects including the sedentary ones exhibit Bedouin features.

Another example of language change given by Versteegh (1993: 72–5) is the development of Juba Arabic in the southern Sudan. This example is significant because Juba Arabic dialect displays ongoing 'decreolising change'[19] in the development of aspectual and agreement marking of the verb. Versteegh refers to a thesis on Juba Arabic (Mahmud 1979), which predicted that in the future the linguistic variety or varieties spoken in Juba would become more and more similar to Khartoum Arabic. Depending on the political situation, which determines the amount of exposure to MSA, Juba Arabic may undergo the same equalising influence of MSA as all Arabic dialects undergo. This may result in a situation where Juba Arabic would be nothing more than a regional variety of general Sudanese Arabic, without any trace of its creole origins. Versteegh concludes that if it is possible for a creolised variety to acquire through a process of semantic change features that are found in normal dialects, one can conclude that the only way to distinguish between a decreolised and a normal dialect is by an analysis of the historical facts connected with those varieties, since the linguistic structure cannot give us any clue to the genetic origins.

The development of Juba Arabic may lead one to start wondering about the real origins of present-day regional varieties. Versteegh concludes that the levelling that takes place in Sudan and the rest of the Arab world proves that the emergence of a regional standard, when it occurs, is identical to the levelling process resulting from the influence of a prestigious variety of speech. A creolised dialect may be decreolised to such a degree that it seems a normal dialect. This is an example of levelling changing a creole into a normal dialect.

If one assumes a creolisation analysis of the development of the dialects (cf. Versteegh 2001), then one has to ask whether levelling has played the major role in explaining the process of decreolisation and the formation of different dialects of Arabic in the Arab world. According to Holes (1986: 221), levelling cannot explain the great differences between modern Arabic pidgins and creoles and the mainstream dialects. He posits that similarities between modern dialects must stem from the main input, which was a range of slightly different dialects which shared similarities as opposed to a unified form of Arabic. Versteegh (2004: 352), on the other hand, argues that the influence of the standard language should not be ruled out completely. One can find examples in the modern Arab world of illiterate speakers who can still produce standard forms (see Palva 1969). This shows that the standard language may still have played a major role in modern Arabic dialects. Versteegh also adds that at all levels hybrid forms such as *b-tuktab* are heard (cf. Bassiouney 2006). In this hybrid form there is an ECA aspectual marker *b-* prefixed to an MSA passive verb form. The influence of MSA is not just related to the spread of education and mass media, but has its religious significance as well, according to Versteegh, as it is used in mosques, for example.[20] Thus the exposure to MSA is almost inevitable.

I want to point out that a number of linguists who studied levelling in Arabic contend that levelling is not necessarily in the direction of MSA. Ibrahim (1986), Abdel-Jawad (1986), Al-Wer (1997) and Gibson (2002) explain that MSA is not a spoken variety, and this is the reason why levelling does not necessarily have to move towards standard Arabic, but could also be directed towards the prestigious vernacular of different countries. Gibson also rejects the term 'prestige' when discussing levelling, since there is an overt and a covert prestige (cf. Trudgill 1972). Another example to support Gibson is provided by Holes (1983a): despite increased literacy and urbanisation in Bahrain, the local language does not move towards classical features. According to Al-Wer (2002: 46), linguistic change in the Arab world is determined by the status of the native varieties, which in turn is determined by the status of the speaker and not the status of standard Arabic; likewise, a higher level of education does not necessarily mean that speakers will use more standard Arabic.

Finally, one has to note that there are degrees of levelling. For example, Egyptians in an inter-dialectal context may accommodate their speech to others and use levelling less than North African speakers. However, as was said earlier, levelling is not necessarily towards Egyptian Arabic in spite of the prestige of this dialect. This is because levelling is dependent not only on prestige but on a number of factors brought together, such as the status of the speaker and the influence of political ideologies. Another example that proves that there are degrees of levelling is given by Versteegh (2001). He posits that the Bedouin dialects in the Arabian peninsula are more conservative than those outside, because they do not allow levelling to the same extent as those dialects outside the peninsula, the most conservative of them all being Najdi Arabic.

According to Al-Wer (1997), the most important feature in levelling which may lead to language change is not education, but frequency of interaction.

Meanwhile, what is needed, according to Versteegh (2004: 355), is 'a much more detailed and fine-grained analysis of the demographic, cultural, and social circumstances of the early period of Arabisation'. In fact, there is an urgent need to study this phenomenon from different perspectives and in relation to different variables such as education, gender, social class, community etc. However, there are relatively few detailed studies on levelling in Arabic.

3.6 CONCLUSION

In this chapter, I have briefly outlined the framework of the study of language variation and change in the west as well as in the Arab world, including a comparison between the methods and findings in the west and the Arab world. The methods used by linguists to study the Arab world are similar to those used in the west. However, there is still room for applying third wave variation studies to the Arab world. Independent variables such as ethnicity and religion are essential in both the Arab and the western worlds. However, in the Arab world the implications of ethnicity and religion are different. Ethnicity is intertwined with historical and political events and with nationalities to a great extent. Religion plays a major role in defining political affiliations, social networks and communities of practice. It is part and parcel of one's identity and sense of belonging, more so than it is in the west. Indeed, religion like any other variable cannot be studied in isolation, but interacts with other variables, whether economic ones (as in the case of Bahrain) or sociopolitical ones (as in the case of Iraq). Social class as an independent variable in the Arab world has been examined by Haeri (1996a, 1996b), but by very few linguists after that. The reason for this is that defining class in terms of income, education, residence etc., as Labov does, does not reflect the situation in a number of Arab countries, in which the tribal system is dominant and in which one's social confidence is derived not from income or education but from the status and strength of the tribe. Indeed there are still countries with a clearly defined social class system, such as Egypt. However, even in Egypt, the interaction between social class and social networks is crucial. This needs to be examined in future research.

A major variable that can distinguish the Arab world broadly from the western world is urbanisation. As was said earlier, there was a huge wave of urbanisation that took place in the Arab world only half a century ago and that changed the demographics of many countries, resulting in linguistic variation and change. Other factors that have been discussed in this chapter and that have helped mould the direction of change and variation in the Arab world are as follows:

1. The discovery of oil in Gulf states led to changes in the communities of practice in countries like Bahrain, Oman, Libya and Saudi Arabia.

2. Social and political upheavals took place in the Arab world after World War I.
3. Wars in the region changed the distribution of the populations of many countries. Examples of the impact of wars on language variation and change are apparent in the case of Jordan and especially of Palestinians in Jordan. Civil wars like that in Lebanon have also left their impact on language variation and change. The Gulf wars must have left a great impact as well, but they have not been examined in relation to linguistic variables yet. The main outcome of wars is the dislocation of a big proportion of the population, which consequently leads to language variation, language change and in some cases language death.
4. The majority of the population of the Arab world is young. This again is a major factor that can influence language.

One fear that comes up whenever one correlates language variation with quantifiable independent variables is that of falling into a circular argument. For example, if we examine linguistic variation in relation to gender and social class, we have to assume that there are linguistic differences between different social classes and there are also linguistic differences that are related to one's gender. Thus, rather than constructing independent variables as they go along, linguists can start by predetermining them and thus lose much of their insight into the real linguistic situation that characterises a specific community.

Another point worth mentioning is that independent variables are themselves different. There are variables that can be shaped and moulded by the individual in relation to the community, and variables that are difficult to change and are assumed as almost uncontrollable. In the Arab world especially one can divide independent variables into two types: fixed independent variables (Chart 3.1) and flexible independent variables (Chart 3.2).

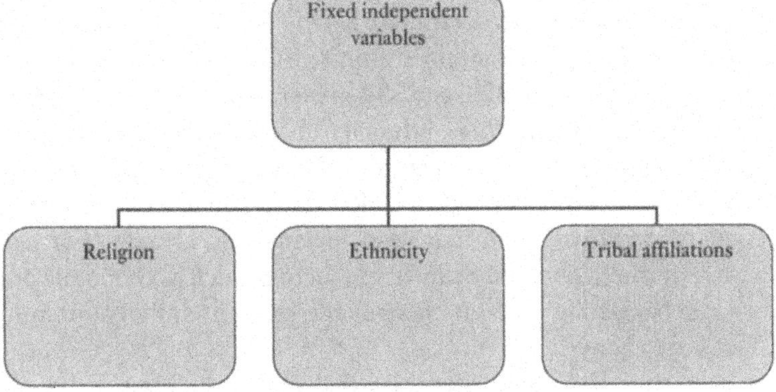

Chart 3.1 Fixed independent variables

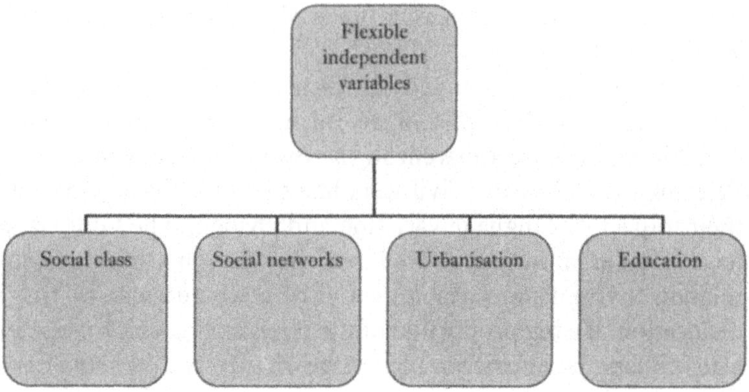

Chart 3.2 Flexible independent variables

As was mentioned earlier in this chapter, religion in the Arab world is not a matter of individual choice. One is born a Muslim, a Christian or a Jew. One is also born a Palestinian, a Kurd, or a Berber. Even if there is intermarriage between different ethnic groups, there is still a difference between them. This difference is the consequence of the way Kurds, for example, perceive themselves and are perceived by others. In tribal communities, the individual may be able to change neither tribal affiliation nor the tribe's status, which mirrors his or her social status.

On the other hand there are flexible independent variables (Chart 3.2). It is possible for an individual to change and modify social class, education or where she or he lives. In Egypt, for example, where there may be a clear social class system, it is still possible to move from one class to another, and this is usually related to education, place of residence and social income to a great extent. Thus a lower-class individual who studies medicine and opens a private clinic may become a famous doctor and take two or more leaps in the social ladder.

Fixed variables create and maintain a community of practice. For example, religion when a dominant fixed variable, as it is perhaps in Lebanon (Sunnis, Shiites and Christians) or Bahrain (Sunnis, Shiites), can help in the creation of a community of practice and the preservation of this community for some time. In other communities, ethnicity or tribal affiliations may be more dominant. Palestinians in refugee camps in Lebanon or Syria form their own community of practice. Flexible variables could initiate change within the community of practice which may lead to language change. For example, social networks when loosened by different factors, such as economic or political ones' or urbanisation when it changes the structure of a community may lead to language change.

There are also independent variables that cannot be classified as fixed or flexible, such as age and gender. These two, like all variables, interact with other variables and are more prominent in certain communities than others.

The diglossic situation in the Arab world adds a new dimension to our understanding of language variation and change in the region. A salient phonological feature such as the *q* is in fact an MSA variable. Its realisation by different speakers in different communities of the Arab world may be related to education and literacy as well as exposure to MSA.

The relation between gender and language change will be discussed in the next chapter. This is because, although gender is one variable that interacts with others, it is an essential one in the study of sociolinguistics and there have been numerous studies concentrating on it. In itself, gender can help us understand the underlying cultural constructs that may be characteristic of the Arab world. There is a huge body of research on gender that cannot be covered in this book. However, gender will be discussed not just as an independent variable which is non-classifiable as fixed or flexible, but also as a discourse variable that sheds light on sociolinguistic aspects of language use.

Note that I have not touched upon pidgin Arabic in this book except in passing, but it is indeed worth studying. Miller thinks that there are nowadays cities with a large component of non-Arabic-speaking populations, which leads to pidgin and creole types of Arabic and to regional dialectal varieties (Miller 2004; Miller and Abu-Manga 1992; Abu-Manga 1999). In Sudan, the non-Arab immigrants speak Arabic but with non-standard Khartoum Arabic dialect. Because of the immigration wave to Gulf cities such as Kuwait, Dubai etc., a new pidgin Arabic has been created.

NOTES

1. Note that this example represents individual language shift: giving up a Berber language or at least adding Arabic to the protagonist's linguistic repertoire, that is, becoming bilingual. This is not exactly what variationists have in mind when they write about language variation and change. However, the example shows the importance of social pressure and extra-linguistic factors in language variation, change and even language death.
2. The reason why their interest is mainly in phonological variables is that these occur frequently. They are also less salient in many ways than lexical or morpho-syntactic variables and thus are less subject to consistent, conscious manipulation. Sound change was the major concern of historical linguistics traditionally (cf. Walters 1988).
3. In fact, Labov used a secondary sample. That is, he eliminated certain categories of speakers from an earlier random sample created for a sociological study called 'mobilization for youth'. Thus the sample was not a hundred per cent random, but it was much closer to a random sample than variationist work has been generally.
4. Labov delineated five categories: casual and careful spoken material, and literacy-based prompts such as reading passages, word lists and minimal pairs.
5. Haeri used networks to recruit subjects, a fact that sometimes makes results less representative.

6. There are also a number of studies of language use in the Arab world that rely on techniques other than the interview for gathering data. These include the study mentioned in the next chapter by Abu-Lughod (1987), who analyses folk poetry, that by Hayasi (1998), who analyses the language use of a TV series, and that by Eid (2002a), who analyses obituaries. Although these studies are not variationist studies, they teach important things about language use and linguistic variation in the Arab world.
7. Studies that rely on statistics relating variation to other social correlates include, in chronological order, Hurreiz's study (1978) of Khartoum and the relation between language, gender, age and education; Owens and Bani-Yasin's (1987) examination of language used by men and women in the Bani-Yasin's tribe Jordanian dialect in relation to level of education and age; and Abu-Haider's (1989) comparison of the language used by men and women in a Baghdad community in relation to language change. There are statistical studies relating gender to social class. Haeri (1992), for example, in her study of Cairene Arabic, provides statistics that compare the linguistic behaviour of men in three social classes with that of women belonging to the upper middle class. She found that the process of palatalisation is associated with the lower middle class; upper-middle-class women tend to avoid it. She also used statistics in the same study to relate gender to age and/or social class. Daher (1999) used statistics that relate gender to age and education, bearing in mind other factors such as word frequency and phonological environment.
8. At the beginning of the twentieth century Sayyid Darwīsh composed a nationalistic song about Egypt, which starts with the following words: '*ʔana l-maṣri:/ kari:m il-ʕunsuri/ bane:t al-magd*' ('I am the Egyptian. I am the one who comes from a noble blessed lineage (ethnicity). I am the one who has built a civilisation (glory)'). In 2005 a young Lebanese female singer sang for Egypt and started her song with the following words '*ʔana maṣri: wa ʔabu:ya maṣri:/ bi-sama:ri: wi lo:ni masri:/ wi b-xiffit dammi: maṣri*' ('I am Egyptian. My father is Egyptian. I am Egyptian because of my colour, my tanned skin and my sense of humour').
9. A famous Jordanian joke is as follows: two young Palestinian men join the army. The military officer asks their names. The first one answers ('*ʔismi ʔa:sim*', my name is *ʔa:sim* [for: "Qa:sim"]'). When the military officer hears the glottal stop rather than the Bedouin Jordanian *g*, he says, 'You speak like a woman. You are now in the army and you must learn to speak like a man.' He then asks the second Palestinian his name. The second Palestinian replies, '*gaḥmad*'. Thus the second Palestinian changed all his glottal stops into *g*s even in the words that should necessarily start with *ʔ* such as the name *ʔaḥmad*, 'Ahmad'. The joke is indeed very significant linguistically.
10. A walk along the row of Christian cemeteries in Alexandria illustrates the confusing variety of Christian denominations: the Latin cemetery borders the Lutheran, which lies adjacent to the cemetery of the Maronites, which is next to the Greek and Coptic Orthodox ones; there are also burial sites for Anglicans, the Armenian Orthodox and so on and so forth.
11. Religion may be regarded in the Arab world as an essential part of one's identity, perhaps more so than in the west. However, as a factor that influences language variation and change it may be equal in importance to other factors like ethnicity. This varies from one community to another.
12. Levelling will be defined in section 3.5.
13. It should be noted that his work predated variationist research and represented structuralist description.
14. I think it has to be admitted that since the independence of many Arab countries, Jews and Christians have decreased in number and ratio because of political climates. Thus communal varieties have to a large degree disappeared. Whether sectarian fighting in Iraq and Lebanon is the outcome of religious differences, ethnic differences or political differences

is not to be discussed here. However, the linguistic reflexes of these conflicts are yet to be studied.

15. For a study of the historic formation of Cairene, see Woidich (1994).
16. The Egyptian delta stretches along the river Nile and does not include Cairo.
17. Oman has of course changed immensely in the past two decades. Holes had already noticed this change, which will be referred to later when discussing language policies in the Arab world.
18. Note that there has been an African American elite class in this community since before the civil war, but Kroch, perhaps replicating the biases of the dominant society, defined the elite in the terms of that society.
19. This term is used by Versteegh. Others do not necessarily label this a creole.
20. Note that the difference between CA and MSA is not discussed in detail here because it does not contribute to the main argument, but see Chapter 1 for a discussion of this difference.

CHAPTER 4

Arabic and gender

> God created Eve from Adam's bent lower rib. That is why women are always twisted. They never talk straight.
>
> An Egyptian Bedouin recounting the story of Adam and Eve, quoted by Abu-Lughod (1987: 124)

4.1 INTRODUCTION

The idea that women never talk straight is an assumption found not only among the Bedouins in Egypt, but also more universally. Holmes (1998: 461) contends that the myth that women talk too much exists in all cultures. Supposedly women do not know their own minds. They hedge and qualify everything they say. As Holmes puts it, they are supposed to be 'indirect and devious' (1998: 461).

However, the presupposition that men and women, because of their sex differences, speak differently should not be taken as a given. The research on gender has moved and developed beyond this presupposition. Holmes and Meyerhoff (2003b: 9) contend that when linguists make generalisations about a community at large, they apply their generalisations to both men and women. Gender is still an essential factor in language variation and change, but, it is a factor that interacts with other independent variables in a community, i.e. it has to be 'put into context' (2003b: 9). Sadiqi (2003a: 312) posits that it is in fact only within a particular culture that 'gender performance acquires meaning.'

This chapter gives an overview of the study of gender in the field of linguistics in relation to Arabic. Gender has been defined by Coates (1993: 4) as 'the term used to describe socially constructed categories based on sex'. On the other hand, gender is perceived by feminist linguists as something that one performs in an interaction rather than something which one has or possesses: 'Gender is not a part of one's essence, which one is, but an achievement, what one does. Gender is a set of practices through which people construct and claim identities; not simply a system of categorising people. And gender practices are not only about establishing identities but also about managing social relations' (Eckert and McConnell-Ginet 2003: 305). Thus gender is the product of social interaction. Individuals construct a gender identity when they interact with other individuals. If we assume that individuals speak differently and have their own repertoire of registers, then we must also assume that the process of 'talking' itself modifies or fixes one's identity and one's social sphere continually (Holmes and Meyerhoff 2003b: 11).

I first (section 4.2) outline briefly approaches to gender studies from a linguistic perspective. Then I discuss gender in the Arab world in general terms, to enable readers who are not familiar with the Arab world to have a grasp of the diversity of Arab countries, and to enable them to appreciate the cultural differences which may also lead to different linguistic contexts between the Arab world and the western one. The two concepts that will be of relevance in this discussion and that will keep re-occurring in this chapter are the Arabs' perception of honour and modesty. The veil as a paralinguistic communicative device is also discussed. Section 4.4 discusses politeness in relation to women. Related to the concept of politeness are terms of address. In section 4.5 I deal with terms of address, names and status. Section 4.6 sheds light on women as narrators in control of language, with an emphasis on poetry. Section 4.7 will investigate the role of gender in language variation and change and will tie up with Chapter 3. In section 4.8 I present a study of the projection of identity in the speech of men and women in Egypt in talk shows. Section 4.9 will deal with the symbolic significance of language in relation to gender. The final section will re-examine language universals in the light of data examined and observations.

4.2 APPROACHES TO LANGUAGE AND GENDER

Sociolinguistic theories that concentrated on gender include the deficit theory, the dominance theory, the difference theory, the reformist theory, the radical theory and the community of practice theory (cf. Sadiqi 2003a for a summary of these). Some of these theories are chronological and some overlap. In this section, I will only deal with four prominent theories: the deficit theory, the dominance theory, the difference theory and the community of practice theory. I will start with the deficit theory and highlight in the process of discussing it Lakoff's contributions to the study of gender in relation to language, since the interest in language and gender has sprung from Lakoff's work on language and gender in the 1970s.

4.2.1 The deficit theory and Lakoff's contribution to the study of language and gender

In 1975, Robin Tolmach Lakoff published her groundbreaking article 'Language and woman's place' (reprinted, with commentary, in Bucholtz 2004). Through her research, she was able to highlight the linguistic dimension of discrimination against women in many cultures, as well as the dominance of men, who practically set the rules.

Lakoff said: 'we will find, I think, that women experience linguistic discrimination in two ways: in the way they are taught to use language, and in the way general language use treats them' (2003a [1975]: 203); hence the idea of dominance and difference, which assumes that women speak differently because they are taught to do so, but also language does not treat them fairly because of men's dominance. She gave examples like the power relation between master and servant: while it was normal to say:

(1) He is a master of the intricacies of academic politics
it is less usual to say
(2) She is a mistress of. . . (2003a [1975]: 204).
'Mistress' had acquired different, sexual connotations, which indicated that women had frequently been treated as subordinate, sexual objects. Another example Lakoff gave was:
(3) He is a professional.
When said about a man, it meant he was a lawyer, doctor etc., but when one said:
(4) She is a professional
it meant she was a prostitute (2003a [1975]: 205).

Lakoff added that a woman is identified in terms of the men she related to. It was normal to ask a woman on occasion, 'What does your husband do?' However, one seldom asked a man 'What does your wife do?' His reply might be, 'She is my wife', and that in itself was a woman's occupation.

According to Lakoff, women's language reflected their marginalisation in society. For example women tended to use indirectness, empty boosters such as 'I am glad you are here', tag questions and hedges such as 'it's probably dinner time' (McConnell-Ginet 2004: 137). Women's language might be deficit because it reflected women's insecurity and powerlessness in society (Freed 2003: 701).

One has to acknowledge that Lakoff wrote her article in the 1970s and that since then, the position of women has changed not only in the US, but in many parts of the world. However, Lakoff has been criticised for a number of reasons: first, some linguists (cf. Mills 2005) claimed that Lakoff relied on anecdotal evidence for her generalisations. Thus there is no evidence that 'all women' used what she called 'women's language'. What Lakoff claimed was women's language could be considered a range of repertoires available to women (McConnell-Ginet 2004: 137). In addition, O'Barr and Atkins (1980) argued that much of what Lakoff had identified as women's features is in fact associated with power as defined by status in courtrooms and is not dependent on the sex of the speaker (cited in McConnell-Ginet 2004: 139). Similarly, Dubois and Crouch (1975), when examining patterns of language use among the participants at a conference, found that male speakers used more tag questions than females. Lastly, Lakoff was understood as placing women in a powerless class which does not conform to the structural classes of society (Hall 2003: 363). This in itself ignores issues such as social status and hierarchical relations in different communities.

4.2.2 The dominance theory

The dominance theory, which was discussed by Thorne and Henley (1975) (see also Freed 2003: 701), assumed a linguistic difference between men and women that is based on power inequality between both sexes. It focused on male dominance, which resulted in women being perceived as unequal to men. According to this theory, norms of society are being formed by men and so are language practices. 'Language differences were identified as part of a structure of unequal access and influence' (Freed 2003: 701).

In fact, the following words, uttered by Jane Austen's Anne in the novel *Persuasion* at the end of the eighteenth century, are a very early explanation of the dominance theory: 'Men have had every advantage of us in telling their own story. Education has been theirs in so much higher a degree; the pen has been in their hands' (1993: 167). Anne summarised the disadvantages of women at her time by mentioning that it was men who dominated history and its writing. They had access to it, and they shaped it. It was also men who were educated while women were not.

When speaking about Arab women, Ghidhdhāmī (2000) posits that women are talked about but never talk. In fact, it is considered better for women not to talk but to listen. This contradicts the claims of both western and Arab cultures that women are chatterboxes who do not know when to keep quiet; which brings us to the distinction between practical behaviour and ideology.

According to Ghidhdhāmī, a woman is the one loved and the one adored; things happen to her, but she does not take the initiative. Again this is the assumption that may be prevalent, which does not necessarily reflect reality. As Freed (2003) puts it, the media, when afraid of change, tries to impose its own fixed ideas about gender differences.

The problem with theories that rely on power is that they tend to oversimplify the definition of power (Sadiqi 2003a: 7). As will become clear later in the chapter, there are many facets of power at different stages of one's life in the

Arab world and they are related not only to gender, but to a number of different, independent factors, including the ones discussed in Chapter 3.

4.2.3 The difference theory

The 'difference theory', or 'cultural approach' as it has also been called, was first formulated by Maltz and Borker (1982), and is frequently associated with Deborah Tannen's work (Tannen 1993: 4; see also Freed 2003: 702). This approach explains linguistic differences between men and women as a result of their being two distinct groups, or even two distinct cultures (cf. Tannen 1994); women and men use different styles and linguistic forms which were developed in same-sex childhood peer groups. The focus of this theory is more on language differences than on power differences. Cameron (2005), however, calls into question the postulation that men and women as groups talk differently. Sadiqi (2003a: 10) also posits that this bicultural model cannot be applied 'cross-culturally'. The difference between men and women cannot be studied in isolation from power relationships (cf. Freed 2003: 701).

The difference theory mainly studies gender by analysing the speech of heterosexual couples, and also it does not concentrate on differences among women themselves; El-Kholy (2002), for example, states that more studies are needed in the Arab world that deal with the dynamics of same-sex power relationships, such as that of mothers-in-law and daughters-in-law in Egypt. There are also men who break our stereotypes and talk as we expect women to talk (Freed 2003). Thus, there is a difference between our expectations as analysts and members of a certain community and linguistic reality. Again this difference is nurtured by the media in order to impose a fixed reality in which women play specific roles that do not change or develop (Freed 2003; see also Cameron 2008).

4.2.3.1 Gender universals

As an outcome of theories that perceive gender as a binary opposition (Freed 2003: 702), Holmes (1998: 468, 472) suggests some language universals related to gender. First, women are more sensitive to the feelings rather than the content of what is said. Men focus on the information. Second, women provide more encouragement, supportive feedback or minimal responses like *mm*, *uh-huh* etc. in conversations between couples (Fishman 1980, 1983), in management discussion groups (Schick-Case 1988), in political debates (Edelsky and Adams 1990), and even in interactions between women and men in laboratory or studio conditions (Leet-Pellegrini 1980; Preisler 1986). Women are more concerned for their partner's positive face needs. They value solidarity. Women tend to use linguistic devices that stress solidarity more often than men (for Mayan Indians see Brown 1980; for Javanese see Smith-Hefner 1988). Third, they also, according to Lakoff (2003a [1975]), tend to use hedges, tag questions, and terms like 'sort of' and 'as you know', which are all signals of uncertainty. Fourth, interruption comes from men, not women. And men tend to speak more. Men want to maintain and increase their power; women tend to maintain and increase solidarity (Holmes 1998: 472). Note that Holmes acknowledges that there are some societies in which this is not true, for example in Madagascar, as will be discussed below. These assumptions about gender will be discussed and challenged throughout this chapter.

4.2.4 Third wave approach to variation studies: community of practice theory

This theory, discussed in detail in Chapter 3, section 3.2.3, can help explain the interaction between gender and other independent variables without resorting to differences among men and women. The theory is built on the concept of a community that is defined according to what is local and practical. Individuals construct their identity in terms of 'allegiance' and 'alliances' (Eckert 2003; Sadiqi 2003a: 10). These 'allegiances' and 'alliances' are not gender specific but community specific. Gender is thus considered not a fixed point that individuals revolve around, but rather a factor in defining and constructing an identity, a factor that evolves and changes with the individual. It is not necessarily the most essential factor in a community. Other factors such as tribal affiliations or social class may be more significant in certain communities in the Arab world.

Sadiqi (2003a: 17), for example, posits that all cultures, to varying degrees, impose control on their members. Moroccan culture is a 'type that strongly constrains the behaviour of men and women'. Sadiqi's postulation about Moroccan culture echoes Eckert and McConell-Ginet's (2004) ideas of allegiances and alliances. Before proceeding further in this chapter, I will attempt to sketch the situation of women in the Arab world briefly, trying throughout to break stereotypes. The concepts discussed below are general and perhaps basic, but needed for a thorough understanding of the relation between language and gender in the Arab world.

4.3 WOMEN IN THE ARAB WORLD: FRAMING AND BACKGROUND INFORMATION

I will start the discussion of women in the Arab world with a quote from Sadiqi (2003a: 212–13) in which she alludes to the fact that it is not helpful to look at Moroccan women as one entity, since diversity within Moroccan society is essential for a clear understanding of women's position in society.

> Granting the existence of some deeply human and universal social values, the components of Western culture are significantly different

> from, and sometimes incompatible with, those of Moroccan culture. The histories, geographies, religions, oralities, social use of languages, social organisations, economic statuses, and political organisations are different. Moroccan women are perceived as one entity in which social boundaries do not seem to count. These women are very much associated with terms 'Arab', 'Oriental. . .'

If it is an oversimplification to speak about 'Moroccan women', then it is indeed almost impossible to speak about 'Arab women', without acknowledging the diversity in their situations and positions. Although, as this chapter will reveal, there may be some underlying similarities in the social concepts that govern gender performance (honour and modesty are cases in point), the disparities, whether economic, political or social, between different communities cannot be overlooked. Thus, while the Arab world is certainly patriarchal to an extent and in ways that may seem greater than in the west, what outsiders may miss is the great diversity of the situations of men and women in the Arab world. This diversity will be discussed below roughly in terms of diversity in education, urbanisation, economy and traditions. Part of the discussion will be devoted, as was said earlier, to the veil and its implications in different communities. Before ending this section I will draw attention to two main concepts related to linguistic gender performance in the Arab world: honour and modesty.

4.3.1 Diversity in education

Because some countries in the Arab world can be characterised as late modernisers (at least with regard to the west), again with great variation across and within countries, we commonly find university professors – male and female – whose parents are illiterate teaching alongside colleagues whose parents were professors or members of the 'liberal professions' (law, medicine etc.). Across and within countries and over the last decades things have been changing rapidly for women. See Table 4.1 for an example of the diversity in literacy rates of women aged 15–24 in eight Arab countries in 1990 and 2004.

The table shows that within the period of 14 years, there was a leap in the literacy level of all the countries presented above. There is also a difference between different countries. Thus, while in Egypt the literacy level of women has increased from 51 per cent to 79 per cent, in Oman it has increased from 75 per cent to 97 per cent in 2004. This is indeed linked to economic and social changes in both countries.

4.3.2 Diversity in urbanisation

While the Arab world is increasingly urban now, as was discussed in chapter 3, rural/Bedouin life, rural/Bedouin ways and memories of rural/Bedouin

Table 4.1 Diversity in literacy rates

Country	Literacy of women aged 15–24 (per cent)	Literacy of women aged 15–24 (per cent)
	1990	2004
Egypt	51	79
Jordan	95	99
Kuwait	87	100
Morocco	42	60
Oman	75	97
Saudi Arabia	79	94
Syria	67	90
Tunisia	75	92

Source: World Bank

ways play roles there that they do not play in the west (cf. Miller 2007). This is because, although urbanisation may be well established in old centres such as Damascus and Cairo, it is a relatively new phenomenon – around fifty years old – in other urban centres such as Muscat, Tripoli or Nouakchott.

4.3.3 Economic diversity

There is likewise the issue of disparity in wealth across the countries. Nearly half of Egyptians live on less than US$2 a day, while the per capita average annual income is US$4,200. The per capita income in Yemen is US$2,400, while it is over US$55,000 in Kuwait and the Emirates and over US$75,000 in Qatar.[1] These economic disparities have great consequences for language use and certainly for issues related to language and gender and how communities function in a wider sense. Note also that in a country such as Egypt, at the beginning of the new millennium, 18 per cent of households were headed by women and not men (El-Kholy 2002: 34), which may not be the case in some Gulf countries, for example.

4.3.4 Diversity in traditions and religious practices

Tradition is perhaps one of the fixed independent variables that play a major role in Arab countries. A number of customs or ways of life that one may associate with religion are in fact associated with tradition. Magic and witchcraft, alluded to in this chapter, are both practices that can go hand in hand with religion, although they may be prohibited by it. Some communities may not perceive any contradiction in practising magic and worshipping God (Kapchan 1996).

One of the highly discussed religious practices is wearing the veil, or ḥija:b as Arabs call it, which constitutes usually covering one's hair and showing only hands, feet and face. For some communities the veil is a tradition, for others it is a religious symbol and for many it is both.

4.3.4.1 The veil

An outsider and an insider to a great extent may fail to distinguish between a traditional dress and a religious one. The connotations associated with veiling are lost for an outsider. Although women may wear the veil as a result of religious conviction, peer pressure or modesty code (discussed below), veiling as an extra-linguistic communicative device has deeper meanings and connotations. It may reflect social class, security, status, defiance, tradition, confidence and age, to name but a few.

Wearing the veil may also be read as displeasure with the politics of the governments of the west as well as those of Arab governments such as those of Egypt or Tunisia which emphasise their secular image. In both Egypt and Tunisia there are jobs in which women are prohibited from wearing the veil. For example, in Egypt, women working as announcers on television are prohibited from wearing the veil, and if they do then they have to accept work behind the screen, as editors or script writers for example, instead of as announcers. Tunisia takes this even further, by prohibiting women working in government offices from wearing the veil during work hours. Thus, in countries like Tunisia women have to take off the veil at work and once outdoors they put it back on. In some Gulf countries women put the veil on when they go out and once indoors they take it off. Veiling is associated with the concept of the public sphere and the private sphere, which will be discussed in this chapter.

According to Abu-Lughod, 'a woman's veil can be manipulated to indicate degree of social comfort' (1987: 127). Note also that wearing the veil is not necessarily a sign of subordination, but may even be a sign of arrogance. In the 1930s and 1940s in Egypt, before the 1952 revolution,[2] there was a strict system of aristocracy and feudality. Aristocratic women had to cover their faces or hair when they went to investigate their lands in the countryside, even if they did not usually do so, so that the peasants do not know what they looked like. Peasants were forbidden to look up and warned to avoid eye-contact with an aristocratic woman. They might even be whipped if they looked up when these women were passing by. For these women, wearing the veil served as a social barrier that separated them from peasants, similar in our times to building high walls to mansions in Egypt or forbidding lower-class members from entering certain quarters of the house. Thus, the veil is not necessarily a sign of piety or modesty, but was once, for a certain class, used to signal social hierarchies. For a detailed discussion of the significance of the veil see Heath (2008).

There are two concepts that help in our understanding of linguistic practices, especially those associated with women. Both concepts have been discussed exhaustively in anthropological studies and both may govern the underlying linguistic performance of most communities, if not all, in the Arab world. These two concepts are honour and modesty.

4.3.5 Honour and modesty

Abu-Lughod (1987) in her anthropological study of Bedouins in Egypt, which will be discussed in detail below, posits that there are two values that represent the core of the moral system of Bedouins. These two values are honour (*ʃaraf*) and modesty (*ḥiʃma*). I think understanding both values helps analysts understand the linguistic choices available to women and the sociolinguistic position of women in the Arab world in general.

Friedrich defines honour as 'a system of symbols, values, and definitions in terms of which phenomena are conceptualised and interpreted' (1977: 284, cited in Abu-Lughod 1987: 86). The key factor that is essential in defining honour is, in fact, self-control. One has to control pain, needs, desires, passions and capricious behaviour. By doing so, one can achieve honour. Thus, honour has to be achieved and/or preserved in a specific community. Abu-Lughod also mentions that freedom from domination, independence, pride and strength to stand alone are all values associated with honour. Honour is also related to respect, and respect is associated with self-image. For example, 'failure to reciprocate gifts, miserliness, can lead to loss of respect' (1987: 92). Abu-Lughod (1987: 105) also differentiates between obeying elders and showing respect to them and being forced to obey superiors, which may entail loss of respect. Superiors are also expected to respect the dignity of others by avoiding aggression and confrontation. 'When a superior publicly orders, insults, or beats a dependent, he invites the rebellion that would undermine his position' (1987: 99). Note also that honour is age specific.[3] All members of a community are responsible for the perservation and achievement of each other's honour.

Modesty, according to Abu-Lughod (1987: 73), is connected to veiling to a great extent, although as I have exemplified, veiling can also be used as a status marker. 'Veiling constitutes the most visible act of modest deference. . .veiling is both voluntary and situational' (Abu-Lughod 1987: 159). Note that modesty is displayed by women in more than one way. Yet it is mainly displayed by ignoring or disregarding anything that calls attention to their sexuality.

Women's modesty is connected to men's honour. However, although Abu-Lughod claims that honour is associated with men and modesty with women, she gives a significant example in which men also care for the modesty code. In the Bedouin tribe that Abu-Lughod studied, men as well as women cover their heads. Men cover their heads as a sign of modesty. Men who do not cover their heads are considered 'brazen and lacking in religion' (1987: 137).

Both concepts of honour and modesty can help explain numerous sociolinguistic cases in which Arab women behave differently from western ones and in which Arab men also behave differently from western ones.

4.4 POLITENESS IN RELATION TO GENDER

In this section I argue against the assumption that women in general are more polite than men and are concerned with solidarity (defined below) while men are concerned with power (cf. Kiesling 2003: 514). I also argue that power is in fact context-dependent, as will become clear below.

There are two concepts that will keep recurring when discussing politeness: power and solidarity. After defining both, I will proceed by defining politeness and face. According to Brown and Gilman (2003 [1987]: 158), 'one person may be said to have power over another in the degree that he is able to control the behaviour of the other. Power is a relationship between at least two persons, and it is nonreciprocal in the sense that both cannot have power in the same area of behaviour.' Power, thus, refers to a hierarchy rank between individuals. Solidarity, on the other hand, refers to the social distance or lack of distance between individuals. According to Brown and Gilman, solidarity is usually the result of frequent contact between individuals as well as marked similarities between individuals. As Brown and Gilman put it (2003 [1987]: 160), 'power superiors may be solidary (parents, elder siblings) or not solidary (officials whom one seldom sees)'.

Politeness is related to power and solidarity. First, politeness reflects a behaviour which 'expresses positive concern for others'. Brown and Gilman distinguish between two kinds of politeness: negative politeness and positive politeness. The first is associated with power and the second with solidarity. Negative politeness aims to preserve the addressee's freedom of action and space (Kiesling 2003: 514). It is a means of underlining the hierarchy and distance between the speaker and addressee. Positive politeness, on the other hand, is associated with solidarity. It highlights the similarities between speakers (Kiesling 2003: 514).

Politeness is usually a means of preserving the face of others and is also context-dependent (Holmes 1995: 21). Face is the public self-image that everyone wants to claim for themselves (cf. Brown and Levinson 1987). Negative politeness and positive politeness aim at preserving the face of self and others or at least making sure it is not threatened. The following two examples (Holmes 1995: 21) will show how context-sensitive politeness is:

(5) Judge to witness in law court:
The witness will please repeat his response to the last question for the benefit of the Jury.

In this formal context the judge preserves the face of the witness by referring to him in the third person and using politeness devices like 'please'. Now note the following example:

(6) Husband to wife at home:
Mm? What was that, love?

The address form 'love' is again a politeness strategy but used in an informal rather than a formal context. In fact it would be inappropriate and face-threatening to use it in a formal context. Also, the direct question reflects the intimacy of the relation and the casual context. The same direct question, if asked in a courtroom, would be face-threatening.

The question is whether there is a direct relation between politeness and the social status of women. Many studies would argue that this is definitely the case because of the lack of power of women; the less power one has in any given interactional context, the more likely one is to be concerned with expressing or displaying politeness, especially negative politeness, explicitly. Deuchar (1989) applied Brown and Levinson's theory of politeness and face to the use of prestigious forms, and posited that powerless people usually monitor face more carefully than powerful ones. They do so by using more prestigious forms that encode status. One usually speaks respectfully to superiors no matter how well one knows them (Holmes 1995).

It is suggested that men in most cultures have more access to power and status than women. They can use more power-related techniques with impunity because their face is already protected. Women, on the other hand, cannot use more assertive techniques when speaking since this may be considered face-threatening. This hypothesis is confirmed by the fact that there were studies that found that women use back-channel responses, simultaneous talk to show interest and support, and facilitative tag questions (Holmes 1995).

However, there are some studies that did not find any differences in the way both sexes use language, or in the degree of politeness they encode (Salami 1991). In fact, Keenan (1974) conducted a study in Madagascar in which it was found that women there are less polite than men. Keenan (1974: 142) also postulates that direct speech in Malagasy is associated with loss of tradition. Men prefer indirectness as an expression of respect. Thus, men's requests are typically delayed and inexplicit. Their criticism is more subtle. Women can be direct and straightforward. They in fact perform tasks such as interacting with strangers more than men do – tasks which, for example, involve buying and selling.

Studies like the last one pose problems. First, does the fact that women seem less polite automatically mean they have more power than women in other communities in which women are more polite than men? The problem with terms like power and politeness is that they can be very general. Thus, while women in all communities are not completely powerless, there are some communities in which women and men divide their share of power in different contexts. So a husband is powerful with his wife, but a mother has more power over the children than the father does, or a husband has power at work, and a wife controls the household, deciding what to cook etc. Although to us this power given by a husband to his wife may seem little and demeaning, the hidden power of women in communities in which men are supposed to be all-powerful cannot be ignored.

In a groundbreaking study that examines the way Moroccan men and women bargain, Kharraki (2001) discusses the concept of politeness and face in relation to both sexes. Brown and Gilman's model of politeness was used. The study analyses more than sixty bargaining exchanges. The conclusion reached was that it is in fact men rather than women who in Moroccan society use more linguistic solidarity devices, i.e. it is men who use more positive politeness techniques than women in bargaining. In fact, women's use of insisting strategies is perceived as 'a daring act of assertiveness' (2001: 623). Men, on the other hand, feel that such strategies could be face-threatening and reduce their social power. Men in this specific community derive their social status not by maintaining hierarchies between them and others, but by emphasising similarities. Women, on the other hand, emphasise their status by appealing to the hierarchical rank. Note the following example of a woman who wants to buy some onions (2001: 623):

(7) Context: a woman wants to buy onions
Setting: a shop
Woman: *baʃ-ḥal* *l-besla* *ʔa* *ḥassan?*
How state the-onion voc Hassan
Greengrocer: *60 doro*
60 doro
Woman: *ʔiwa ma-tebqa-ʃ tejri mor l-meʃtarijja rexxes ʃwijja/*
Yes neg-be-neg run from the-buyers **reduce**- a little
letnin *tkun xir* *rebʕin* *doro*
Monday to be only forty doro
Greengrocer: *ma-fi-ha-ʃ* *ʔa ḥajja*
Neg-in-her-neg voc ḥajja

Woman: How much are these onions, Hassan?
Greengrocer: Sixty doros
Woman: Oh! Don't send your customers away! Reduce the price a little! On Monday, they cost only forty doros.
Greengrocer: There is not much profit in it, hajja!

In this example, the woman does not use a greeting or any form indicating solidarity. She does not use any forms indicating endearment, like *ḥabibi* 'my love', *ʕazizi* 'dear' etc., as is often done in such interactions. These forms of endearments are also forms of solidarity. Rather, the interaction opens with a woman's straightforward question:

(8) Woman: *baʃ-ḥal l-besla ʔa ḥassan?*
How state the-onion voc Hassan
Woman: How much are these onions, Hassan?

Then she makes a demand with the hope of getting a good price. There are no 'polite' terms such as 'please' etc. In some cultures, such behaviour would be considered abrupt and rude.

Sellam (1990: 90) posits that, in general, the way Moroccans make requests is different from the way the speakers of English do, for example. The woman in this example is not particularly rude. In fact, this exchange does not result in any damage to the face of the greengrocer or the speaker. His reaction to her does not carry any insult. Insisting is another strategy of bargaining with vendors used by women. Other strategies also include repetitions, oaths or threatening to buy from another seller (Kharraki 2001).

Now note the following example of a man who wants to buy some watermelons from the same greengrocer (2001: 622):

(9) Context: a man wants to buy watermelon from a greengrocer, who is a close neighbour
Setting: shop
Man: *Manssalamu ʕalikum/ delliʕ hada ʕal ḥassan/*
I greet on- you/ watermelon this good Hassan
Man: Peace be upon you. What wonderful watermelon you have there Hassan!

At first sight, this difference between the way men and women bargain in this specific Moroccan community may seem bewildering. From the examples given by Kharraki (2001), women are much more assertive than men when bargaining and much more persistent. This may be, as Kharraki puts it, to demonstrate their skills as housewives. It may also have larger implications for the power spheres of both sexes in this community. As was said earlier, power is context-sensitive. However, the interaction between the women and the street vendors in Morocco is not just a manifestation of politeness and power relations. It is in fact a manifestation of the intricate relation between politeness as a communicative device and independent variables discussed in Chapter 3, such as social class, tribal affiliations, ethnicity, age and so on and so forth. Social class and status are at work in the above examples. From my observations, upper-middle-class women in Egypt, when bargaining or arguing with men from a lower class who are serving them, like the porter, caretaker, the street vendor etc., can seem very rude to an outsider, using insults and a higher pitch and omitting greetings altogether. Men from the same class deal with the situation differently, being calmer, using greeting terms and rarely using verbal insults. This is indeed worth studying and may yield surprising insights into the power relation between men and women.

Although independent variables like social class could explain why women in the Moroccan context were not concerned with the face of the greengrocer, independent variables are not enough to explain why men from the same social class act differently. An examination of the way men and women are expected to behave in an interaction is indeed needed, and studies of the implications of different face-saving strategies employed by both are also needed, before one can reach definite conclusions. There are other communities that are similar in this respect, like the one mentioned above by Keenan (1974) in Madagascar.

To sum up, since power is context-dependent and since it is almost impossible to make generalisations about politeness, then one has to concentrate on defining the different contexts which may have been taken for granted so far and which may render the argument about women, men and politeness strategies clearer.

Related to politeness, as was said earlier, are terms of address. In section 4.5 I shed light on both names and terms of address and their relation to status, gender and identity.

4.5 'MISTER MASTER': NAMES, STATUS AND IDENTITY

How we label ourselves and others is significant because it can 'offer a window on the construction of gendered identities and social relations in social practice' (McConnell-Ginet 2003: 69). In this section I examine terms of address and names in relation to specific communities, and I also correlate methods of referring to both men and women to the underlying structures of a number of Arab societies, bearing in mind that there may be a coherent concept of social order in all Arab communities that dictates a specific way of using terms of address and names. As McConnell-Ginet (2003: 72) puts it, referring to others is basic not just in conveying information, but also in maintaining the social structure of a community.

Ever since Mahfouz published his classic 'Cairo Trilogy' in the 1960s (2001), women have been angry in Egypt and elsewhere in the Arab world at the way the wife in the novels (especially the first one, *Bayn al-Qaṣrayn* ('Palace walk')) is treated. Though we are not interested here in the way the husband hypocritically managed his life and how he betrayed his wife with impunity throughout the novel, I am very interested in the choice of terms of address between the husband and wife. The wife, Amīnah, is careful throughout the novel to address her husband as *si:* 'mister' and never to look him in the face or argue with him. He, on the other hand, always addresses her as 'Amīnah' and is much more confrontational and tyrannical. It is no coincidence that his first name is *Sayyid*, meaning 'master'. Thus throughout the novel, his wife refers to him as 'mister master'.[4]

The relationship between them can be neatly explicated in terms of Brown and Levinson's theory of power and politeness (1987). Amīnah, the wife, has little if any power, has to maintain her face as much as possible, and has to preserve the face of others. The husband, Sayyid, has much more power; he does not have to pay attention to face within their relationship, and he can flout all the rules without threatening his face. His face is already protected because he is a man. It is the wife who has to try to use more polite forms to protect her face.[5]

In the case of Amīnah there is a clear case of power differences. Whether names and terms of address are always a reflection of power relations between men and women is a crucial issue. This is what I will try to discuss in the next paragraphs. Again, as with everything pertaining to gender, the answers are not always clear; the case of Amīnah and Sayyid, which was very clear cut, will not be repeated often in real-life data without complications or other implications. In addition, cases in which terms of address involve two men or two women may not necessarily reflect power. One should not just take interactions between pairs of adults – one female, the other male – as the quintessential or perhaps only context to try to analyse or understand gender (Holmes and Meyerhoff 2003b).

Parkinson (1985), in a study of terms of address in Egypt, did not find significant differences in the way men and women used these terms. Terms of address were more sensitive to other factors including class, age and occupation. Although this study is now more than twenty years old, it can help us assess the linguistic situation in Egypt more scrupulously. Parkinson noted that:

> Knowledge of the proper use of terms of address is, therefore, as important to the overall success of a communication as knowledge of the conjugation of verbs would be. The terms give the entire communication its social setting and tell addressee how the rest of the communication is to be taken or understood. . .the terms of address maybe peripheral to the syntax of ECA, but they are central to the process of communicating in ECA. (1985: 225)

He gives the following example to show the importance of terms of address in communication in Egypt and perhaps in the whole Arab world: a group of men who were entering a shop in Cairo saw an artist in shabby and paint-stained clothes. They started addressing him as *ya rayyis* 'hey boss'. The man was angry and ignored them. Once they entered the shop they realised the man was not a painter but an artist. They were very embarrassed and said:

(10) *la: muʔaxza ya baʃmuhandis/ ma-kunna:-ʃ ʕarfi:n*
'Please don't take offence, engineer, sir, we didn't know.' (1985: 224)

Terms like engineer, doctor, or Pasha (an old Turkish title; in the time of the monarchy in Egypt it was given by the king to aristocrats) are used loosely in Egypt. A male police officer could be addressed as a Pasha, a male or female nurse or student of medicine could be addressed as doctor, a male or female graduate assistant is also addressed as a doctor (meaning professor as well) and a male mechanic could be addressed as an engineer. Terms such as *ʕamm* 'uncle' are used by both children and adults with male older workers like drivers and porters.

Problems can arise from addressing someone by a term that denotes a lower status, as in the example above. Note also that painters in Egypt are usually men. It would not have been possible to make this mistake had the paint-stained person been a woman, because a woman would have been expected to be an artist or an engineer. In the same way, a police officer is always a Pasha (even though titles were abolished after the 1952 revolution in Egypt), but a woman is not usually called a Pasha because there are few female police officers in Egypt.

Parkinson likewise studies terms like *ḥagg* and *ḥagga*, which refer to someone who has made the pilgrimage to Mecca. These terms, according to Parkinson, are used to address men and women equally. Although they are terms of respect, they can replace 'mother' and 'father' when parents get older. They can also appear alone or with the first name. Note the following example (1985: 152): a working-class man aged 55 asks a working-class male aged 17 about the destination of a bus in Cairo. Here is the answer of the 17-year-old male:

(11) *la: ya ḥaggi miʃ bi-yru:ḥ it-taḥri:r*
'No pilgrim it doesn't go to Taḥri:r square'

The next example (1985: 152) is that of a 55-year-old working-class wife and her 60-year-old husband: the husband is standing in the street, and the wife sees a bus coming towards him, so she yells:

(12) *taʕa:la hina ya ḥagg*
'Come over here, pilgrim'

It is not clear whether these people addressed as pilgrim have done the pilgrimage or not. The term pilgrim is used to strangers and/or intimates to show respect.

Now note this example (1985: 153): two older, upper-class female neighbours meet by chance at the door of the building:

(13) *ʔizzayyik ya ḥagga layla*
'How are you, pilgrim Layla?'

The neighbour uses the first name of her neighbour Layla because she has known her for a while. She could have used *ḥagga* without the first name as well.

Again, all the above examples show that both terms, *ḥagg* and *ḥagga*, are used by both sexes. There is no evidence that women feel insecure and thus use terms of address more (as Trudgill suggested in 1972). In the following example the term *ha:nim*, which is a Turkish term that means 'gentlewoman' or 'lady', is used by a pickle salesman in the market to an upper-class woman to denote respect and formality.

(14) *ʔaywa ya sitt ha:nim ʕayza bika:m?*
'Yes madam, how much worth (of pickles) do you want?' (1985: 167)

In this example it is clear that the status of both speaker and addressee in Egypt is indeed much more significant than their sex.

Some of what has to be accounted for is found in cases where men and women behave similarly, which is something the variationists discussed later in this chapter seemed to overlook. Abu-Lughod (1987: 154), in her study of Bedouin women of the western desert of Egypt, claims that they must try to be modest. This implies hiding their sexual or romantic attachments. This is reflected in the way women address their husbands; they do not use their husbands' first names but refer to them as 'that one', *haða:k*, or if they are affectionate, 'the old man', *ʃa:yib*, or 'the master of my house', *ṣaḥib be:ti*. This is what they do when others are around or when they are in formal situations. It seems as if this situation is not very different from the one described by Mahfouz, which was supposed to have taken place in Egypt at the beginning of the twentieth century and not in the 1980s. However, as was said earlier, the situation is not as simple as it seems. One can claim that women in these societies have less power than men and have to maintain their face by using terms of address and thus being more polite. The only problem is that men in a lot of Arab societies, including the Bedouin ones, do not refer to their wives by name in formal gatherings either, as Abu Lughod also noted in her study.[6]

Hachimi (2001: 43) reports that husbands in Morocco would refer to their wives as *mallin ddar* 'owners of the house' or *drari*, which literally means 'children', and which refers, in that context, to both 'children' and 'wives'. It is only non-traditional married women who are referred to by their names. Mothers are addressed and referred to with terms such as *ḥajja* (*ḥagga* in

Egypt), again a term of respect for one who has made the pilgrimage, *lalla* 'mistress' and *frifa* 'lady with noble blood'. Hachimi also notes that while in other Arab communities, mothers are addressed as 'mother + name of her eldest son', e.g., *ʔumm ʔaḥmad* 'mother of Ahmed' (cf. Minai 1981), this is not the case in Morocco. When addressed by strangers, a woman in Morocco could be called *madame* followed by their husband's name, 'Mrs + husband's name', although legally women in the Arab world do not take their husbands' family name, but keep that of their birth family, which is usually their father's family name. Moroccan educated men in embassy receptions, for example, introduce their wives as *madame* 'madam', very rarely as *mrati* 'my wife' or by her first or family name (Sadiqi 2003a: 134). Again this is related to the honour and modesty code.

The way a woman refers to herself is context-dependent (Sadiqi 2003a: 135). In Egypt a woman could use 'madam' + her husband's first and last name when ordering food via the phone, for example, or when in contact with people she does not know, whether men or women. A woman uses her first and last name at her workplace and when buying or selling her properties. This pertains not only to the honour and modesty code discussed above, but also to the power the name has, as will be discussed below.

Terms of address can be used to mark the distance between females and males who could be potential sexual partners (Sadiqi 2003a: 79). In communities in which honour and modesty are two essential factors that, combined, define an individual's worthiness, as was explained earlier, the way individuals are addressed is loaded with meaning. In Egypt when two close male friends converse and ask about each other's wives, they do not use the first name of the wife, since this might imply a violation of the honour and modesty code by the male friend. A man could ask his friend 'how is madam so and so (first name)?' or 'how is the *ḥagga* (no first name) (*al-ḥagga*)?'.etc. Interestingly enough, when two female friends converse they can use each other's husbands' names. This shows again that the modesty code is not exclusive to women, but manifests itself differently in the interaction between men and women. However, these observations need to be studied systematically.

From a different perspective, sadness at the loss of women's names, whether the women are dead or alive, and perhaps the implications for loss of identity with the loss of name, are discussed in an unprecedented study by Eid (2002a), which is based on obituaries as a source in three communities: Egyptian, Persian and American. She obtained her data from three major newspapers, *Al-Ahram* (Egyptian), *Ettela'at* (Iranian) and the *New York Times* (American). Her data was collected for one-month periods at ten-year intervals from 1938 until 1998. Eid (2002a) uses statistics that parse different kinds of information, such as use of the names of the deceased (whether men or women), use of professional titles (for the deceased and their relatives), and use of the names of relatives of both men and women (whether the relatives are male or female).

She measures the impact of gender, culture and time independently and combined on obituaries. Of the dead women she studied, she writes:

> I remember their names, except those women who lost theirs in the world of obituaries. . .I will always remember the joy I felt every time I found more Egyptian women with their names, American women with their professions, and Iranian women mentioned at all. (2002a: 281)

Her study implies that women in Egypt are identified in obituaries not by name but by their relation to different males and perhaps even females in their lives. Thus a woman who dies is known as the mother of so and so, the wife of so and so etc. This practice also means that by herself, she may not be identified at all. Whether or not obituaries reflect society may not be clear, but the fact that obituaries are written by members of society is already evidence that they at least reflect our ideal belief about what society should be like. In that 'society' a woman is not 'someone', but the mother, daughter, wife, sister of someone.

In obituaries, Egyptian women were the only group who in 1998 still appeared without a name 10 per cent of the time, while 100 percent of Iranian women's names have presentation in 1998 obituaries. When it comes to occupation and professional titles, the space belonged to Egyptian men, who occupied 94 per cent of occupation space (space devoted to discussion of professional life) and 97 per cent of professional title space, while social space remained the domain of women in Egyptian obituaries (63 per cent in 1998). In American obituaries, women and men were represented equally, although there was still a difference in professional space even in the 1990s. Only 36 per cent of American women had their occupations mentioned and only 8 per cent of American women had their professional titles mentioned. In obituaries at least, women were, thus, lagging behind in professional titles in the three countries.

In comparing the treatment of Egyptian and American women in obituaries in 1998, Eid observes that what an Egyptian woman loses after she dies is her first name. What an American woman also loses alive and dead is her last name if she is married. A dead American woman may have her maiden name given in parenthesis, if at all. A dead Egyptian woman may or may not have her first name mentioned, but even if she has her first name mentioned, her daughter's name may not be. She may only be defined as the wife of such and such, and in most cases her mother's name will not be mentioned. Eid gives examples of inconsistencies sometimes depending on different individuals, but the overall picture seems to be consistent. Women's first names in Egypt are preferably not mentioned in obituaries, while women's maiden names in America are again preferably not mentioned, and if mentioned then not bold-faced but in parenthesis.

Again, if names are part of one's identity then women seem to give up much of their identity in most cultures, although one has to note that given their cost, obituaries will appear for only some of the deceased, whether males or females. However, the symbolic nature of names does not stop at being markers of one's identity, but may play an even more subtle role.

4.5.1 Names and why they are hidden

In Egyptian culture names hold power, especially the first name of a mother. The power I am referring to here is not just linguistic in nature but in fact magical. Although religion in the Arab world is taken seriously by members of all religious communities, Egyptians – whether Christians or Muslims – still tend to believe in magic and supernatural forces. For example, in rural areas specifically, women may resort to magic, usually performed by an older person who is reputed to be in touch with jinn (spirits), to solve marriage problems, to cause harm to enemies, to make a man impotent, to bear children, to make a married couple get divorced and so on and so forth. Magic can be used to inflict harm or solve problems. However, to use magic on someone, especially in a harmful way, this person's mother's first name is needed. A mother's name is more like an Achilles heel, a vulnerability, and over time it has also become something both shameful and yet sacred.

To elaborate on this point, a mother's name, especially if the mother is dead, is not mentioned except with the immediate family and definitely not to people that are not to be trusted. A father's name does not hold the same power. For example, when praying for her children, a mother would use the child's first name followed by 'son of (mother's name)', e.g., Ashraf son of Fāṭima. Thus, it is quite common for elderly women when asked about their mother's name to give a false one consistently, especially to young children who might reveal the secret to other grownups, who might then use the name to cast a spell on the elderly woman or on her offspring. Thus, refusing to use a woman's first name, whether she is alive or dead, is culture-specific and may have to do with the power the name has rather than the power women lack. So wedding invitations usually include the name of the bride and her father but not her mother's name, and the name of the groom and his father but not his mother's name.

Sadiqi (2003a) discusses, in her sociolinguistic study of Moroccan women, fortune telling, witchcraft and black magic. Although she does not go into details of how names are used in the three practices in Morocco, she emphasises the importance of the three practices in the Moroccan community. She posits that 'the three practices are very real in Moroccan culture as they are believed to offer "solutions" and "remedies" to weak, problem stricken literate and illiterate men and women that are victims of social stress that they cannot handle' (2003: 73).

The importance of witchcraft and magic is not exclusive to Egypt and

Morocco but is found in the Arab world at large.[7] The implications of this for women and how they are addressed are indeed crucial for a more thorough understanding of the interaction between gender and language in Arab communities. One needs a study that evaluates all the implications of women's names. However, there is no study that does this to date.

In this section I have only briefly touched the tip of an iceberg. There is much more to be studied in the way women are addressed and the way they address others, as well as in the way they retain or give up their names, or have them taken from them. The answers, as always, are not clear, but that should only make the journey of discovery worth making. What is obvious, though, is that despite the great differences and disparities of many sorts we find between Arab communities, there are sound reasons for claiming that these communities in fact have a culture in common at some profound level and that this culture is manifested in the two interlinked values: modesty and honour. Although both take different shapes in different communities across the Arab world, they are at the core similar and essential for a successful communicative process.

In section 4.6 I show how women as narrators survive in parallel to men and use similar themes and forms in their narration.

4.6 WHEN A CHICKEN CROWS LIKE A COCK: WOMEN NARRATORS

Al-Farazdaq, the famous medieval Arab poet (641–742), once said of a woman who recites poetry:

(15) *ʔiða: ṣa:ḥat id- daja:jatu ṣiya:ḥa d-di:ki*
fa-ðbaḥu:ha:
'If a chicken crows like a cock,
slaughter her.'
(Ghidhdhāmī 2000: 154)

Though the number of female Arab poets is less than the number of male poets, there are still some remarkable female poets who have decided to 'crow like a cock', beginning with the pre-Islamic female poet al-Khansāʾ (Tumāḍ ir bint ʿAmr, d. 634 or 661) and up until today. What is interesting about the poetry of al-Khansāʾ is that in theme it is not that different from the poetry of men. Although al-Khansāʾ does not describe any weaponry in detail, as male poets often do,[8] she does use the same forms and grammatical constructions and almost the same themes as her male peers. These similarities are interesting, since, as detailed below, studies done on women's poetry from a linguistic point of view, as well as studies of women who just recite poetry rather than compose it, have not come up with much evidence that there are any major differences between the themes or the forms of poems created by men and women. Some marginal differences have been detected, but none pertaining to women specifically. Whether the case is different in other cultures is worth investigating. In this section I will summarise some of the major studies done across the Arab world on women's poetry and women's prose from a linguistic perspective. Note that the three studies, which I will examine in more detail below, depend on folk genres of poetry rather than high-culture poetry which is in MSA and which is perhaps less spontaneous or less representative of the ordinary people. I will then shed light on a study conducted by Eid (2002b) that examined women's prose.

First, Stillman and Stillman (1978) used various genres of songs in order to study the language of women in relation to society. They concentrated on women's songs in Morocco. Songs sung in women's gatherings during work or play were analysed, or these sung on semi-religious occasions such as weddings, circumcisions and death. These songs were called *ʕarabi* by members of this community. The researchers also examined songs dealing with topics that are of interest to women rather than men.

Stillman and Stillman (1978) studied the Jewish community of Sefrou, a provincial town in Morocco that lies 18 km south of Fes. In the 1940s the community comprised 6,000 Jews, i.e. one-third of the population of Sefrou. In 1972, when the fieldwork began, there were only 200 Jews left, the others having emigrated mainly to Israel. They retained their own distinctive dialect, the Sefriwi dialect of Jews.[9] The female poet whose poems Stillman and Stillman analysed, Simḥa poni, was an illiterate married woman in her fifties. Like most Arabic folk poetry, her verses were sung, not recited. She composed while singing using specific formulaic expressions. Stillman and Stillman also examined singing duels, which were similar to a war of words (contests) between women. One woman composed her verse from some cue in the last line of the opponent's verse, and then the duel continued. This competition could get personal, as when one refered to the other woman's husband etc. Simḥa specialised in *mawwa:l*, which is a kind of poem or song that originated in Iraq and is sung throughout the Middle East.

The themes that occurred were usually melancholic ones, like separation, loneliness, unrequited love and exile. These themes do not differ depending on gender, according to the researchers, but rather seem like traditional Andalusian themes.[10] Another motif found in these Moroccan songs is that of the Andalusian garden. Note the following example:

(16) *tmenni:t gelsa maʕa: ġza:li: fil-ʕarṣa*
l-ʕarṣa xa:liya ma: fiha-r-rbba
'I wish I could sit with my gazelle in a garden,
a deserted garden whose owner is not there.' (1978: 73)

Stillman and Stillman compared themes and structures used by women to those used by men and concluded that both men and women refer to gardens, baths, high ceilings and windows in their poetry. Not only is there no clear difference between the poetry of men and women, but also there are almost no differences between the poetry of Jews and non-Jews, i.e., Muslims. Stillman and Stillman posit that, 'There is nothing in the content of the "ʕarabi" as sung by our poetess which could be identified as particularly Jewish, with the exception of the occasional mention of personal names, such as David'[11] (1978: 74).

Abu-Lughod (1987), whose work was referred to earlier, has studied the social function of the Bedouin poetry of men and women in Egypt. She concentrated on the sociolinguistic and pragmatic significance of poetic discourse in a Bedouin tribe in the western desert in Egypt called Awlād ʿAlī. She studied how poetry and songs were used by men and women to express different attitudes and feelings ranging from love to anger and defiance, and how poetry also defines and redefines the degree of intimacy between individuals.

This study is crucial in a number of ways. First, although Abu-Lughod did not mention it by name, she indirectly and very early on used the social networks approach for collecting her data. She used her Muslim background as an asset in her research, and also her father's background in Egypt. She was both an insider and an outsider. She was an insider because she shared with the Bedouins their Muslim identity[12] and stayed with them long enough to be able to participate in their daily rituals without them feeling uncomfortable, and an outsider because she was not from that community herself, and therefore was allowed to ask questions and behave differently. She claimed to have taken the role of 'an adoptive daughter' (1987: 15). Note that she started her fieldwork mainly as an anthropologist but ended up with a study on the discourse significance of poetry in that community. We can read her work as ethnography of communication. Still, the methods she used to integrate in that community were not different from those used by others, like Haeri (1996a).[13] In fact, at the onset of Abu-Lughod's study, her father accompanied her. She said that as an Arab, he realised that being a young unmarried woman travelling by herself on an ambiguous mission was not going to help her in her research (1987: 11). He knew his culture well and knew that she would not be able to gain the trust of the community if she arrived on her own, and thus would have a hard time convincing them to open up and feel at ease with her. In her behaviour, she appealed to the half-Arab identity she had, and behaved with respect towards the culture of the community.

It was clear to Abu-Lughod from the beginning that as a woman she would not have many liberties, but she would be able to enjoy an intimacy with other women that would eventually open new doors for her. Similarly, early on she became aware of the great importance of poetry in the community under investigation, an importance that surpassed all her expectations. While staying in the house of one of the seniors of the tribe, a shepherd's wife helping in the household recited a poem about despair in love. Abu-Lughod, in all innocence, read it to the *ḥajj* (the senior person she was staying with), who was usually a calm, helpful man. Suddenly his attitude changed and he became angry and asked her who had recited the poem to her. He was afraid that it had been his wife, and that the poem had been a reflection of her feelings towards him. The *ḥajj*'s senior wife[14] scolded Abu-Lughod for having revealed something as sensitive as a woman's poem to a man (1987: 11). Abu-Lughod then realised that poetry in this community was used 'as a vehicle for personal expression and confidential communication' (1987: 26).

Abu-Lughod focused specifically on poems called *ġinna:was*, which are little songs similar to lyrical poems but also similar to the American blues in content and emotional tone. They are mostly about romantic love. They describe a feeling and are usually 'personal statements about interpersonal situations' (1987: 27). This kind of poetry exploits sound elements like alliteration, intonation and rhythm to a great degree. Words, for example, are usually repeated in reverse order. Note the following example:

(17) *damʕ za:d ya: mawla:y*
xaṭar ʕazi:zi fi wa:n iz-zaʕal
'Tears increased, oh lord.
The beloved came to mind in the time of sadness.' (1987: 179)

In the above poem

fi wa:n
in when
'in the time'

is repeated nine times.

ʕazi:zi	*fi wa:n*	*iz-zaʕal*
beloved me	in when	the-sadness

'beloved in the time of sadness'

is repeated twice. The order is reversed, as in:

fi wa:n	in the time
fi wa:n	in the time
fi wa:n iz-zaʕal	in the time of sadness
fi wa:n	in the time
ʕazi:zi fi wa:n iz-zaʕal	beloved in the time of sadness

fi wa:n	in the time
fi wa:n	in the time
ʕazi:zi fi wa:n iz-zaʕal	beloved in the time of sadness

Although these poems are rarely sung by men in public any more, but are usually sung by women at weddings and on similar occasions, both men and women recite poetry about their beloved ones, though in different settings and mainly without the other sex's being present. Much of Bedouin life remains sex-segregated to a great extent, more than life in urban centres such as Cairo or Alexandria. The following poem was recited by a jilted man and reveals feelings of grief and pain caused by loss. When it was recited to women of the community by Abu-Lughod, they were touched by it.

(18) *ʕazi:z lil-kfa: ma: ha:n*
sayya:tha: xaṭa: wa:jʕa:tni:
'Her bad deeds were wrongs that hurt
Yet I won't repay them, still dear the beloved.' (1987: 189)

Similar themes occur in a poem recited by a woman:

(19) *ðahabit ge:ʃun l-awla:f*
kanni:ba zini:ni: yji:bhum
'I have lost their tracks, the loved ones
perhaps my singing will bring them.' (1987: 242)

Here the power of poetry is called upon by the woman, and indeed poetry is powerful in this community. Abu-Lughod states that both men and women lead two parallel lives: a public one and a private one. There are codes of behaviour that they have to maintain, among them the modesty code and the honour code. Poetry, the domain of the private life, can violate all codes as long as it remains private. Men and women of the community express through poetry weaknesses that may violate the honour code and romantic love that may violate the modesty code. Both men and women share poems only with friends and close kin. Poetry is not to be shared with men or women across different generational or status lines. The public and private spheres, are distinct and well defined. In the public sphere the two codes discussed in section 4.3, honour and modesty, have to be maintained.

Abu-Lughod's study is an eye-opener in many respects. First, it reframes and analyses values like honour and modesty, within the framework of a specific community, and in so doing correlates how both concepts can be used in different parts of the Arab world. Second, she draws attention to the nuanced nature of the relation between men and women, the public sphere and the private sphere, and an individual and a community. Although Abu-Lughod does not state clearly in her study the complex nature of the power relation between men and woman in the Arab world at large, she refers to the spheres that men and women control and adjust.

Rosenhouse (2001) studied the narrative structure of stories narrated by Bedouin and sedentary male and female speakers from Israel, specifically that of a type of folk story dealing with fantastic events and characters. The analysis focused on linguistic elements like clause structure, number of words per clause, verb tense use and demonstratives. The sixteen stories were of the same type and from the same dialect area; eight were narrated by males and eight by females. Rosenhouse concluded that there were inter-gender and inter-group differences, but also similarities. In fact, the differences between Bedouin and sedentary dialect narratives were much less than Rosenhouse expected. There were also a large number of occurrences of the *yifʕal* form[15] used as part of a modal structure in all the data, to give vividness to the story and to express the present tense. One difference between men and women was that women used demonstratives more than twice as often as did men. However, there were no other major differences noticed.

Eid (2002b) examined eight female modern Egyptian writers and the various ways they use both MSA and ECA in their work. The women writers varied in the way they used ECA and MSA. Some used only MSA, even in dialogues, while others used both, or just ECA. The study did not compare female writers to male writers, but makes it clear that there was no obvious tendency for women to use ECA or MSA. According to Holes (2004: 376), a number of Egyptian male writers have exploited the diglossic situation by using both MSA and ECA in their novels in both narration and dialogue, among them Yūsuf Idrīs (1927–91). Although there are a number of studies in the Arab world that deal with the themes of women writers, there are few studies if any that deal with the language variation of women and men writers in the Arab world. There is a great need for such studies.

In this section I have examined some linguistic studies that concentrate on women as narrators of poetry (poets) or prose (writers). In fact, none of the studies discussed demarcates a clear and crucial difference in the way men and women use language in narration. Perhaps there is none. More studies are needed, however, before one can reach this conclusion. What is worth mentioning is that in poetry the differences between men and women, whether real or imaginary, are blurred. Poetry in different communities in the Arab world creates an ideal world in which both men and women can express their weaknesses and needs. From al-Khansāʾ in pre-Islamic poetry to the women in the western desert in Egypt, women have found a means of expressing themselves, an outlet through art. Abu-Lughod (1987: 185) calls poetry 'a discourse of defiance'. Perhaps it is so.

In sections 4.4–4.6, I have concentrated on women in relation to politeness; terms of address, names and status; and women as narrators. In the next section I examine linguistic variation between men and women in more detail.

4.7 LANGUAGE VARIATION AND CHANGE IN RELATION TO GENDER

I argue that quantitative sociolinguistic research tends to treat gender as a given and then examine variation between males and females; categories such as social class, ethnicity and sex are treated as clear and simple categories that can be used directly to account for variation within a community. This in itself, as was mentioned in Chapter 3, is an oversimplification.

I first (section 4.7.1) give an overview of studies on language variation in relation to gender in general, and then (section 4.7.2) concentrate on studies done on the Arab world. Finally, I question some earlier claims about language variation between men and women in the Arab world.

4.7.1 An overview of studies on language variation in relation to gender

There is a claim in the western world that women use more prestigious language forms than men. Women, especially in the lower middle class, took the initiative in the introduction of new prestigious forms of many of the phonological variables studied in the US, UK and other industralised societies such as Sweden (cf. Romaine 2003). Men initiate change from below (Labov 1990).

This may first be related to economic and social factors. Nichols in 1983 conducted a study in two small villages in South Carolina in which three groups were examined. Nichols was able to link the patterns of linguistic variation to the economic positions of men and women in the community. The poorer/working-class women were interacting with speakers of more standard varieties of English far more than their husbands. Women used more prestigious norms because of the differences in profession and economic exposure of men and women. James and Drakich (1993) argued that the use of prestigious linguistic forms by women is related to the economic opportunities available to them. That is to say, if one sex is exposed more often to the prestigious forms of language because of the jobs they hold or their social and economic circumstances, they will eventually use more prestigious norms.

To the extent that such a claim is valid, it may account for the fact that women's speech in working-class communities in the west has been found to be closer to the standard than men's. Lower-working-class women are in contact with middle-class people more. However, this factor cannot be considered an essential one in language choice, since Holmquist (1985) found that young men in a Spanish village were exposed more to standard Spanish[16] than were young women, because the men worked more outside the community and because they spent time in the military service; yet women in that community still used more prestigious forms. This pattern of behaviour may be related to Milroy's concept of social networks, discussed in Chapter 3. Men in the Spanish village have more dense and multiplex networks than the women, although they may come from the same class. In fact, it is not always men who have the strongest social networks. Cheshire (1982) revealed that older women in a Welsh community were the ones who used more non-standard forms of speech; she accounts for this finding by pointing out that they had the strongest social networks. The theory of market forces and the theory of social networks complement each other, since both depend on interaction between people. Still, although the idea of social networks is valid in explaining the differences between the two sexes, it is not enough in itself to account for all cases of differences.

Even in studies that examined language change in bilingual communities, women seem to be initiating a change towards the more prestigious variety. Gal (1978a) studied a Hungarian village in Austria in which social networks and market forces interact strongly. Gal posited that young men and young women there did not differ in their type of social networks. None the less, women still used the prestigious variety, standard German. Gal (1978a) states that the reason for this is that women feel less loyal to the community than men do. In fact the major independent variable in that case was not sex but 'peasantness' of network, peasantness being defined in local terms: having cows and chickens. Younger women had fewer peasant networks because they had a goal of speaking German without an accent – the goal of the youth but not their elders – which increased the likelihood that young women could marry a German-speaking, urban, middle-class men and leave their current peasant lifestyle. Their life would then be materially easier. Their use of standard was a way of showing their attitude towards being peasants. They in fact chose not to be peasants, and this was symbolised by their language choice.[17]

Women in the western world were assumed to be more status conscious and less secure in their social positioning (cf. Romaine 2003). According to Trudgill (1972), language is used as a symbolic means of securing social status. He claims that women have a less secure position in society, are subordinate to men, and as a result use more prestigious forms. This is an overgeneralisation and has been criticised in a great number of studies (cf. Holmes and Meyerhoff 2003a). Romaine gives the example of women in Sweden, which is a country famous for gender equality, and in which women still use more prestigious forms than men. Nordberg and Sundgren (1998) conducted a comparison of gender differentiation across two generations, first in 1967 and then again in 1996, in a town called Eskilstuna in central Sweden, about 110 km from Stockholm. They concluded that gender differentiation in most of the variables had not changed. They examined six morphological variables. Women were still using more prestigious forms than men, although, as was said earlier, women's status in Sweden is secure. Thus, correlating the use of prestige with social security is not always viable.

Women are supposed to use language as a means of gaining respect and influence. Gaining respect and influence means asserting one's membership in all the social groups to which one belongs. If, for example, one belongs to a group that uses a prestigious-standard variety, using this variety may be a way of gaining respect in that group. Eckert (1998) examined the speech of two groups of girls in a Detroit high school. She found that the working-class group spoke a less prestigious variety than the middle-class group. This was because the latter group did not need to rebel against society. They considered society a means of asserting their identity. In fact, women can use language as a way of gaining respect, if they cannot do so in a more direct way. Salami (1991) found that Nigerian women do not use a more prestigious language than men because they do not need to gain respect. There is already a high level of participation by them in the society.

The most important interpretation of studies done on the west, and the one that concerns us directly, is that lower-middle-class women tend to use more prestige forms to compensate for their socially insecure position (cf. Labov 1982; Trudgill 1972; Paulston and Tucker 2003). However, Labov (1982: 201) claims that this is not the case in the Near East and South Asia and that in these areas women are not necessarily more conservative than men. Labov may not have taken account of the difference between a prestige variety and a standard one (see Chapter 1). Many linguistic studies in the Arab world have shown that for most people at least in urban areas there is a prestige vernacular, the nature of which depends on many geographical, political and social factors within each country. In Egypt, for example, for non-Cairenes it is Cairene. It is usually the urban dialect of the big cities. There is also a standard variety, MSA. This linguistic situation does not exist in western societies, with the consequence that at first glance the results reached by some western linguists concerning language and gender seem to contradict those reached by some linguists in the Arab world.

The fact that linguists like Daher (1999) provide evidence that specific women of a specific background in a particular locale may not use some standard features of language does not contradict the findings of Labov and others, since women may still use the prestige form of language, which, as was said earlier, is different from the standard one. Note also the claim made by Abu-Haidar (1989: 479) that young women in the Arab world are more sensitive and innovative than old and young men to linguistic changes. Abu-Haidar's interpretation is in line with the claim made by Labov (1972b: 243) that women are more sensitive than men to prestige patterns.

In section 4.7.2 I will first give an overview of linguistic studies that ntrate on variation and then examine a selected number of them in il.

4.7.2 An overview of linguistic variation in relation to gender in the Arab world

Studies that concentrate on phonetic, phonological and prosodic features are mentioned chronologically. First, Roux (1952) examined the differences between men's and women's speech in Morocco in relation to specific consonants, such as *s*, *z* and *r*. Hurreiz (1978) in his study of Khartoum also examined the use of intonation. Royal (1985) studied the relation between pharyngalisation, class and gender in Egypt. Al-Khateeb (1988) studied a number of consonants used in Irbid in Jordan, which include *q*, *k* and *t*, and one vowel, *a*. He studied them in relation to gender, education and age. Trabelsi (1988) studied the use of diphthongs and monophthongs in relation to gender in Tunisia. Al-Muhannadi (1991) studied the articulation of some segments including the *q* in the speech of Qatari women. He found that certain segments characterise the speech of the Bedouin community while others characterise urban speech.[18]

I will now examine some of the studies on variation in more detail. Walters (1991) made a quantitative sociolinguistic study of Arabic as spoken in Korba, a small Tunisian town, to examine sex differentiation there. He compared and contrasted his findings with western studies. To collect his data, he used a male Tunisian teacher of French and a female student of language. The issue was also to see whether the sex of the interviewer mattered. He was interested in phonological variables, especially the *ima:la*, vowel raising (palatalisation, produced by a rising movement of the tongue towards the prepalatal region).[19] He found that *ima:la* is used by older people, less educated people and females. It is considered a feature of the dialect of Korba which is now looked down upon, especially when used outside Korba and with Tunisians from other areas.

Daher (1999) examined *θ* and *ð* as MSA variables realised differently in Damascene Arabic. He measured the way both phonological variables are realised by men and women. In Damascene Arabic the variables would be realised as *s* and *z* respectively. He found that men tend to realise them more in their standard form (which is different from the prestige form), *θ* and *ð*, than women did.

Daher's methods were very effective. He tried to overcome the observer's paradox in more than one way. He was aware that it is difficult to elicit spontaneous speech in the presence of a tape recorder. The recorder makes the informants more conscious and thus they use more MSA than they usually do. Daher made sure the interviewer was familiar with the culture, had the trust of the informants, and was a member of the speech community. The informants were mostly either friends, family members or co-workers. The setting was their homes, where other family members were present. Daher then ignored the first five minutes of the interview. He started by asking about personal experiences, memorable stories, hobbies at school, television in Syrian society, and society in general. In fact, stories with lasting memories worked well, such as those about a journey on foot from Beirut to Damascus, a marriage, an accident etc. His informants had all finished at least elementary education. He found that speakers who realised the two variables in their MSA form were speakers whose professions entailed much use of the written language, i.e. they were mainly men. He claims that 'men are more likely than women to approach the standard variant as a speech norm' (1999: 180). This situation is stable; there is no change in progress taking place. MSA is used in major institutions such as law, education etc. Because of that it is associated with men, who have more access to education and more access to professions.

In another study (1998), Daher examined another phonological variable realised differently in Damascene Arabic and SA, namely the uvular variable */q/*, which is realised as a glottal stop in Damascene Arabic. His study was based on thirty hours of tape-recorded sociolinguistic interviews with twenty-three men and twenty-three women. The informants were classified into three levels of formal education, i.e. elementary school, high school and college degree, and into three age groups, i.e. 15–24, 25–39 and 40–70. He found that men tended to favour the connotations and usage of *q*, while women avoided its connotations and usage. The *q* variable was being introduced into the dialect through education. And since, according to Daher (1998: 203), education was 'traditionally the domain of a small male elite', women did not use the *q* as much as men. In fact, according to him, even educated professional women tended not to use it because the glottal stop is associated more with urbanisation and modernisation, while *q* was associated with men and rural speakers. He concluded that men and women in that context approached different norms, since MSA and the vernacular were two sets of norms instead of one.

The attachment of women to the urban variables and to modernisation is common for studies done on the west (cf. Romaine 2003), and studies done on Arabic. Al-Wer (1999) reached a similar conclusion in her study, discussed in chapter 3, of the Palestinian and Jordanian dialects used by men and women in Jordan. She concluded that indigenous Jordanian women responded to the urban prestige norms more than men did. This was because, for them, according to Al-Wer, urban Palestinian women represented finesse (1999: 41). Palestinian women appeared more liberated, more modern and better educated than Jordanian ones. Havelova (2000) reached a similar conclusion in the study he conducted in Nazareth. He posited that it was gender more than religion directing phonological variation. When examining the realisation of the MSA *q* variable, he found that women used the glottal stop more, while men tended to use the rural variant *k*.

In a different vein, Haeri (1996a) was interested in the variation within Cairene Arabic between men and women, especially in the processes of fronting and backing. She noted that data from ten different communities in Cairo, Egypt, suggests that women take the lead in fronting processes, and she posed the question of whether this variation between men and women is anatomical in nature or social. She concentrated specifically on two variables: the degree of pharyngealisation and apical palatalisation. Pharyngealisation is a secondary articulation which involves the backing of the tongue towards the pharynx (cf. Jakobson 1978 [1957]), while palatalisation is a fronting process that involves tongue fronting as well as raising (cf. Bhat 1978; Haeri 1996a: 106). She contended that social class plays an important role in this variation between men and women. She concluded that men have heavier pharyngealisation than women perhaps in order to sound tough and manly (1996a: 107), while weak or no pharyngealisation is characteristic of women in general and upper-middle-class men and women in particular (cf. Royal 1985). Although strong pharyngealisation is a process found in CA, it tends to be avoided by women. For women, weak pharyngealisation is associated with the upper classes, civilisation etc., while strong pharyngealisation or backing is associated not just with men but with men from the lower classes. Haeri (1996a) found that in Cairo it is in fact middle-class women who initiate change. Variables associated with upper-middle-class women tend to become prestigious norms associated with refinement, thus become models for lower-class women who have social ambition.

Tables 4.2 and 4.3 summarise some of Haeri's findings with regard to palatalisation and the use of the MSA phonological variable /*q*/.

The tables show that class and gender interact as independent variables in Egypt and influence linguistic variation. However, an MSA variable such as the /*q*/ is used more frequently by men than women across almost all classes.

Table 4.2 Strong palatalisation in female speakers in Cairo, by social class

Class		Strong Palatalisation	Weak palatalisation	Total tokens	% of total tokens
Lower middle	N %	697 44	877 56	1574	41
Middle middle	N %	322 40	478 60	800	21
Upper middle	N %	266 28	688 72	954	25
Upper	N %	30 6	469 94	499	13
Total	N %	1315 34	2512 66	3827	

Table 4.3 Use of /q/ by male and female Cairene speakers, by social class (average number of tokens per 1,000 words)

Class	Female speakers	Male speakers
Lower middle	0.37	3.14
Middle middle	7.60	8.20
Upper middle	4.91	8.59
Upper	3.57	9.76

There are other studies that also found that young, educated, middle-class women use more foreign lexical items than men do (cf. Lawson-Sako and Sachdev 2000 for a study done on Tunis).

The above studies all indicate, first, that women sometimes do not have access to education and professional life to the same extent as men do and thus their use of MSA is less than that of men. This interpretation echoes Jane Austen's claim in her novel *Persuasion* that we discussed at the beginning of this chapter. On the other hand, when women have a choice between the prestigious urban variety, a rural variety and MSA, they are more prone to choose the urban variety as a symbolic means of asserting their identity.

Haeri (1996a: 307) claims that 'studies of gender differentiation have shown that women who have equal levels of education to men use features of classical Arabic significantly less than men' (see also Haeri 2006: 529). Note that Mejdell (2006) found that this generalisation did not apply to some of her female informants.

In the following paragraphs I will show the limitations of quantitative variation studies that rely on gender as an independent factor:

- Variation research that relies on gender as a variable starts with categorising people into males and females and places them into fixed social classes, which may yield circular arguments, as was discussed in Chapter 3. Language in this case will just be a reflection of already existing social identities rather than a construction of identities and communities (Romaine 2003). Research against this kind of categorisation includes Goodwin (2003), Eckert (2003) and Holmes and Stubbe (2003).
- Two key factors in the variation of speech between men and women, according to Romaine (2003: 109), are 'access' and 'role'. The amount of access that women have to the prestige language and the role that they play in their community are significant in their language use. Both factors have to be considered before any conclusions about variation and gender can be reached.
- Variationists claim that in the Middle East women move away from the prestige forms (cf. Romaine 2003). This is not necessarily true and may

be the result of the confusion between standard and prestige which was discussed in Chapter 1, and which will be alluded to again in the next section.

- In addition, use of language may have a discourse function and is not just an outcome of social factors. For example, according to Larson (1982) women use more standard in Norway when they want someone to do something or when they want to persuade.

4.8 PROJECTION OF IDENTITY IN THE SPEECH OF EDUCATED WOMEN AND MEN IN EGYPT: EVIDENCE FROM TALK SHOWS – A CASE STUDY

This study has two purposes. First, it examines the use of MSA and ECA in talk shows. I shed light on code choice and code-switching by women specifically in relation to identity. Second, the study examines assertiveness techniques such as interruption and floor-controlling by women.

To reiterate variationist studies done on the Arab world all indicate, first, that women sometimes do not have access to education and professional life to the same extent as men do and thus their use of MSA is less than men's. On the other hand, when women have a choice between the prestigious urban variety, a rural variety and MSA, they are more prone to choose the urban variety as a symbolic means of asserting their identity.

In spite of the fact that talk shows may not be representative as stratified samples of variationist research should be, talk shows can help demonstrate that certain general conclusions about the use of MSA by educated women should not be drawn: This study aims to provide another perspective, one that shows that educated women with access to MSA in fact can and do use it in certain contexts for a discourse function and to project a specific identity on themselves. The question that this study poses is why women and men use MSA when they do. It also shows that in specific contexts, Egyptian women are as assertive as men if not more.

My data consists of fifteen hours of talk shows. The analysis includes five talk shows. Two are exclusive to one group, males or females and not the other. Note that all the participants are in the same age group, 45–55.

In programmes in which there are exclusively men or women, there is still no difference in the way MSA is used by each. The quantity of MSA is related to the role the speaker wants to take and which part of his or her identity he or she appeals to. The use of the phonological variable *q* specifically was not exclusive to men. Both women and men use *q* and sometimes it is women rather than men who do so.

4.8.1 Description of data

The talk shows examined are the following:

1. *kala:m nawa:ʕim* 'Women talk': Four women from different parts of the Arab world discuss current issues in the Arab world and the world in general (no announcer).
2. *ma wara:ʔ al-ʔaḥda:θ* 'Beyond events': Four men from different parts of the Arab world discuss current events in the world (male announcer).
3. *ḥiwa:r ad-dustu:r* 'The constitution dialogue': Educated men and women from Egypt discuss changes to the Egyptian constitution. Sometimes there are three men and one woman, and sometimes two men and two women (male or female announcer).
4. *il-buyu:t ʔasra:r* 'Home secrets': Usually two men and two women from Egypt discuss family problems in Egypt (female announcer).
5. *qabla ʔan tuḥa:sabu* 'Before you are held accountable': A group of men and women, two and two, usually from Egypt, discuss a current problem with religious implications (female announcer).

4.8.2 Categorising the data

In this study, I try throughout to distinguish broadly between ECA and MSA as distinct code levels. The main difficulty encountered by a linguist dealing with two languages or two varieties that are closely related, like MSA and ECA, is to differentiate clearly and consistently between them. This is because MSA and ECA have a number of shared vocabulary, syntactic and morphological features. If we put to one side the absence of case and mood endings, some utterances could be classified as either ECA or MSA. Therefore it was difficult at times to make a clear distinction between them.

After an initial survey, I categorised my data on the basis of counting MSA and ECA variables, whether lexical, morphological, phonological or syntactic. The categories start from MSA and move gradually and quantitatively to ECA. Note that in case the participants come from different parts of the Arab world and use a different colloquial from MSA, the categories are still able to help us in our understanding of the choice of variety. In these cases I replaced ECA with the variety used, so instead of categorising an utterance as basically ECA, I categorised it as basically SCA, for example.[20] These seven categories are in the following order:

MSA
MSA with insertions of ECA
Basically MSA
Mixture of MSA and ECA

Basically ECA
ECA with insertions of MSA
ECA

As was said earlier, I measured these categories by counting the MSA percentage of variables in the speech of the participants: (see Table 4.4).

Note that the category 'MSA' has a wider range than the category ECA; MSA has 80–100 per cent MSA variables, while ECA has 0–10 per cent MSA variables. This is because my data is spoken and something as subtle as the quality of a vowel can render a morpheme or word ECA in the counting process.

I have categorised my data using these seven categories because I attempt to show how code choice and social motivations are related and how, in a stretch of discourse that is basically geared towards one variety rather than another, the speaker's motivations may be different. In a stretch of discourse which is geared towards MSA, the speaker's relationship to the audience and projection of self may be different from one that is geared towards ECA. Again, whether and how code choice substantiates and expresses pragmatic variables of this kind is handled more insightfully if the speaker's code is first carefully analysed and divided into different categories on the basis of form alone. Therefore, this rough categorisation is an important first step to enable us to get to grips with how and why a speaker moves from using one kind of Arabic to using another.

The categorisation above has of course no formal status as either a linguistic or a social construct, the only purpose being to help arrive at an understanding of how the dynamics of switching between MSA and ECA, the 'poles' at either end of a stylistic line, take place. I do not claim that the notion of categories occurs in the mind of Egyptians when speaking, nor that these are in any sense consciously 'used' by Egyptians. The only operational difference between my 'categories' is in the quantity of MSA or ECA features, regardless of whether these features are phonological, morpho-syntactic or lexical in nature. The basis of my division is simply the quantity of features from both codes in a given stretch of discourse.

Table 4.4 Categorisation by use of MSA variables

Category	Use of MSA variables (%)
MSA	80–100
MSA with insertions of ECA	70–80
Basically MSA	60–70
Mixture of MSA and ECA	40–60
Basically ECA	20–40
ECA with insertions of MSA	10–20
ECA	0–10

I exemplify below the features used to distinguish between MSA and ECA.

4.8.2.1 Lexical features

There are certain lexical items and expressions which are markers of one code rather than another. For example, the verb 'to go' in MSA is *ðahaba*, while in ECA it is a different lexical item altogether, *ra:ḥ*. This type of item is the easiest to spot. For example in programme 2 in the series 'Before you are held accountable', the male journalist, who speaks 'basically ECA', uses a number of quintessentially ECA expressions and vocabulary.

(20) *fi ḥa:ga*
'there is something'

(21) *ʔa:h*
'yes'

The MSA counterpart of these words and expressions is different:

(22) *huna:ka ʃayʔan*
'there is something'

(23) *naʕam*
'yes'

On the other hand, in programme 2 in the series 'Home secrets', the female judge, who speaks 'MSA', uses many quintessentially MSA lexical items.

(24) *naḥnu*
'we'

(25) *nabḥaθ*
'we search'

The ECA counterpart of these lexical items and expressions would be:

(26) *ʔiḥna*
'we'

(27) *nibḥaθ*
'we search'

Note that there is a large amount of vocabulary shared between the two codes, and sometimes the difference between two lexical items, one in ECA and the other in MSA, is only a low-level phonological one, as in examples (25) and (27) above. The only difference between the MSA and the ECA realisations of the same verb is in the vowel pattern and syllable structure.

It is by no means clear whether differences on the phonological or lexical level are more salient. This needs further research and a large amount of data.

4.8.2.2 Morpho-syntactic features

Case and mood marking are purely MSA morphological features. If a speaker consistently uses case and mood endings, this indicates that her or his utterance is stylistically 'high flown'. It is noteworthy, however, that in spoken MSA in Egypt, people tend to drop case and mood endings except in the most elevated (especially religious) discourse. So in Egypt the criterion of case and mood marking has limited usefulness in deciding which code is being used, since it is so rare. On the other hand, the aspectual/mood marker *b* or the tense marker *ḥa* are features that are characteristic of ECA, with a different counterpart in MSA, and their use is a sign that a speaker has moved in the direction of ECA.

There are numerous other significant morpho-syntactic differences between MSA and ECA. There are major differences in the way in which negation, deixis, tense and aspect are realised in ECA and MSA. There are also other significant differences in the expression of syntactic processes such as relativisation and interrogation.

The following examples illustrate how ECA and MSA morpho-syntactic features can combine. Note this example from programme 2 in the series 'Home secrets', in which the female judge uses a number of salient MSA morpho-syntactic features:

(28) *al-aḥka:m iʃ-ʃarʕiyya wil- qa:nuniyya wil-qada:ʔiyya θa:bita/ θubu:tan la yaqbal/ wala gadal wala muna:qaʃa*
'Legislative, legal and procedural rules are fixed so as not to allow any scope for argument or discussion.'

She uses case marking in *θubu:tan* 'fixed', accusative. She also uses the MSA negative marker *la* in *la yaqbal.*

Now note the following example from programme 2 in the series 'Before you are held accountable', in which the male journalist uses the ECA plural demonstrative *do:l* and follows ECA structure by having the demonstrative after rather than before the noun it modifies as in MSA.

(29) *il-fataya:t do:l*
'These girls'

The MSA counterpart would be

(30) *ha:ʔula:ʔi al-fataya:t*
'These girls'

In the MSA counterpart the demonstrative precedes the noun.

4.8.2.3 Phonological features

As was said above, some lexical items are shared by both varieties and the only factor that causes them to be classified as ECA rather than MSA is that they are phonologically ECA. The vowel pattern may be different, or the realisation of consonants; see example (27) above.

Note also the following example from programme 2 in the series 'Before you are held accountable', in which the female director uses the MSA *q* instead of the ECA glottal stop.

(31) *al-faqr*
'poverty'

In the following example from programme 2 in the 'Home secrets' series the vowel quality marks this word, spoken by the female journalist, as ECA rather than MSA.

(32) *ʃe:ʔ*
'something'

The MSA counterpart would be

(33) *ʃayʔ*
'something'

4.8.3 Detailed description of the data

***kala:m nawa:ʕim* 'Women talk'**: Four women from different parts of the Arab world discuss current issues in the Arab world and the world in general. There is no announcer present.

Programme 1 broadcast November 2006
Topic: Religion and tolerance
Duration: 1 hour and a half

Woman 1: Saudi; basically SCA
Woman 2: Lebanese; basically LCA
Woman 3: Egyptian; ECA
Woman 4: Syrian; Syrian Colloquial Arabic (SYCA)

Programme 2 broadcast December 2006
Topic: Divorce rates in the Arab world
Duration: 1 hour and a half
Woman 1: Saudi; SCA with insertions of MSA
Woman 2: Lebanese; LCA
Woman 3: Egyptian; ECA with insertions of MSA
Woman 4: Syrian; SYCA Arabic with insertions of MSA

ma wara:ʔ al-ʔaḥda:θ **'Beyond events'**: Four men from different parts of the Arab world discuss current events in the world. There is a male announcer.

Programme broadcast December 2006
Topic: The economic influence of China on the world
Duration: 1 hour
Male announcer: ECA
Male minister of foreign affairs: Basically MSA
Male economic expert: ECA with insertions of MSA
Male businessman: ECA with insertions of MSA

ḥiwa:r ad-dustu:r **'The constitution dialogue'**: Educated men and women from Egypt discuss changes to the Egyptian constitution. Sometimes, there are three men and one woman, and sometimes two men and two women. There is a male announcer.

Programme 1 broadcast October 2006
Topic: The changes in the Egyptian constitution
Duration: 1 hour and a half
Male announcer: Basically ECA
Female professor of law: Mixture of MSA and ECA
Male professor of law: Basically ECA
Male politician: Basically ECA

Programme 2 broadcast November 2006
Topic: Imposing emergency laws in Egypt
Duration: 1 hour and a half
Female announcer: Basically ECA
Female judge: Basically MSA

il-buyu:t ʔasra:r **'Home secrets'**: Usually two men and two women from Egypt discuss family problems in Egypt. There is a female announcer.

Programme 1 broadcast October 2006
Topic: Women who betray their husbands
Duration: 2 hours
Female announcer: ECA with insertions of MSA
Male psychologist: ECA with insertions of MSA
Female psychologist: ECA with insertions of MSA
Female social worker: ECA with insertions of MSA

Programme 2 broadcast December 2006
Topic: The new forms of marriage in the Arab world
Duration: 2 hours
Female announcer: Basically ECA
Female judge: MSA
Female journalist: Mixture of MSA and ECA
Male journalist: Basically ECA
Male writer: Mixture of MSA and ECA

qabla ʔan tuḥa:sabu **'Before you are held accountable'**: A group of men and women, two and two, usually from Egypt, discuss a current problem with religious connotations. There is a female announcer.

Programme 1 broadcast October 2006
Topic: Marriage and the treatment of women
Duration: 2 hours
Female announcer: Basically MSA
Male religious scholar: Basically ECA
Female religious scholar: Mixture of MSA and ECA

Programme 2 broadcast December 2006
Topic: Street children
Duration: 2 hours
Female announcer: ECA with insertions of MSA
Male professor of psychology: ECA with insertions of MSA
Male journalist: ECA with insertions of MSA
Female professor of sociology: ECA with insertions of MSA
Female director: ECA with insertions of MSA[21]

If we exclude the women who are not Egyptian, then we are left with 16 Egyptian women and 13 Egyptian men to compare and contrast for the purpose of this study. Tables 4.5 and 4.6 summarise the categories they use.

Table 4.5 Male speakers (number: 13)

Number of speakers	Code choice
0	MSA
0	MSA with insertions of ECA
1	Basically MSA
1	Mixture of MSA and ECA
5	Basically ECA
5	ECA with insertions of MSA
1	ECA

Table 4.6 Female speakers (number: 16)

Number of speakers	Code choice
1	MSA
0	MSA with insertions of ECA
2	Basically MSA
3	Mixture of MSA and ECA
2	Basically ECA
7	ECA with insertions of MSA
1	ECA (Egyptian colloquial Arabic)

Although the tables suggest that there is a difference in the way both men and women use MSA – in the programmes analysed, women use more MSA than men – because of the limited amount of data, I do not want to draw definite conclusions. However, it is clear that women do not use less MSA than men.

4.8.3.1 Factors examined

In addition to the role that language form plays in projection of identity, which will be discussed in detail below, the following factors are also important in determining the code used by men and women in talk shows:

- *Education background*: When the announcer presents the participants, she or he usually mentions their profession, and whenever the participants speak, their professions and names are written on the screen. All participants have been educated at university level and beyond.
- *Intended audience*: The programmes are broadcast on the Arab satellite dish. Thus the audience is Arabs everywhere, even outside the Arab world.
- *Subject matter*: The subject matter is important in the sense that sometimes women are expected to be experts in specific topics, such as

marriage problems or street children. However, there is still a limit to the importance of subject mater, since, as will be clear in the data, in programmes that discuss a political issue, women can still be assertive. This is more dependent on how women perceive themselves, whether they perceive themselves as experts in the subject matter or not. This is when education also interacts with professional life and form of language.

- *The role of the announcer*: The programme announcers in the programmes selected play a minimum role and do not interfere in the interaction except rarely. These are discussion programmes and usually it is up to the participants to take turns. The announcer starts by posing the question and rarely interferes after that.

4.8.3.2 Data analysis

Eid (2007) posits that the media, especially the broadcasting media, has a large role to play in 'negotiating the relationship between the two varieties': MSA and ECA. It 'creates in between spaces that serve as excellent sites for the negotiation of identities. It does so by bringing public content into the privacy of the home and taking private content to the public view to audiences that are local and, when aired over satellite channels, global as well.' (2007: 405). This is true for the data presented in this study, in which the speakers also use code-switching to negotiate identity. Talk shows specifically are an opportunity for women to compete with men on a professional level and to re-define their identity according to context.

The relation between form and function with regard to the use of MSA is highlighted by Holes (2004: 344). He posits that:

> In any passage of Arabic speech, whether monologue or conversation, one cannot track, still less make sense of, the moment-by-moment, unpredictable changes in language form unless one is also aware of co-occurrent changes in the ideational content of the discourse and the interpersonal relationships of the participants, as perceived by the participants themselves. Changes in the form of what is said are a complex set of signals – the rules of which have yet to be worked out – of these underlying changes.

Note the following example taken from programme 2 in the series 'Before you are held accountable', which is broadcast on the religious channel Iqraʔ 'Read'. The setting is a garden and, in addition to the female announcer, there are two men and two women. One man is a professor of psychology, the other is a journalist. One woman is a professor of sociology while the other is the director of a non-governmental organisation that takes care of street children.

The topic for discussion is street children. Two participants, one man and one woman, hold PhDs. I have chosen this excerpt because it occurs in the middle of the talk show, when speakers are supposed to be more relaxed about being on television.

I will use the following abbreviations to refer to the men and women:

Male professor of psychology: M-P
Male journalist: M-J
Female professor of sociology: F-P
Female director: F-D

(34) **M-P**: *il-ḥubb axba:ru ʔe:h ʕandukum// bi-yitkallimu ʕan il-ḥubb//*
'How about love? Do they speak of love?'
F-D: *a:h tabʕan bi-yitkallimu ʕan il-ḥubb/ fi: minhum yaʕni fi ʔiṭa:r al-zawa:g/ tabʕan fil bida:ya b-tibʔa ḥassa ʔinni huwwa illi ḥa-yintaʃilha/ lakin il-maʃa:ʕir bardu/ ma-btibʔa:-ʃ mustaqirra/ ya dukto:r ha:ʃim/ liʔanni hiyya bi-tḥibbu taḥt ḍaġṭ muʕayyan/ wi waḍʕ muʕayyan/ lamma b-yiṭlaʕ nadl wi yixli bi:ha/ ha:ðihi al-maʃa:ʕir bi-tatabaddal tama:man/ fa yi:gi waḥid ta:ni/ al-munqið/fa yinqiðha min waḍʕ ʔa:xar/ fa tḥibbu huwwa/ wa ha:kaða//*
'Yes of course they speak of love. Some of them speak of love within the frame of marriage. Of course at the beginning the girl feels that the man is her saviour. But also, Dr Hashim, her feelings are not stable, because she loves him under certain pressure and certain circumstances. When the man proves to be a scoundrel and jilts her, these feelings she had for him change completely. Then another man comes, who plays the role of the saviour who also saves her from another situation. So she falls for him and then it goes on like that.'
M-J: *le:h fi bint b-tihrab min it-tafakkuk il-ʔusari / wi fi:h bint bi-tistaḥmil//*
'Why is there one girl who runs away from a disintegrated family and another who can put up with it?'
F-P: *ʕala ḥasab bardu iʃ-ʃaxṣiyya illi ʔitrabbit guwwa il-bint/ fi ʔawwil sanawatha/ yaʕni . . .*
'This is also dependent on the girl's acquired personality in her first years. I mean . . . '
M-J: *yaʕni bi-taʕtamid ʕala do:r il-ʔusra*
'So it depends on the role of the family.'
F-D: *miʃ ʃarṭ ʔinn yiku:n iṭ-ṭifl ṭifl ʃa:riʕ/ mumkin yiku:n min guwwa il-be:t.*
'It is not necessary that the child lives in the street for him to be a street child, he can be living with his parents still.'
M-J: *fi ḥala:t kiti:ra giddan lil-tafakkuk/ ʔawwalan mumkin il-be:t nafsu bardu . . .*

'There are different cases of disintegration. First, maybe the home itself is also . . . '
F-D: *mumkin yibʔa gaww il-be:t ṭa:rid*
'The atmosphere at home may be repulsive.'
M-J: *fikrat iṣ-ṣala:ba in-nafsiyya/ yaʕni iṭ-ṭifl bi-yitḥammil walla ma-b-yitḥammil-ʃi/ fi ʔatfa:l ʕanduhum/ yaʕni fi haʃa:ʃa fil mawaḍi:ʕ di/ wi fi ʔatfa:l mumkin bi-yistaḥmilu/ wi yiqawmu/ ʔila ʔa:xiru// bas fi ḥa:ga tanya yimkin ʔaʃa:rit liha dukto:ra ʃahinnda/ wi hiyya fikrat il-faqr/ yaʕni ʔistiġla:l ha:za il-faʔr il-mawgu:d ʕand il-fataya:t do:l . . .*
'The concept of psychological strength refers to whether the child can bear his circumstances or not. There are children . . . I mean there are children who are weak in that respect. Other children can put up with this and can struggle against it etc. but there is something else that perhaps Dr Shahinda referred to, which is the concept of poverty. I mean taking advantage of the poverty of these girls . . . '
F-D: *ʔana baʕṭarid ʕala ha:ða ik-kala:m/ maṣr ṭu:l ʕumraha balad faʔi:ra.*
'I object to what you have just said. Egypt has always been a poor country.'
M-J: *ʔismaḥi li-bass akammil ig-gumla . . .*
'Just allow me to finish my sentence . . . '
F-D: *wi ṭu:l ʕumraha balad faʔi:ra/ ʕumrina kunna bi-nismaʕ ʕan banatna fil-ʃa:riʕ//*
'And Egypt has always been a poor country. We never heard of our girls living in the streets.'
M-J: *wara:ʔ kull mustaġill fi wa:ḥid bi-yistaġillu/ da ṭabi:ʕi/ lakin ʔa:h fi taġayyura:t ḥaṣalit fi mugtamaʕna ʔaswaʔ b-kti:r giddan min it-taġ ayyura:t illi ḥaṣalit zama:n/ wil- tafakkuk il-ʔusari/*
'Behind everyone who is exploited, there is someone who exploits them. This is natural. Yes there are changes that took place in our society, changes that are much worse than the ones that happened before and also the disintegration of families.'
F-D: *il-ʔaxras da b-yiʃaġġal bint ʕandaha ʔarbaʕ sini:n wi huwwa ma-b-yiʃtaġal-ʃ le:h// yaʕni ʕayzi:n. . ...*
'Why does this dumb (unable to speak) man make a 4-year-old girl work for him while he does not work? So we want . . . '
M-J: *ʔiḥna b-nitkallim ʔan system ʔigtima:ʕi . . .*
'We are speaking about a social system . . . '
F-P: *ma hiyya il-ʔusra mutafakkika/*
'But it is a disintegrated family.'
F-D: *min ʔigma:li ʔarbaʕ tala:f ṭifl/ ṣannafna ḥala:t il-faqr faqat/ ṭiliʕ il-faʔr bas ʔarbaʕa fil-miyya/ al-faqr faqat ka-ʕa:mil wa:ḥid/ ma-fi:-ʃ ḥa:ga ʔismaha al-faqr faqat/ il-ʕawa:mil il-ʔiqtiṣa:diyya/ maʕa*

t-taʕli:m/ il muʕamla is-sayyiʔa/ / ʕadatan lamma titfakkak il-ʔusra/ ʕadatan il-ṭifl la bi-yuqbal hina/ wa la bi-yuqbal hina/ /
'We have a total of 4,000 children. We classified cases of poverty only. We found that poverty is only 4 per cent. Poverty is only one reason. It is not only about poverty. Economic factors in addition to education and abuse are important. Usually when the family is disintegrated, the child is not accepted by both parties.'

In this example, the interaction between the two men and women is in fact an eye-opener in many respects. The announcer was not really involved in the interaction at all. So it was up to the participants to take turns. While the dialogue goes back and forth between men and women 17 times, women take control of the floor 9 times while men take control of the floor 8 times of the interaction. There are two who specifically control the floor, the F-D and the M-J, but still it is clear that women in this example are not less assertive than men. The interaction starts with the M-P asking the F-D a question about love and its importance for street girls. F-D considers herself the expert among all participants since she is the director of an organisation that deals directly with street children. She gives her answer. It is up to the participants to direct the interaction. Then another man, M-J, asks the second question and the interaction goes on. F-D is the only woman who asks a question and it is in fact a rhetorical one, when she wonders why a dumb man would make a 4-year-old girl work for him. Thus, men ask two questions while women only gave propositions, as F-D does at the end of this example, when she gives numerical evidence of cases of poverty between girls to support her argument.

The women in our example do not hedge. In fact F-D interrupts M-J and states clearly that she objects to what he said. While M-J refers to F-P as 'Dr Shahindah', his title is never used by any woman.

One has to bear in mind that these are all well-educated women, and judging from the way they dress they are also upper-middle-class women. They are still conservative in their outfit: F-D wore a head scarf, while F-P did not, but she was still wearing a long-sleeved dress.

All the speakers in this part use ECA with insertions of MSA. Counting the MSA and ECA features used by both men and women revealed no differences between them in this talk show. Let us consider in detail some MSA and ECA features, whether phonological, morpho-syntactic or lexical. If we consider the use of the MSA phonological variable *q*, we find there is no clear difference in its use between men and women in the above example.

Note that there are words that cannot be pronounced with a glottal stop, for example *il-ʔiqtiṣa:diyya* 'economic', which is used by F-D. F-D uses *q* five times and uses the glottal stop twice, as in *faʔr* 'poverty' and *faʔi:ra* 'poor'. M-J does not only use *q*. He uses it once in *il-faqr* 'poverty' and then he uses the glottal stop for the same word.

Throughout the data there is no tendency for women to stick to the glottal stop while avoiding *q*. In fact the *q* occurs 116 times by women and 98 times by men in positions which permit either the MSA *q* sound or the ECA glottal stop. This may indicate that women in talk shows use more MSA features than men. However, such a postulation needs more data.

F-D uses MSA demonstratives, as in:

(35) *ha:ða ik-kala:m*,
dem det-talk
'what you have just said'

She also uses MSA negation with an MSA passive verb and an ECA aspect marker, the *b*-, as in

(36)	*ʕadatan iṭ-ṭifl*	*la*	*bi-yuqbal*	*hina/ wa*	*la*	*bi-yuqbal*
	Usually det-child	neg	asp-msg-pass-accept	here/and	neg	asp-msg-pass-accept

hina
here
'Usually the child is not accepted by both parties'.

The form of language used by F-D is a marked choice, as Myers-Scotton (1998) calls it, that emphasises F-D's identity. It is marked because it occurs in a context in which ECA demonstratives were used. Just before she starts speaking, M-J used an ECA demonstrative.

(37) *il-fataya:t do:l*
det-girls dem-pl

F-D considers herself the expert among all participants, and, as is clear in the content of what she says, she thinks that she is more knowledgeable than the man. Her use of MSA demonstratives is to highlight her disagreement with what M-J claims, that poverty is the cause of the increase in the number of street children. She interrupts him and states that she objects to what he says. She uses the MSA demonstrative system to do that. Also, when stating facts about the reasons why some children become street children, she uses the MSA negative system as well as the MSA passive form albeit with the ECA *b*-prefix (see example 34). The ECA counterpart would be

(38)	*iṭ-ṭifl*	*miʃ*	*bi-yitʔabal*	*hina wa la hina*
	The-child	neg	asp-msg-pass-accept	here and neg here

'the child is not accepted by both parties'

The choice of MSA features in the woman's speech is related to the identity she projects on herself, which is her identity as a social reformist and a director of a non-governmental organisation for street children.

What is also worth mentioning is that M-J uses the English word 'system' while neither female switches to English at all.

Now note the following example from programme 2 in the series 'Home secrets', in which a female judge starts speaking in MSA to the audience as well as the participants. She wants to make a point that 'secret marriages' and 'temporary marriages', though they may be widespread in the Arab world, are in fact against religion and humanity. Note that she is wearing not just a head scarf but also gloves, which are symbols of ultra-conservative Islamic dress.

(39) **Female judge:** *naḥnu fi zaman/ furiḍa ʕala l-marʔa ʔan tubtaðal/ wa yuġṭaṣab gasadaha/ wa naḥnu gami:ʕan nabḥaθ/ min an-na:ḥiya al-ʃarʕiyya/ walla min an-naḥya iq-qa:nuniyya/ al-aḥka:m iʃ-ʃarʕiyya wil-qa:nuniyya wil-qada:ʔiyya θa:bita/ θubu:tan la yaqbal wa la gadal wa la muna:qaʃa/*

'We live at a time when women are expected to be abused, when women's bodies are raped, while we are all still investigating whether this is allowed according to jurisprudence or law. Legislative, legal and procedural rules are fixed so as not to allow any scope for argument or discussion.'

The female judge in this example uses MSA rather than ECA (except very rarely), although the interaction that has been going on was not in MSA. She, however, uses MSA morpho-syntactic features like negation, as in

(40)

la yaqbal	*wa*	*la gadal*	*wa*	*la muna:qaʃa*
neg 3msg-accept	and	neg argument	and	neg discussion

'not to allow any scope of argument or discussion'
in contrast to the ECA

(41)

miʃ	*bi-yiʔbal*	*wa*	*la gadal*	*wa*	*la munaʔʃa*
not	asp-3msg accept	and	neg argument	and	neg discussion

'not to allow any scope of argument or discussion'

She also consistently uses the *q* phonological variable and never the glottal stop. Even the pronoun she starts with is an MSA pronoun, *naḥnu*, as opposed to the ECA equivalent, *ʔiḥna* 'we'.

The fact that the interaction that has been taking place before between the female journalist and the male journalist was not in MSA is significant in this example. Unlike the female judge, the female journalist's code is categorised as a mixture of MSA and ECA, the male journalist speaks basically ECA, and the male writer speaks a mixture of MSA and ECA. The negotiated manner of speaking in the programme is not MSA. Thus the female judge's use of MSA represents again what Myers-Scotton (1998) calls a marked choice, a choice not expected by the participants or the audience (see Chapter 2). This example can also be explained in terms of indexicality, which was discussed in Chapter 2 and will be defined again here for the sake of clarity: indexicality is a relation of associations through which utterances are understood. For example, if a specific code or form of language presupposes a 'certain social context, then use of that form may create the perception of such context where it did not exist before' (Woolard 2004: 88). If a code is associated with the authority of courtrooms and this code is then used in a different context, it will denote authority. The language of the speaker would then be considered an authoritative language (Silverstein 1998: 267 cited in Woolard 2004: 88). This is exactly the case in the example of the female judge. By using MSA, a language associated with authority of several kinds – religious, legal/governmental – as well as education, the female judge lays claim to all MSA indexes. These indexes can help shape her projection of identity as well. By using MSA the woman is assigning herself the elevated status of an authority on the subject matter and a religious scholar as well as a legal expert. If one examines the content of what she says, one will notice that she is stating facts and giving powerful conclusions. MSA gives her postulations an air of authority.

She is also assigning herself the role of the commentator on the frame of events, the all-knowledgeable, sophisticated, educated woman.

This is exactly what happens in parliament in Egypt, when a member of parliament speaks MSA rather than ECA. By using a code different from the one expected and used thus far by other members, which is usually a mixture of MSA and ECA, the speaker is also appealing to a specific part of his or her identity and laying claims to all MSA indexes.

Compare the above example to the following one, which is by a male member of the Egyptian parliament, given in January 1999 in the People's Assembly (Majlis al-Shaʿb). The speaker voices his opinion about the sanctions imposed on Iraq.

The speaker, as it were, removes himself from his surroundings and party affiliation, and says that he wants to speak as an Arab and an Egyptian. He asks the parliament members as well as the head of parliament to remember the famous slogan of Muṣṭafá Kāmil (1874–1908), the Egyptian national hero, who said that one should never make concessions about the rights of one's country. The speaker wants to highlight the importance of supporting the Iraqis, because they are suffering harsh penalties as a result of sanctions which, in his view, are quite unfair.

(42) *b-ṣifaṭi ʔalmuwa:ṭin sa:miḥ ʕaʃu:r ʕuḍwi maglis iʃ-ʃaʕb/ ʔallaði yantami: ʔila ʃaʕbi miṣr wa ʔila l-ʔumma l-ʕarabiyya/ wa ʔargu ʔan taḥðif ʔayyat*

ʔintima:ʔ ḥizbi li ʔaw liġayri fil-ḥadi:θ ʕan haðihi l-qadiyya/ siya:dat ir-raʔi:s kullama rattabtu ḥadi:θan fi ha:ða l-mawḍu:ʕ ḍa:ʕa minni/ faqat/ ʔiltaṣaqa fi ðihni ʔalʔa:n qa:lat/ wa maqu:lat/al-waṭani al-kabi:r muṣṭafa ka:mil/ ʕindama qa:l/ ʔinna man yatasa:maḥa fi ḥuqu:qi bila:dihi wa law marratin wa:ḥida/ yaʕi:ʃ ʔabad iḍ-ḍahr muzaʕzaʕ il-ʕaqi:da/saqi:mu l-wigda:n

'I speak as the citizen Sāmiḥ ʿĀshūr, the member of parliament, who belongs to the Egyptian people, and to the Arab nation, and please disregard my affiliation to any political party, and disregard the affiliation of others, when discussing this issue. Speaker, whenever I prepare a speech about this topic, I lack the words. There is only one thing that still sticks in my mind right now, and that is the saying of the great national hero, Mustafa Kamil, when he said, "whoever concedes the rights of his country to someone even once, lives ever after faltering in his beliefs, and will always remain weak to the core".'

Note that the speaker himself says that he does not speak as a member of parliament belonging to a specific party, but as an Egyptian and an Arab. Therefore, he wants people to perceive him as such, with no regard to his political affiliations.

At the beginning, the speaker does not refer to himself by saying 'I am Sāmiḥ ʿĀshūr'; he rather starts by 'as the citizen Sāmiḥ ʿĀshūr, the member of parliament, who belongs to the Egyptian people, and to the Arab nation.'

In this speech, the parliamentarian could speak ECA or a mixture of MSA and ECA, and this does happen in parliament in Egypt (cf. Bassiouney 2006), but he attempts to stick to MSA. The female judge in example (39) likewise does not refer to her own personal opinion, but starts with the all-inclusive 'we' and then starts postulating about women's plight in our time.

In examples (39) and (42), the use of code is not an arbitrary one. It is a result of the role the female judge and the male member of parliament project on themselves by using all MSA indexes. He projects on himself the role of 'the archetypal Egyptian', or 'the archetypal Arab'. He is not speaking as an individual member of parliament any more, but rather as a kind of 'abstract voice' speaking for the historical record. She projects on herself the identity of the authoritative figure. They both use a code that reflects their identity. Thus, the code used is not related to the gender of the speaker but to the projection of identity in the part of the speaker.

Returning to the discussion of programme 2 in the 'Home secrets' series, the reply to the female judge does not come from one of the men present but from another woman, the famous Egyptian journalist Iqbāl Barakah. She does not use MSA only as the female judge does, although she still uses MSA features. Her utterance is categorised as a mixture of MSA and ECA.

(43) **Female journalist:** *il-mugtamaʕ il-ʕarabi yuʕa:mil al-marʕa ka-ʃe:ʔ/ fa ʃe:ʔ*
ṭabi:ʕi ʔinnaha tataḥawwal fi yo:m min il-ʔayya:m ʔila silʕa tuba:ʕ wa tuʃtara// il-qawani:n sabta/ di muʃkilitna//
'Arab society treats woman as a thing. So it is quite natural that one day women become goods to be bought and sold. Indeed laws are fixed and that is our problem.'

There are ECA features like the demonstratives, as in *di muʃkilitna* 'that is our problem'. Also, the vowel in *ʃe:ʔ* is the ECA *e:* rather than the MSA *ay*. However, the verb is in MSA, *yuʕa:mil* 'to treat'; the ECA counterpart would be *bi-yiʕa:mil*. Once more the switching between ECA and MSA is used to draw attention to what is being said. The MSA verb emphasises the point made by the female journalist that women are treated as goods in Arab society. In fact all the verbs in this extract are in MSA: *yuʕa:mil* 'to treat', *tataḥawwal* 'to become', *tuba:ʕ* 'to be sold' and *tuʃtara* 'to be bought'. The last two verbs are in the MSA passive form. After she states her facts clearly, she ends her postulation with an ECA demonstrative phrase

(44) *di muʃkilitna*
dem problem-ours
'that is our problem'

ECA here is the marked code since it is juxtaposed with the MSA verbs. Code-switching between MSA and ECA serves to get her message through more effectively.

The male journalist is then asked by the announcer to give his opinion. He uses less MSA than either women. In fact, by counting MSA and ECA features, one can deduce that he uses a variety which is categorised as basically ECA.

(45) **Male journalist:** *ʔana ba-tkallim ʕan iz-zo:g/ tayyib ma l-sitt hiyya ig-guzʔ it-ta:ni/ il-wagh it-ta:ni lil-ʕumla.*
'I am speaking about the husband. But women are also the other half. They are the other side of the coin.'

He uses ECA features like the aspectual marker *b* in *ba-tkallim*, and ECA lexical items, as in *sitt* for 'woman' instead of the MSA *marʔa*.

The man is then interrupted by the female journalist, who starts defending the woman whose problem is being discussed.

(46) **Female journalist:** *waḥid ʔusta:ð fil gamʕa*
'He is [the husband] a university professor.'

The female journalist observes that the husband who deceived his wife was in fact a professor, so he has to take all the blame, and thus it was easy for him to deceive a girl and marry her secretly.

The male journalist then answers:

(47) **Male journalist:** *ʔiḥna ʕandina na:s ma-tʕallimit-ʃ wi lakin ʕandaha mabdaʔ*
'There are people who have no education whatsoever but who have principles.'

The male journalist wants to stress that deceiving is not related to level of education. He uses ECA negation in *ma-tʕallimit-ʃ* 'who have no education'.

Again, this example shows that both men and women manipulate MSA and use it as a symbol of their identity, authority and expertise. MSA is also, sometimes, juxtaposed with ECA to leave the utmost effect possible on the audience. In a study conducted by Bassiouney (2005–9) in which thirty advertisements from national Egyptian television channel (1) were analysed, it was concluded that the use of MSA is not related directly to the gender of the speaker but rather to the nature of the product and the target demographic. Although commercial language is special in nature, it is still important to note the linguistic forms used by men and women in relation to the diglossic situation in Egypt and other Arab countries.

4.8.3.3 Identity and code choice

Human identity is defined by Lakoff (2006: 142) as 'a continual work in progress, constructed and altered by the totality of life experience. While much of the work in support of this belief concentrates on the larger aspects of identity – especially gender, ethnicity, and sexual preferences – in fact human identity involves many other categories. Identity is constructed in complex ways, more or less consciously and overtly.' Lakoff points to the variability of identity at different stages of one's life and in different contexts. One's identity is made up of more than one part; a mother can also be a professor, a wife, an administrator, a politician, a friend, an Egyptian, a Muslim, an Arab and so forth. As Lakoff says, an individual is a member of a 'cohesive and coherent group' as well as an individual (2006: 142). Bastos and Oliveira (2006: 188) emphasise the fact that identity is both 'fixed' and 'continuous', in the sense that individuals perceive themselves differently in various situations or contexts. Identity is also manifested through language use, as is the case in the data analysed.

When discussing the use of code choice by women, linguists tend to concentrate on the disadvantages of women in the public sphere, while ignoring how code choice can be used as a means of attaining power by women and asserting their identity. Cameron (2005: 496) discusses how women are marginalised globally in public spheres and how women are silenced in public contexts or denied access to the 'language literacies and speech styles' needed to enter the public domain. Sadiqi (2006: 647), when discussing language and gender in the Arab world, postulates that women had to struggle to be able to enter the public arena. While this may be true, her other statements are too general. She claims that although literate women have a 'less detached attitude' towards MSA, they, like illiterate women, are not encouraged to be in the public sphere' and use MSA less than men. She also postulates that MSA is the 'male domain', since it is the language of the public sphere and the institution.

The data presented in this study reveals that this may not be the case in all contexts and for all Arab women. When women are in the public sphere, which occurs frequently in Egypt, especially in the media, they use the opportunity to establish their status and identity, and MSA is one of the tools used by them to define and clarify these.

In addition, according to Cameron (2005: 139), as people, whether men or women, are interacting with one another they are also adopting particular 'subject positions' and assigning positions to others. Thus, when a woman is talking she is also assigning herself a position, such as teacher, expert, professional and so forth. She is also assigning positions to the others she talks to; she may choose to express solidarity with them, claim distance from them or even condescend to them. The definition of subject positions is similar to that of identity given by Bean and Johnstone (2004), who contend that identity is formed by our experiences and set of memories and, more importantly, by the projection of our experiences and memories on the way we express ourselves. If having an identity requires 'self expression', then individuals have to resort to all their linguistic resources to express their identity (2004: 237). The linguistic resources available to women in the programmes analysed include code choice and code-switching. Bolonyai (2005: 16–17) in a study of bilingual girls, shows how they intentionally and strategically use their linguistic resources to exhibit their power. They use code choice to position themselves in a dominant position. This can be done by switching to English to show their expertise and knowledge. Switching to English is used as a control mechanism and a power display. Switching is also a means of asserting their superior identity. Again, this is exactly what women do when they switch to MSA in the programmes analysed.

Finally I will discuss in more detail the second point that the study makes, which is that in talk shows Egyptian women can be as assertive as men, if not more.

4.8.3.4 Interruption and assertiveness

Interruption is different from overlap. Interruption is defined as simultaneous talk that involves the violation of rules of turn-taking. It may also convey lack of care on the part of the interrupter for the face of the other participant. It usually takes place in the middle of a clause or sentence rather than at the end. Overlap, on the other hand, is not considered a violation of the turn-taking system, and could be used to support an argument, as a transition device, or to show involvement. It is not usually a contradiction of what has been said before, and it takes place at the end of a clause rather than in the middle of it (Cheng 2003: 34; see also Tannen 1994; Romaine 1998). While interruption can be considered a face-threatening device, overlap is usually a supportive device that denotes solidarity. Note also that the notion of interruption presupposes an idealised world in which turn-taking always takes place at the end of a clause, which is not always the case in actual conversations (Romaine 1998; Tannen 1994).

In example (34), as was said earlier, the announcer was not really involved in the interaction at all. So it was up to the participants to take turns. While the dialogue goes back and forth between men and women 17 times, women control 9 times and men control only 8 times in the interaction. There are two who specifically control the floor, the F-D and the M-J, but still it is clear that women in this example are not less assertive than men. This is true for all my data.

4.8.3.4.1 Difference between overlap and interruption
Two examples of overlap follow.

(48) **F-P**: *ʕala ḥasab bardu iʃ-ʃaxṣiyya illi ʔitrabbit guwwa il-bint/ fi ʔawwil sanawatha/ yaʕni . . .*
'This is also dependent on the girl's acquired personality in her first years. I mean . . .'
M-J: *yaʕni bi-taʕtamid ʕala do:r il-ʔusra*
'So it depends on the role of the family.'

This is an example of an overlap rather than an interruption. M-J uses overlap to support and clarify what is said by F-P. There is no contradiction and he speaks after the sentence filler *yaʕni* 'I mean'. Note also that the speaker pauses after *yaʕni.* Thus, he does not interrupt F-P in the middle of a clause.

(49) **M-J**: *fi ḥala:t kiti:ra giddan lil-tafakkuk/ ʔawwalan mumkin il-be:t nafsu bardu . . .*
'There are different cases of disintegration. First maybe the home itself is also . . .'
F-D: *mumkin yibʔa gaww il-be:t ṭa:rid*
'The atmosphere at home may be repulsive.'

This is another example of an overlap. M-J pauses after *bardu* 'also', and F-D clarifies and summarises his point, without any threat to his face.

Examples of interruption now follow.

(50) **M-J:** *fikrat iṣ-ṣala:ba in-nafsiyya/ yaʕni iṭ-ṭifl bi-yitḥammil walla ma-b-yitḥammil-ʃi/fi ʔatfa:l ʕanduhum/ yaʕni fi haʃa:ʃa fil mawaḍi:ʕ di/ wi fi ʔaṭ fa:l mumkin bi-yistaḥmilu/ wi yiqawmu/ ʔila ʔa:xiru// bas fi ḥa:ga tanya yimkin ʔaʃa:rit liha dokto:ra ʃahinnda/ wi hiyya fikrat il-faqr/ yaʕni ʔistiġla:l ha:za il-faʔr il-mawgu:d ʕand il-fataya:t do:l . . .*
'The concept of psychological strength refers to whether the child can bear his circumstances or not. There are children . . . I mean there are children who are weak in that respect. Other children can put up with this and can struggle against it etc. but there is something else that perhaps Dr Shahinda referred to, which is the concept of poverty. I mean taking advantage of the poverty of these girls . . . (this is the first part of a clause; the speaker is interrupted before he finishes the sentence).'
F-D: *ʔana ba-ʕṭarid ʕala ha:ða ik-kala:m/ maṣr ṭu:l ʕumraha balad faʔi:ra.*
'I object to what you have just said. Egypt has always been a poor country.'
M-J: *ʔismaḥi li-bass akammil ig-gumla . . .*
'Just allow me to finish my sentence . . . [This should be modified by an adjectival demonstrative *di* 'this', which the speaker could not say, because he was interrupted again.]
F-D: *wi ṭu:l ʕumraha balad faʔi:ra/ ʕumrina kunna bi-nismaʕ ʕan banatna fil-ʃa:riʕ//*
'And Egypt has always been a poor country. We never heard of our girls living in the streets.'

M-J is interrupted by F-D twice in the middle of the sentence and she states clearly that she objects to his claims. First, M-J realises he is being interrupted and he asks her to allow him to finish his sentence. However, F-D interrupts him again and continues with her argument that she does not agree with him. F-D's assertiveness is clear in her interruptions and her general postulations about Egypt.

(51) **F-D:** *il-ʔaxras da b-yiʃaġġal bint ʕandaha ʔarbaʕ sini:n wi huwwa ma-b-yiʃtaġal-ʃ le:h// yaʕni ʕayzi:n . . .*
Why does this dumb man make a 4-year-old girl work for him while he does not work? So we want . . . '
M-J – *ʔiḥna b-nitkallim ʔan system ʔigtima:ʕi . . .*
'We are speaking about a social system . . . '

In this example, M-J interrupts F-D again in the middle of the clause, by reminding her of the aim of the conversation that he thinks that F-D may have digressed from.

Note the following example from programme 1 in the series 'The constitution dialogue', in which there is only one woman and three men. The woman interrupts the man when she does not like what he is saying, and asserts her identity by reminding him that she is a professor of law and knows exactly what she is talking about. Her assertive way is defined by her interruption and by re-stating what he already knows about her occupation.

(52) *ʔismaḥ li-/ ʔana dokto:ra fil-qanu:n*
Allow me/ I professor in law
'Excuse me, I am a professor of law.'

ʔismaḥ li- is not used in this context politely but as a defiance device. The man in fact backs down and shows his solidarity by saying:

(53) *laʔa l-ʕafu ya dokto:ra.*
No forgiveness voc professor
'Yes of course, forgive me, professor.'

By using her professional title he is also emphasising her status and acknowledging her power.

In the last example below, from programme 1 in the series *qabla ʔan tuḥa:sabu* 'Before you are held accountable', which discusses different forms of marriage in the Arab world, a male religious scholar seeks help from the female announcer because he has been interrupted twice by a female religious scholar.

(54) **Male religious scholar:** *hiyya bi-tʔaṭiʕni: dilwaʔti/miʃ ʕa:rif akammil kala:mi/ ġe:r raʔyi al-ʃarʕ. . . .*
'She is interrupting me. I cannot finish what I am saying. This is different from the opinion of legislative law . . . '[First part of a clause]

(55) **Female religious scholar:** *argu:k tira:giʕ al-qara:r al-ṣa:dir ʕan maglis al-buḥu:θ al-isla:miyya fil-azhar/ al-laði: ʔursila li wiza:rit al-ʔadl/ tarak li-ʔuli: al-amr min man yatawallu:na al-qara:r fi miṣr al-batti fi ha:ða al-amr/ al-raʔyi al-laði yaḥẓa bi-aġlabiyya laysa xaṭaʔ ʕala l-mustawa al-ʃarʕi:/*
'Please revise the decision of the research syndicate at Al-Azhar University, which was sent to the ministry of justice. The decision gave members of government the authority to decide the best way of dealing with the law. If a suggestion is endorsed by the majority then it cannot be wrong in legislative terms.'

I want to note that words such as *argu:k* 'please' in (54) or *ʔismaḥ li-* 'allow me' when used in Egypt in contexts such as talk shows, are not considered

Table 4.7 Number of interruptions and overlaps initiated by women and men

	Men	Women
Speakers	13	16
Interruption initiated by	27	33
Overlap initiated by	48	58

polite terms but rather detaching and challenging ones. On the other hand, the expression used by the male politician, *al-ʕafu* 'forgive me' in (53), demonstrates negative politeness as defined earlier in this chapter. Table 4.7 shows the total number of interruptions and overlaps initiated by men and women in all the data analysed in my study.

As in the example of Moroccan women bargaining, Egyptian women on talk shows do not appeal to solidarity but rather to power. They are indeed assertive.

I have not analysed interruption and assertiveness in detail here but rather wanted to give the reader a feel of the linguistic situation. I also wanted to argue that women and men are not two independent/homogeneous entities. They interact on a daily basis and when they do, it is not always gender that is the governing factor.

4.8.4 Conclusion

In this study I argue that, first, there is a direct relation between the code used by speakers and the projection of identity which is manifested clearly in the examples analysed. Therefore, it is not possible to measure the frequency of MSA features in the speech of women in the public sphere without understanding which part of their identity they appeal to. Moreover, this is true for both men and women. The women in the programmes are as educated and as exposed to MSA as the men and they do not have any problem in using MSA.

Second, code-switching is used by both men and women as a linguistic device to leave the utmost effect possible on the audience. Thus when switching minimises the costs and maximises the rewards of the speaker, the speaker resorts to it, since, as Myers-Scotton claims, this is the main aim of the speaker in most cases (Myers-Scotton 1993: 110; 2006). Assertiveness goes hand in hand with the projection of identity on the part of the speaker.

The diglossic situation in Egypt can be used by women to show their authority and expertise and to appear emphatic and assertive. Once more I want to emphasise that in this study I do not aim at making generalisations, but rather at questioning them. Although talk shows are a special kind of data, they still represent women in the public sphere.

4.9 THE SYMBOLIC USE OF LANGUAGE

The symbolic significance of language has been and will be discussed throughout the book. In fact, most acts of language choice by both men and women are a symbolic act of some sort. If, for example, women are seen in a culture as a symbol of tradition and the transmitters of history, then they may want to preserve this role by using a specific variety, and not necessarily the most prestigious one.[22] Miller (2004) posits that in established Arab cities where the old urban vernacular has been replaced by a new one, it is older women who retain linguistic features of the old dialect. Still, in other situations of language contact and change, young women tend to acquire features faster than do older women. Eckert (1998) states that one cannot make a generalisation like the one that posits that women are more or less conservative than men; it is only that women use 'symbolic resources' more than men to 'establish membership and status' (1998: 73). It could also be that women evaluate and use the symbolic resources differently.

An interesting example of the symbolic use of language is that by women in the Thonga community in South Africa; they are more respected in traditional Thonga culture than in Zulu culture. It is thus not surprising that they use the less prestigious language, Thonga, as a way of rebelling against the loss of power and respect which is associated with Zulu for them. Men, on the other hand, use the more prestigious Zulu language (Herbert 2002: 321–4).

In a study conducted by Hoffman (2006) about Berber language use by women, it is women who have the role of maintaining Berber and preserving it. Before discussing Hoffman's study in detail, I will first give some background information about the linguistic situation in Morocco, which is discussed in detail in Chapter 5, but which needs to be outlined here.

According to Sadiqi (2003a: 218–29) the languages/varieties used in Morocco and their associations are as shown in Table 4.8.

Sadiqi divides the use of language between men and women according to domains and contexts. It is appropriate in specific contexts to use a specific variety or language and in others to use another.

According to Hoffman, at a time when political and economic factors shape women's linguistic practices, it is still rural Berber women who carry the burden of speaking the language and remaining monolinguals. If the language is to continue, it falls to women to pass it on because they are monolingual caregivers. The Tashelhit language community of south-western Morocco was specifically examined. Tashelhit Berber speakers reside in the Anti-Atlas mountains and Sous valley. Note that in public it is urban Berber men, who are usually bilingual in Arabic (Standard and colloquial) and Berber languages, who are the prominent figures in the Amazigh rights movement for valorising and preserving the language (Demnati 2001, cited in Hoffman 2006: 146). The reasons why these women are practically monolingual and do not speak

Table 4.8 Languages and varieties used in Morocco and their gender associations

MSA	Moroccan colloquial Arabic	Berber varieties	French
The language of the high institution and usually associated with *men* rather than women because of the contexts in which it is used, and in which men play a prominent role.	The language associated with both *men and women*. It is used in the public and private domains. It is used in the media, in trade transactions, in education, in television soap operas and in films.	The language associated with *women*. There are more monolingual women who speak Berber varieties only than men. This may be due to the high illiteracy rate of women compared to men, to the use of Berber by mothers to their children, and to its association with home, folk culture and personal identity for Berbers in general. Men still use Berber but they are mostly bilingual in Berber languages and Moroccan Arabic. However, the contexts in which Berber languages are used are associated more with the private sphere, home and nostalgia than with the public one.	The language associated with *men and women*. It is a language linked to financial gain and economic opportunities. Note that urban upper and middle class men associate French with business and administration, while urban upper-middle class women associate it with everyday use and socialisation.

any Arabic, although this in fact affects their access to resources, is because of the closer relation they have to the land. In the Anti-Atlas mountains, women are the agriculturalists and men are considered unfit to farm, but more suited for clean city work (2006: 156). Note that although men are not attached to the land they are still attached to the language, since it serves as a symbol of belonging to a tribe and a community.

Hoffman discusses the example of a study done on Mexican Nahuatl women by Hill and Hill (1986; Hill 1987), in which it was demonstrated that women use their heritage language more than men and are expected to do so by both men and women. The same is true for the Berber women analysed.

They use fewer Arabic loan words and borrowings than men even when they are familiar with Arabic, especially in counting and identifying colours, two domains where Arabic prevails with males. These women are 'romanticised' by men and considered the carriers of heritage. Their language is seen as pure. They use high pitch and loud volume index, seen as denoting femaleness, confidence, boldness, assertiveness and bravado (Hoffman 2006: 158, 159). These are all features that are supposed to be lacking in Arab women. Such features are used in popular music, as performed by Fatima Tabaamrant, where high pitch indexes and a roughness in women are admired. Although females in that community are seen as being authentic, they are also known for having very poor schooling, and being completely detached from the Arabic-speaking community, which may be economically superior.

In a similar vein, the following study conducted by Walters is an example of a study that reveals how language can be used as one of the symbolic resources for women. Walters (1996b), in his paper 'Gender, identity, and the political economy of language', studies a diglossic community and a bilingual one simultaneously. He studies foreign wives coming from England, Canada or the USA married to Tunisian men and living in Tunisia. These wives have integrated themselves into a new community. To some extent their status in this community is predetermined by certain factors, such as them being native speakers of English and their husbands' position in this community, as well as their in-laws' positions. However, there is still room for these women to shape and modify their status. The language used for communication can serve as one of the symbolic means of modifying a status.

The women have three if not four options. There is the option of not learning any new language and communicating in English, which is not practical. There is the option of learning MSA, and there is also the option of using French, which is supposed to be the language of educated Arabs in Tunisia, thus the more prestigious language than TCA; or they can use the Tunisian colloquial dialect, which is in practice the best instrumental language available to them for their daily lives. By learning TCA they can do their shopping, communicate with their in-laws, and get involved in Tunisian culture in different ways and probably to different degrees. The women generally spoke French well. Some also knew some TCA, in response to the linguistic demands and possibilities of daily personal and professional life, in ways that are profoundly linked to their class positions and family situations as well as their status as educated native speakers of English. French, on the other hand, was associated with economic market forces and economic pressure, since French could enable them to find jobs, or perhaps because for them French is more related to English and thus easier to learn – French is a Romance language written in Roman script, unlike Arabic (MSA and TCA), which is a Semitic language. Besides, there are no sufficient teaching facilities for Tunisian Arabic, unlike, for example, SA, which, as was said earlier, may be another option for these women. The interesting thing about this study is that these women are expected to learn Tunisian Arabic to interact with family and friends, but some still prefer French as a symbolic means of keeping their distance and not getting involved in family conflicts. French also serves as a symbol of their power and prestige. One of the goals of the study was to highlight the differences in outcome despite the similarities in the social positions of these women.

Hoffman claims that women in general as both individuals and members of groups either initiate language change, by adopting an instrumental language and abandoning their ancestral one, as occurred in Gal's study of Austria (1978a), or decide to take on the role of authentic symbols of heritage. They become so not just through language but also through their dress codes, cooking and songs. The situation Hoffman describes is similar to that of female Peruvian Quechua speakers. These women can keep their hold and control over their status in their communities by maintaining the language (cf. Harvey 1994: 55).

It is worth noting that women's use of language may be symbolic in some cases, but, women themselves could be regarded as a symbol, and this is reflected in language. For example, in literature, poetry and songs, Egypt is presented as a woman whose honour men have to fight to reclaim or preserve (Baron 2005: 47). The city of Beirut is portrayed as a woman in Nizār Qabbānī's poem with the title 'Bayrūt sitt al-dunyā' 'Beirut, mistress of the world'. Related to this, Eckert and McConnell-Ginet (2004: 167) suggest that women are usually appointed to jobs that enhance a company's symbolic image, such as those of a secretary, flight attendant or receptionist. Being regarded as a symbol themselves implies that women are expected also to preserve the symbol by different means and some of these means, are related to language use and maintenance.

So far, all these studies have concentrated on women. Indeed, as will become clear in Chapter 5 below, language is a powerful symbol for both men and women.

For example, Eisikovits (1987) analysed the speech of working-class male adolescents in Sydney, and found that there is a change in their language when talking to close friends of the same age and when talking to the interviewer. With the interviewer they use even more non-standard forms intentionally as a symbol of their independence and anger at the social norms. They talk 'with defiance and bravado' (1987: 56–114).

To conclude, I will highlight the points discussed:

- The association of women with tradition is not absolute but can change, in the same way as women's role in a specific community is subject to change.
- The linguistic choices available to women are also not absolute but are limited by a number of factors, such as their access to a language or

variety, the context and domain in which they can use this language or variety, and their ability to learn a different language or variety (as is the case with the Anglophone wives of Tunisian men discussed above).

- Language can be used as a symbolic resource for both men and women, although women have been studied more than men in relation to language.

4.10 GENDER UNIVERSALS RE-EXAMINED

If we re-examine the gender universals discussed by Holmes (1998), then indeed we will find that in the Arab world, as is the case in the west and indeed in all cultures of the world, women are still subordinate to men in one way or another, and this fact is reflected in language use. However, it is wrong to assume that women do not fight directly or indirectly in all cultures to assert their power, perhaps sometimes in an unexpected way.

Kharraki's (2001) study about Moroccan women bargaining and being less polite than men challenges one language universal. Likewise, data presented on Egyptian women and men in talk shows exemplifies how women can interrupt, challenge and control the floor as much as men if not more. Again, this challenges another language universal.

There are numerous ways in which women in the Arab world can invoke power. One of them is age. Eckert (2003: 369) alludes to the fact that gender has to be studied in relation to age. Arab women in general gain status by aging. Abu-Lughod (1987) mentioned, for example, that Bedouin women in the western desert in Egypt tend to show their faces more and veil less when they have higher status or when they are older. A mother's status is much higher than a young woman's. The formidable power of mothers in the Arab world is reflected in language to a great extent. Mothers, by praying for or cursing their children, are thought to be able to give happiness or inflict misery. This is indeed done through language. A mother can pray for her son and her prayers are believed to have the utmost effect, and the opposite is likewise true. To give an example, a 1960s Egyptian film called *al-Shumū ʿal-sawdāʾ* ('Black candles') asserts the linguistic power of mothers. The film is about a blind poet who cannot save his girlfriend from capital punishment because of his blindness, which was the result of an accident. In a moment of despair, the blind poet starts saying to his mother desperately and tearfully that this is the first time in his life that he feels disabled and weak. He breaks down and starts cursing his fate. At that point the mother is moved, and looking into the sky she says:

(56) *ya rabb/ daʕwa min ʔalb ʕumru ma faqad il- ʔamal wala il-ʔima:n bi:k*'
Voc God/ prayer from heart never neg lost the hope nor the-faith in-you

'Oh God. This is a prayer from a heart that never lost hope or belief in you.'

Two minutes later in the film, the blind poet looks at his hands and screams, 'I can see! I can see my hand!' Although this may sound absurd to a westerner, most Egyptians do not find the events absurd at all, but very believable. In a quarrel between a mother and her children, a mother can always issue the threat of cursing her children, which is almost as effective as issuing them a threat of death. Thus words spoken by a mother are powerful and must be taken seriously.

In the classic Egyptian novel *al-Watad* ('The tent peg'), by Khayrī Shalabī (1986), we have a powerful, rural, illiterate mother who holds the family together. Even though the husband is alive, he is never in the forefront; decisions are taken mainly by the mother. The mother's power is reflected through her language choice. Since in literature a writer can redefine reality with impunity, in the last chapter of the novel the uneducated peasant mother, Fāṭimah, speaks in MSA. The children reply to her in ECA, although we know that this could not have happened in reality. Because it would be almost impossible for an uneducated, peasant mother on her deathbed to start speaking pure MSA, Egyptian readers also take this use of MSA to be indicative of the power mothers have; recall the discussion of the association of MSA with authority. Similarly, the son's reply is always in ECA since he does not have any power over the mother. Note the following example, in which the eldest son tries to placate the mother by telling her not to take what his young brother said seriously:

(57) صلي على النبي يا حاجة بقى..سيبك منه هو يعني الكلام عليه جمرك؟

ṣalli ʕala in-nabi:	*ya*	*ḥagga baʔa/*	*si:bik*	*minnu/*
Pray for the-prophet	voc	ḥagga be/	leave-you	from-him
huwwa	*yaʕni*	*ik-kala:m*	*ʕale:h*	*gumruk/*
he	mean	the-talk	on-him	customs

'Invoke God's blessing on the Prophet, *hajja*, please do not think of what he said. He is just saying nonsense. His words do not count.'

The elder son tries to calm his mother by asking her to invoke God's blessing on the Prophet and not to take heed of what her younger son said in moments of anger. He speaks in ECA. By asking her to pray to the Prophet he takes the initiative in the reconciliation that the mother seems to refuse by replying in MSA.

It is noteworthy that the son does not address his mother as 'mother', but as *ḥagga*, (although she has not made the *ḥajj*, 'pilgrimage'), which brings us back to the power and status affiliated to terms of address. In contrast to the 'mister master' situation that we discussed in section 4.5, here it is the son who acknowledges his mother's power and status, which she gained by age and which makes her not just a mother but a *ḥajja*. The relation is in fact very formal, and it is the son who cares about preserving her face and not vice versa.

The mother then starts telling her children her life story and her achievements; all this is done in MSA.

(58) لقد دخلت هذه الدار وهي مجرد جدران..كانوا لا يوافقون على زواج أبيكم مني..و كنت وحيدة أبوى..و لم أكن فلاحة..فزرعتهما أشجارا و خضروات..و قال جدكم لأبيكم كيف تتزوج بنت أرملة لا عائلة لها؟

laqad	*daxaltu*	*ha:ða*	*ad-da:r*	*wa*	*hiya*	*mugarrad*	*gudra:n/*
Already	enter-1sg-perf	this	the-house	and	she	only	walls

ka:nu:	*la:*	*yuwa:fiqu:n*	*ʕala*	*zawa:g*	*ʔabi:kum*	*minni:/*
be-3mpl-perf	neg	3mpl-agree	on	marriage	father-yours	from-me

wa	*kuntu*	*waḥi:dat*	*ʔabawayyi/*
and	be-1sg-perf	lonely	parents-mine

wa	*lam*	*ʔakun*	*falla:ḥa/*	*fazaraʕtuhuma:*	*ʔaʃga:ran*	*wa*	*xuḍrawa:t*
and	neg	1sg-be	peasant/	plant-1sg-they	trees-acc	and	vegetables

wa	*qa:la*	*gaddukum*	*li-ʔabi:kum/*	*kayfa*
and	say-3msg-perf	grandfather-your-pl	to-father-your-pl	how

tatazawwag	*bint*	*ʔarmala*	*la:*	*ʕa:ʔila laha:/*
2msg-marry	girl	widow	neg	family to-her

'I had come to your grandfather's house when it was just walls. They did not approve my marriage to your father. I was an only child and I was no peasant then. Since then, I have planted trees and vegetables. Your grandfather then asked your father how he can marry a mere widow with no family.'

This is an example of the hidden power of women in Egypt. Women may compensate for the loss of power in some contexts by asserting their power in others, e.g. with their children. Again, although this is a piece of fiction, it is one that tries to mirror society and a countryside community, in which the mother runs the household and presumably, though not realistically, speaks MSA.

In different contexts women may have more power than men. As the studies above show, in Morocco women seem to be more assertive in bargaining than men. For example, in Egypt a woman with her male driver has more power and can be more assertive than her husband. So while with a husband the women may or may not abide by all the universals discussed above, like hedging, using tag questions, interrupting less, caring about face etc., this may not be the case with a son, a subordinate man or a vendor. With what women consider their social inferiors they manage face differently. More studies are definitely needed to examine the language of women in different contexts.

Also, in some parts of the Arab world there is a hierarchy that cannot be ignored which may depend on tribe, class, education etc.

Another way in which women can reclaim their power is by reversing old sayings to their benefit. Hachimi (2001) gives the example of Moroccan women who are now aware of the sexist implications of folk wisdom in Morocco. They reverse the meaning of old sayings. For example, *klma dlʕyalat* 'women's word', which is an expression that is used to mean that a woman's promise cannot be taken seriously, is now used by women in Morocco to emphasise that a promise will be carried out beyond doubt.

Indeed language universals are culture- or community-specific to a great extent, in the same way as politeness strategies and face-threatening strategies are also both culture- or community-specific and context-specific.

I will conclude this section with a quotation from Kapchan (1996: 2), who conducted an anthropological study on women who work in the market in Beni Mellal, a provincial capital in Morocco with a population of 350,000. Kapchan concluded that women use the same linguistic strategies to gain power and status as men in the market. She posits about one of the women who sell goods in the market:

> She speaks of the cure of the viscera. She ingests her product on the spot to demonstrate its safety and efficacy, and offers her audiences samples. She swears by God, invokes the authority of the written word, and encourages her audience to put their belief in the herbs and to leave the rest, the responsibility to her. Her presence in the Suq is anomalous. She is a mother and breadwinner, aggressive and crafty in the skills of the marketplace. She speaks to men as well as to women forthrightly and with authority, using public genres of speech.

4.11 CONCLUSION

Analysts, studying the relation between language and gender, should begin with the assumption that gender will rarely stand alone but will interact in complex ways with other social variables, both fixed and flexible, such as class, education, ethnicity etc. Likewise, they should assume that the range of behaviours engaged in by women and men are not independent – no more Mars and Venus – but overlap and are highly contextualised.

In comparing and contrasting sources and methods used to study gender by linguists, it has been concluded that the sources used by linguists in the Arab world are varied to some degree, (from obituaries to women in the market), but much research remains to be done. For example, we need more studies that examine job interviews, like the one that examines verbal interactions between men and women using recordings of several job interviews in Dutch companies (Bogaers 1998). Studies that concentrate on the media and how women are represented there linguistically are also needed.

When it comes to the methods used in studying language and gender, one finds that linguists studying the Arab world use the same techniques as their western counterparts: they concentrate on quantitative studies, they use social correlates and statistics, and finally they also try to overcome the observer's paradox (cf. Coates 1993 for an overview of some western studies on gender). However, the linguists discussed above, as well as others studying gender in the western world, could not overcome the observer's paradox completely. As Haeri (1992: 106) posits, 'Investigating interactions between iconic values based on sex differences and social structure is an inherently difficult task, and the data that would be required to examine completely the issue are not available.'

In addition, linguists studying language and gender need to expand their horizons and include more studies that examine gender in relation to code-switching, for example, like the study done by Walters (1996b) in Tunisia, and indeed the diglossic situation should be considered more in studies done on the Arab world. Further, pragmatic studies that examine the language of men and women in relation to politeness are needed. For example, Keating (1998) studied women's roles in constructing status hierarchies, by examining honorific language in Pohnpei, Micronesia. Similar studies need to be done on the Arab world; although Arabic does not have true honorifics, it has other means of showing status and hierarchies.

It was also concluded in this chapter that there are two main approaches to studying gender from a linguistic perspective. The binary approach to gender assumes that men and women, because of the way they are brought up and treated in their community, are two different groups and as such there are differences in their linguistic performances. The construction approach assumes that men and women together form and are formed by a community, which in turn is constructed and modified by independent, fixed and flexible variables. Individuals, whether men or women, within this community project an identity on themselves which is usually reflected in their linguistic performance. These two approaches are summarised in Charts 4.1 and 4.2.

The myth of men and women as two altogether different entities exists because we nourish it. Reality is different but indeed also shaped by the myth (cf. Cameron 2008).

When discussing politeness, names and terms of address, and women as narrators, it was clear that extra-linguistic independent variables, both fixed and flexible, can help explain the sociolinguistic performance of both men and women. Evidence from data from talk shows, as well as evidence from different studies that concentrate on the performance of women in the Arab

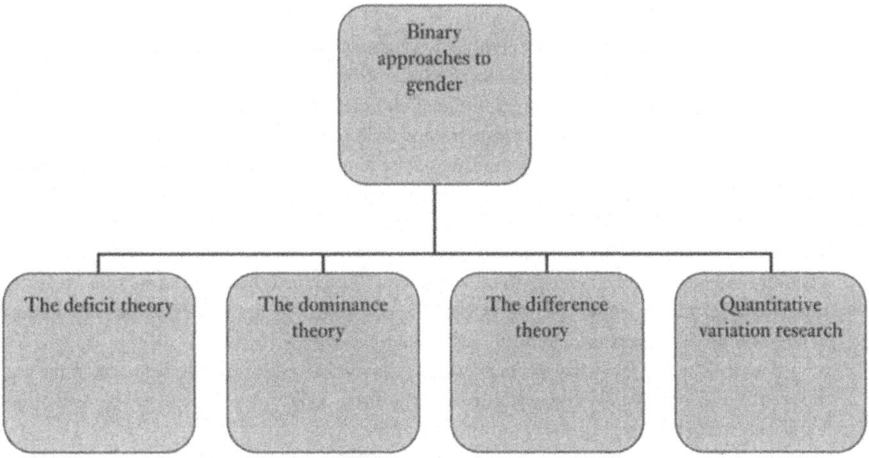

Chart 4.1 Binary approaches to gender studies

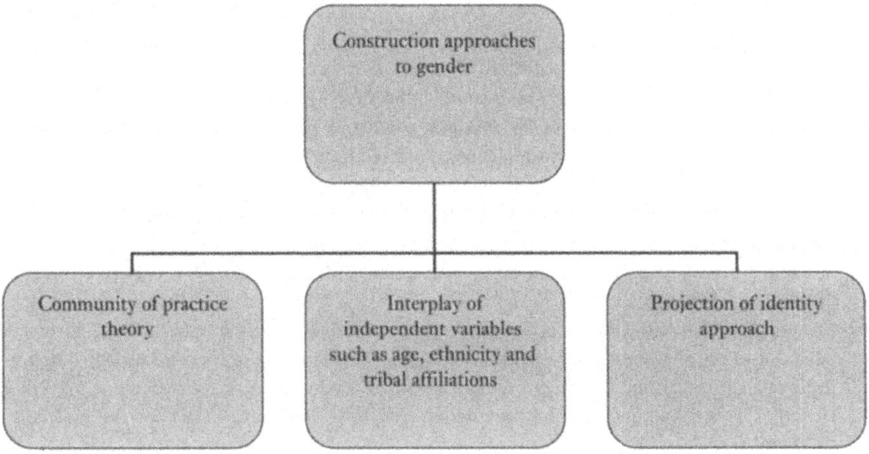

Chart 4.2 Construction approaches to gender studies

world, reveals the intricate nature of concepts such as politeness and variation in language use.

The social status of women continues to change, especially in the Arabic world, as the result of the exposure of women to the outside world, education, work etc. (cf. Haeri 1996a; Kapchan 1996; Daher 1999; Sadiqi 2003a).

NOTES

1. Countries like Qatar, Kuwait and the United Arab Emirates depend largely on a huge number of imported workers, some from elsewhere in the Arab world and some from poorer developing countries.

2. The 1952 revolution will be discussed in detail in Chapter 5.
3. Baron (2005) highlights the problem of translating terms such as honour, *ʃaraf*, from Arabic. The term honour may entail high rank, nobility, distinction, dignity etc. Arabs use the term honour to refer to national honour. For example, it is common for a country to be seen metaphorically as a woman whose honour has to be preserved by its citizens.
4. Whether it was the norm at the beginning of the twentieth century for women to address their husbands as mister + first name is difficult to prove. In Egyptian films of the 1930s and 1940s, women are divided into those who use a term of address when addressing a husband and those who do not. Men are also divided into those who use terms of address with or without the wife's first name and those who do not. There are examples of men using terms such as *ḥagga* 'one who does the pilgrimage', *ʔumm* 'mother'+ first child's name, and *ha:nim* 'lady' with no first name attached to it; cf. note 6 below.
5. It was established earlier that women in the Arab world are not powerless and there are different kinds of power. However, the example from Mahfouz is indeed exaggerated and shows an extreme case of tyranny on the part of men.
6. In Egyptian films of the 1930s and 1940s, aristocrats never addressed their wives by their first names but as *ha:nim* 'lady' or the like; cf. note 4 above.
7. It is worth noting that witchcraft and magic are more common in African Arab countries than Asian Arab ones. Thus, Morocco, Egypt, Tunisia and Sudan specifically rely more on these forces and devise ways of dealing with them than do Gulf countries. This may be related to the African identity of these countries more than their Arab one.
8. Pre-Islamic poetry usually starts with predictable themes, such as a man praising his tribe or his sword, which is a symbol of his strength, pride and honour. In addition, a poet usually recalls the glorious past with nostalgia and feels sad for the loss of home and family.
9. see Chapter 3 for a discussion of communities, language variation and religion.
10. Unrequited love is one of the most prevalent themes of Arabic popular music.
11. David: in Arabic, *dawu:d* would be the name used. Although Muslims could refer to David as well, since he is mentioned in the Qur'an as one of the Prophets, Jews possibly refer to him more frequently.
12. It is difficult for someone who is not a Bedouin to have an insider status. She, however, shares specific characteristics with the Bedouins such as her Arab origin and her religion. She had also been familiar with the culture of the Bedouins early on when she travelled with her father. Being an 'insider' in a Bedouin society is a complex issue (cf. Al-Torki and El-Solh 1988).
13. Both Abu-Lughod and Haeri were women and both were culturally Muslim.
14. Since this community practises polygamy, a senior wife is usually the oldest and first wife of the man and is usually given more status than other wives.
15. Examples of this form are: *yiṭlaʕ* 'to go out, or climb the stairs', *yiʃrab* 'to drink', *yiftaḥ* 'to open'.
16. In all the above studies a standard language, whether German, Spanish or English, is basically equivalent to the most prestigious variety in Arab countries, that is, Cairene Arabic in Egypt, Damascene Arabic in Syria etc. In fact, in the Arab world there is only one standard, which is MSA as opposed to the different vernaculars.
17. Note that this is a study of language change and not just of variation.
18. Studies that concentrate on the lexical variation between men and women include Hurreiz (1978), which compares and contrasts the use of specific expressions by men and women in formal and informal situations in Khartoum. Morpho-syntactic studies include Jabeur's (1987) study of diminutives in the urban dialect of Rades. In addition, Owens and Bani-Yasin (1987), in their study of the Bani Yasin tribe of Jordan, examined the use of concord in the speech of men and women. Phonetic, phonological and prosodic features have been

studied by a number of linguists. For example, the consonant *q* used in Arabic and its realisations have been studied by Kanakri (1984) in relation to Jordanian Arabic. Jabeur (1987) in his study of Rades also examined the realisation of *q* as *q* in the urban dialect and as *g* in the rural one.

19. For a full description of the phenomenon see Fleisch (1971).
20. This study does not analyse inter-dialectal communication, communication between people who speak different dialects in the Arab world. This is indeed a topic worth a study of its own.
21. Note that the speakers do not necessarily accommodate their speech to that of the announcers. Thus, the accommodation theory (Giles et al. 1987), though relevant in any kind of communication, does not play a major role in this study.
22. It is worth noting that women will not necessarily accept the role assigned to them by a community. There may be a difference between what women really do with language and what they are expected to do.

CHAPTER 5

Language policy and politics

> Standard Arabic speaking:
>
> They have accused me of bareness in the prime of my youth.
> I would that I were barren, so that I should not suffer the
> words of my enemies.
>
> I have encompassed the book of God in word and meaning.
> And have not fallen short in any of its verses and exaltations.
>
> I am the sea; in its depths pearls are hidden.
> Have they asked the diver for my shells?
>
> I see the people of the west full of power and might.
> And many a people have risen to power through the power of
> their language.
>
> Ḥāfiẓ Ibrāhīm (1871–1932)

In his poem about Arabic, by which he meant SA, Ḥāfiẓ Ibrāhīm sums up the feelings of the majority of Arab intellectuals about the language. Arab governments in their struggle for freedom from colonising powers often appealed to language as a shield for their identity.[1] It is indeed true that the power of language reflects the power of its people. Still, the struggle is not always fair, nor is it always fruitful. In February 2007, the Arab League held a conference to discuss the future of SA with emphasis on teaching it to children. The conference was the collaborative work of many parties: the Arab Council of Childhood and Development, the Arab League (AL), the Arab Gulf Programme for United Nations Development Organisation, UNESCO, the Kuwaiti Fund for Arab Economic Development, and the Islamic Organisation for Education, Science and Culture (ISESCO). The reporter of the event for *al-Ahram Weekly* wrote '"The Arab Child's Language in the Age of Globalisation", a three-day conference held at the Arab League last week, focused on the role of language in shaping identity and how to promote its unity among future generations' (Abdel Moneim 2007). Indeed, the conference echoed words written powerfully by Ḥāfiẓ Ibrāhīm (above) almost a century earlier.

Note that throughout this chapter the distinction between MSA and CA will not be maintained and both will be referred to as SA. This is because this chapter deals mainly with ideologies related to identity, politics and language policy, and since native speakers do not make this distinction it would be both confusing and imprecise to make it in this chapter specifically.

5.1 THE POWER OF LANGUAGE

Language can be used as an instrument for communication, but it can also be used as a symbol of one's identity. If we just think of language as a means of communication then we underestimate its power. Language policies may reflect a conflict within a country or may trigger one. Thomason (2001) mentions the fact that many a time an armed conflict is caused by language policies. For example, in 1976 there were anti-Apartheid riots in Soweto, a township outside Johannesburg, in South Africa. The riots were triggered by a government decision to enforce the law that required the use of Afrikaans as a medium of instruction in some schools. In Sri Lanka there were also riots triggered by the conflict about the use of Sinhalese and the use of Tamil. According to Thomason, 'Language serves as a powerful symbol for discontented groups' (2001: 47).[2]

This symbolic significance of language can help explain why advocates for SA, which is not the spoken dialect of any Arab country, struggled to maintain it amidst colonisation, modern technology and globalisation. Yet the path of SA advocates was not always smooth, and the differences among different Arab countries in their attitudes towards it are as different as the history and environment of each country.

To be able to appreciate fully the discussion on language policy in the Arab world, one has to resort to political science, sociology, psychology, anthropology and history as well as sociolinguistics. However, this chapter aims to give a snapshot of different language policies in the Arab world, implemented ones and even unimplemented ones, and of the ever-evolving relation between language, ideology, nation and state in the Arab world. The chapter starts (section 5.2) with a definition of language policy. Section 5.3 examines the general concept of nation and juxtaposes it with that of state. Then the relation between the Arab nation and language is discussed. Because both ideologies and policies in the Arab world have been shaped by the history of colonisation in the area, mainly British and French colonisation, in section 5.5 I compare and contrast French and British patterns of colonisation and their impact on ideology and policies. Some countries are examined in detail: Algeria, Morocco, Tunisia, Syria, Lebanon, Egypt, Sudan, Israel and the Palestinian territories. The linguistic situation in Libya and the Gulf countries is also referred to (section 5.6), and in section 5.7 there is a discussion of Arabic language academies and their main objectives. Section 5.8 provides a case study of two interviews with two presidents of Arab countries Syria and Yemen. The relation between SA and politics is highlighted in this section. Section 5.9 concentrates on the concept of linguistic rights with reference to the Arab world, and finally English and globalisation are discussed in section 5.10, before the conclusion to this chapter.

Note that Arab countries are diglossic, as was mentioned in Chapter 1. This will again add more complexity to the language policies adopted in the Arab world. The languages in competition for official status may include a colloquial, SA, a foreign language and/or a language spoken by a significant minority such as Berbers in Morocco. However, in the twenty-three countries in which Arabic is the sole or joint official language, it is SA that has this status rather than any of the vernaculars.

5.2 WHAT IS LANGUAGE POLICY?

I will start the discussion of language policy with a quotation from Wright which sums up beautifully the main components of language policies in the Arab world in particular and in the world at large.

> Language policy is primarily a social construct. It may consist of various elements of an explicit nature – juridical, judicial, administrative, constitutional and/or legal language and may be extant in some jurisdictions, but whether or not a policy has such explicit text, policy as a culture construct rests primarily on other conceptual elements – belief systems, attitudes, myths – the whole complex that we are referring to as linguistic culture, which is the sum totality of ideas, values, beliefs, attitudes, prejudices, religious stricture, and all the other cultural 'baggage' that speakers bring to their dealings with language from their background. (2004: 276)

To illustrate Wright's definition, consider these two anecdotal incidents, one mentioned by Spolsky (2004) and the other by a Syrian acquaintance of mine. Spolsky (2004: 1) starts the first chapter in his book about language policy with the story of a 56-year-old Turkish woman who was refused a heart transplant by a doctor in a clinic in Hanover, Germany, with the claim that her lack of

German, which is common among some Turkish immigrants in Germany, would act as an impediment to her recovery process. The clinic supported the doctor's decision by explaining that because the woman did not speak German, she might not understand the doctor's orders, and might thus take the wrong medicine. As Spolsky argues, doctors and clinics make language policy 'when they decide how to deal with language diversity'. The doctor, because of his 'linguistic culture', was in fact implementing a policy in which Turkish immigrants have, and are expected, to learn German.

When discussing the role of SA in education in Syria, a Syrian acquaintance spoke about how crucial SA is in Syria and how vigorously schools promote it. He then recalled his childhood years in primary education in Damascus in the 1980s, when his maths teacher lowered his grade by two marks although he answered all questions correctly. When he asked why this was the case, the teacher then answered that he had made one mistake in SA by giving a noun the wrong case marking. Although this was a maths exam and not an Arabic one, and although the student did not even make a spelling mistake but a grammatical one, and a very common one at that, his grade was lowered by the teacher. The teacher was again implementing a policy here, by deciding to highlight the importance of SA. These two anecdotes suggest that policy, as Wright posits, is a cultural construct. It is the sum of beliefs, attitudes, values and even misconceptions at times that individuals have accumulated from their community.

However, language policy may also 'consist of various elements of an explicit nature – juridical, judicial, administrative, constitutional and/or legal'. Language policy usually refers to 'a set of planned interventions supported and enforced by law and implemented by a government agency' (Spolsky 2004: 5). The key factor in language policy is the power and legitimacy to enforce a policy. Power in that case refers to both political power and economic power. Language policies always try to push forward an official language.

An official language is usually the language used in government offices in official contexts and documents, and the constitution clearly states that it is official. As Wright (2004: 243) puts it, it is a language with 'muscles'; it is supported by the institution and by a legal written document; it is something *de jure*. A national language, on the other hand, is the language of cultural and social unity. It could be used as a symbol to unite and identify a nation or a group of people (Holmes 1992: 52). It does not necessarily have to have an official status.

Factors related directly to language policy are language ideologies, language practices and language planning. The three will be defined below.

5.2.1 Language ideologies

The term language ideologies refers to the belief system that is prevalent in a specific community about language and language use. Ideologies are perhaps the 'cultural constructs' that Wright refers to in the quotation above. These beliefs influence language practices and motivate them. As was clear from the two anecdotes above, ideologies are crucial for the implementation of a policy. They usually form the basis for language planning processes. In fact they can also form the basis for modifying language policies (Spolsky 2004: 14). Although in most countries there is more than one ideology, one ideology is usually dominant. Spolsky posits that 'language ideology is language policy with the manager left out, what people think should be done. Language practices, on the other hand, are what people actually do' (2004: 15). Where people use a language is important in its maintenance. Thus, there are domains for language use such as home, workplace, religious worship places, government offices, schools and so on and so forth (Spolsky 2004: 43). Language practices are sustained in these domains.

The difference between practice and ideology is significant in the Arab world especially. For example, in 2008, Māzin al-Mubarāk, a scholar of SA and a member of the Language Academy in Syria, called for a reinforcement of the status of SA, and for an effort to eradicate the use of the colloquial gradually in Syria. The plan to rid Syria of all colloquials, according to him, included awareness programmes for the whole family to teach parents how to deal with the challenges of introducing SA at home with their children; making sure newspapers have a section with full case marking for children to read and learn from; improving the SA of media announcers; increasing the number of songs, plays and films in SA as opposed to the colloquial ones; and encouraging children's competitions for writing poetry, novels and short stories in SA by offering them prizes. Al-Mubarāk even went as far as suggesting that both the public and private sectors in Syria should start refusing work presented to them in colloquial even if this work were soap operas, advertisements or signposts. Al-Mubarāk's ideology may be in line with the political agenda of Syria as well as a belief in the slogan 'one nation, one language', which will be discussed in section 5.3. However, his ideology is to a great extent a symbolic one which is almost impossible to implement, given that the colloquial is the spoken language used by Syrians in most domains including home, group interaction and schools (if not an SA class), and in most soap operas and songs.

On a similar note, in the conference referred to at the beginning of this chapter, which took place in February 2007 and which was concerned with the future of SA, the reporter stated the following:

> ISESCO Secretary-General Abdel Aziz Al-Twigrii spoke of 'language pollution', the condition whereby the influence of foreign languages – those of economically predominant countries – corrupts Arabic, especially among children. One study released at the conference found that the language of advertising and the commercial world has a

> corrupting effect – with the use of colloquial and foreign words written in Arabic script. Another, carried out on Libyan children, found that dialect and foreign expressions were far preferable among them than SA. This can undermine the language in use for 15 centuries and leave Arabs exposed to 'cultural invasion'; it is a mistake to let dialect prevail at the expense of the Arabic tongue. (Abdel Moneim 2007)

The last postulation in that quotation, that 'it is a mistake to let dialect prevail at the expense of the Arabic tongue', is indeed significant. Dialect, meaning the colloquial Arabic of Arab countries, is considered a corrupted version of SA. SA is the 'Arabic tongue', the real language; dialects are not Arabic. The postulation ignores the fact that dialects are in fact the spoken languages in all Arab countries while SA is not the spoken dialect of any of the Arab countries mentioned. Ideology is again tied closely to politics. Perhaps ideology in both the Syrian case discussed above and the conference reported here do not adhere to reality. However, an ideology is significant even if it is a 'romantic notion' like the one mentioned here: that SA can prevail and be the daily language used by all Arabs. As Hill and Mannheim (1992: 382) argue, language ideology may remind us that cultural concepts analysed by linguists are usually subjective and contentious. Language ideologies especially are used as political, religious or social weapons in conflicts, as will become clear throughout this chapter (cf. Schieffelin et al. 1998).

Related to language ideologies is the symbolic function of language as opposed to its instrumental function. Suleiman (2003: 174) discusses the power of the symbol. As stated earlier, the fact that SA has survived for such a long time even though it is not a spoken language may have to do with its power as a symbol. For example, Algeria tried to impose SA as a symbol of its identity. French in Algeria was associated with the colonial power and the seven years' war to gain independence. To assert its identity Algeria imposed SA. On the other hand, French had been an instrumental language for almost a century; France had been in Algeria from 1830 and Algeria was considered part of France. French had been imposed and used then to play the Arabs against the Berbers. It was the language used in government offices and schools and as a means of communication. The proper role of 'Arabic' had been among the issues in the struggle for independence long before the war began. Its declaration as an official language was almost purely symbolic – no texts, few teachers, as will become clear when discussing Algeria below. Part of Arabic's symbolic import was also the Arab Muslim identity of a country with a significant Berber minority.

Language policies have to take into consideration both functions of language, the symbolic and instrumental, otherwise the policy will be lacking. This is not an easy task, however, especially with the instrumental function that English is gaining worldwide. Note that according to Wright (2004) a language policy will not work if it clashes with feelings of identity and communities.

Economic factors are also related to language ideologies. Governments can try to impose languages as much as they like, but unless their plans reflect the economic reality, they will not be appealing to the people. A language plan that does not include French in Morocco, although Morocco's main economic dealings are with the west, and especially France, will not reflect the economic reality.

Before concluding this section about ideology, I want to refer to a concept that will keep recurring whenever one examines language policies, and which is related directly to ideology: the concept of language attitude. Walters (2006b: 651) posits that 'language attitudes are psychological states related in complex ways to larger abstract language ideologies'. Because of this it is difficult to elicit the real attitude of people in a straightforward questionnaire. There are a number of methodological problems related to attitude, one of which is the representativeness of the data collected. For example, in the next sections some language attitude surveys will be mentioned which were mostly done on university students or high school students; neither group represents the majority of the population in Arab countries, or necessarily the attitude of the masses of the population. Another methodological problem is that people who answer these questionnaires may answer from a prescriptive perspective; what they think they should do as opposed to what they actually do. The anecdote in Chapter 1 in which Ferguson met a scholar who claimed he only spoke SA, but then replied to the phone in colloquial, is a case in point (cf. Walters 2006b for a full discussion of methodological problems). As Walters puts it, for a methodology to be effective, the researcher has to be trained in psychology. However, such surveys are still useful as guidelines for a prevalent ideology or signs of group discontent with a specific policy.

5.2.2 Language practices

Language practices have been juxtaposed with language ideologies in the last section. Practices refer to the habitual selection that individuals make within their linguistic repertoire (Spolsky 2004: 9). Thus, faced with three words that mean 'computer' in Egypt, *al-ḥa:sib al-ʔa:li:*, *ḥasu:b* and *kompiyu:tar*, Egyptians use *kompiyu:tar*. By doing so, they are consciously or unconsciously selecting a lexical item that will directly affect language policy. The sum of all lexical, morphological, syntactic and phonological patterns used by individuals comprises their language practices.

Language practices are sometimes more significant than language policies. If a policy works against language practices, there is no guarantee that it will be successful. For a policy to be successful, it has to lay claim to both language practices and language ideologies. As was said earlier, individuals in a community, their assumptions about language and their linguistic habits, make a policy even when there is no written one (Spolsky 2004: 9).

5.2.3 Language planning

Language planning refers to the efforts to manage, modify or influence the habitual practice of individuals as part of a community. There are two kinds of language planning: status planning and corpus planning: Status planning refers to the process of selecting a language or variety for use. Corpus planning is the process by which the language or variety selected is codified, i.e. choices are made to standardise spelling, grammar, lexicon etc. Spolsky (2004) gives the example of Serbians who wanted to codify their language by making sure Croatian elements were omitted and replaced by Serbian ones.

In multilingual countries, many languages compete to gain official status. But in practical terms assigning a language an official status is a costly task. It means that the government has to provide services and information in this language or languages. In Canada, for example, a number of minorities would like their languages to gain the official status French has. These languages include Italian and Chinese. To plan for an official language (status planning), the planners have to bear in mind the function the language will have. They have to agree on the form of language that will be codified, and then they have to codify it, thus securing its grammar and vocabulary (corpus planning). Finally they have to make sure that the language will be accepted and the attitude of the people using it will be positive (cf. Lambert 1999; Spolsky 2004).

Corpus planning is a complicated issue, and if there is more than one language involved in the process, then the task is even more complicated. Lambert (1999) discusses the need for teaching materials and teachers trained in the languages concerned and in language teaching pedagogy. Then there is the problem of the selection of which language to teach at each educational level. This is usually subject to fierce political negotiation. There is also the need to layer the languages used in schools and provide instruction in different languages at different levels of the education system. Finally there is the issue of adult learning and designing curriculum to fit adult needs (Lambert 1999: 21).

Thomason (2001) gives an example of how policy can be different from planning. In 1920 the state of Nebraska declared that English was its official language, at a time when German was used as the medium of education for some students; because of anti-German feelings at the time of World War I, the state created this law. It was in fact never implemented.

To conclude this section, I would like to point out again that a policy does not have to be written to be implemented and that a policy is not necessarily clear to all members of a community. For example, in the USA there is an implicit disagreement as to which policy is used. Some may argue that the

USA adopts a monolingual policy since there is low level of recognition of any language other than English. Others may argue that the USA encourages multilingualism since there is legal official support of other languages. There is neither a written policy in the USA, nor an agreement about which policy is being implemented (Spolsky 2004).

5.3 NATION AND STATE

Guibernau (2007: 11) defines a nation as 'a human group conscious of forming a community, sharing a common culture, attached to a clearly demarcated territory, having a common past and a common project for the future, and claiming the right to rule itself'. Guibernau's definition is perhaps difficult to quantify since a perception of what constitutes a common culture, a common collective perspective of the future, and a common feeling of autonomy is subjective to a great extent. Terms like culture are also difficult to define. Would the culture of Kuwait have enough components in common with that of Tunisia? Or even would Djibouti share a culture with Syria? It could be that Arab countries, for example, share some underlying psychological perception of values and beliefs. In the preceding chapter, values such as honour and modesty were discussed as underlying values that distinguish Arabs from westerners.

I do not aim to examine thoroughly what a nation is, but just to give the reader an idea of how a nation could be defined. One of the major factors in defining a nation seems to be the psychological dimension of belonging to a community. A nation is also attached geographically to a specific territory and may have a specific religion. A nation may have its way of perceiving itself in relation to history, which may or may not be a true perception; a nation will have its own myths (Grosby 2005). Note also that a national identity may remain buried for years and can then be resurrected at times of crises or major historical turning points (Guibernau 2007).[3]

A nation as opposed to a state does not necessarily have clear borders nor the legitimacy that a state may have. 'The state may be loosely defined as a structure that, through institutions, exercises sovereignty over a territory using laws that relate the individuals within that territory to one another as members of the state'(Grosby 2005:22). A state may also have citizens from different nations. For example, Britain is a state with different nations such as the Welsh nation, and the Scottish nation (Guibernau 2007).

5.3.1 The relation between nation and language

It is assumed that the emphasis on language as a defining factor of a national identity started to bloom during the nineteenth century with the work of the

German philosophers Herder and Fichte and the French Renan. Germans related language to a shared cultural heritage. Also, one of the bases of the French revolution was a shared cultural contract between citizens and a nation built on a homogeneous oral and written language that united this nation (cf. Miller 2003; Spolsky 2004; Wright 2004). However, according to Grosby (2005: 70) the relation between nationalism and language is much older than that. He gives the following two examples: in Israelite tradition there is evidence that suggests that differences in language were understood as indicating distinctions between native Israelites and foreigners. Similarly, in 1312 in Poland, there was a supposedly German-led revolt of Cracow against Lokietek. Although the revolt was not successful and was put down, anti-German sentiments developed. The instigators were then trailed and their guilt was determined by whether or not they could correctly pronounce such Polish words as *soczewica* 'lentil', *kolo* 'wheel' and *mlyn* 'mill'. The person who mispronounced any of these words was judged to be either German or Czech and hence guilty.

5.3.2 The Arab nation

The Arabic word *ʔumma* is equivalent to 'nation', while *watan*, on the other hand, refers to a 'country' as opposed to a nation. A common usage of *ʔumma* is to refer to *al-ʔumma al-ʕarabiyya* 'the Arabic nation' and *al-ʔumma al-ʔisla:miyya* 'the Islamic nation'. The latter, as will be discussed below, is a universal term rather than particular to a specific community with a shared culture and history.

In the Arab world, as is the case in the west, a nation can also be defined in terms of different factors, including but not limited to language, religion, geographical environment, historical background, colonial history, values etc. Linguists and intellectuals disagree as to which of these factors is the most essential. In fact, each factor is manipulated politically at different stages in history. For example, the Syrian nationalist Anṭūn Saʿādah (d. 1949) held the view that the environment plays the most essential role in shaping the national character (cf. Suleiman 2003: 219).

However, in the twentieth century, the relation between the Arab nation and SA has been in the forefront in government constitutions, in language academies, among Arab intellectuals and in the media more broadly. National unity was assumed to be achieved through linguistic unity and, thus, multilingualism was perceived as a threat to national unity (Miller 2003: 3). According to Suleiman (2003) there are writers who emphasise the relation between nationalism and language. Consider, for example, the work which Ibrāhīm al-Māzinī (1889–1949) published in 1937 (cited in Suleiman 2003: 198), in which he argued that language is a factor that defines a nation. Similarly, al-Anṣārī and al-Anṣārī in their book *al-ʿUrūbah fī muqābil al-ʿawlamah*

('Arabness in the face of globalisation') (2002) emphasise the relation between the Arabic language and the Arab nation. They posit that:

> What differentiates the Arab world or the Arab nation from all other nations and states in the world is language. Statistics show that Arabic is the third biggest language, not in terms of its speakers, but in terms of the countries that adopt it as its official language. Arabic comes after English and French. However, countries that use French or English as their official language are scattered all over the world, while countries that adopt Arabic as their official language comprise one geographical entity that stretches from the ocean to the gulf. (2002: 37)

Note that in ancient times the only true 'Arab' was the Bedouin Arab, and kinship and lineage as much as language were important means of identification (Miller 2003: 3). Miller also contends that in pre-modern states there was no correlation between language and nation; the elite of a country could be speaking a different language from the commoners. In the Ottoman period, for example, it was religious affiliation rather than language that defined the nation. However, I think it is worth mentioning at this stage that the relation between nation and language must have started earlier than the modern period in the Arab world. The fact that the elite spoke a different language is not a criterion for judgement, since the elite in some Arab countries nowadays may frequently still speak a language other than Arabic, even if they know Arabic, as is probably the case in some Gulf countries, in Egypt,[4] Morocco or Algeria, and still there is a belief in the slogan 'One nation, one language' held by many. People could speak a language while thinking they speak another; consider again the anecdote mentioned by Ferguson in Chapter 1 and the case of the Syrian scholar Māzin al-Mubarāk mentioned earlier in this chapter. As was said earlier, common beliefs about what constitutes a nation are not necessarily realistic. A nation could be built on language ideology rather than language practice, as long as the ideology is a vessel for forming a sense of belonging between members of a specific community. As was mentioned earlier, there is a psychological component to a national identity. However, I do agree with Miller that an Arab is now defined differently from how it was defined in the early Islamic period.

The Arabs' perception of the Arab nation is very complicated and possibly needs a book by itself (cf. Suleiman 2003). Some Arabs perceive themselves as belonging to a nation because they have a common colonial history, they occupy a specific geographical space, they share nostalgia for a glorious past and they speak 'Arabic'. The Arab nation is not a political entity but an ideological one, in the same way as the idea of 'one nation, one language' is also sometimes only ideological. In a survey conducted by Egyptian professor Muḥ sin Khiḍr (2006) to examine feelings of Arabness among Egyptian university graduate students from different fields of study, the professor presented a questionnaire to 270 students, in medicine, science, humanities and business, about whether they thought there would ever be a unified Arab nation and, if this did indeed happen, what this nation would look like. More than half of the students gave optimistic answers such as:

- One day there will be a unified Arab nation with no borders.
- This unified nation will have the same education system, and the same governmental system.

Some students went as far as saying that this nation, once united, should coordinate its architectural infrastructure and paint all houses the same colours.

It is noteworthy still that Egyptians' perception of their Arabness is very complicated and correlates with different political and historical changes.

The Arab nation is represented by the Arab League (AL). When compared to the EU, the AL as an ideological construct seems at first different in some respects. Both Guibernau (2007) and Ricento (2006: 55) contend that the EU comprises countries with different perceptions of history, different languages and a different way of looking at the universe. Consider, for example, the differences between Greece and Sweden. However, the EU is relatively functioning as a political and economic power. The AL is different since it comprises the Arab nation. The AL, defines itself in its website as an association of countries whose peoples are Arabic speaking. Its objectives are to strengthen relations among the member states, coordinate their policies and promote their interests. Guibernau (2007: 115) calls the EU a non-emotional identity. I would call the Arab league 'an ideological emotional identity' first and foremost, and this is not a political statement but a sociolinguistic one, as will become clear in the discussions below.

Nationalism in general has a bad reputation and has been accused, sometimes rightly, of a number of atrocities over history and a number of cases of intolerance: the murder of innocent civilians in the Balkans, in Kashmir or in Kurdistan are all examples of governments or people who were not ready to compromise their concept of a nation (Grosby 2005: 116). On the linguistic level, the Arab nation has been accused of promoting linguistic intolerance (cf. Miller 2003). Although Arabic is associated with Islam, and although politics in some countries is associated with Islamic radical movements, the Islamic nation is a universal one where kinship, language and territory are surpassed (Grosby 2005). The Arab nation as an ideology is built as was said earlier, on a number of factors, prominent among which is language. Religion is not a main component since not all Arabs are Muslims, and even the Muslim Arabs are not all Sunnis. Diversity, whether, economic, cultural or historical, is still dominant in the Arab world, and language seems like the safest haven for nationalists. Note that the harshest linguistic policies towards minorities have come from secular states; Turkey is a case in point (Miller 2003: 4). Linguistic rights will be discussed in detail in section 5.9. However, in the next section I will first list countries with Arabic as the official language.

5.4 COUNTRIES WITH SA AS THE OFFICIAL LANGUAGE

Table 5.1 lists all countries with SA as the sole or joint official language, as well as the other languages used in these countries.

Apart from four countries, Comoros, Chad, Djobouti and Somalia, Arabic is the sole official language of all countries in this table.

5.5 FRENCH VERSUS BRITISH PATTERNS OF COLONISATION AND THEIR RELATION TO LANGUAGE POLICIES

By the beginning of the twentieth century the majority of Arab countries were under either the British or French mandate. In 1916 Britain and France negotiated the Sykes-Picot agreement in which most of the Arab world, excluding Saudi Arabia and North Yemen, were divided between France and Britain. France controlled the Mediterranean coast of North Africa and what is now Syria and Lebanon, while Britain controlled Iraq, Transjordan, Egypt and the Sudan (Mansfield 2003).

Most of the structures of these countries were established during the colonial period, and were shaped to correlate with British and French systems. Thus systems of education, government, politics, economics and even the architecture were influenced by either Britain or France. The indigenous Arab linguistic, religious and cultural traditions were downplayed and ignored by the colonising power (cf. Findlow 2001; Shaaban 2006: 694.)

After independence Arab countries followed a policy of Arabisation. SA was a symbol of an identity that had been suppressed for years. For a great number of Arab intellectuals immediately after independence, SA was a language of independence, tradition, a glorious past, and even the language in which a sound moral system could be explained and maintained (cf. Saʿdī 1993).

However, the use of foreign languages, French and English specifically, is still prevalent in the Arab world, even more so than at the time of colonisation, for different reasons. Some of these reasons are related to economic needs and market forces, as is the case with countries that depend on tourism for their hard currency, such as Morocco, Tunisia and Egypt, or countries that depend on France as their main trading market, such as Morocco. Although most of the reasons why parents in the Arab world are keen on teaching their

Table 5.1 Countries with Arabic as the joint or sole official language

Country	Official language[a]	Languages used[b]
Algeria	Arabic	Arabic, Chaouia, French, Kabyle, Tachelhit, Tamazight, Taznatit
Bahrain	Arabic	Arabic, English, Farsi, Urdu
Chad[c]	French, Arabic	Arabic, Daza, French, Gulay, Kanuri, Maba, Sara, Zaghawa
Comoros	Shikomor, Arabic, French[d]	Arabic, French, Shikomor
Djibouti	Arabic, French	Afar, Arabic, French, Somali
Egypt	Arabic	Arabic, Armenian, Domari, Greek, Nubian
Iraq	Arabic	Arabic, Azeri, Farsi, Kurdish, Turkmen
Jordan	Arabic	Arabic, Armenian, Chechen, Circassian
Kuwait	Arabic	Arabic, English
Lebanon	Arabic	Arabic, Armenian, English, French, Kurdish
Libya	Arabic	Arabic, Nefusi, Tamashek, Zuara
Mauritania	Arabic	Arabic, Fulfulde, Soninke, Tamashek, Wolof
Morocco	Arabic	Arabic, Draa, French, Spanish, Tachelhit, Tamazight, Tarifit,
Oman	Arabic	Arabic, Baluchi, English, Farsi, Swahili
Palestinian Territories	Arabic	Arabic, Domari
Qatar	Arabic	Arabic, English, Farsi
Saudi Arabia	Arabic	Arabic, English
Somalia	Somali, Arabic	Arabic, Gabre, Jiddu, Maay, Mushungulu, Somali, Swahili,
Sudan	Arabic	Arabic, Bedawi, Beja, Dinka, English, Fur, Nuer
Syria	Arabic	Arabic, Armenian, Assyrian, Azeri, Kurdish
Tunisia	Arabic	Arabic, Berber languages/dialects, French
United Arab Emirates	Arabic	Arabic, Baluchi, English, Farsi, Pashto, Somali
Yemen	Arabic	Arabic, Mehri, Somali

Notes:

(a) UNESCO, (unless otherwise indicated), http://portal.unesco.org/education/en/ev.php-URL_ID=20183&URL_DO_TOPIC&URL_SECTION=201.html; last accessed 18 April 2009.

(b) UNESCO (ibid; Versteegh et al. (2006–70); Moseley and Asher (1994). This list should be treated as a rough guide.

(c) Chad, although not a member of the Arab League, is a partly Arabic-speaking country.

(d) Source: Constitution of the Comoros Islands: http://www.beit-salam.km/article.php3?id_article=34; last accessed 20 October 2008.

children a foreign language, and learning one themselves, are to a great extent utilitarian (Shaaban 2006), there are still symbolic connotations of the use of French in North Africa, for example. As will be discussed in the next section, Berbers in Algeria, after efforts towards complete Arabisation that did not take account of Berber languages, made a point of using French as a symbol of their objection to Arabisation policies, and because for some of them French is associated with open-mindedness and rationality (see the subsection on Algeria below).

Before proceeding to compare and contrast French and British patterns of colonisation and how these were reflected in language use and language policies, it is important to mention that with regard to language policies and the relation between politics, history and language, scholars as well as politicians and even members of different countries may find it difficult to be objective. One writes from a specific background and with a specific ideology. As Spolsky mentions in the preface of his book on language policy, 'it is hard to conceive of a scholar who is strictly neutral' (Spolsky 2004: ix). Suleiman likewise starts his book *A war of words* (2004) by claiming that he writes with both a Palestinian and a British identity, and that language is part and parcel of one's identity. It is not surprising, then, that one can find scholars who discuss language policy in Algeria from very different perspectives and who reach very different conclusions. Thus, while Holt (1994) may claim that the Arabisation policy in Algeria was successful to some extent, Benrabah (2007a) claims that the Arabisation policy in Algeria was a disaster at all levels. This example is just to illustrate the complexity of the issues at hand. This complexity cannot be dealt with in detail in one chapter, but is referred to throughout.

5.5.1 French patterns of colonisation

French in France is not just perceived as a language of a particular nation; it is an instrument that reflects universal values of rationalism and clarity of expression. (Holt 1994). The aim of French colonisation was to assimilate the colonised people (Chumbow and Bobda 1996). Thus the colonies were known as African French territories of France overseas. France tried to eradicate SA from all its North African holdings by making French the official language in all public domains, including administration, public life and education (Alexandre 1963). Being civilised entailed learning French, and it was only the elites who did so.

However, the linguistic and political situation was different in Syria and Lebanon, which were under French mandate from 1916 until 1946. French was not the sole official language, but both SA and French were declared official languages, although in practice, French dominated in education and administration (Shaaban and Ghaith 1999).

5.5.1.1 North Africa

Spolsky posits that:

> The proclamation of national monolingualism, on the principle of 'one nation, one state, one language' in a language other than that of the previous colonial power, was and remains an obvious method of asserting real independence. A number of nations tried to do this. (1994: 133)

Again in this statement the relationship between politics and policies is highlighted. However, the backlash of colonisation, which according to Spolsky is always the declaration that each nation has only one language, does not reflect reality. North African countries (Algeria, Morocco and Tunisia) provide examples of this.

In 1950 France's colonial holdings in North Africa were still untouched and constituted the largest single Francophone area in the world. A number of years later France's control over the three countries ended (Morocco and Tunisia: 1956; Algeria: 1962), although the presence of French was still strong. French had been the only official language of the three countries, in both educational and administrative environments. Even Islam, which might have given people the chance to use SA, was suppressed (Sirles 1999: 118). Thus these countries were left to fend for themselves after independence and forge a language policy as independent nation-states.

5.5.1.1.1 Algeria

Languages used in Algeria: SA, Algerian Colloquial Arabic, Berber languages/dialects (Chaouia, Tamazight, Kabyle, Taznatit, Tachelhit and French)
Biggest minority[5]: Berbers 25 per cent
Colonisation: 1830–1962

The postulation that 'Through language people can be controlled and political power exercised' (Miller 2003: 3), finds no stronger evidence than in the case of Algeria. France tried ruthlessly and meticulously to eradicate SA there. Algeria, in return, after independence tried ruthlessly and meticulously to eradicate French and resurrect SA. This task met some huge challenges, and because of the intricate relation between language, religion, political affiliations, ethnic identity – Berber versus Arab – and social economic factors, the opinions of scholars about the language situation in Algeria are diverse and not devoid of a political stand.

In this section I illustrate the relation between ideology and practice in Algeria, trying in the meantime not to take any stands.

ALGERIA BEFORE INDEPENDENCE

Algeria was under French rule for 132 years (1830–1962). According to Holt, 'one hundred and thirty years of language and educational policy determined by an outside power have evidently left deep scars' (1994: 25, see also Kaplan and Baldauf 2007). The attitude of the French when they colonised Algeria was to turn it into part of France on the other side of the Mediterranean (Stora 2001).

France's policy in the early years of colonisation was to suppress the indigenous culture rather than replace it with a French one. France attacked the structure of society; the French depended on military pacification of the Algerians and tried to break up important families and tribes. They also played the Berbers and Arabs against each other.[6] The French seemed as if they mainly wanted to marginalise Algerians rather than assimilate them; their policy was based on exclusion rather than inclusion. This exclusion was based not on race but on language and religion. On the social and religious level, they made the Muslim judicial system subordinate to the French one (Holt 1994: 34).

In 1848 Algeria became formally part of France (cf. Stora 2001: 6), with French as the official language. To achieve their aim of eradicating SA, the French took hold of the religious endowments which provided the financial base for education and closed all Qur'anic schools, allowing education only in French ones. Education was related to religion and usually run by Muslim religious institutions in which one of the means of learning SA for children was memorising the Qur'an. Thus the old education system in Algeria collapsed.

If one examines the level of literacy before and after colonisation, the result will be somewhat shocking. According to Gordon (1978) the level of Arabic literacy at the onset of colonisation was 40–50 per cent. This is definitely high at that time given that the teaching methods were very basic and printing was not in use. According to Holt, things deteriorated so quickly that when the French left Algeria, 90 per cent of Algerians were illiterate (Holt 1994: 28–9).

In 1847 Alexis de Toqueville sums up the plight inflicted on Algerians by the French as follows:

> Muslim society in Africa was not uncivilised; it was merely a backward and imperfect civilisation. There existed within it a large number of pious foundations, whose object was to provide for the needs of charity or for public instruction. We laid our hands on these revenues everywhere, partly diverting them from their former uses; we reduced the charitable establishments and let the schools decay, we disbanded the seminaries. [. . .] Around us knowledge has been extinguished, and recruitment of men of religion and men of law has ceased. That is to say we have made Muslim society much more miserable, more disorganised, more ignorant, and more barbarous than it had been before knowing us. (2001: 140–1)

If we put aside the judgemental comments about Algerians, we are left with a description of the dire situation inflicted by France on Algeria, especially that pertaining to religion, education and literacy. Perhaps such a description is useful in explaining the growing importance of religion as well in Algeria, as a reaction to French policies.

In the first half of the twentieth century, Algerians began to develop a sense of nationalism which circulated around SA, and which came as a reaction to France's political, social and educational policies. The majority of Algerians spoke colloquial Algerian Arabic and/or Berber. The Algerians resorted in their religion and history and found a great tradition in Islam, literary works and SA. Religion and personal identity became connected to SA. Although by then Algerians were mostly illiterate, they were still exposed to SA through Muslim scholars and Qur'anic recitations. Algerians began their struggle early and before their independence. In 1931, seven years before Arabic was decreed a foreign language by France, the Algerians formed the Algerian Association, which became the strongest defender of Arab and Muslim culture and a major provider of education in Arabic.

In 1931, Aḥmad Tawfīq al-Madanī's book *Kitāb al-Jazā'ir* ('The book of Algeria') was published, in which he declared: 'Islam is our religion, Arabic our language and Algeria our fatherland' (al-Madanī 1931). French was considered by the nationalists a symbol of colonisation and oppression.

In 1933, preachers were banned from preaching in SA in mosques. Then Algerians began setting up a system of private schools. Religion became a symbol of national unity which included Berbers and Arabs (Holt 1994). Nevertheless, Arabic was officially decreed a foreign language in 1938 (Tigrizi 2004).

France's policy helped eradicate Arabic, but failed to eradicate national identity and failed to establish French as a national language. What really helped establish French was contact between the French-speaking population from France living in Algeria and the Algerians. The two factors that played a major role in establishing French were, according to Holt (1994), immigration and urbanisation. From 1914 to 1954 two million Algerians lived in France. The amount of French lexis which has entered colloquial Algerian Arabic during this period is vast (for example, words like 'firmli' and 'infirmiere'). In addition there were more than one million French, Italian and Maltese people living in Algeria. Algerians had to interact with them and the language of interaction was usually French (Sirles 1999).

ALGERIA AFTER INDEPENDENCE

After 132 years of anti-colonial and strong nationalistic feelings piling up, and after seven years of a bloody war with the French, Algeria gained its independence from France in 1962. Algeria suffered the most severe effects of colonisation linguistically, and yet it is still the country in the Maghreb that sought most ardently to pursue Arabisation. Algeria was left with 10 per cent literacy in Arabic and/or French. Yet according to Sirles (1999) more than half of the Algerians spoke French, and more than three times as many were literate in French as in Arabic. However, Benrabah (2007a) gives different figures for literacy in French specifically. According to Benrabah, Algerians literate in SA were around 300,000 out of a population of 10 million. However, 1 million (10 per cent) of the population were literate in French and 6 million (60 per cent) were able to speak French. (cf. Gallagher 1964: 148; Gordon 1978: 151; Benrabah 2007a: 230).

According to Mostari (2004), after independence Algeria was committed to the policy of Arabisation. Arabisation was encouraged by Algerian nationalists and political leaders who were trying to carve a niche for themselves amidst a French-speaking elite (Mostari 2004: 26). In September 1962, Ben Bella became the president of the Democratic Republic of Algeria, and the constitution of the country was set in October of 1963. The preamble of that constitution (dated 10 September 1963) stated that:

> Islam and the Arabic language have been efficient means of resistance against the attempts of the colonial regimes to de-personalize the Algerian people. Algeria needs to affirm that Arabic is its national and official language, and that it draws its main spiritual force from Islam; and yet, the Republic guarantees to all that their views and beliefs shall be respected, and that all shall be free in their religious worship. (Tigrizi 2004: 291)

However, as will be clear below, Arabisation was faced with big obstacles.

In the mid-1960s the then Algerian president Houari Boumedienne[7] pushed for a programme of complete Arabisation (Djité 1992: 21). Because after the war most foreigners left, there was a shortage of teachers. Algeria requested 12,000 teachers from France but got only 4,000. SA was introduced for seven hours per week in primary schools. But there was still the major problem of lack of teachers. In 1964, 1,000 Egyptian teachers were brought in. Because of strong nationalist movements among the Egyptian teachers that perhaps not all Algerians shared, and because of traditional methods of teaching, the outcome of bringing teachers from Egypt was less than perfect. Benrabah claims that the colloquial Egyptian Arabic that the Egyptian teachers spoke was difficult for Algerians to comprehend (Benrabah 2007a: 230).

By September 1967, the minister of education, Taleb Ibrahimi, intiated complete Arabisation of grade two in primary education. Note that the system of education corresponded to the French one, in which students spend five years in primary education, four years in middle school and three years in secondary education (Benrabah 2007a: 231).

In 1968 a law was passed declaring that civil servants were required to demonstrate ability in SA. Within three years Arabic courses were set up within the various ministries. Yet in 1975 all ministries were still carrying out their work in French.

Arabic became the official language. Islam became the state religion in 1976. However, French remained the language of higher education and administration (Holt 1994). By 1979, French was introduced at fourth grade and English as a secondary mandatory foreign language at eighth grade (Benrabah 2007a: 232). All the time unofficial private bilingual schools, French/Arabic, not endorsed by the government, were still functioning, specially in Algiers (cf. Benrabah 2007a).

According to Sirles (1999), this forced Arabisation in education was disastrous. It produced half a generation of Algerians who went through an ill-trained, understaffed system of Arabic-language education during these early years. However, French was then not the language of colonisation any more, so the number of Algerians receiving education in French grew.

During the following years, from 1979 onward, a large part of cultural life was Arabised, including primary and secondary education and many humanities faculties at universities. Broadcasts on radio, television stations, public signs and the judicial system were Arabised as well. Still, the centre of power remained French.

The next president of Algeria, Chadli Benjedid (in office 1979–92), declared the further expansion of Arabic. In 1980 he appointed a militant Arabist to head the nation's higher council of national language, and in 1984 he called for the establishment of an Arabic language academy in the country (Sirles 1999).

The graduates of Arabised degree programmes expected jobs, but did not find any (Holt 1994: 38). By the mid-1980s people realised the discrepancy between language policy and linguistic reality. Algeria managed to change primary and secondary school curricula even in technical areas and the sciences (Mostari 2004; Benrabah 2005, 2007a). It also achieved success in requiring sound competence in Arabic as a condition for government employment. But the private sector was different, so graduates of government universities could not find jobs. Students in Arabised universities staged a two-month strike demanding employment. The minister of the interior issued a directive to employers to end their discrimination against Arabised students, stating that credentials and not language should be the basis of employment. 'Employers began hiring token Arabised students on the condition that they also spoke fluent French' (Saad 1992: 137).

In 1990 there were demonstrations at the University of Science and Technology at Bab Ezzouar. Students who were not competent in French due to their public education system were demanding the immediate Arabisation of the entire curriculum. Political leaders sided with them but no change really happened. Still, French newspapers circulated more than Arabic ones (Sirles

1999). In 1991 a tough law stated that Algeria would be completely Arabised by 1997, and a law was issued stating that anyone who signed a document written in any language other than Arabic would pay a fine of about 40 to 200 dollars (Benrabah 2005: 425).

The partial success of Arabisation created demands the state could not or would not meet (Holt 1994). The question of language now appeared in political debates, and SA was used in nationalist and Islamist movements as a source of authenticity and identity. Politics once more played a role. If Islamic fundamentalists were to get the upper hand in government then Arabisation would be pursued with even more zeal. If, on the other hand, strong economic and financial resources took control, then French would be back with even more force than before (Sirles 1999).

In 1999 President Bouteflika (1999–) admitted that Algerian culture is plural and was using French publicly. He then received a letter from members of the council for Arabic language warning him against 'public use of French and the Franco-phone lobby in the presidency' (Benrabah 2005: 382).

THE PRESENT-DAY SITUATION

Currently schools teach all subjects including science, maths and technical subjects in Arabic. French is a foreign language taught at second grade for approximately five hours a week (Cherfaoui 2004: 2; cf. Temim 2006). At university level, medicine, engineering and all technical subjects are taught in French, which is a major problem for students who are not trained to use French. Humanities subjects, such as philosophy, history and geography, are taught in Arabic. Social sciences, such as business administration, economics and political science, are taught in both Arabic and French. In mid-2005, the minister of higher education declared that 80 per cent of university first year students failed their final exams because of linguistic incompetence (Allal 2005: 13; Maïz and Rouadjia 2005: 13.) The minister declared that government schools did not equip students with the linguistic competence to study in French.

In an attitude survey conducted by Benrabah (2007a) during April–May 2004, in which 1,040 Algerian secondary school students were given a questionnaire to answer, 55.3 per cent wrote that they preferred learning French to SA; only 37.6 per cent preferred SA, and 1.3 per cent preferred Tamazight. Benrabah (2007a) found in another survey that 75 per cent of Algerians supported the idea of teaching scientific subjects in French in schools. The results of these surveys are related to the function of French as an instrumental language with economic importance. However, the informants used are still few and do not represent the majority of Algerians. The problem with surveys that examine attitudes is one of thoroughness first and foremost and then one of deducing a true result from the informants, who may be under some pressure or imagine that they are under some pressure, especially in a country such as

Algeria in which speaking a language may be perceived as making a political statement (see section 5.2.1 and cf. Walters 2006b).

BERBERS IN ALGERIA

In Algeria there is more than one language/dialect of Berber, namely Chaouia, Tamazight and Taznatit. Of all the Berbers in Algeria, Kabylians in the north-west of the country are the most prominent group (Mostari 2004).

There was a stronger than expected backlash after independence from the Berber-speaking tribes, who, as we have said, make up about 25 per cent of the population. They began an armed struggle against the authorities in 1962–3 after forming the Socialist Forces Front (FFS), which was opposed to Arabisation policies in Algeria (Mahé 2001: 442). Taleb Ibrahimi, who was minister of education in 1967, informally allowed Moulad Mammeri, a Berber/Kabylian writer and academic, to restore the chair of Berber studies at Algeirs University. However, this was not enough recognition of the Berbers' linguistic rights, which were ignored after independence. Berbers began a linguistic resistance movement by banning their children from speaking (colloquial) Arabic at home and making a point of speaking French in shops, cafés and restaurants (cf. Kahlouche 2004: 106; Mahé 2001: 471). For the Berbers, SA was unable to deliver a democratic secular ideal. Berbers demanded recognition and freedom of expression. More unrest broke out in 1988, which was again supressed by the government (Tigrizi 2004).

According to Tigrizi (2004), President Chadli Benjedid adopted a new constitution on 13 February 1989 which highlighted Algeria's political pluralism but did not take account of Berber rights. In fact, the preamble of that constitution read:

> Algeria, as land of Islam, as integral part of the Maghreb, as Arab, Mediterranean and African country prides itself on the glory of its Revolution of November 1st, and on the respect which this country has acquired for itself through its commitment to the promotion of justice in the world. (Tigrizi 2004: 293).

Once more, Algeria emphasised its Arab and Muslim identity.

However, strikes were on the rise from the 1990s (Mostari 2004). In 1999 President Bouteflika claimed that it was up to the Algerians to make Tamazight a national language but not an official one. In 2003 Tamazight was declared a national language. In 2004 the president described it as a dividing factor (Lewis 2004). He then declared openly in 2005 that there would be only one official language and not two. Tamazight was adopted as a national language by the National Assembly on 8 April 2003 (Benrabah 2007a). In 2004 Abderrazak Dourari became head of the institute for the planning of Tamazight. From 2005 onwards, Tamazight has been introduced in the first three years in middle school for three hours a week (Benrabah 2007b: 77).

Benrabah (2007a: 226) claims that the enforcement of SA as the only official language is the main cause of the rise of fanaticism, civil war, unemployment and the failed education system. He adds that the regime in Algeria is 'An authoritarian regime allergic to pluralism whether cultural, political or linguistic' (2007a: 248), because the regime seems to prefer one subgroup over all others. Benrabah's claims make his political stand clear and do not just reflect a linguistic stand. As was said earlier, it is indeed difficult to remain neutral when discussing such an issue.

It would be simplistic to think that multilingualism will solve all problems in Algeria, including unemployment, poverty, fanaticism and political frustration (see section 5.9). In the case of Algeria the linguistic situation reflects political tension rather than creates it. It is easier for intellectuals to be outspoken about linguistic diversity, a safe topic compared to other political ones. In order to understand the complexity of the situation one has to realise that diversity and conflicts were perhaps to a great extent part of Algeria before independence as well.[8]

For example, Saʿdī, a Berber himself, claims that France implanted sectarianism in Lebanon and has been trying to do the same thing in Algeria. According to him, it is France that supports the Berber movement financially, and its aim is to destroy Algerian unity and make sure that the French language will prevail at the expense of SA. By playing SA against Berber, France makes French the saviour and the most neutral language of the three (Saʿdī 1993: 205). Saʿdī's claims show that there is division among Berbers themselves and that the situation is not solely a linguistic one, but mainly viewed as a political one.

To conclude this section, I posit that an ideal policy will not only reflect the multilingualism of a community, but also reflect the political and economic realities of a community. In a similar vein, Algerian writer Amīn al-Zāwī claimed that Algeria should start thinking of French as 'a prize of war' which can serve as a gateway to modernity (al-Zāwī 2006).

Still, SA is important for Algeria, since it can act as a unifying factor and one that relates Algeria to its past and its neighbours. Even before independence Arabic was a symbol of identity and a political tool to confront colonisation, sometimes without a practical programme to implement its spread.

The problems of education faced in Algeria are first and foremost problems of lack of resources. Government education in the Arab world at large is far from perfect because of this lack. The fact that schools in Algeria fail to bring out students who master SA is not because SA is impossible to master and not because the diglossic situation renders people inhibited, but because the methods are lacking and the money spent on teaching in government schools is very little. Private education is always another alternative, as in most of the Arab world. However, the problem with Algeria specifically and North African countries in general is the linguistic discrepancy between schools and universities. The fact that schools teach science and maths in Arabic and universities suddenly teach technical subjects in French is indeed a peculiar problem pertaining to North Africa.

5.5.1.1.2 Morocco

Languages used in Morocco: SA, Moroccan Colloquial Arabic, Berber languages/dialects (Tachelhit, Draa, Tamazight, Tarifit), French and Spanish
Biggest minority: Berbers 45 per cent
Colonisation: 1912–56

Morocco is a country with Arab-speaking and Berber-speaking populations. According to Ennaji (2002), Berbers make up 40 per cent of the population; Faiq (1999) states that Berbers make up 45 per cent of the population. In present-day Morocco the Berber languages/dialects, French, SA, Spanish and at least five varieties of Moroccan Arabic are used. The main conflict in language policies is between the roles assigned to SA, Berber and French, although Spanish is important in areas that were occupied by Spain in the north and the Moroccan Sahara (Ennaji 2002).

Again, as in Algeria, in Morocco also we encounter the problem of the discrepancy between language used as an instrument and language used as a symbol. Morocco too is a country in which French constitutes the 'elite language', and this has an effect on Arabisation.

A HISTORY OF THE FRENCH COLONISATION OF MOROCCO

French colonisation started in Morocco in 1912. In fact, France was following the principle held by most colonisers, including England, as will become clear later: the principle of divide and rule. For example, the decree known as *le Dahir berbère*, relating to the recognition of a separate justice system for the Berber tribes, and passed in 1930, was widely seen as a measure to divide Morocco into two parts: a Berber part and an Arab one. The decree was met with opposition from both sides (Ennaji 2002: 71).

French was then imposed as the medium of instruction in schools, government, administration and the media. SA was used only in religious and traditional activities (Ennaji 2002). According to Gill (1999: 124), the French had neither the intention of educating the whole population nor that of modernising them.

Note that the length of the French colonisation in Morocco was only 44 years. Morocco gained its independence in 1956. This period of colonisation is relatively short compared to Tunisia's, which was colonised for 75 years, or Algeria's, which was colonised for 132 years.

Morocco was also different from Algeria in the quantity of the French colonial population living there. There was only a small French colonial population of around 350,000 (Belal and Agourram 1970: 142) among a 'native' population of around 5 million (Houtsma et al. 1913–36: VI/590, "Morocco"). This colonial population was concentrated on the coasts of Morocco along the Mediterranean and the Atlantic. While the great majority of Algerians and Tunisians lived along the coasts, the majority of Moroccans at that time did not. Moroccans were scattered throughout the country and not concentrated in specific areas. Moreover, many major cities, like Fes, Meknès and Marrakesh, are not on the coast. Therefore, there was very little contact and interaction between Moroccans and their colonisers. Thus it comes as no surprise that after independence, the first official population count in 1960 showed that only one in fourteen Moroccan Muslims could speak French; only 6 per cent were literate in French and twice as many were literate in Arabic. It was reported that proficiency in spoken colloquial Arabic was about 80 per cent, indicating that a good portion of Berbers, had mastered spoken colloquial Arabic (Sirles 1999: 120).

THE SITUATION AFTER INDEPENDENCE

During the twenty years following independence the country's political leadership made decisions and then reversed them (Sirles 1999). The two main reasons for this change were lack of teaching materials and resources, and shortage of trained teachers. There was also the fear that Arabisation would lead to a rise in Islamic fundamentalism similar to what happened in Algeria (Shaaban 2006).

Ḥammūd (2000) divides Morocco's Arabisation policy into five stages. In the first stage, from 1958 to 1967, Arabisation was launched, but French still played an essential role. The first stage is described in the next paragraphs.

Sirles (1999) declares that all members of the major cabinet of the first government of post-dependence Morocco, except the defence and interior ministers, had not been educated in France at the university level. In spite of that, Morocco's new minister of education, Muḥammad al-Fāsī, started the process of Arabisation in 1957 by Arabising subjects at the primary level. To do so he had to bring teachers from the Middle East, mainly from Egypt. This is because, as in Algeria, Morocco was not prepared for this process; it did not have enough teachers trained in SA (Ennaji 2002). Again as with Algeria, there were problems with the colloquial Arabic the teachers used, which was incomprehensible for some Moroccans, and the Egyptians' Nasserist politics orientation was also a problem. The government then changed its policy two years later concerning introducing SA in primary education (Sirles 1985: 202–55 passim).

In 1966 the new minister of education, Mohamed Benhima, declared that Arabisation in Morocco had failed to improve the standards of education, the general level of students' achievement and students' knowledge of SA and/or

French. He posited that French should be kept for instrumental purposes to meet the needs of modernity, science and technology. This policy met with negative reactions from different groups. At that point in time Morocco was in a critical situation. The nationalist, pan-Arabist Istiqlāl party was calling for Arabisation. There had been Berber riots for three years (1957–60) calling for the official recognition of Berber (Faiq 1999). A spokesman for the only Moroccan trade union stated in the press in 1966 that due to the faltering of Arabisation, public education would be limited to the elite (Ennaji 2002).

Basically, Morocco found itself caught between two conflicting policies: universalisation and Moroccanisation. Universalisation means expanding education to more students, which increases the need for more teachers. Moroccanisation means using Moroccans rather than foreigners as teachers. Since most Moroccan teachers and educators were educated in France, the process of Arabisation was doomed at that stage (Sirles 1999: 120).

The second stage was from 1968 to 1972, and during this period the government managed to complete Arabisation for the elementary cycle (Ḥammūd 2000; Ennaji 2002). In the 1970s the new minister of education, Azzeddine Laraki, gave a new impetus to Arabisation. He aimed to implement Arabisation completely in education and administration.

The third stage was from 1973 to 1977. During that stage, social studies in the secondary schools were all Arabised. During the fourth stage, from 1978 to 1980, there were efforts to Arabise all secondary school subjects. During the fifth stage, from 1981 to the present, all secondary school subjects including science subjects and maths have been Arabised.

FRENCH IN MOROCCO

The socioeconomic environment encourages the use of French rather than SA. Morocco, for example, trades mainly with France. King Hassan II himself reflected these conflicting feelings towards Arabisation. He was praising Arabisation at the same time that he was establishing political and economic ties with France. There was also the feeling that French was the elite's language; the leaders continued to send their children to French schools. This made Arabic seem as if it were the language of the masses, not the upper classes or the elites (Sirles 1985: 236–7).

Note that just like English in Egypt, as will be clear below, French gained more status even though right after independence it was spoken only by one in fourteen Moroccans, as was said earlier. The reasons for this are economic, political and geographical in nature. According to Sirles (1999), although Morocco is part of the Arab world, it followed a different policy in its economic and political development. Its policies were quite independent of other Arab countries'. For example, its largest export commodity, which is phosphates, is exported mainly to France and the USA. It is also a country that depends on tourism to a great extent.

Migration was also crucial in the increase of the French presence in Morocco. Urbanisation eventually led to contact with French. At the end of French rule more than two-thirds of the population lived in towns and villages under 5,000 in population; then millions migrated to coastal cities where there was a strong French influence. For example, Casablanca increased in its population from less than 1 million to more than 2.3 million in the twenty years after independence (Sirles 1999: 127).

THE PRESENT-DAY SITUATION

As in Algeria, the university level has still not been Arabised in Morocco. French is still the medium of instruction in the schools of medicine, engineering and science (Ennaji 2002: 75, see also Shaaban 2006). Ennaji argues that the reason why French is still dominant today in these schools is that all reference books in these subjects are either in French or in English. There is a lack of teachers who are trained to teach these subjects in SA.

The linguistic discrepancy between school and university led to frustration in the young generation. For example, there have been student strikes at the University of Fes since 1990–1, when the first Arabised science students reached university level and could not deal with French textbooks. Many of them eventually decided to change to the faculty of letters to study Islamic studies or French because they could not take scientific courses in French. In the academic year 1998–9 students at the faculty of science and technology boycotted exams for one term because they were unable to assimilate course material in French in time for exams (Ennaji 2002: 77; see also Marley 2004).

Currently French is taught from third grade in public schools in Morocco. However, there are also government-supervised private bilingual schools in which French is taught side by side with SA, and maths and science are taught in French while the history of Morocco and civics are taught in SA. There is also a third kind of schools which do not comply to government standards. In these private schools, French is the main language of instruction and Arabic is taught as a second language or even a third one, after English. These are usually the schools where the elites send their children.

However, English is also entering the picture, with the opening of American schools in Morocco which again do not comply with the government standards and where SA is again a second or third language. In 1995, the American-accredited Al-Akhawayn University opened in Ifrane (Shaaban 2006). As in Egypt, the Gulf countries and Tunisia, English in Morocco is thus coming at full force.

In present-day Morocco there are at least two conflicting attitudes towards Arabisation, without even taking account of the Berbers' attitude: that of the 'Arabisants' and that of the 'Françisants'. The Arabisants are usually Arabic-educated intellectuals, politicians, lawyers and teachers educated in the Middle East, mainly at Al-Azhar University. For them Arabic education is essential because Islam and Arabic have been used as a weapon to confront colonisation (cf. Bensadoun 2007). The right-wing Istiqlāl party exemplifies this attitude. Ennaji also believes that 'the Muslim fundamentalists go even further to claim that only classical Arabic is worth teaching and learning because it reflects Muslim tradition, beliefs and values' (Ennaji 2002: 75). The Françisants are usually the French-educated elite. They may hold positions in higher education, public administration and the private sector. They prefer French and SA to monolingual Morocco with only SA. They think bilingualism can provide Arabic with new terminology that can be translated or transferred to Arabic, and thus can in its own way reinforce Arabisation. Note that some also prefer French to learning SA altogether.

In two questionnaires by Ennaji (2002) in which the attitudes of 112 university students and 19 of their teachers at the Institute of Technology in Fes towards SA and French were elicited. It was suggested that the majority of students were not in favour of Arabisation. The reason they gave is that it is difficult to master SA or to use it for science and technology. They also preferred bilingualism, because they felt there are two domains that need two languages: French should be used for science and technology, and Arabic for the humanities and literature. For them French could be used as a 'tool' for meeting the needs of the modern age and might enable them to move forward economically and socially (Ennaji 2002: 83). Note, however, that choosing science students specifically is bound to yield this predictable result, since, as is clear throughout the section on North Africa, it is students of science who suffer the discrepancy between school and university. In addition, 28 per cent of the students were bilingual Berberophones. The problematic issues encountered with language attitude surveys in general are also encountered in this survey.

Ennaji (2002: 83) contends that 'The linguistic rivalry is emerging as a hidden struggle for cultural identity and the revival of Arab-Muslim values and beliefs.' Thus, Arabic is emerging with a new motive in mind, and a new status. Sirles (1999) posits that the Arabisation policy may create a new group of leaders and businessmen who depend on Arabic rather than French to conduct their transactions. However, Sirles argues that what goes against this is Moroccan dependence on the west for most of its trade and hard currency. It is quite apparent that all these policies do not consider the importance of Berber, nor do they try to incorporate it in any plan. None the less the status of Berber and the way that Morocco deals with it are worth studying as well.

THE STATUS OF BERBER AND LANGUAGE POLICY

Berbers were bilinguals before and after colonisation. As far as Berbers are concerned, Arabic Morocco was preceded by centuries of Berber Morocco. The constant call for Arabisation since independence in 1956 has antagonised the Berber speakers and emphasised feelings of identity among them (cf.

Faiq 1999; Thomason 2001). The status of the Berber dialects/languages in Morocco shows a clear case of the discrepancy that can occur between language policies and real linguistic situations. The policies in Morocco until very recently did not take account of Berber dialects or seek to standardise them. Thus, the preamble of the 1996 constitution states: 'Le Royaume du Maroc, Etat musulman souverain, dont la langue officielle est l'arabe, constitue une partie du Grand Maghreb Arabe' ('The kingdom of Morocco, a sovereign Muslim state, of which the official language is Arabic, forms part of the greater Arab Maghreb').[9] The policy was that the purity of Arabic is something to be preserved. It is the language of the country and its religion. Again, this policy in essence ignored the multilingualism that existed in Morocco long ago, even before the French colonisation in 1912 (cf. Ennaji 2002; Thomason 2001).

In 1994 the king of Morocco decreed that Berber dialects would be taught at least in primary education. Plans had been drawn up and associations were being established for that purpose. In the same year, Moroccan television started a daily broadcast of 10-minute news bulletin in each of the three Berber dialects: Tachelhit, Tamazight and Tarifit (Faiq 1999). In 2003 Tamazight was introduced in 300 elementary schools all over the country. However, even now Berber languages are not recognised in the constitution (Errihani 2006). Marley (2004) posits that Morocco has to face the multilingual situation it is in without limiting its struggle to implementing SA.

Even though the relation between Arabs and Berbers in Morocco was not always harmonious, they were able to exist together for centuries, although Berber languages/dialects had been undermined. If we think of language as a symbol of identity then there must be a reason why the language issue did not cause conflict in Morocco. This is in fact because the allegiance of some Berbers is to the tribe and Islam before the state. The king of Morocco cleverly manipulates this allegiance. By calling himself *ami:r al-muʔmini:n* 'the commander of the faithful', which is a classical Islamic title, he derives his legitimacy from Islam and from being a *sharīf* (i.e. a descendant of the Prophet). He refers to a large community that surpasses ethnicity (Faiq 1999).

Morocco is still struggling with its multilingualism more than fifty years after independence. Thomason describes the language situation in Morocco by stating:

> Morocco, a country long regarded by the outside world as a coherent and tolerant one, is going through a period of great flux . . . it is apparent that the Berbers of morocco have embarked . . . on a process of historicising their territory and territorializing their history. (Thomason 2001: 151)

It is worth mentioning, however, that Berbers did not use the Arabic script to write their dialects/languages, which were mainly oral ones. Although the

Arabic script was used among Tachelhit speakers, Berbers decided to use the Tifinagh script to codify their language. This script was only used in emblems and short texts like epigraphs before this (Aissati and Kurvers 2008). Berber languages/dialects are now emphasised as a symbol of a distinct identity, and using Arabic script may be a threat to this identity (see section 5.5.2.2 for a similar phenomenon in Sudan).

Note also that in a survey conducted by Marley (2004) in which 159 secondary school students were asked to rate their attitude about bilingualism, SA and Tamazight, 84 per cent of the students preferred bilingualism in French and SA to monolingualism in SA, and only 10.1 per cent found it useful to learn Tamazight. However, Marley argues that this is because the survey was conducted in Khouribga –which is an area with no Berbers.

5.5.1.1.3 Tunisia

Languages used in Tunisia: SA, Tunisian Colloquial Arabic, Berber languages/dialects and French
Biggest minority: Berbers 1 per cent
Colonisation: 1881–1956

Tunisia was occupied by France for 75 years. Berbers in Tunisia, unlike in Morocco, constitute only 1 per cent of the population. They in fact do not have any political representation (Faiq 1999).

TUNISIA AFTER INDEPENDENCE

After independence, literacy rates in French and Arabic were in rough parity, and about 40 per cent could speak French (Gallagher 1964: 134). In fact Arabisation would have been easier in Tunisia than in Algeria because its Berber population was very scattered and small, and their presence was not seen as an impediment to the process of Arabisation (Sirles 1999: 120). Arabisation, at least at the beginning, was not a political issue in Tunisia, unlike in Algeria. President Habib Bourguiba stressed biculturalism and strong ties with France and the west. His government was pro-western. This pro-western tendency may have been decreased by the Palestine Liberation Organisation (PLO)'s moving to Tunis in the 1980s and early 1990s. This must have influenced the overt embracing of the west.

Competence in French is still considered prestigious in Tunisia. Language attitude surveys in Tunisia of French–Arabic bilinguals show that they prefer French newspapers and journals (Sirles 1999; see also Daoud 2007).

Bourguiba, at the beginning of his presidency, was a strong supporter of Arabisation, and then he changed his attitude and favoured French. Although Arabisation was gradual, the policy was not always consistent. French was delayed to the fourth grade and then brought back to second grade and then delayed to third grade.

In 1999 the Tunisian government declared that all administration would be arabised by the year 2000. There was also a call to Arabise computer software and databases in all public institutions.

Arabisation of science, mathematics and technical education up to ninth grade was achieved in 1997 (Daoud 2002). Scientific and technical subjects in secondary school and university are still in French. It is worth mentioning that Tunisia was reputed to be more successful than other Arab countries in training teachers and producing Arabic textbooks (Shaaban 2006).

Tunisia is still struggling with different ideologies. In 1996 there were large demonstrations calling for the ousting of the education minister and the changing of the university curriculum towards more Arabic (Sirles 1999).

Over the last twenty years Arabic has become more dominant than French in Tunisia. It is now used in government documents, official forms and letters, and shop signs. However, French is still dominant in banking documents, insurance documents and medical documents. Wholesale and retail shops still issue receipts in French. Thus, although the 1980s generation has been growing up with more Arabic around, especially in education, French is still playing a major role in Tunisia, perhaps a role that is only threatened by the spread of English (Daoud 2007: 275).

Again in Tunisia, as is the case in other countries in the Arab world, politics plays the major role in language policies. Sirles (1999: 122) posits that 'politics appear to play the central role in the future of Tunisian language planning'. There are challenges from the religious movement that Tunisia has to face and that could change its policies.

5.5.1.1.4 Conclusion to language policy in North Africa

According to Gill (1999), Arabic has a symbolic significance and French an instrumental significance. Arabic – SA in this case – is associated with Islam, nostalgia and the glorious past, and is also a unifying factor, while French and to a great extent now English are the languages of technology and science. As long as French still holds social prestige, as it does in Morocco, Algeria and Tunisia, then it will survive. Berber languages/dialects are now gaining status, although Hoffmann (1995) highlights the possible consequence of the rise of regional languages, as in the case of Catalan in Spain. The speakers of these indigenous languages, who were long suppressed, may establish oppressive tactics against non-speakers. However, there are a number of North African scholars who argue that what can help Morocco's language policies, for example, is an acknowledgement and appreciation of language diversity (cf. Ennaji 2002: 84). The system should be inclusive rather than exclusive. SA does not exclude French, vernacular or Berber languages/dialects.

Each country is different when it comes to the linguistic situation, the past, the environment, the history and length of colonisation, and the ethnic groups and their sizes. Therefore, any language policy should take into account all of these factors. For example, while Morocco is 45 per cent Berber, Tunisia is only 1 per cent Berber. The situation in Tunisia is thus different. Nevertheless, as long as the west controls the economic and technological world, policies of Arabisation are challenged and Arabic is sometimes perceived as if it is at odds with the modern world. Gill (1999: 134) posits that language policies in North Africa are sometimes at odds with socioeconomic reality. In the absence of an economic outlet, language policy should accompany socioeconomic change rather than create it.

There will be more discussion and comparisons of North African countries at the end of the section on French patterns of colonisation, when both Syria and Lebanon have been discussed.

5.5.1.2 Syria and Lebanon

As was said earlier, following the Sykes-Picot agreement of 1916, Syria and Lebanon became part of the French mandate. France was already notorious in Syria because of its policies in North Africa. Thus Syrians demonstrated hostility towards the French. Although anti-Turkish feelings were on the rise in Syria, most Syrians did not perceive their salvation in France. However, according to Mansfield (2003: 156), only the Maronites in Mount Lebanon thought of France as a protector. The British government at that time regarded France's control over Syria as 'excessive' (Mansfield 2003: 181). In 1919 a General Syrian Congress, meeting in Damascus, demanded the recognition of Syria's independence but failed to achieve its aim. In the same year Syria launched a futile attack on French positions on the Lebanon border. With North African and Senegalese soldiers, and with tanks and planes, France seized Damascus in July 1919.

In 1920 General Gouraud issued the decree of 31 August, in which he declared the creation of *le Grand Liban* (Mansfield 2003: 182). This which consisted of Mount Lebanon, the Biqāʿ plain to the east, and the coastal towns of Tripoli to the north and Sidon and Tyre to the south. The majority of the inhabitants of Lebanon were then Christians (see Chapter 3).

5.5.1.2.1 Syria

Languages used in Syria: SA, Syrian Colloquial Arabic, Kurdish, Armenian, Azeri, and Assyrian
Colonisation: 1916–46

Syria's population is composed of several ethnic groups, including Arabs, Druze, Kurds and Armenians. There are also several religions and religious sects in Syria, namely Sunni Muslims (c. 70 per cent of the population), Alawis (a Shiite sect, estimated at 9–15 per cent), Christians (c. 12 per cent) and Druze, as well as a dwindling Jewish community.

During the French mandate in Syria (1916–46), Syria was regarded by France as a focus of Arab nationalism (Mansfield 2003: 182). The situation in Syria was more like that in Egypt than that of North Africa. Although SA was suppressed in Syria, as was said earlier, and both administration and education were officially conducted in French, this did not have the same effect in Syria or Lebanon as in North America for a number of reasons. First, the position of Arabic in both Syria and Lebanon was strong because of the missionary schools that had opened at the end of the nineteenth century. These missionary schools, which represented different churches in the west, taught SA in addition to their own language. For example, the Catholic school taught French and Italian in addition to SA, while the Presbyterian and Anglican schools taught English in addition to SA.

Second, the Syrian Arab Science Academy was established in 1919, with the goal of providing SA with the technical terms needed for modernisation (Shaaban 2006: 699), the same year that the general congress demanded the recognition of Syria's independence. Third, the geographical location of Syria enabled it to interact more with neighbouring Arab countries, and its relatively short colonial history helped Syrians and Lebanese retain their knowledge of SA. In fact, Syria gained its independence from France almost six years before Egypt gained full independence from the British occupation. Because of all the above reasons, France's position in Syria was not as strong as its position in its North African territories. As was said earlier, Britain was reluctant to allow France to seize Syria. In 1930 the French government agreed on a constitution that made Syria a parliamentary republic with France retaining control over security and foreign affairs.

During the French mandate the University of Damascus was established (1923), with its teaching mainly in Arabic. Syria proclaimed its independence and declared SA the sole official language in 1946. After independence, a feeling of patriotism and nationalism was on the increase. There was also Syria's desire to regain territory split off by the French. SA became dominant; it was the symbol of unity. Although there are Kurds in Syria, who constitute 10 per cent of the population, their language is not on the agenda of language policies there. For example, Syria replaced Kurdish place-names with Arabic ones (Spolsky 2004). In that sense the ruling Syrian government is similar to the governments of Morocco and Algeria, since they suppressed other languages (in their case Berber languages) in favour of one official, unifying language.[10]

The government in Syria managed to Arabise all university subjects including science, maths and technical fields such as engineering and medicine (Shaaban 2006). According to Miller, Arabisation in science is more advanced in Syria than in any other country (Miller 2003). However, in Syria as in most Arab countries English is gaining status as a global language (Shaaban 2006).

SA AND POLITICS IN SYRIA

The reasons why Arabisation in Syria has been a thorough and an efficient process in both schools and universities are related to the political ideologies of the Syrian government. The ruling Baath party adopts a secular socialist policy. This party belongs to the Shiite sect of the Alawis. According to Kedar, Alawis' Islamic credentials are not held in high esteem by the Orthodox Muslims of the Sunni majority (Kedar 1999: 142). The Alawis, though a minority in Syria, are thus ruling Sunnis, the majority, and other religious groups and sects, and have been ruling Syria for more than three decades. The party's ideology has been to emphasise the 'Arabness' of all Syrians. The president has been and is called *qa:ʔid al-ʔumma* 'leader of the nation'. Kedar also notes that Syria's official name is al-Jumhūrīyah al-ʿArabīyah al-Sūrīyah 'the Arab Republic of Syria'. The Arab element is thus prior to the Syrian one. The Syrian press describes Syria as *qiblat al-ʕuru:bah* 'the direction to which all Arabs should direct their faces for prayers'. The *qibla* (the direction to which all Muslims turn their faces during prayers) is supposed to inspire unity among Muslims, and thus referring to Syria as the *qibla* of Arabs reflects Syria's role of inspiring unity among Arabs. The Syrian government has fostered the image of Syria as a strong opponent to western hegemony and ideologies, and the Syrian press has also blamed the other Arab states for betraying the cause of the nation (Kedar 1999).

5.5.1.2.2 Lebanon

Languages used in Lebanon: SA, Lebanese Colloquial Arabic, Armenian, Kurdish, English and French
Colonisation: 1916–46

According to Mansfield (2003: 202), a substantial part of the population of Lebanon after the partition of Syria and Lebanon rejected French control at least on an emotional level, and regarded themselves as part of an Arab nation. The sectarian political system imposed by the French – the president was to be a Maronite, the prime minister a Sunni Muslim, and the president of the Chamber of Deputies a Shiite (cf. Mansfield 2003) – was weakening feelings of national identity within Lebanon but not eradicating them.

The education system at the time of the French mandate remained in the hands of missionary schools, and higher education was exclusively provided by the Jesuit Université Saint-Joseph (established. 1875) or the American University of Beirut (AUB, established. 1866), a Presbytarian institution. The Université Saint-Joseph taught – and still teaches – in French, while the AUB used Arabic for a short while in all subjects, even in medicine, but now uses mainly English (cf. Mansfield 2003; Shaaban 2006: 699).

Currently French is associated with the Christians in Lebanon, and English is associated with the Muslims. In a survey conducted by Shaaban and Ghaith

(2002: 558) of students' perception of the ethnolinguistic vitality of SA, French and English, university students regarded French as a 'symbol of sectarian conflicts'.

As in other parts of the Arab world, Lebanon's elite, whether Muslims or Christians, prefer private education to public. In private schools, maths, science and technical subjects are taught in French or English, and humanities subjects are taught in SA. In addition to the AUB and Saint-Joseph, there is also the Beirut Arab University, co-founded in 1960 by the Lebanese Jamʿīyat al-Birr wa-al-Iḥsān, and Alexandria University. The Lebanese university's close ties with Egypt are evident in the fact that its operations were moved to Alexandria during the civil war (1975–90), and its degrees are awarded jointly with Alexandria University. Technical subjects, science and maths at university level are taught in a mixture of SA and English, as in Egypt, while humanities and social sciences are taught in SA.

5.5.1.3 Conclusion to French patterns of colonisation

French colonisation began and ended at different times in different countries and had different effects. However, Tables 5.2–5.4 show that the education systems in countries colonised by France, perhaps with the exception of Syria, have been influenced largely by colonisation. Algeria, which was considered a province of France for 132 years and which France was not ready to give up without a 7-year struggle, has the largest sum of Arabic lessons of all the countries discussed. While, even Syria teaches 10 hours of Arabic for the first year of primary education students, and 2 hours of English, Algeria starts with 14 hours of Arabic, and no French until second grade. Teaching SA in Algeria was a reaction to the long, severe involvement by the French in managing both the country and the linguistic situation. Both Tunisia and Morocco were protectorates of France and perhaps managed to overcome feelings of bitterness towards France. Note that when Morocco and Tunisia gained their independence there were more people who spoke and read French than in Algeria.

In Morocco the difference in hours between Arabic and French is levelled out in the second cycle of primary education and in secondary education. In Tunisia, again, the difference in hours is largely levelled out between Arabic and French at the end of primary education and throughout secondary education. In Algeria, from the sixth year of school (collège), the difference between both is levelled out. Algeria now teaches Tamazight as a second foreign language for three hours a week from the sixth year of school, for three years.

In Lebanon, French or English is the first foreign language taught to students from their first year of school. The number of hours devoted to French/English and Arabic is very similar starting from primary education. Note that, in Lebanon, schools adopt either French or English as the first foreign

Table 5.2 Language of instruction by subject and educational cycle: Morocco, Algeria and Tunisia

Subject	Morocco			Algeria			Tunisia	
	Primaire (6 yrs)	Secondaire collégial (3 yrs)	Secondaire qualifiant (1+2 yrs)	Primaire (5 yrs)	College (4 yrs)	Lycee (3yrs)	Ens de base (9 yrs)	Ens secondaire (4 yrs)
Arabic	Arabic	Arabic	Arabic	Arabic	Arabic	Arabic	Arabic	Arabic
French	French	French	French	French	French	French	French	French
History	Arabic	Arabic	Arabic	n/a	Arabic	Arabic	Arabic	Arabic
Maths	Arabic	Arabic	Arabic	Arabic	Arabic	Arabic	Arabic	French
Sciences	Arabic	Arabic	Arabic	Arabic	Arabic	Arabic	Arabic	French

Table 5.3 Weekly hours per language in primary and secondary education: Morocco, Algeria and Tunisia

Year	Morocco[a]							Algeria[b]										Tunisia[c]					
	Enseignement fondamental				Enseignement secondaire (1+2 yrs) Ara 6			Ecole primaire (5 yrs)		Collège (4 yrs)				Enseignement secondaire (3yrs)				Ens de base (9 yrs)			Ens secondaire (3 yrs)		
	Premier cycle (6 yrs)		Second cycle (3 yrs)																				
	Ara[d]	Fre	Ara	Fre	Ara	Fre	FL2	Ara	Fre	Ara	Fre	Tz	Eng	Ara	Fre	Eng		Ara	Fre	Eng	Ara	Fre	Eng
1	11	-	6	6	5	5	4–5	14	-	5	5	3	3	3–5	4–5	2–3		11.5	-		4.5	3.5	3
2	11	-	6	6	2–5	4–5	3–6	12	3	5	5	3	3	4–5	3–4	3–4		11.5	-		4.5	3.5	3–4
3	6.5	8	6	6	1–5	4–5	3–6	11	4	5	5	3	3	3–7	3–4	3–4		10	9		0–5	2–4	3–4
4	6.5	8						8.3	5	5	4	-	5					10	9.5				
5	6	8						7	5									7	11.5				
6	6	8																7	11				
7																		5	4.5	2			
8																		5	4.5	2			
9																		5	5	2			

Notes:
[a] UNESCO (2007)
[b] Benrabah (2007b: 95–8)
[c] Daoud (2007: 268–9)
[d] Ara=Arabic; Fre=French; FL=Foreign Language; TZ=Tamazight.

Table 5.4 Weekly hours/periods per language in primary and secondary education: Lebanon and Syria

Year	Lebanon[a]								Syria[b]					
	Primary education (6 yrs)		Middle school (3 yrs)			Secondary school (3 yrs)			Basic education (9 yrs)			Secondary education (3 yrs)		
	Ara[c]	Fre/Eng	Ara	Fre/Eng	FL2	Ara	Fre/Eng	FL2	Ara	Eng	Fre	Ara	Eng	Fre
1	7	7	6	6	2	5	5	2	10	2	–	5	3	2
2	7	7	6	6	2	3–6	3–6	2	9	3	–	5–7	3–4	2–3
3	7	7	6	6	2	2–6	2–6	2	8	3	–	4–8	4–5	4–5
4	6	6							8	3	–			
5	6	6							7	3	–			
6	6	6							7	3	–			
7									6	3	2			
8									6	3	2			
9									6	3	3			

Notes:
[a] UNESCO (2007). Numbers represent periods of 45 minutes.
[b] Syria, Ministry of Education (2008). Numbers represent periods of unspecified length.
[c] Ara=Arabic; Fre=French; Eng=English; FL2=Second Foreign Language

language depending on the region/religious affiliation. In Syria, the first foreign language is in fact English and not French, and is usually taught for only 2–3 hours a week from the beginning. The hours of Arabic and English are not equal while Arabic is taught for 6–10 hours, English is taught for approximately 3.

Of all the countries colonised by France, it is only Syria, and perhaps parts of Lebanon, that adopt English as the first foreign language and not French. This again shows that the political agenda of France in Syria and Lebanon was different from that in North African countries.

The political struggle in each country was and is different in nature and may take the shape of an ethnic struggle for equal rights, as in the case of Berbers in Morocco and Algeria; a religious struggle – fundamentalists versus secularists in Algeria, and Christians versus Muslims in Lebanon; or even an ideological struggle, as in the case of Syria, with the political party ideology of pan-Arabism and political hegemony.

This section has examined how language policy interacts with extra-linguistic factors such as political struggles for independence, ethnicity, religion and urbanisation (as is the case in Morocco) and economic forces. Although the outcome of colonisation is different in each country, the repercussions, whether political or linguistic, are still dominant.

5.5.2 British patterns of colonisation

The British, unlike the French, did not aim at assimilating their holdings in the Arab world, nor did they consider their Arab colonies part of Britain. Consider the following quotation from Lord Palmerston (d. 1865), British prime minister 1855–8 and 1859–65, which summarises the attitude of at least a part of the British establishment before the colonisation of Egypt.

> We do not want Egypt or wish it for ourselves, any more than any rational man with an estate in the north of England and a residence in the south would have wished to possess the inns on the north road. All he could want would have been that the inns should be well-kept, always accessible, and furnishing him, when he came, with mutton-chops and post-horses. (Ashley 1879: II 337–8)

Britain regarded Egypt as the 'inns' on the road rather than as a province or a territory overseas, and although English was declared an official language along with Arabic in Egypt, Sudan, the Palestinian territories and Israel, Britain lacked the zeal to implement its policy, and had no interest in the linguistic situation as such.

For the British, being civilised did not entail learning English specifically but learning and speaking a European language. Thus only a European language should be used and recognised as the language of education (Spolsky 2004). The British aimed at weakening SA by promoting the vernacular, as will become clear below. For the British, the diglossic situation was inhibiting and difficult to understand. Thus Britain tried hard to raise the status of the colloquial at the expense of SA. They believed that children should learn the language they speak, which in the Arab world would be the colloquial/vernacular. In fact, this was also their policy in India, where they used the vernacular of each area for elementary education and English for secondary education (Spolsky 2004). However, Britain's encouragement of the colloquials was not without a political aim as well. In addition, Britain forged colonial policies that stressed the separateness of African and European identities.

5.5.2.1 Egypt

Languages used in Egypt: SA, ECA, Nubian, Armenian, Greek, Domari
Colonisation: 1882–1952

Egypt is different from North Africa when it comes to language policy and the position of SA. In the 1950s and 1960s Egypt took the lead in propagating both independence in the Arab world and SA (cf. Mansfield 2003). The idea of the Arab nation was very concrete in that period. Although the influence of English or French is not as strong as it was in North Africa, the British occupation did try to weaken SA, as was said earlier.

EGYPT BEFORE INDEPENDENCE

Egypt was occupied by Britain for seventy years, from 1882 to 1952. The British administration aimed to weaken Arabic from the beginning of the occupation (Shraybom-Shivtiel 1999). To do so they first introduced English and French as the required languages in the education system. Second, they elevated the status of ECA rather than SA by emphasising the distinctiveness of the Egyptian identity as opposed to the Arab identity. They were aiming to eradicate any Egyptian national aspirations and to tighten their grip on Egypt.

To achieve the first goal of establishing foreign languages as the medium of education, the British administration announced in 1888 that the language of instruction in all schools was to be either French or English. Their explanation for this was that Egypt was moving towards a European style of development and that this development is technological and scientific in nature. During this period Egypt's elite began to send their children to foreign schools, whether English, French or German, i.e. schools in Egypt using these languages as the language of instruction. The demands for the revival of SA were met with harsh criticism of its weakness as a living language. Its grammar and vocabulary were thought to be fossilised. The methods of teaching SA were also criticised for being tedious and difficult. SA was seen as a language taught by repetition and memorisation and not fit for the contemporary needs of society (Shraybom-Shivtiel 1999).

At that time key figures in the British administration were calling for the use of Egyptian Arabic (ECA) as a written language and also its use as the official language to be used in civil affairs. Lord Dufferin, special envoy of Her Majesty's government in Egypt and British ambassador to the Ottoman Empire, when ordered to provide a plan for Egypt's reorganisation, devoted part of his report to the problems with Arabic and to expanding the colloquial. At that time, foreign orientalists in the Arab world showed a strong interest in the colloquial. Carlo Landberg (swedish) wrote about the Syrian dialect, Louis Jacques Bresnier (French), was interested in the Algerian dialect, and J. Seldon Willmore (British) in 1901 wrote a grammatical analysis of Egyptian Arabic. Orientalists started opening schools to teach colloquial (Shraybom-Shivtiel 1999: 134). The Egyptians then seemed to be encouraging what the British were doing. During the initial period of British rule in Egypt, the Egyptians 'meekly and willingly accepted British guidance and supervision' (1999: 134).

At the same time that the British were seeking to weaken the role played by SA, Egyptian national identity was being revived and shaped by other factors. This identity was not, however, always associated with SA. According to Suleiman (2003: 175–6), several external factors helped shape this identity:

1. *The 1919 revolution, in which Muslims and Christians were united:* The Egyptian leader Saʿd Zaghlūl (1860–1927) and his colleagues were arrested by the British mandate on 8 March 1919 and exiled to Malta days after he demanded full independence for Egypt from the British. Women took off their veils to demonstrate side by side with men, both Muslims and Copts. The revolt resulted in the death of 1,000 Egyptians and 36 British and Indian soldiers. A month later, in April 1919, on the recommendation of the new high commissioner, Lord Allenby, Saʿd Zaghlūl and his colleagues were released from detention and returned to Egypt. To Egyptians this was one of the first times that the British complied with their demands, which enhanced their feelings of patriotism and confidence.
2. *The creation of a parliamentary democracy in 1922–23:* Britain declared Egypt independent in 1922 but with four stipulations – reservations that limited its sovereignty. In 1923 parliamentary democracy was established, though most of the power was still in the hands of the British and the monarchy. Martial law was also lifted.
3. *The pride Egyptians felt in their past and pharaonic history as a result of the discovery of the tomb of Tutankhamen in 1922:* In the Valley of the Kings

at Luxor, the British Egyptologist Howard Carter discovered the tomb of Tutankhamen with all treasures and the mummy untouched.

4. *The ending of the caliphate by the Turkish leader Mustafa Kemal Atatürk in 1923:* After this, King Fuʾād of Egypt made a discreet attempt to become the leading Muslim figure and the caliph, but gave it up when he met with no encouragement (cf. Haag 2003: 280–3).

Egyptians felt a direct psychological and racial link between modern-day Egyptians and their pharaonic ancestors (Suleiman 2003: 176). They felt they were different from other Arabs with whom they shared a language, which is SA. They also felt different from their co-religionists, mainly Muslims. They had the belief that 'Egypt's great powers of assimilation have enabled it to absorb waves of immigrants and to stamp their mental make-up with the indelible imprint of its character' (2003: 176).

Some intellectuals began to argue that Egyptian Arabic was the true language of Egyptians rather than SA, which is the language stressed by all Arabs. For example, Nīqūlā Yūsuf raised the issue in 1929. He posited that Egypt has its own environment, which is very different from the Bedouin environment in which Arabic is spoken. Arabic, meaning SA, was for him a desert language not suitable for the modern needs of Egypt (Suleiman 2003: 178). Similarly, Salāmah Mūsá (1887–1958) 'declared that SA is a dead language which cannot compete with the colloquial as the true mother tongue of Egyptians' (Suleiman 2003: 182). Suleiman notes the fact that Mūsá declared this statement not in ECA, but in SA. Suleiman contends that in that sense Mūsá is similar to those who advocate the use of SA as a spoken language, but who never use it themselves. Mūsá was convinced that Arabs were less advanced than Egyptians, so there was no use in retaining their language. SA, according to Mūsá, was a poor language, artificial, difficult and backward. He proposed a solution using the Roman alphabet to write colloquial language. As far as science was concerned, this would enable Egyptians to borrow words from European languages and keep up with modern technology.

However, at that point there were still intellectuals who were quite aware of the possible dangers associated with abandoning SA altogether. Some proposed modernising SA to make it more receptive to lexical borrowing from colloquial and other languages. One of the initiators of this move was Luṭfī al-Sayyid (1872–1963). He suggested creating a middle language between standard and colloquial. Others, like ʿAbd Allāh al-Nadīm (1844–96), who was a journalist, warned Egyptians against abandoning the standard. In his article 'Language loss in surrendering the self' he called upon Egyptians to hold on to Arabic instead of surrendering themselves to foreign languages. This was all at a time when the British were emphasising the importance of colloquial and foreign languages in schools (cf. Suleiman 2003: 174).

THE BEGINNING OF THE ARABIC REVIVAL IN EGYPT

According to Suleiman (2003), the attitude of Egyptians had changed by the late 1930s. Muḥammad ʿAllūbah, an Egyptian journalist, declared that Egypt was an Arab country because of the Arabic language. This change is reflected in the layout of his newspaper, *al-Siyāsah al-Usbūʿīyah* ('Weekly Politics'). The cover page used to appear with pharaonic decorations. The Islamic dates were only on the inside pages. In 1930 the pharaonic decorations were replaced by caricatures and the Islamic dates were on the front page (Husayn 1983 vol. 2: 172, cited in Suleiman 2003: 180).

In fact, even before the 1930s, there were calls for the revival of Arabic. At the time that Egyptians were reshaping their identity, a number of them began to realise the significance of SA. Shraybom-Shivteil (1999) postulates that by the beginning of the twentieth century, with the start of the process of liberation from foreign rule and the rise of nationalist aspirations, Egyptian intellectuals felt a need to deal with the issue of SA. There was definitely an awareness that it was an issue. The first person to begin the change in language education policy was Saʿd Zaghlūl, when he was minister of education between 1906 and 1910. He aimed at replacing English with Arabic as the language of instruction in schools even though Arabic then could not meet the needs of science. His aim of introducing it was a crucial first step that came amidst nationalist calls for the revival of Arabic. The beginning of the century also witnessed the establishment of Fu'ād I University in 1908 (later to become Cairo University). The committee decided unanimously that the official language of instruction would be Arabic.

The call to reform Arabic to meet modern needs came quite early in Egypt as compared to other countries, and included calls to modify grammar, script and spelling. There were also some radical ideas like eliminating grammatical rules entirely, getting rid of the dual system and the suffix of the feminine plural. King Fu'ād, although he himself did not know Arabic well, was very aware of its importance. He established the Academy of the Arabic Language in 1932. The king intervened personally in the reform of the language. He proposed the simplification of Arabic letters upon the recommendation of the British orientalist Denison Ross, who had new letters designed for use at the beginning of a sentence similar to capital letters in Latin orthography. These letters were called crown letters and they were designed to facilitate mastery in reading and writing (Shraybom-Shivtiel 1999: 136). This proved to be a failed experiment. Despite all these efforts the situation did not change. As late as the 1940s foreign languages were still the primary means of instruction except in religious schools, which were under the supervision of al-Azhar University. Private schools excluded Arabic while public schools used it in a very limited manner, and they themselves were limited in number (Shraybom-Shivtiel 1999).

In the meantime, a key figure appeared in Egypt who had a great influence on the revival of Arabic. The writer Ṭāhā Ḥusayn (1889–1973) was himself educated at al-Azhar University. In his book *Mustaqbal al-thaqāfah fī Miṣr* ('The future of culture in Egypt', 1938), he called for the establishment of Arabic in foreign schools – those schools that were run by non-Egyptians and not under government supervision (Shraybom-Shivtiel 1999). According to Suleiman (2003), Ṭāhā Ḥusayn believed in Egypt's national identity as built not on religion but on the political, geographical and historical environments. He, like Mūsá, looked to Europe as a model. He also believed in the significance of the modernisation of language. Yet he and Mūsá had different attitudes towards SA. Ḥusayn held the belief that 'Muslims (more accurately, Muslim rulers and elites) . . . understood that religion is one thing and politics is another, and that the first basis for establishing political unity is common interests' (1944: 21, quoted in Suleiman 2003: 191). He stressed the importance of language as the medium for thought and modernisation.

According to Ḥusayn, Egypt, which was known for moderation, should aim at integration with the west and not at assimilation. Therefore, one of the policies of the state should be to make sure that SA was taught in all private foreign schools in Egypt. He called for the elimination of all teaching of foreign language in the primary stage in state schools. He was aware that SA was dreaded as a subject, and he thought this was so because of the concentration on grammar as a means of teaching (Suleiman 2003: 193).

Ḥusayn thought there was a difference between teaching about the language and teaching of the language. Thus, the parrot-like learning style used to study grammar and rhetoric was not valid. According to him, because language should have a creative role, SA had to be simplified without being compromised. Ḥusayn remained throughout an ardent supporter of SA. This is because, according to him, if Egyptians ignored SA, they would cut themselves off from their past and their Arab literary heritage. He still had problems with al-Azhar, where he studied, because it was the sole authority in grammar teaching and teacher training. He even claimed that the Coptic church should make sure that it used good Arabic (meaning SA), since Arabic was part of Egypt's national identity, but was not limited to Egyptian national identity (Suleiman 2003: 194).

In the early 1940s Ḥusayn Haykal was appointed minister of education; private foreign schools were instructed to teach their pupils Arabic, Egyptian history and geography. Still, the primary language of instruction in these schools remained a foreign language. However, Shraybom-Shivtiel posits that 'the introduction of Arabic as a required language constituted a turning point in Egypt's national education system' (1999: 137).

EGYPT AFTER INDEPENDENCE

After the 1952 revolution[11], Nasser had in mind the goal of making education accessible to everyone by offering it free to all the population, and making primary education compulsory. In addition to that, according to Shraybom-Shivtiel, 'Egypt, in its efforts to achieve national unity during the 1950s and 1960s, positioned literary Arabic (SA) at the core of its educational system and utilised it as the cornerstone in the development of the image of the young generation in the Arab World' (1999: 131). Nasser had the goal of helping other Arab countries achieve independence and emphasising similarities rather than differences among all Arab countries. SA was to play a major role as a unifying force in defining the Arab nation at that time[12]. Shraybom-Shivtiel (1999) argued that in order for Egypt at that time to achieve national unification, it had to emphasise joint heritage and modern political needs. A logical result of the 1952 revolution was a change in both the attitude and the approach towards Arabic. To enhance the pan-Arab movement and to build a nationalist feeling among the new generation of Egyptians, schools began teaching Islamic resources, classical Arabic literature and poetry. A new image of Egypt was being formed: that of Egypt as part of the Arab nation (Faksh 1980).

Nasser himself, when addressing the United Nations on 28 September 1960, said, 'We announce that we believe in a single Arab nation. The Arab nation was always united linguistically. And linguistic unity is unity of thought' (Dajānī: 1973: 119–37). During this period, the idea held before the revolution that called for the simplification of SA grammar and spelling disappeared. Colloquial lost its status once more, and became only the language of daily life. In fact, SA was encouraged as the language of academics, intellectuals and educated people. The Arab Academy of Language worked hard in creating scientific terms in Arabic. Universities began teaching SA even in science faculties. In 1960 the Egyptian minister of education, Kamāl al-Dīn Ḥusayn, called on the Arabic Language Academy in Cairo to recommend that only SA be spoken at universities[13] (Shraybom-Shivtiel 1999).

According to Shraybom-Shivtiel, SA at that time, although not a spoken language, became the spoken language of the elite in some domains/contexts, such as lectures or formal gatherings and to discuss specific topics as well. It gained a new status for some intellectuals which replaced the status of foreign languages. If this were the aim of the revolution, then it was to a great extent achieved, since SA was not just the official language, but also gained the status of a prestige language, which carries political significance.[14] Note that SA had been a discredited language during foreign rule (1999: 138).

However, the call for Egypt's identity distinct from that of the Arab world, and the importance of colloquial, may have been ignored for some time but they were never forgotten. Twenty years later, after Nasser's death in 1970, and the peace treaty with Israel in 1979, Egypt was ostracised by the rest of the Arab world. The feeling that Egyptians are different from Arabs was beginning to be fostered once more. According to Suleiman, the writer Lūwis ʿAwaḍ (1915–90) called for a distinct identity for Egyptians which should be reflected in their language. He called for this in a book published during the time of the presidency of Anwar Sadat (1970–81), when Egypt 'veered towards an "Egypt first" policy in response to the Arab boycott following its peace treaty with Israel in March 1979' (Suleiman 2003: 198). ʿAwaḍ tried to separate the language factor from national identity and the political sphere. According to him, Egypt had been under colonising powers for about 4,000 years. These colonisers were different: Greeks, Romans, Arabs, Turks and British, to name a few. By returning to its pharaonic past, Egypt could regain its sense of creativity. This could be done by the creation of an Egyptian language. He even went so far as to say that the use of the glottal stop in Egyptian Arabic is caused by the racially bound physical constitution of the Egyptian vocal tract, a claim that is patently false (Suleiman 2003). In fact, this 'Egypt first' policy was also reflected in the education system in Egypt, starting from 1980 and continuing to the present day. Egyptian children were taught in their social studies classes that their affiliation is first to their country, Egypt, then to the nation, the Arab world, and finally to their religion, in most cases Islam (see ʿAbd al-Kāfī 1991; Khiḍr 2006).

THE PRESENT-DAY SITUATION

Currently there are two educational systems in Egypt: a public one and a private one (see Chart 5.1). The public one does not fill all labour-market jobs; there are two different markets for the public and the private systems. SA is taught more in the public schools, while the private system concentrates on foreign languages much more. The largest employer requiring moderate to advanced knowledge of SA is the state. Government posts, like those of Arabic teachers or those whose jobs involve reading and writing in SA, need knowledge of SA. However, even the degree of this knowledge required varies from one job to another. For example, working in a state hospital as a physician, nurse, director of public relations, agent and secretary all require different levels of language skills (Haeri 1997).

Haeri (1997) poses the question of how much knowledge of SA is needed in jobs which by and large are more attractive and better paid than government jobs. By that she means jobs like those of an owner of a small or large business: construction, boutique, pharmacy, television production, doctors in private clinics and hospitals, teachers in private schools who do not teach SA etc. She gives the example of a diplomat who does not master SA and depends on his secretary for writing official documents in SA. Haeri posits that the upper classes do not receive their education in SA. They may have knowledge of it, and they can use standard words in their speech depending on context as borrowed words. In that sense, Egypt is different from, for example, the USA, where there are also two different systems of education that possibly aim at different labour markets, but where in both systems the standard language, which is English, is taught. According to Haeri, this situation in Egypt does not favour SA. Haeri says:

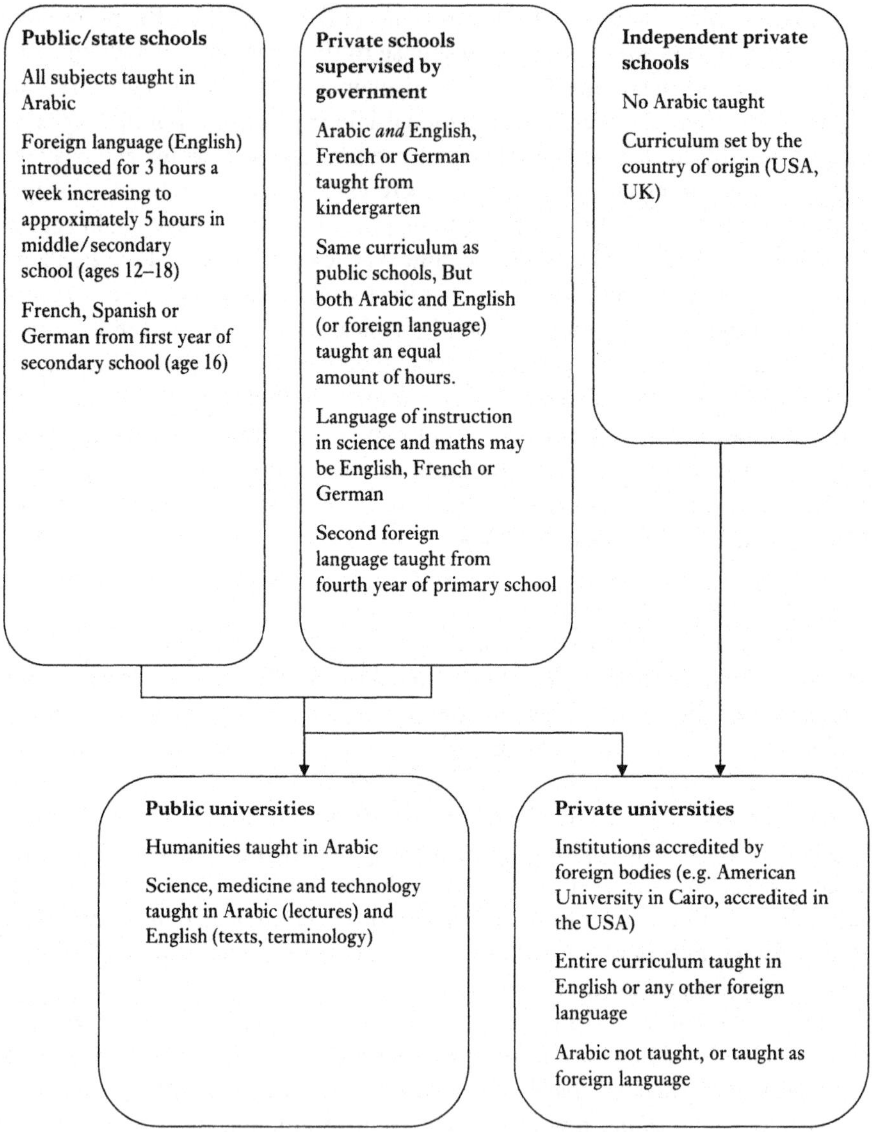

Chart 5.1 The education system in Egypt

> It appears that by and large members of the upper classes in Egypt are not the ones who know the official language the best or use it the most. In fact, speaking with a number of Egyptian sociologists and anthropologists, I was told that I should use the criterion of foreign language school attendance as central to my classification of speakers. (1996a: 162–3)[15]

Egypt is a country that is dependent on tourism to a great extent for its economic growth (Schaub 2000). It has been reported that the largest group of foreign tourists is in fact from the UK. According to the American University in Cairo career advising and placement services office, the number one criterion for finding a decent job is being able to demonstrate proficiency in English (cf. Russell 1994: 147). In addition, since Sadat adopted the open-door economic policy, Egyptians have been very keen on learning English. The role of English in the Arab world will be discussed in detail in section 5.10. However, Chart 5.1 gives an idea of the organisation of the education system in Egypt.

It is noteworthy that al-Azhar, though criticised by Ḥusayn, has played a role in maintaining SA, and the Academy of the Arabic Language, which existed much earlier than other academies in the Arab world, must have played a role as well. Egypt was under a different colonising force and suffered a different kind of discrimination against standard from the discrimination that North African countries have suffered. However, Shraybom-Shivtiel summarises the relation between policies and politics when he postulates that 'the history of modern Arabic, therefore, serves as a microcosm of the development of Egypt's socio-political image in the modern world' (1999: 138).

5.5.2.2 Sudan

Languages used in Sudan: SA, Sudanese Colloquial Arabic, Dinka, Bedawi, Beja, Nuer, Fur and English (and see list in the section below). Of all Arab countries, Sudan has the most languages used (Mugaddam 2006).
Ehno-linguistic make-up: Southern peoples 34 per cent (Nilotic and Nilo-Hamitic, Sudanic linguistics groups – Dinka, Nuer etc.); Arabised peoples of the north 40 per cent; non-Arabised peoples of the north 26 per cent (Beja, Fur, Nuba etc.) (Lesch 1998: 17).
Colonisation: 1882–1956

In an article which is more political than linguistic, Sharkey (2008) discusses language policies in Sudan, and how these policies reflect the unbalanced political power in the country between the northern and the southern parts. Sharkey posits that the current language policy of Sudan in which SA is the sole official language will not be conducive to national unity but in fact to divisions within Sudan (2008: 43).

Yokwe (1984) had argued more than twenty years earlier that the language policy of Sudan does not take account of the southern languages. He claims that 51 per cent of the Sudanese people speak Arabic as their mother tongue, 20 per cent speak Arabic as a second language, but only 5 per cent of southerners speak Arabic as a second language. According to him, there are 136 languages spoken in Sudan, of which 114 are Sudanese and the rest are foreign, including English. Although in Khartoum 96 per cent of the population speak Sudanese Colloquial Arabic, in the south this is not the case. Among the languages spoken in the south are: Acholi, Aja, Avokaya, Bai, Baka, Banda-Mbrès, Banda-Ndélé, Belanda Bor, Belanda Viri, Beli, Berta, Boguru, Bongo, Didinga, Dongotono, Feroge, Gbaya, Gula, Indri, Kakwa, Lango, Lokoya, Lopit, Luwo, Mandari, Mangayat, Njalgulgule, Nuer, Shilluk, Suri, Tennet, Thuri, Toposa and Zande[16] (see also Yokwe 1984: 153). In the north the Coptic church uses SA, while the Roman Catholic church uses Sudanese Colloquial Arabic and the Anglican churches use colloquial Arabic if it is the language of the community they are in.

BEFORE INDEPENDENCE

The British relied on Egyptian officers to govern Sudan from 1924 onward. The British also tried to block the spread of Arabic in the south by attempting a southern policy/closed district policy in 1930–46. Under this policy Britain claimed that the Negroid Africans of the south were culturally and racially different from the northerners, who claim to be Arab. As a result, the southerners could either be separated from the northerners or be integrated into what was then British East Africa (corresponding roughly to the territory of present-day Kenya) (cf. Yokwe 1984; Miller 2003). On the other hand, the British did not have a plan for teaching the different languages of the south. Teaching in southern Sudan was left in the hands of missionaries and was done by these missionaries first in the different vernaculars and then in English at higher levels (Miller 2003). This system corresponds to the linguistic ideology of the British, which was to teach in the child's vernacular mother tongue and then in English. Once more the British were not trying hard to promote English but to weaken SA. The rate of literacy in the south remained low compared to the north (Miller 2003).

The British policy in the south did not succeed in eradicating Arabic, which still served as a lingua franca, but did succeed in creating an English-speaking Christian elite. In 1946 the closed district policy ended.

The Report of the International Education Commission on Secondary Education in the Sudan of 1955 estimated that it was a 'waste of time and energy to teach the south their own vernaculars [i.e. their languages] in schools with no reading material available to them and no written literature, since in that case students could not pursue any reading after they left school'. The same fact was emphasised even after independence in a UNESCO report in 1963. The report added that even if Latin script were used for these languages, teaching them would still be a futile task (Yokwe 1984).

AFTER INDEPENDENCE

Sudan gained its independence from British rule in 1956 and Arabic was declared the sole official language of Sudan. According to Miller (2003: 11), there may have been an underlying ideology in the Sudanese government then that Arabic language and culture are superior to the southern African culture.

As early as 1963, an organisation called The Sudan African Closed Districts National Union sent a petition to the UN complaining that Arabic had replaced the vernacular languages which were taught at lower elementary schools. They argued that children should begin with their native language, not a foreign one (a position that was advanced strongly by the 1953 UNESCO declaration entitled *The use of vernacular languages in education*). In 1972, after the Addis Ababa agreement which put an end to the first civil war between the north and south, the regional government formulated a comprehensive policy which acknowledged the use of the spoken languages. In rural areas the spoken languages are used in the first four years of school, and SA is introduced only orally.

Economic and political inequality, and religious, cultural and racial differences, may be some of the reasons for the conflict between the southern and northern parts in Sudan. However, for the southerners Arabic is associated with the north and with Islam (Miller 2003: 16).

The different languages used in Sudan, especially in the south, are the oral vehicle for folklore, traditions and local beliefs. These languages are used in communicating with family and friends. In the urban part of southern Sudan, Sudanese colloquial Arabic is used in the markets, schools and offices (see Mugaddam 2006). It also serves as a lingua franca. Although Arabic has a role in the towns in the south, it barely exists in the villages. As was noted earlier, the Sudanese languages are used in the first four primary school years in the south. In the north, at all levels of education English is used as a foreign language introduced at middle school and Arabic is the main language of instruction. There is no room for other local languages (Sharkey 2008). This emphasis on SA is because the government highlights Arab political unification which is based not on colour or religion but on language. According to Yokwe (1984) southerners have been resisting this policy since the nineteenth century. However, Sudan is still struggling with the problem of acknowledging so many languages. Politicians, whether in the south or the north, may have to resort to Arabic since it is already the official language. As Yokwe (1984) puts it, southerners may have to accept Arabic not as a symbol of submission, but as a practical solution.

THE PRESENT-DAY SITUATION

In the north, the government is still committed to Arabisation. Elementary, middle and secondary schools have been completely Arabised, including scientific and technical subjects. In 1991, higher education was formally Arabized throughout Sudan, although English remains a compulsory core subject at Khartoum University[17]. Also in 1991, Sudan established the Higher Authority of Arabisation (HAA) in order to establish SA as the language of instruction at universities in scientific and technical areas. The HAA's mission was to coin technical terms, to establish a SA scientific library and to encourage translation and scientific publications in SA (Shaaban 2006).

The relation between the political conflict in Sudan and language ideologies is highlighted by scholars in the field who are either for or against Arabisation. Those against it claim that Arabisation is a catalyst in the civil wars in southern Sudan from the 1950s onward, and the conflict in Darfur that erupted in 2003. Sharkey (2008: 28) postulates that having one language as the official language does not lead to unity but to resentment. She calls for the government's acknowledgement of the diversity within Sudan, including the linguistic diversity. Sharkey criticises the government's linguistic ideologies by positing that 'this Arabism is ideological, meanwhile, in the dictionary sense that it has inspired and justified a schema of actions or policies that are implicitly or explicitly adopted and maintained regardless of the course of events' (Sharkey 2008: 28).

However, even Sharkey herself acknowledges that in spite of resentment feelings in the south of Sudan, Arabic (at least colloquial Arabic) is still spreading, especially in Darfur, and not for political or ideological reasons, but for practical ones, such as contact, trade and market forces.

It is worth mentioning that southern Sudanese, like Berbers in Morocco, decided to codify their language (corpus planning) in a script other than the Arabic one. In Morocco it is Tifinagh script, and in Sudan it is Latin script, even though there were attempts by Egyptian teachers in the middle of the twentieth century to teach southern Sudanese languages in Arabic script (cf. Sharkey 2008).

5.5.2.3 Palestine and Israel

At the beginning of this chapter, I mentioned the fact that language policies do not always go hand in hand with language planning. One of the crucial factors that influence language policies is language contacts. In fact contact is more relevant than schools and curricula. This is the case in Israel and Palestine. While Arabs may not want to learn Hebrew in schools in the Gaza Strip and the West Bank, they learn it from contact with Israelis, often in prison in fact (Spolsky and Shohamy 1999). In Israel economic factors also play a major role, so while Israeli Jews do not feel the need to learn Arabic, Israeli Arabs feel the need to learn Hebrew. In fact the situation in both Israel and Palestine is crucial to our understanding of language policies because sometimes policies do not reflect reality and, in spite of political animosity, language contact leads eventually to language learning. I discuss the situation in Israel, then that in the Palestinian Territories.

5.5.2.3.1 Language policy in Israel

According to Spolsky (2004), the move to revive Hebrew in Palestine started in the 1890s. Hebrew began to be taught in the schools such as Zikhron Yaakov and Petach Tikvah. From 1890 onwards a political campaign started in Britain to have Hebrew recognised as an official language. The codification of language was fast and efficient. Dictionaries were written, grammars codified and academies established. This is why Sirles (1999: 118) says that language policies apart from those of Hebrew can claim only modest success. In fact, Hebrew was recognised after World War I by the British mandate as an official language. It was used in the main public and private schools of the Jewish community, serving as a lingua franca among immigrants from many backgrounds. It was spread by a 'strong ideological campaign' (Spolsky 1994: 227). The British army entered Jerusalem in 1918, and prior to this date English and Arabic were the official languages. Britain added Hebrew as the official language and gave the Hebrew-speaking and Arabic-speaking communities responsibility over their own educational systems, with little or no financial support. According to Spolsky and Shohamy (1999), the Hebrew speakers seized this opportunity and used it to support the spread of Hebrew. Although Arabs and Jews had separate school systems, there was language contact between them, mainly with the Jews learning Arabic (Amara 2003).

In 1948 Hebrew became the national language and dominated all other official languages. English was dropped from the list of official languages and only Hebrew and Arabic remained. Israeli Arabs continued to use their vernacular in speaking and SA in their schools, but also had to learn Hebrew formally in schools as a required subject and informally at home (Spolsky 1994: 228). However, 'official language use has maintained a *de facto* role for English, after Hebrew but before Arabic' (Spolsky 1994: 227; cf. Fishman et al. 1977). For example, Spolsky says that 'if public notices are bilingual they tend to be more often in Hebrew and English than in Hebrew and Arabic' (1994: 227).

There were plenty of Hebrew courses for new immigrants. Hebrew became the language of government, parliament, television and radio stations. There is also an Arabic-language radio station, and the government television station broadcasts Arabic three and half hours daily. However, according to Spolsky and Shohamy (1999), English has more status and Arabic is somewhat discriminated against (Spolsky 1994: 228). Spolsky and Shohamy (1999: 119) posit that Israeli Arabs' main complaint is not that their language is not taught in schools, because it is in fact taught in schools, and they are also keen on learning both English and Hebrew, but that their language is not used in signposts and the provision of Arabic subtitles and programmes on Israeli commercial television.

Spolsky and Shohamy (1999:119) mentioned three court cases in their study. In the first one, a group of Arabic speakers in Haifa requested the city authorities to have Arabic added to signposts that are in Hebrew and English. In the second case, a local Arab developer had asked to require the city authorities in upper Nazareth to permit him to display advertising posters written in Arabic only, rather than enforcing a municipal code requiring that two thirds of a poster be in Hebrew. In the third case, the ministry of public roads was asked to add Arabic to road signs. According to Spolsky and Shohamy (1999: 119), these three cases have clear political undertones; by asserting their linguistic rights, the Arab Israelis are trying to assert their identity (Spolsky 1994: 228). The court resolved the three cases without the need to resort to the constitution, which states that Arabic is an official language. In the first case, the municipality agreed to add trilingual signs in Hebrew, English and Arabic in its plan over the next years. In the second case, the Arabic signs were permitted, and in the third case, the ministry agreed to make the changes.

It is noteworthy, however, that a large portion of the population is bilingual or multilingual. Among the languages spoken in Israel are different varieties of Arabic from North Africa, Egypt, Syria, Iraq and Yemen. Yiddish is also used among older immigrants from Eastern Europe and ultra-orthodox Jews who refuse to use Modern Hebrew. Among the other languages used are Russian, and the Jewish varieties of Amharic among Ethiopian Jews. To deal with the complicated language situation, the Israeli Ministry of Education supervises 2,500 vocational, agricultural and comprehensive schools, 2,000 with Hebrew as the language of instruction and 500 with Arabic. In the Arabic-language school areas, Hebrew starts from the third grade and continues as a main subject until twelfth grade. A new Hebrew curriculum with emphasis on the communicative aspects of language rather than on literature and culture is being suggested (Amara 2007).

As for the Jewish schools with Hebrew as the language of education, the teaching and learning of Arabic are a problem. Spolsky (1994) contends that this is because of the diglossic situation, which makes it difficult to decide which variety to teach – standard or vernacular – and also because of the attitude towards Arabic.

In June 1986 Yitzhak Navon, then minister of education – and himself fluent in Arabic – created a new policy of teaching Arabic as a compulsory subject in seventh to twelfth grades. SA was to be taught as a compulsory subject, with colloquial as an option, in the fourth year. Until then Arabic, meaning SA, in Jewish schools had been compulsory for three hours a week for grades 7–9, and optional for grades 10–12. Whether or not policies of teaching Arabic are successful depends on the political situation (Spolsky 1994: 232), and according to Spolsky and Shohamy (1999) few students ended up mastering Arabic, for a number of reasons. First, three hours a week is not enough to reach proficiency levels. Second, students were taught SA and not the spoken variety, and they were usually taught in Hebrew. Finally, a negative attitude towards the language does not usually help in the process of learning. For Jews in Israel Arabic is the language of neighbouring countries, a number of which are not on good terms with Israel, and the language of Palestinians in the Gaza Strip and the West Bank as well as Israeli Arabs. The small minority who master Arabic, according to Spolsky and Shohamy (1999: 146), may either work for the intelligence service or become orientalists at the university.

However, Spolsky (1994) speculates that Arabic as a minority language will be maintained among Arabs because of neighbouring countries, although among Jews it remains a marginal language. It may be a spoken vernacular at home among groups of immigrants, or a school subject, but it may remain no more than that. Spolsky contends that bilingualism in Israel is uneven, because while Arabs master Hebrew and even English sometimes, Israelis do not master Arabic.

This uneven bilingualism is significant since it shows that language reflects political power, ideologies and economic factors. In the case of Israel, only Israeli Arabs need to learn Hebrew, since it will help them develop their careers and participate more fully in the country in which they are citizens.

5.5.2.3.2 Language policy in the Palestinian Territories

Amara (2003) posits that the ideal policy in the West Bank and Gaza Strip would be one in which Arabic was maintained for relations with Arab countries, but also the need for both Hebrew and English was considered. Amara posits that since Israel is a reality Palestinians live with, then it is essential for them to learn its language. English will also be used for communication with the western world. Meanwhile, the end of Ottoman rule in Palestine in 1917 brought about changes in all areas, including language (Amara 2003: 319).

In 1948 Israel was established on most of Palestine's land except the West Bank, which was annexed to Jordan, and the Gaza Strip, which became the responsibility of Egypt (Amara 2003: 219). After 1948 the Jordanian curriculum was in force in the West Bank, and the Egyptian curriculum in the Gaza Strip. This was the case even during the Israeli occupation. From 1967 to 1994 Israel occupied these two areas. English then served as a lingua franca between Palestinians who did not know Hebrew and Israelis who spoke no Arabic. English was viewed as a neutral language (Al-Masri 1988). Note that some older Palestinians had learned Hebrew during the British mandate through contacts with Jews. The use of Hebrew in the West Bank and Gaza stopped after 1948, but after the 1967 occupation contact between the two was re-established. Hebrew began to be learned informally. It became the main language of business and trade between Israelis and Palestinians. For example, Palestinian workers in the Israeli labour market learned spoken but not written Hebrew. After the Intifada (the late 1993 Palestinian uprising against Israeli forces), Hebrew was in fact taught in prisons. Knowledge of Hebrew was instrumental and work-related. It was also being taught at private institutions (Amara 2003).

Then when the Palestinian authorities took over both areas, there was a need for an independent Palestinian policy. Arabic became the official language of Palestine, and English was used as a second language because of its status as a global language. It is mainly used in institutions of higher education. The first Palestinian curriculum for general education in 1996 emphasised the status of English. There was a proposal to teach English from first grade in all government and private schools, which is now being implemented. English is taught for approximately three hours in the first years of school.

Amara argues that, although the attitude towards it is negative, Hebrew is needed as a functional language given the political situation (Amara 2003: 218). Hebrew is taught at universities in the Arabic departments, but not spoken Hebrew, only written (Hamed 1995 cited in Amara 2003: 224). The Palestinian workers who experienced life in Israel can speak Hebrew much better than students who studied it at university. There has been a proposal to teach Hebrew as a third language in schools, but it has never been implemented. French was also considered (Amara 2003).

5.5.2.4 Conclusion to British patterns of colonisation

In the previous section, we examined four countries colonised by Britain: Egypt, Sudan, Israel and the Palestinian Territories. These countries suffer from different problems and have different political systems and different language policies and ideologies. In Egypt, perhaps more than any other Arab country, the competition between SA and ECA has been highlighted by a number of intellectuals, some preferring the symbolic significance that the colloquial carries to that carried by SA. In August 2006, a Coptic Christian multimillionaire launched a new, private, Egyptian satellite channel called O-TV. The channel's distinctive feature is its use of ECA for all domains, even in news broadcasts, a domain associated exclusively with SA. As was expected, there were Egyptians who were in favour of the idea of using ECA in the news and claimed that this is the only channel that highlights Egypt's distinct identity. However, the fact that the channel is owned by a Coptic Christian and uses ECA met with scepticism from others. Blogs started discussing the pros and cons of using ECA in the news for the first time in Egypt. The Muslim Brotherhood website accused the channel of aiming at an audience of rich Egyptian youth and of encouraging the breakdown of language in Egypt. Using ECA in the news was regarded as a conspiracy, and an impractical one at that, since it is hard to read the news in colloquial, almost needing more effort than to read it in SA. (Kamal 2008)[18]. It is clear that the issue of ECA versus SA in Egypt is far from resolved.

The problem in Egypt that may have a direct effect on SA is the clear gap between the elite and the masses (Table 5.5). The elite send their children to private schools, in which they learn English, French or German, and the masses can afford only state schools, in which Arabic is the main language of instruction. With Egypt now moving into a capitalist system and privatising most of the companies owned by the government, knowledge of SA is downplayed and knowledge of English specifically is becoming a must. Since the government is basically failing to provide any jobs, the private sector will set the rules. Due to privatisation, a whole generation who were working for the

Table 5.5 Weekly hours/periods per language in primary and secondary education: Egypt, Sudan and Palestinian Territories

Year	Egypt[a]							Sudan[b]				Palestinian Territories[c]			
	Primary education (6 yrs)		Middle school (3 yrs)		Secondary school (3 yrs)			Basic education (8 yrs)		Secondary education (3 yrs)		Basic education (10 yrs)		Secondary education (2 yrs)	
	Ara[d]	FL1	Ara	FL1	Ara	FL1	FL2	Ara	Eng	Ara	Eng	Ara	Eng	Ara	Eng
1	12	3	7	5	6	6	3	10	–	4	4	8	3	5	5
2	12	3	7	5	4–8	4–8	3	9	–	4	4	8	3	5	5
3	12	3	7	5	4–8	4–8	3	9	–	4	4	8	3		
4	11	3						9	–			8	3		
5	11	3						9	3			7	4		
6	11	3						9	3			7	4		
7								9	7			7	4		
8								9	7			7	4		
9												7	4		
10												5	4		

Notes:
[a] UNESCO (2007). Numbers represen periods of 45 minutes.
[b] UNESCO (2007).Numbers represent periods of 40 minutes. The informal use of the spoken languages in rural areas (P.000) is not shown.
[c] Palestinian National Authority, Ministry of Education (1998).
[d] Ara=Arabic; FL1=First foreign language; FL2=Second foreign language; Eng=English.

government were forced into early retirement by the private companies that bought the companies where they used to work, with the result that a new generation will take over for which SA does not play a major role. A new phenomenon in Egypt is the great number of private universities that are opening up beside the American University in Cairo, and the increase in private schools that are not supervised by the Egyptian Ministry of Education and in which SA is basically not taught at all. Thus, there is a new generation of Egyptians who are highly educated and who speak ECA but who are illiterate in SA because in their private schools SA is not taught at all. This seems the most pressing problem for Egypt today.

Sudan, on the other hand, suffers from an ethnic, religious and political conflict that is reflected linguistically in the southerners' opposition to Arabic. The conflict in Sudan is mainly about distribution of resources and power, but also about projection of identity, and whether the identity of Sudan is that of an Arab country or an African one, a Muslim country or a Christian/multireligious one. While Sharkey (2008: 21–2) accuses the Sudanese government of imposing an Arab identity on Sudan only to become a member of the Arab League and get the help of Gulf countries, northern Sudanese intellectuals emphasise the Arab origin of Sudan.

In Israel and the Palestinian Territories, the status of Arabic is a reflection of an ongoing political conflict whose outcome, as Spolsky and Shohamy posit (1999), will play the major role in determining the direction of language policies there. Currently, according to Spolsky (2004), Arabic is regarded by Israeli Jews either as the language of the enemy, or as the language of neighbouring countries that are not all at peace with Israel. And yet, it is also the language of the biggest minority group in Israel, who interact with and participate in different domains of life in Israel. As for the Palestinian Territories, Arabic is the language that connects them to their past and to their neighbours.

In all the above discussion, Britain's linguistic role was not prominent. Britain's political one was. Nevertheless, English has gained a status in all the countries discussed above. English managed to forge its own role, as the language of the elite in Egypt, as the neutral lingua franca for Israelis and Palestinians, and as the safe haven for southern Sudanese instead of Arabic. Unlike France, Britain did not try to establish its language in the colonies discussed above: English established itself. This statement will be discussed in detail in section 5.10.

5.6 LANGUAGE POLICIES IN OTHER PARTS OF THE ARAB WORLD

In section 5.5, I examined the relation between language ideology and language policies in North African countries, Syria, Lebanon, Egypt, Sudan, Israel and the Palestinian Territories. Libya, although a North African country, is different from the countries we have analysed. It was occupied by Italy in 1911. At the time, Italy tried to impose Italian as the language of instruction in schools, but this policy was not successful for a number of reasons. First, there was strong local resistance most of the time. Thus there was no time for people to assimilate and learn the language. In addition, few Libyans attended the schools where Italian was the language of instruction. In fact, at that time few Libyans attended schools of any kind. After the 1969 revolution, a strong Arabisation policy began (Pereira 2007). SA became the language of instruction at all educational levels and at universities for humanities subjects. Yet English is still taught in schools and used at universities in science and technology subjects, in addition to SA (Spolsky 2004).

In the Gulf countries, the present linguistic situation is critical. Due to immigration to these oil countries, a vast number of language minorities exist. A great number of people in these countries are multilingual as a result of significant but marginalised foreign minorities. For example, in Bahrain, one third of the population of 650,000 is made up of foreigners. Although Arabic is the official language, there are large minority groups, like the Persians. Thus there are 50,000 speakers of Persian, 20,000 speakers of Philippine languages, and 18,000 speakers of Urdu. Kuwait has a population of 2 million, over half of whom are foreigners. Oman has a population of 2,400,000, a high proportion of which is again made up of foreign workers. In 2001, the population of Saudi Arabia was 22.7 million, 5.3 million of whom were non-nationals. Although there is a policy of indigenisation in labour, foreigners still constitute a large group in these countries (Spolsky 2004: 141).

One cannot speculate how and whether language policies in these countries will change because of the significant minorities present in them. But since we have shown that it is language contact and interaction that lead to the preservation and learning of a language, then one can predict that these countries will have to take account of their minorities, who are usually there to stay, in spite the fact that they may be contract workers. My gut feeling is that English, in addition to Pidgin Arabic. will serve as a lingua franca in these countries and may act as an instrumental language, and as such will over time gain more status than Arabic, whether standard or colloquial.

In the United Arab Emirates (UAE), the government has decided to implement a law for the protection of Arabic, SA. When the deputy minister of culture, Bilāl Budūr, was asked by journalists how an Arab country produces a law to protect its own language, he replied that Arabs have become a minority in the UAE, in which at least ten languages are spoken, Arabic is the fourth language spoken at the moment, and English is the main lingua franca. Of the population of the UAE, 65 per cent are non-Arab foreigners; the indigenous population makes up only 15 per cent. Sharjah, the capital, has already imposed a law that requires all government offices to use Arabic for their oral and written transactions. The rest of the Emirates is still in the process of forming a similar law (Maḥāmidīyah 2007).

5.7 THE ROLE OF LANGUAGE ACADEMIES IN THE ARAB WORLD

There are at least five language academies in the Arab world: the Arab Academy of Damascus, established in 1919; the Arabic Language Academy in Cairo, established in 1932; the Iraqi Academy, established in 1947; the Arabic Language Academy of Jordan, established in 1976, and the Arabic Language Academy in Libya and in Algeria, which is not functioning at the moment.

The idea of creating an Arabic language academy sprang up first in Syria and then in Egypt at the beginning of the twentieth century and was inspired by the French Academy, which was founded in 1635 with the goal of prescribing rules for the French language in order to purify it and make it capable of treating the arts and sciences. Currently the aim of the French Academy is still to guard the French language, by producing standardised grammars and dictionaries (Spolsky 2004: 64).

The main purposes of all the Arabic academies are the preservation of the Arabic language and the development of Arabic to meet the needs of modern society in all domains of human knowledge (Sawaie 1986: 57, 2006). The academies are also responsible for the creation and standardisation of scientific terms (cf. Khalīfa 1977) and the Arabisation of terms from other languages. Examples of this from the Arabic language academy in Cairo are the word for telephone, which is either *ha:tif* or *tilifo:n*, and the word for bank, which is either *bank* or *maṣraf* (Sawaie 1986).

Each academy focuses on a different aspect in the process of preserving Arabic, meaning SA, and each academy changes its focus over the years. The academy of Damascus started with the following goals (Sawaie 2006: 635):

1. the simplification of literary work to make it accessible to the public
2. the establishment of a national public library
3. the coinage of technical and scientific terms
4. the publication of an Arabic journal
5. support for Arabic research and publications.

In 2001 the academy realised the need to unify technical terms across the Arab world and to find methods of simplifying SA grammar. The academy also aimed at encouraging Syrians and Arabs more generally to use SA in all domains of life, and at finding means and ways to curb the spread of dialects (Sawaie 2006). This last goal of the academy of Damascus is not shared as enthusiastically by the other academies. Although the ideology comes up in intellectual arguments in Egypt from time to time, it is not as dominant as it is in Syria, for political reasons (see discussion of Syria above).

The Cairo academy has the following goals (Sawaie 2006: 635):

1. the maintenance of Arabic (SA) by making sure it has new terminology for science and technology
2. the editing of classical texts and manuscripts
3. the compilation of dictionaries and the publishing of a journal.

Note that currently membership in the Cairo academy is not restricted to Egyptians or even Arabs but is open to all scholars who excel in maintaining SA (Sawaie 2006).

The academies in Damascus and Iraq have been more concerned with aspects of historical linguistics and literature, while the academy in Cairo has been concerned with developing materials in SA morphology, grammar and coinage of scientific and technological terms. All the academies have produced a yearly journal, although this has not always been regular because of economic and political difficulties (Sawaie 2006).

The academies base their words on *qiyās* 'analogical derivation', which is the formation of words according to existing word patterns. This enables the academies to produce new terminology and new words from existing roots. For example, one of the forms approved by Cairo Academy in the 1930s was *fiʕa:la*, which denotes professions like *ṭiba:ʕah* 'printing', *jira:ḥah* 'surgery' etc. Dictionaries are then produced with the new forms

One problem with all these academies is that there is no guarantee that writers in particular and society in general will follow their recommendations, since the academies lack any authority. In March 2007 the chair of the Cairo Academy, Fārūq Shūshah, stated in *Akhbār al-Adab*, the literary magazine of Egypt, that the role of the academy was diminishing because of its lack of authority. He proposed that the recommendations of the academy should be imposed on all mass media in Egypt and should be declared compulsory by them. Whether this is possible or not is another question.

Another problem is the lack of coordination of activities between the different academies. Thus, each academy may coin a different term for the same concept. An example of this lack of coordination is the fact that during the political unity between Syria and Egypt, 1958–61, the two countries' academies were united, but when the political unity broke up, the academies also broke up. Again, politics plays a major role in forming policies and influencing language. Members of the academies were aware of this problem; a call for the unification of all academies was established early on, in 1956, and again in 1971 when coordination between the academies in Egypt, Syria and Iraq was more prominent. In 1977 the Jordanian academy followed suit. Now two members of each academy meet, headed by a president, to standardise forms and arrange conferences. For example, a conference on SA legal terminology took place in Damascus in 1972, one on SA oil terminology in Baghdad in 1973, and another on SA Arabic medical terminology in Tunis in 1992. Currently the academies are still suffering from political disagreement and lack of resources and financial support. After the last war in Iraq (beginning in 2003), it is still not clear whether the academy in Iraq will function again (cf. Sawaie 2006).

5.8 SA, POLITICS AND THE ACHING NATION: A CASE STUDY

Throughout this chapter the relation between SA and politics has been examined. In this section I give a current example of the symbolic role of SA in defining a nation and serving political aims. I contrast two interviews with two Arab leaders: the Syrian president Bashshār al-Asad and his Yemeni counterpart ʿAlī ʿAbd Allāh Ṣāliḥ. The markedness theory as developed by Myers-Scotton (1998, 2006) will be used to explain the data, as well as the concept of indexicality as explained by Woolard (2004).

The first example I discuss is an extract from an interview held with the current president of Syria immediately after the Hezbollah–Israel war that took place in Lebanon in summer 2006 (broadcast on Al-Jazeera). The role of Syria in supporting Hezbollah was discussed, but more importantly so was the role of Iran in the war. Iran is not an Arab country and yet it has a very close relationship with Syria, which at the moment is one of the ardent believers in the Arab nation and the slogan 'one nation, one language', which was nearly dead after the death of the Egyptian president Nasser in 1970[19]. The Syrian president, as was said earlier, is referred to in the Syrian media as 'the leader of the Arabs'. Syria has always emphasised the importance of SA in both its schools and universities. Given that there are still both Christians and Jews in Syria beside Muslims, it is indeed language that can be the unifying factor: Syria has only 70 per cent Sunni Muslims, 12 per cent Christians (mostly Orthodox and Greek Catholic), and 18 per cent other minority groups including Jews and Druze. This again helps us understand why Syrian intellectuals emphasise SA so much and have the ambition of SA replacing the colloquial one day. Arabic is the unifying factor in a country that does not emphasise its religious identity and has a political system that tends towards socialism (see section 5.5.1.2 above on Syria).

The president of Syria, whether in interviews or speeches, speaks in SA, unlike the president of Egypt, who switches between SA and ECA. Example (1) below is crucial not only because of the topic discussed, but also because the president, when interviewed by an Egyptian journalist who switches throughout the interview between SA and ECA, sticks to SA only. By doing so, as will become clear below, he lays claims to all the authoritative powers of SA and confirms his support for the Arab nation even if collaboration with Iran is necessary. Once more, SA becomes a symbol for the identity of Syria and the nation in general.

(1) **Interviewer:** *ʔayna ʔi:ra:n min ha:za iʃ-ʃarq il-ʔawṣaṭ ig-gadi:d// ʃarq ʔawṣaṭ gadi:d/ il-la:ʕib ir-raʔi:si fi:h/ amri:ka w- ʔisraʔi:l/ zayyi ma kunna bi-nʔu:l/ ʔam il-la:ʕib ir-raʔi:si fi:h ʔi:ra:n/ ʔam il-ʕarab//*
'What is the role of Iran in this new Middle East? Who is the main player in this new Middle East? Is it the USA and Israel as you mentioned? Or is it Iran? Or is it the Arabs?'

The question asked by the Egyptian journalist is not in SA. He uses ECA, as in *bi-nʔu:l*, which has the ECA aspectual marker *b-* as well as the ECA glottal stop rather than the SA *q*. The reply of the president, who is not reading, is in fact in SA with case and mood markings. He also uses SA negation, demonstratives and syntactic structures.

The unmarked code in this interview is established by the interviewer as a mixed code of both SA and ECA. This is usually the code used in interviews in the media by interviewees who are not usually reading, even if the interviewer uses SA. When the president replies in a specially elevated variety of SA that many, including the journalist, would not be able to produce extemporaneously, he is in a sense appealing to all the connotations of SA, especially the legitimacy associated with it. SA is then a marked choice that has an effect on the audience (on markedness, see Chapter 2, section 5.2.1). Applying the indexicality concept as developed by Woolard (2004) to this interview, we find that each code presupposes and is associated with a social context: a mixture of SA and a colloquial by the interviewee is associated with political interviews, while SA is associated with public political speeches. If SA is then used in a different context, such as in a political interview, the speaker who uses it lays claim to all the indexes of SA, including the authoritative ones.

(2) **President:** *ma yuhimmuni huwa l-ʕarab/ tabʕan ʔisraʔi:l la:ʕib raʔi:si min xila:l ʕudwa:n/ il-wulaya:t il-muttaḥida la:ʕib raʔi:si/ min xila:l mawqiʕha ka quwwa ʕuẓma:/ wa min xila:l daʕmaha al-ġe:r maḥdu:d l-israʔi:l/ amma bi-nisba l-ʔi:ra:n fa hiya dawla fi haðihi al-manṭiqa munðu l-ʔazal/ munðu t-ta:ri:x// la:kin ʔana ʔuri:du ʔan ʔaqu:la/ ʔin ka:nat ʔi:ran la:ʕib raʔi:si/ al-muhimm/ ʔan nara ʔannana al-ġa:ʔib ar-raʔi:si ka-ʕarab/ ʕan as-sa:ḥa as-siya:siyya fi manṭiqatina/ ha:ðihi hiya an-nuqṭa allati yajib ʔan nara:ha// ʔahamm/ min ʔan nuḍi:ʕ waqtana fil ḥadi:θi/ ʔan ʔi:ra:n talʕab dawr yajib ʔan yakbur aw yaṣġur/*
'I am interested in the Arabs. Of course Israel is a crucial player because of its attacks as an enemy. The USA is a crucial player because of its role as a super-power and its unlimited support for Israel. As for Iran,

it has been a country in this region for a long time, since the beginning of history. But I want to mention that if Iran is the main player we have to understand that we as Arabs are the main absentee in the political arena in our region. This is the point that we have to understand. This is more important than wasting our time wondering whether the role of Iran should be less or more.'

When declaring that his main interest is the Arabs, it is SA that the president uses. For whatever role Iran plays, it is Arabs who are crucial to him and whom, at least in this public statement, he expresses his concern about. The contrast between him and the announcer is salient to the audience.

Note the sentence in example (3), in which the announcer uses the glottal stop and ECA structure:

(3) *zayyi* *ma* *kunna* ***bi-nʔu:l***
like that be-2pl-perf asp-2pl-say
'as you mentioned'

Now contrast example (3) with example (4), in which the president uses the SA *q:*

(4) *la:kin* *ʔana* *ʔuri:du* *ʔan* ***ʔaqu:la***
But I 1sg-want-ind that 1sg-say-sub
'But I want to mention that'

The Syrian president uses mood marking, as in:

(5) *ʔana* *ʔuri:du* *ʔan* *ʔaqu:la*
I 1sg-want-ind that 1sg-say-sub
'I want to mention'

He also uses case marking as in:

(6) *fil- ḥadi:θi*
in-det-talk-gen
'in wondering (speaking about)'

However, the agenda of the Syrian president is very different from that of the Yemeni one, for example. While Syria derives its power from Nasser's belief, mentioned earlier, that the Arab world is united linguistically, the Yemeni president derives his legitimacy partially from his claim that Yemen, unlike its Gulf neighbours, is a democratic country. The president of Yemen projects an identity of a democratic ruler and his words are aimed at a non-

Yemeni audience first and foremost. In a similar context, the Yemeni president, unlike the Syrian one, uses a number of features from his dialect and does not attempt to stick to SA.

Example (7) is taken from an interview with the Yemeni president that took place in 2007 (on Al-Jazeera). The interviewer uses SA only and is formal in addressing the president; he addresses him with the 'you' plural, for example, much as one would do in French or German. The issue for discussion is the corruption that is prevalent in Yemen and whether or not the president has taken measures to curb it. The fact that the interviewer uses SA only is not a surprise, since interviewers usually prepare their questions beforehand and can read them from a piece of paper as well. This interviewer has a piece of paper to read from. However, as was said earlier, use of both SA and a colloquial by the interviewee, who is not supposed to have prepared the answers and who is not reading from a piece of paper, is common in political interviews. By using a mixture of SA and colloquial Yemeni, the president is using an unmarked variety rather than a marked one. He, unlike the Syrian president, is not laying claims to the indexes of SA.

(7) **Interviewer:** *sa-ʔuʕṭi:k baʕḍ al-amθila min da:xil al-ḥizb al-ḥa:kim nafsu/ ʕala ma yabdu/ huna:k ʔazma fi l-balad/ ḥatta al-ḥizb al-ḥa:kim yuʕtabar guzʔ min al-ʔazma/*
'I will give you some examples of personnel in the ruling party itself. It seems there is a crisis in the country. Even the ruling party is considered part of the problem.'
President: *naḥnu naʕtadd inni ha:ða al-balad balad dimugra:ṭi:/ wa huwa ʃamʕatun muḍi:ʔa fi l-manṭiga/ hada maʕru:f/ wi ʔayyi balad dimugra:ṭi/ il-go:l fi:ha akθar mimma huwa ḥagi:ga/ il-go:l fi:ha/ aw al-ḥakyi fi:ha ʕakθar mimma hiya ḥagi:gi/ le:ʃ/ liʔanni fi:ha dimugraṭiyya/ ʔiða balad ma-fi:ha dimugra:ṭiyya/ ma ḥada yigdarr yiḥki: ʕan il-fasa:d/*
'We appreciate the fact that this country is a democratic one. It is a beacon of light in the region. This is a known fact. In any democratic country, some of what is being said is untrue. Some talk or some of the gossip is beyond the truthful. Why? Because there is democracy. If there is a country that does not have democracy, no one can speak about corruption.'
Interviewer: *bil-ḍabṭ*
'Exactly.'
President: *ma ḥada yigdar yiḥki: ʕan il-fasa:d/*
'No one can speak about corruption.'
Interviewer: *ṣaḥi:ḥ*
'True.'
President: *ʔiḥna . . . / ʕadad min il-muxa:lifi:n da:xil il-taḥgi:ga:t/ wi fil niya:ba il- ʕa:mma/ niya:bit il-ʔamwa:l il-ʕa:mma/ ṭayyib*

> *ma-tigdar-ʃi tijarrimhum aw tiʕlin ʕanhum/ ʔila fi ḍo:ʔ ma yagirrah il-gaḍa:ʔ// ma-tigdir-ʃ/ lakin ʕadad min al-murtakibi:n da:xil il-niya:ba bil-ʕaʃara:t aw il-ʕiʃrina:t min muxtalaf muʔassasa:t id-dawla/ ha:da waḥdih/.*
> 'We . . . /A number of the perpetrators are under investigation, and before the general prosecutor, and the state finance bureau. Well, you cannot hold them accountable, or report on them, except in the light of that which the courts establish. You cannot, but some of the perpetrators are before the general prosecutor, tens, twenties of them from all the different institutions of the state. That is one.'

The Yemeni president, unlike the Syrian one, uses only colloquial negation, as in *ma-tigdir-ʃ* 'you cannot' (repeated), to defend himself against the interviewer's accusations of corruption in Yemen. The use of colloquial negation may be to add emphasis to the denial by the president of the existence of such corruption. The use of colloquial morpho-syntactic features is highlighted by the use of SA morpho-syntactic features by the interviewer, such as the use of the *sa-* future marker with the SA verb *sa-ʔuʕṭi:k* 'I will give you'. Phonologically, the president consistently uses the *g* realisation of the *q* variable even in words like *dimugra:ṭiyya* 'democracy', which is now used widely with the *q*, and does not occur with a glottal stop in countries that use a glottal stop instead of the *q*, like Egypt and Syria. He even starts the last section of (7) with the colloquial pronoun *ʔiḥna* 'we', rather than the standard one, *naḥnu*.

The use of SA by the Syrian president is in line with the political and ideological agenda of Syria. It comes as no surprise that Syria is very keen on promoting SA in schools and universities while Yemen does not show the same enthusiasm. An increasing number of private schools in Yemen now teach science and maths in English rather than Arabic. The emphasis on SA as a unifying factor is waning in Yemen. In fact, the president in this interview is to a great extent differentiating himself from his neighbouring Arab countries that are not democratic in nature. I am not implying that SA is not democratic; what I am trying to imply is that the emphasis by the president in that interview is not on the unity of the nation that speaks one language, but rather on distinguishing himself from the rest of the nation which has a different political system. It would be surprising if he used SA as the Syrian president did, since the topic is not 'we Arabs', but rather how 'we Yemenis' are democratic. The expected unmarked choice is what the president of Yemen uses: a mixture of SA and colloquial.

It is worth mentioning that although the topic of discussion is different, the setting of both interviews is similar.

To conclude this section, I have contrasted the two presidents to show that the political undertones of language choice are not to be ignored. While considering language policies in the Arab world, one has to also consider the political agenda of different countries. In the Arab world there may be an underlying ideology that 'we speak one language', but within the nation as such there are different political systems and different political ideologies, which are sometimes reflected in language choice.

5.9 LINGUISTIC RIGHTS AND POLITICAL RIGHTS

Some linguists (Fishman 1967; Fishman et al., 1968; more recently Spolsky 2004: 58) distinguish three 'types' of nations. The first is that of, monolingual mono-ethnic and ethno-linguistically homogeneous nations with insignificant minorities. This type is now rare, although Lambert (1999) lists Japan as belonging to it. The problem with deciding whether a community is mono-ethnic or not lies in the decision whether a minority is significant or not – a decision that is surely subjective, and potentially politically motivated. For example, Berbers in Tunisia represent only 1 per cent of the population, and may be considered by some as a non-significant minority, and by others as a significant one.

The second type of nation in this scheme is that of 'dyadic' or 'triadic' nations, in which two or three ethno-linguistic groups live side by side and share almost equal linguistic power, in Belgium, Switzerland and Canada. The third type of nation is the 'mosaic' or multi-ethnic nation in which more than three linguistic groups exist. Nigeria and India are examples of this type. In fact, more than half the countries of the world have five or more ethnic groups. However, usually, as Grin (2005: 449) suggests, ethnically, culturally or linguistically different groups compete over both material and symbolic resources within a given social, economic and political sphere. One of the most thorny issues is linguistic rights and obtaining an official status for a language.

The Declaration on Cultural Diversity of UNESCO's general conference, which took place in Paris on 2 November 2001, states the following:

> All persons should therefore be able to express themselves and to create and disseminate their work in the language of their choice, and particularly in their mother tongue; all persons should be entitled to quality education and training that fully respect their cultural identity; and all persons should be able to participate in the cultural life of their choice and conduct their own cultural practices, subject to respect for human rights and fundamental freedom[20].

The actions that are recommended to achieve equal linguistic rights for everyone include protecting the linguistic heritage of different communities by encouraging and supporting linguistic diversity.

Having the right to use and express oneself in one's mother tongue is in fact a moral right, but a costly one. As Grin posits, if a language policy is fair, it should include all languages of the major minority groups, and for this to happen, 'some members of society are likely to lose, while others win from the policy, and even if all win, some will win more than others' (Grin 2005: 455). For example, the estimated cost of the move from monolingualism to bilingualism in the Basque Country and Guatemala was 4–5 per cent per capita of spending in the system (cf. Grin 2005: 454). The conflict between languages is also a conflict over resources and how they are used, for example whether for better schooling, housing or bilingual education (Grin 2005). This may explain why the results of attitude surveys in which informants, mainly students, in Algeria and Morocco were asked about the usefulness of learning Tamazight, as opposed to SA or French, were usually unfavourable towards Tamazight (Marley 2004; Benrabah 2007a). Most of the areas the informants came from had few if any Berbers, and these informants did not see the need of learning an extra language even if spoken by a significant minority (see sections 5.5.1.1.1 and 5.5.1.1.2 above on Algeria and Morocco). This again throws light on the complexity of the relation between linguistic rights and actual policies.

In addition, as Wright (2004: 243) puts it, for a minority group to impose their language as an official language, or even make sure their language is used in education, they have to have some political weight; otherwise they are completely dependent on the majority of the people to respect their will. However, if the majority has a different ideology altogether then this is not possible. Usually in multi-ethnic nations, there is uneven bilingualism, in which the minority group is bilingual in their language and that of the majority, while the majority group is monolingual. For a minority group to stick to learning only their mother tongue is almost like ostracising themselves. According to Wright, the price to pay in such cases is marginalisation within the state, which is usually too high a price.

Note that for Berbers, for the southern Sudanese and for Israeli Arabs, linguistic tolerance is correlated with political tolerance, cultural participation and more democratic involvement in the government. Language is again a symbol which is impregnated with meanings and connotations. Language reflects identity and values associated with this identity whether these values are moral or practical in nature: values such as equality, power, dominance and progress. However, the ideology of correlating multilingualism and linguistic tolerance with political systems remains a mere ideology with its own exaggerations, misconceptions, assumptions and myths. Linguistic tolerance is never easy to achieve and assigning individuals their linguistic rights is not always straightforward, because of the reasons discussed above. In democratic countries such as Germany, Switzerland, the UK and Austria, to name but a few, minorities are still struggling for their linguistic rights.

Stevenson (2005: 157), when discussing minorities and linguistic rights in Austria, refers to the strict policy that Austria has with regard to the imposition of German. All migrants have to learn German within a certain amount of time, by taking specific courses; if they fail to complete the courses for three years, they have to pay a fine of 200 Euros. However, if they do not complete the courses within four years of entering Austria, their residence permit is not renewed. According to Wright (2004: 199), 'linguistic space is only opening up for territorial rather than migrant groups'. Wright gives the example of a law passed by the Labour government in Britain at the beginning of the new millennium, when there was worry among members of the government that immigrant children were not assimilating well. The new law stated that it was the duty of the immigrant to become competent in English.

Correlating linguistic rights with democracy may seem simplistic at times. It is more viable to correlate linguistic rights with political ideologies and the projection of identity. SA provides the symbol that countries and governments need. It provides the symbol for those Arabs who want to belong – Sudanese, Algerians, Moroccans, Tunisians – and those who want to lead – Egyptians, Syrians, and recently some Gulf countries (cf. Mansfield 2003: 249 for a discussion of Egypt's aspirations to Arab leadership).

Another important aspect of the relation between language policy and politics in the Arab world is diglossia. Diglossia has been accused of hindering Arabisation processes, of causing an increase of illiteracy levels and even of promoting and sustaining non-democratic systems. McFerren (1984: 5) identified diglossia as the cause of the failure of Arabisation in North Africa: 'Diglossia remains the single greatest impediment to Arabisation in the Maghreb.' Similarly, the following is Haeri's conclusion to her book *Sacred language, ordinary people*

> Beyond its use for religious purposes, most Egyptians find speaking and writing in classical Arabic difficult, especially given the dire state of pre-college education. The official language thus acts as an obstacle to their participation in the political realm. There is of course no suggestion here that this is the only reason for absence of democracy in Egypt. But the language situation makes a strong comment on the nature of politics in that country. There seem to be deeply entrenched political interests in having classical Arabic to be the sole official language. (Haeri 2003: 151)

Note first that the call to use colloquial instead of SA in education has been promoted by colonising powers, especially the British (see section 5.5.2.1 above on Egypt). This call is associated in the mind of native speakers in general and intellectuals in particular with colonisation and orientalist thinking. When the call to use the colloquial instead of SA in writing and in school subjects comes from non-Arabs, the scepticism is even greater (cf. Walters 2006b). For Arabs such calls are considered a conspiracy to divide the Arab nation. It is SA that, as Walters puts it, 'is the glue holding the Arab culture and the Arab world together' (2006b: 660). In a hypothetical world, if each Arab country started using its own colloquial in domains in which SA was used, then in fifty years, all Arab countries would be detached from SA, and the common SA literature which was read by all Arabs would be incomprehensible for a young generation trained only in colloquial. Whether Arabs would still understand each other is difficult to predict. Possibly some of them might still be able to communicate since Arabic satellite channels are now broadcast worldwide with all dialects of the Arab world.

An incident that is of relevance to this discussion took place in the year 2000 in France. The French minister of education decided Arabic should be taught as an optional language in some secondary schools, given the great number of North Africans in France (estimated at 5 million). He decided to use the colloquial dialect of Morocco. Nāṣir al-Anṣārī, then director of the Institut du Monde Arabe, sent a letter to the minister of education in France at the time, Jack Lang (minister 2000–2), in which he argued that teaching Moroccan colloquial Arabic instead of SA was not the best option for students. His letter argued the following: teaching Moroccan colloquial Arabic would not be fair to the other North Africans who do not belong to Morocco, such as Algerians and Tunisians, who have a different dialect, and who comprise a large portion of the North African minority. He also mentioned that since there are different dialects within Morocco, it would be problematic to choose one of them, even if it were the prestigious one, for some it might not carry the same prestige. On the other hand, teaching SA would be of more benefit to the students at many levels. First, most of the curriculum of Arab countries for primary education is similar in content. This would connect the minority group to their Arab roots and ensure that the students would have the same ability to understand news bulletins in SA, read literature in SA, and write in SA. Al-Anṣārī asked the French minister to reconsider his decision in the light of all these arguments (al-Anṣārī and al- Anṣārī 2002: 40).

While al-Anṣārī was mild in his reaction, other Egyptian intellectuals were not. Egyptian scholar Yūsuf ʿIzz al-Dīn (2006) accused France of religious intolerance and posited that France's policy with regard to teaching colloquial has a political dimension. Once more he emphasised that SA gathers Arabs together and colloquials divide them.

In addition, there is also the psychological aspect, which is difficult to ignore, Arabs do not consider their colloquial another language. It is still Arabic; whether it is good Arabic or bad Arabic that they speak is a moot point. The fact that they do not consider SA a different language is significant. For example, expressions like *al-lahga al-miṣriyya* 'the Egyptian dialect', or *al-ʕa:mmiyya al-miṣriyya* 'Egyptian colloquial Arabic', are used by intellectuals in Egypt to refer to ECA. However, the average Egyptian when asked what she or he speaks would reply automatically 'Arabic'. Children watch *Sinbad* translated into SA without complaining that the language is incomprehensible.

In addition, using two varieties, a standard one and a colloquial one, in different domains is not uncommon. Germany is also a diglossic community, and even if Hochdeutsch (Standard German) is spoken (while SA is not), some Germans end up writing in Hochdeutsch, though they never speak it. What Haeri (2003: 152) calls a 'highly uneasy relation to the self' that develops in Egyptian children, because they grow up hearing that the language they speak is bad and has no grammar, is in fact an ability to adapt to and later even manipulate the linguistic situation. Egyptian children do not think in terms of bad and good, although this is difficult to prove without psychological data. Children are trained to think in terms of domains: in the same way as there is a public domain and a private domain, there is an SA domain and an ECA domain. Children could think in terms of good or bad if their parents, for example, forbade them to speak colloquial with them or in front of others, which does not happen in any Arab country that I know of, even if Arab scholars say otherwise. Given the cases studied in this book in which the diglossic situation provided an opportunity for speakers to project their identity and leave an effect on their audience, I would consider diglossia, once more, an asset rather than an impediment. As one can deduce from all the discussion above, diglossia is dragged into the conflict without capturing the fact that diglossia itself is linguistic diversity, and by eliminating it we are suppressing a linguistic richness in Arab societies.

5.10 ENGLISH AND GLOBALISATION

When discussing language policies in Egypt, I mentioned the vast influence of the privatisation move that has taken place in the last decade in Egypt, resulting in parents rushing to teach their children English so that they can find jobs in the private sector, since the public sector now fails to provide the same jobs and security it used to. Walters (2006b: 660) discusses the influences of a globalised economy which is based on Anglo-American capitalism, and which has little to do with culture or politics and everything to do with economic/market forces on the linguistic situation in Arab countries.

Universities in which the medium of instruction is English are being established throughout the Arab world, including countries in which French played a major role, such as Morocco and Tunisia. Spolsky (2004: 87) posits that Tunisians are keen on learning English now even more than French. As Shaaban (2006: 703) puts it, 'although the Arabists insist on their children acquiring a good basis in Arabic, and the others insist on a good French education, both parties are espousing English as a language of education in Arab societies'.

When it comes to scholarship and technology, computer manuals, for example, are written in English, and scholars who want to be recognised internationally, even French scholars, have to publish in English. Even France with its systematic language policy cannot stand in the face of the spread of English within French society (Spolsky 2004). Crystal (1987: 358) contended more than twenty years ago that 'over two-thirds of the world's scientists write in English, three quarters of the world's email is written in English, of all the information in the world's electronic retrieval systems 80per cent is stored in English' (see also Luke et al., 2007). Arab societies are following what Fishman calls their 'common sense needs and desires', and these needs are not necessarily related to their colonial past (1997: 639). There are changes affecting the world at large, whether social, political or economic, and related directly to globalisation. Language is just another domain in which these changes are reflected (cf. Bourdieu 2001).

In fact, globalisation makes one wonder once more to what extent official language policies influence language practices. Britain has no constitution that states that English is the official language, and the USA has nothing about language policy in its constitution (cf. Spolsky 2004: 223). Still, English is dominant in both countries and is spreading to the whole world. Note that the fact that the policy is not written does not mean it is not implemented. As was mentioned at the beginning of this chapter, a policy is implemented by members of a particular community even if not written, as long as there is tacit agreement as to what this policy is.

5.11 CONCLUSION

I will conclude this chapter with the following comment by Wright (2004: 225): 'Language is a robust marker of group membership and one that is not easily changed.' Arabs are still struggling with how to define themselves, as a group and/or individually, and how to belong to a group and still project a different identity. Language is at the heart of this struggle. The instinct to belong is what nations are usually built on (Grosby 2005). However, as has been clear throughout this chapter, Arab countries are as different as they are similar and attitudes are as diverse as they are coherent: Arab Muslims, Arab Christians, Syrians, Egyptians, Lebanese, Algerians, to name but a few, are also struggling with the ideology of what they are 'supposed to be' and what they really are. It is not easy to separate the two and perhaps one should not attempt it, since both forge an identity.

The interplay between ethnicity, as in the case of Berbers or southern Sudanese, religion, as in the case of Lebanese Christians and Lebanese

Muslims, politics, as in the case of Arab Israelis, and language is indeed complex and cannot be covered in one chapter. I aim only at giving a snapshot of language policy, ideology, practices and politics.

Most Arab countries except Iraq, where Kurdish had been acknowledged regionally for decades, have Arabic and only SA as their official language. This does not reflect the linguistic reality, but may have many political, ideological and symbolic undertones.

In this chapter I have discussed language policies in general and then examined the situation in some Arab countries in detail (sections 5.2–5.5). One of the factors essential to language policies is language contact. Fishman (1997: 194) argues that: 'endangered languages become such because of the lack of informal inter-generational transmission and informal daily life support, not because they are not being taught in schools'. If we examine the language planning process used by the caliph ʿAbd al-Malik in the first centuries of Islam[21], we find that one of the reasons why Arabic spread so fast, replacing other languages, is that Arabs were in contact with the people they conquered; they built cities and settled in them. This is in effect urbanisation. Also, economic factors are important. Arabs at the time were in control of the economy of these countries. They eventually became advanced scientifically and economically. Wright (2004: 113) discusses how Arabic was used as a lingua franca to understand the scientific concepts developed in the age of the caliphates. Scholars from non-Arabic-speaking countries had to learn Arabic. Gill (1999) mentions that the success of a language is dependent on economic factors as well as the prestige associated with the language. At present, English, French, Spanish and to a lesser extent German are important for people in the Arab world. The status of English is rising fast, especially in countries where tourism provides a substantial amount of hard currency, such as Egypt, Morocco and Tunisia.

As for education in the Arab world, the discrepancy between high school and university level in Arab countries is a big problem. In many countries, especially North African ones, education in public high schools is mainly in Arabic, but science faculties use French as the medium of instruction. This can be an impediment to students. Arab countries have to face this problem one day. Either Arabic has to catch up and be used more in science, which is not an easy task, or English and French will remain the languages of the elite and the educated in Arab countries. English has been referred to as 'a killer language' (cf. Fishman 2002). Fishman thinks this is not a precise term, since it is people who give the language the status it has. If indeed English is a killer language, then where does that leave SA, a language that is not even spoken by anyone as a vernacular? Why did SA survive and confront colonisation, modern technology and the widespread use of English?

Indeed, religion has a vast role to play in the survival of SA. But there is also the romantic belief among users of Arabic and Muslims in the appeal and superiority of their language, as is evident in the poem cited at the beginning of this chapter. Schiffman (1996: 69) points to the perceived 'sacredness of Arabic', while the entry for 'Koran' in the *Concise encyclopedia of Islam* summarises the traditional Muslim position neatly:

> Muslims consider the Koran to be holy scripture only in the original Arabic of its revelation. The Koran, while it may be translated, is only ritually valid in Arabic. This is connected with the notion of Arabic as a 'sacred'. Language itself is sacred, because of its miraculous power to communicate and to externalise thought. (Glassé 1989: 46)

For Muslims words are powerful; they are divine. Indeed, to fight a curse one has to use words, Arabic words mainly from the Qur'an. The *Encyclopedia* (Glassé 1989: 46) adds that Arabic, though 'originally a desert nomadic dialect, has maintained a fresh directness that makes it a more suitable vehicle than many others'. The writer attributes this freshness to the relationship between words and their roots, and to the Qur'an's use of simple statements (cf. Wright 2004: 69). The *Concise encyclopedia of Islam* further notes that:

> Simple statements, which are the rule in the Koran, open, under the right conditions of receptivity, into astonishing and vast horizons; the world is reduced to ripples in consciousness. These and other qualities make Arabic an incomparable medium for dialogue between man and God in prayer. (Glassé 1989: 47)

Wright argues that these attitudes towards Arabic (SA) affect language policy-making in the Arab world and the Islamic world in general (2004: 70). She contends that all language policies are culturally specific. To a great extent this is true, although again, it is difficult to define the term 'culture'. Culture in this sense is the shared historical and geographical background of a group of people who also have the same set of values and beliefs. These beliefs may or may not be religious ones.

The call to save MSA is still heard in all parts of the Arab world. In 2007 Dr Yūsuf ʿIzz al-Dīn, a renowned professor and scholar, as was mentioned earlier, said in the Egyptian literary magazine *Akhbār al-Adab* (Nūr 2007) that it is our duty as Arabs and patriots to confront the conspiracy against us to weaken SA. His words echo words spoken a century ago, but perhaps the mission to preserve SA and the struggle to save it are just at their onset.

NOTES

1. Wright (2004: 224) discusses how communities suffering from colonisation, or who have suffered from colonisation, consider language an 'identity marker'.

2. Suleiman (1999: 11) tries to examine how 'political conflict in the Middle East, whether inter-ethnic or inter-nation, is related to language policies'.
3. Around the second half of the twentieth century, when most of the Arab countries gained their independence, the idea of the Arab nation was at its zenith and Nasser, the then president of Egypt, was hailed as the leader of Arabs and of Arab unity (Haag 2003).
4. In the documentary film *Four Egyptian Women* (1996), a female Egyptian professor who was then about 50 years old claimed that she only spoke French to her family and Arabic to the servants, and when she read the Qur'an for the first time, it was in French and not Arabic. It is also common for rich families in Egypt now to address their children in English and have nannies who only speak English at home.
5. Figures on minority are given only for some countries, as the degree of importance of these groups differs from one country to another.
6. Note that in 1830 the Jewish community of Algeria comprised some 25,000 persons, most of whom were quite poor (see Stora 2001).
7. President Boumedienne ruled for three decades of relative peace, although his regime was authoritarian. The diversity within Algeria was hidden under the surface and only came out again in 1989 (Stora 2001).
8. From 1989, new political movements became strong nationalist, liberal, radical, Islamist and even communist. In 1992, the military forces intervened to end an election that would have been won by opposition Islamists of the Front Islamique du Salut (FIS). Politicians do not agree as to whether it would have been better to let democracy take its course or to intervene (cf. Stora 2001).
9. Source: Morocco, Ministry of Justice, *Constitution*, http://www.justice.gov.ma/fr/legislation/legislation.aspx?ty=1&id_l= ; last accessed 30 October 2008.
10. In fact, apart from Iraq, where Kurdish is acknowledged regionally and has been for a long time, no country acknowledges Kurdish. Iraq acknowledges Kurdish in the Kurdish region; in Iraq, street names are written in both languages, for example. This is not the case in other countries such as Syria, Armenia or Turkey (Spolsky 2004).
11. Nasser with his Free Officers (army officers) started their bloodless coup on 26 July, 1952 to get rid of the monarchy and the British presence in Egypt. The coup was welcomed by a great number of Egyptians who regarded it as a new beginning and an end to a corrupt era. King Farouk was ordered to abdicate in favour of his son and to leave Egypt. For a short time after, his son was named king, before Egypt was declared a republic in 1953 (cf. Haag 2005).
12. Nasser is described by Mansfield (2003: 278) as 'an Egyptian who developed a genuine belief in the movement to unite the Arabs, of which he saw Egypt as the natural leader'.
13. This was not really implemented by students. However, the ideology is very similar to that proposed by Māzin al-Mubarāk (p. 000).
14. This status that SA obtained at that time may explain why Ferguson, in his analysis of diglossia (1972 [1959]), mentioned that SA is the language used in mosque sermons, university lectures and political speeches. This is not the case today, but since his article was first published in 1959, it may reflect the sentiment of the time. In addition, Badawi's levels may also reflect the attitude of Egyptians at the time (see Chapter 1 above for his classifications).
15. See Chart 5.1 to understand why Haeri was classifying speakers in this way.
16. See Ethnologue, 'Sudan', http://www.ethnologue.com/show_country.asp?name=sd, last accessed 30 October 2008.
17. See University of Khartoum website, http://www.uofk.edu/index.php?id=825, last accessed 30 October 2008. 'The second phase of Arabicization was formally started in 1991. Arabic replaced English as medium of instruction in all Sudanese Universities and higher institutions of learning.'

18. See http://www.ikhwanonline.com/Article.asp?ArtID=39000&SecID=294, last accessed 1 November 2008.
19. Part of the Nasserist ideology was the issue of who would lead the Arab world.
20. See UNESCO, http://unesdoc.unesco.org/images/0012/001271/127160m.pdf; last accessed 11 Novermber 2008.
21. See Versteegh (2001) for a discussion of the process of Arabisation at the time of Islamic conquests.

General conclusion

In this book, I have first shed light on the diglossic situation and the main groups of dialects in the Arab world. It was established at the beginning that the distinctions made by linguists between CA, MSA and the different vernaculars are not necessarily accepted by native speakers and in some cases not even trusted, as was shown in Chapter 5, in which there were native speakers who were sceptical about linguists and politicians, especially non-Arab ones, discussing their language and linguistic situation. The relation between language and ideology is very much in the forefront of the minds of native speakers. Arabic, in its entirety, is a major means by which people in the Arab world can endow themselves with a sense of belonging and manifest different facets of their identity.

When discussing the structural constraints and discourse functions of both diglossic switching and code-switching, it was apparent that the diglossic situation is more complex than the bilingual one, and that theories that can be applied neatly to bilingual code-switching are challenged by diglossia. In fact, when discussing code-switching, diglossic switching was also examined. When concentrating on quantitative variationist studies in the Arab world, levelling and diglossia were still relevant. MSA phonological variables like the *q* were juxtaposed with dialectal ones in Egypt, Bahrain and Jordan, to name but a few. Diglossic switching was found to have a discourse function for educated women in talk shows. It was also seen as a means of highlighting political affiliations and agendas in the case of the interviews with the Syrian and Yemeni presidents analysed in Chapter 5. Diglossia thus remains in the weft and warp of any sociolinguistic study in the Arab world. Studies that concentrate on dialects rather than MSA still refer to the diglossic situation and still compare and contrast MSA variables with dialectal ones. It is diglossia, or rather the conscious obsession with diglossia by native speakers of Arabic as well as linguists working on Arabic, which distinguishes the Arab world from the western one and distinguishes studies conducted about the Arab world from their western counterparts.

Linguists working on the Arab world realised that a blind application of methods and theories constructed for the west would not work for the different Arab countries. However, the methods of collecting data used in the west were to a great extent adhered to by linguists working on the Arab world. The findings were indeed different in a number of ways. First, the dynamics of change and variation in the Arab world are different because of the way communities are structured and maintained. Independent variables such as religion, ethnicity and class tend to be defined differently in relation to the Arab world. One essential factor that plays a major role in the study of variation and change in the Arab world is urbanisation, especially in countries such as Libya, Oman and Bahrain where urbanisation is both recent and rapid.

The interaction between gender and other independent factors is also examined in this book. Gender is not necessarily the main defining factor that influences change and variation. In the Arab world, men and women together form and are formed by a community, which in turn is shaped by independent fixed and flexible variables.

I started this book with the catchphrase 'the earth speaks Arabic' which triggered a number of unanswered questions that this book has attempted to answer at least partially. I end this book with the same phrase but with a different speculation about its connotations. There are two facts that render Arabic inclusive in many respects. The first is the non-distinction between CA, MSA and the colloquials by the mass of native speakers who may think they speak Arabic, perhaps bad Arabic, but still perceived by many as a corrupted version of the same language as that of the Qur'an. An aggregate picture of Arabic is prevalent. The second fact that this book has tried to capture is the diversity of the Arab world, whether religious, historical, political, ethnic, social or economic. This diversity in itself renders Arabic an inclusive, common component of different communities. Tribes, religious groups, upheavals, rapid urbanisation, wars, civil wars, social and political changes, dislocation of large groups, ethnic minorities, varied ethno-geographic and historical backgrounds are all characteristics of the Arab world that are reflected directly or indirectly through language.

The Arab world is a place where individuals play different roles through language choice and code-switching. It is a place where intellectuals have at least two varieties available to them, and a place where people can add to the two varieties a different language all together; a place where the struggle for independence and social justice has been going on hand in hand with a linguistic struggle to maintain and develop standard Arabic, and the struggle for democracy and civil rights has been going on hand in hand with the struggle to acknowledge other languages and not just standard Arabic. Language has been used as a political tool to the utmost.

The Arab world is also a changing place; some Arabs have been changing from pearl divers to oil traders and from Bedouins to city dwellers. It is changing from a place where older women were the carriers of tradition to younger women setting the course of events and taking control of their linguistic choices.

I have aimed throughout this book to set the reader thinking about different linguistic issues pertaining to 'Arabic' in its entirety. By challenging and discussing different approaches to Arabic sociolinguistics and perhaps sociolinguistics in general, I have aspired to add freshness and vitality to the field. Both Arabic and Arabs will remain a fertile ground for investigation in sociolinguistics. There is still more that needs to be unfolded and examined.

Bibliography

ARABIC TITLES

'Abd al-Ghanī, M. (1986), *Ṭāhā Ḥusayn wa-al-siyāsah*, Cairo: Dār al-Mustaqbal al-'Arabī.

'Abd al-Kāfī, I. (1991), 'al-Taʿlīm wa-baththal-huwīyah al-qawmīyah fī Miṣr', PhD thesis, Cairo University.

al-Anṣārī, N. and M. al-Anṣārī (2002), *al-ʿUrūbah fī muqābil al-ʿawlamah: ʿAnāṣir li-naẓarīyah jadīdah*, Cairo: al-Hayʾah al-Miṣrīyah al-ʿĀmmah lil-Kitāb.

al-Madanī, A. T. (1931), *Kitāb al-Jazāʾir*, Algiers: s.n.

al-Qaʿīd, Y. (2004), *Qismat al-ghuramāʾ*, London: Dār al-Sāqī.

Badawi, S. A. (1973), *Mustawayāt al-ʿArabīyah al-muʿāṣirah fī Miṣr: Baḥth fī ʿalāqat al-lughah bi-al-ḥaḍārah*, Cairo: Dār al-Maʿārif.

Dajānī, A. M. (1973), *ʿAbd al-Nāṣir wa-al-thawrah al-ʿArabīyah*, Beirut: Dār al-Waḥdah.

Ghidhdhāmī, ʿA. M. (2000), *Thaqāfat al-wahm: Muqārabāt ḥawla al-marʾah wa-al-jasad wa-al-lughah*, Casablanca: al-Markaz al-Thaqāfī al-ʿArabī.

Ḥabīb, M. and Q. Shaʿbān (1983), *Tadrīs al-lughah al-Arabīyah fī al-marḥalah al-ibtidāʾīyah fī al-bilād al-ʿArabīyah*, Beirut: Dār al-Kitāb al-Lubnānī.

Ḥammūd, S. (2000), 'Taʿrīb al-taʿlīm wa-al-siyāsah al-lughawīyah fī al-Mamlakah al-Maghribīyah bayna al-māḍī wa-al-ḥāḍir', in K. Shaʿbān (ed.), *al-Lughah wa-al-taʿlīm*, Beirut: al-Hayʾah al-Lubnānīyah lil-ʿUlūm al-Tarbawīyah, 91–120.

Ibrāhīm, Ḥ. (1980), *Dīwān Ḥāfiẓ Ibrāhīm*, Cairo: al-Majlis al-Aʿlā lil-Thaqāfah.

'Izz al-Dīn, Y. (2006), 'Wājib qawmī wa-waṭanī yadʿūnā lil-taṣaddī li-hādhihi al-muʾāmarah: Al-ʿāmmīyah tuhaddid bi-indithār al-ʿArab', *Akhbār al-Adab* 622 (19 March), http://www.akhbarelyom.org.eg/adab/issues/662/1001.html, accessed 4 January 2008.

Kamāl, W. (2008), 'Sāwīrus wa-rāʾiḥat al-māl fī qanāt OTV', *Ikhwān Online*, http://www.ikhwanonline.com/Article.asp?ArtID=39000&SecID=294, accessed 10 November 2008.

Khalīfah, 'A. (1977), 'Majmaʿ al-lughah al-ʿArabīyah fī al-muʾtamar', *al-Lisān al-ʿArabī* 15(3): 19–22.

Kharyush, A. (2002), 'Dawr majmaʿ al-lughah al-ʿarabīyah al-Urdunnī fī taʿrīb al-taʿlīm al-ʿilmī al-jāmiʿī fī al-Urdunn', *Majallat Majmaʿ al-Lughah al-ʿArabīyah bi-al-Qāhirah* 97: 145–79.

Khiḍr, M. (2006), *Min fajawāt al-ʿadālah fī al-taʿlīm*, Cairo: al-Dār al-Miṣrīyah al-Lubnānīyah.

Maḥāmidīyah, ʿA. (2007), 'Qānūn li-ḥimāyat al-lughah al-ʿArabīyah qarīban fī al-Imārāt', *al-Jazera*

Online (13 July), http://www.aljazeera.net/News/archive/archive?ArchiveId=1063226, accessed 12 November 2008.

Mahfouz, N. (2006), *Rasā'iluhu: Bayna falsafat al-waḥdah wa-dirāmā al-shakhṣīyah*, Cairo: al-Dār al-Miṣrīyah al-Lubnānīyah.

Mubarāk, M. (2008), 'Māzin Mubārak ʿadwan fī Majmaʿ al-Lughah al-ʿArabīyah', *Shurufāt*, http://www.moc.gov.sy/index.php?d=30&id=1351, accessed 29 November 2008.

Mūsá, N. (1987), *Qaḍīyat al-taḥawwul ilā al-fuṣḥā fī al-ʿālam al-ʿArabī al-ḥadīth*, Amman : Dār al-Fikr.

Nūr, M. (2007), 'Fārūq Shūshah: Miṣr bilā sulṭah lughawīyah . . . wa-al-majmaʿ 'yuhātī' wa-lā aḥad yasmaʿ', *Akhbār Al-Adab* 714 (18 March), http://www.akhbarelyom.org.eg/adab/issues/714/0200.html, accessed 4 January 2008.

Saʿdī, ʿU. (1993), *al-Taʿrīb fī al-Jazāʾir: Kifāḥ al-shaʿb ḍidda al-haymanah al-Frankūfūnīyah*, Algiers: Dār al-Ummah.

Shalabī, Kh. (1986), *al-Watad*, Cairo: Dār al-Fikr.

Shukrī, M. (2000), *al-Khubz al-ḥāfī: Sīrah dhātīya riwāʾīyah*, London: Dār al-Sāqī.

al-Zāwī, A. (2006), 'al-Lughah al-faransīyah ghanīmat ḥarb nadkhul ʿabrahā ilā al-ḥadāthah', *Akhbār al-Adab* 702 (24 December), www.akhbarelyom.org.eg/adab/issues/702/0904.html, accessed 4 January 2008.

TITLES IN EUROPEAN LANGUAGES

Abdel Moneim, A. (2007), 'Pickled tongue', *al-Ahram Weekly* 834 (1–7 March), http://weekly.ahram.org.eg/2007/834/cu5.htm, accessed 4 January 2008.

Abdel-Jawad, H. (1986), 'The emergence of an urban dialect in the Jordanian urban centers', *International Journal of the Sociology of Language* 61: 53–63.

Abdel-Malek, Z. (1972), 'The influence of diglossia on the novels of Yuusif al-Sibaa'i', *Journal of Arabic Literature* 3: 132–41.

Aboheimed, I. A. (1991), *Linguistic analysis of diglossia in Arabic and its implications for teaching Arabic to non-Arabs in Riyadh (Saudi Arabia)*, [Leeds]: [s.n.].

Abu-Haidar, F. (1988), 'Male/female linguistic variation in a Baghdadi community', in A. K. Irvine, E. B. Serjeant and G. R. Smith (eds), *A miscellany of Middle Eastern articles: In memoriam Thomas Muir Johnstone (1924–83), Professor of Arabic in the University of London, 1970–82*, London: Harlow, 151–62.

— (1989), 'Are Iraqi women more prestige conscious than men? Sex differentiation in Baghdadi Arabic', *Language in Society* 18: 471–81.

— (1991), *Christian Arabic of Baghdad*, Wiesbaden: Otto Harrassowitz.

— (1992), 'Shifting boundaries: The effect of Modern Standard Arabic on dialect convergence in Baghdad', *Perspectives on Arabic Linguistics* iv: 91–106.

— (2002), 'Arabic and English in conflict: Iraqis in the UK', in A. Rouchdy (ed.), *Language contact and language conflict in Arabic: Variations on a sociolinguistic theme*, London: RoutledgeCurzon, 286–96.

Abu-Lughod, L. (1987), *Veiled sentiments: Honor and poetry in a Bedouin society*, Cairo: American University in Cairo Press.

Abu-Manga, A. (1999), *Hausa in the Sudan: Process of adaptation to Arabic*, Cologne: R. Koppe.

Abu-Melhim, A. R. (1991), 'Code switching and linguistic accommodation in Arabic', *Perspectives on Arabic Linguistics* v: 231–50.

Ageron, C. R. (1991), *Modern Algeria: A history from 1830 to the present*, London: Hurst.

Agius, D. A. (1996), *Siculo Arabic*, London: Kegan Paul International.

Aissati, A. and J. Kurvers (2008), 'Language policy and literacy', unpublished paper presented at the 17th Sociolinguistics Symposium, Amsterdam, 3–5 April 2008.

Aitchison, J. (2001), *Language change: Progress or decay?*, 3rd edn, Cambridge: Cambridge University Press.

Al Batal, M. (2002), 'Identity and language tension in Lebanon: The Arabic of local news at LBCT', in A. Rouchdy (ed.), *Language contact and language conflict in Arabic: Variations on a sociolinguistic theme*, London: RoutledgeCurzon, 91–115.

Alexandre, P. (1963), 'Les problèmes linguistiques africains vus de Paris', in J. Spencer (ed.), *Language in Africa*, Cambridge: Cambridge University Press, 53–69.

Al-Khateeb, M. A. A. (1988), 'Sociolinguistic change in an expanding urban context: A case study of Irbid city, Jordan', PhD thesis, University of Durham.

Allal, M. A. (2005), 'Que fait-on de l'université algérienne?', *El Watan* (2–3 December), 13.

Al-Masri, N. (1988), 'Teaching culture in the foreign language classroom with particular reference to the Gaza Strip', Master's dissertation, University of Salford.

Al-Muhannadi, M. (1991), 'A sociolinguistic study of women's speech in Qatar', PhD thesis, University of Essex.

Altoma, S. J. (1969), *The problem of diglossia in Arabic*, Cambridge, MA: Harvard University Press.

Al-Torki, S. and C. El-Solh (1988), *Arab women in the field: Studying your own society*, New York: Syracuse University Press.

Al-Wer, E. (1991), 'Phonological variation in the speech of women from three urban areas in Jordan', PhD thesis, University of Essex.

— (1997), 'Arabic between reality and ideology', *International Journal of Applied Linguistics* 7(2): 251–65.

— (1999), 'Why do different variables behave differently? Data from Arabic', in Y. Suleiman (ed.), *Language and society in the Middle East and North Africa: Studies in identity and variation*, Richmond: Curzon, 38–58.

— (2002), 'Education as a speaker variable', in A. Rouchdy (ed.), *Language contact and language conflict in Arabic: Variations on a sociolinguistic theme*, London: RoutledgeCurzon, 41–53.

— (2003), *Variation and change in Jordanian Arabic*, London: RoutledgeCurzon.

— (2004), 'Variability reproduced: A variationist view of the [ḍ]/[d] opposition in modern Arabic dialects', in M. Haak, R. De Jong and K. Versteegh (eds), *Approaches to Arabic dialects: A collection of articles presented to Manfred Woidich on the occasion of his sixtieth birthday*, Leiden: Brill, 21–31.

— (2007), 'The formation of the dialect of Amman: From chaos to order', in C. Miller, E. Al-Wer, D. Caubet and J. C. E. Watson (eds), *Arabic in the city: Issues in dialect contact and language variation*, London: Routledge, 55–76.

Amara, M. H. (2003), 'Recent foreign language education policies in Palestine', *Language Problems and Language Planning* 27(3): 217–32.

— (2007), 'Teaching Hebrew to Palestinian pupils in Israel', *Current Issues in Language Planning* 8(2): 243–57.

Appel, R. and P. Muysken (1987), *Language contact and bilingualism*, London: Arnold.

Arnold, J., R. Blake and B. Davidson (eds) (1996), *Sociolinguistic variation: Data, theory, and analysis*, Stanford, CA: Center for the Study of Language and Information.

Ashley, E. (ed.) (1879), *The life and correspondence of Henry John Temple, Lord Palmerston*, London: Richard Bentley & Son.

Attia, M. F. (2005), 'Seeing through advertisements: A feminist stylistic approach in Arabic and English discourse', *al-Logha* 5: 43–74.

Auer, P. and A. Di Luzio (1984), *Interpretative sociolinguistics: Migrants, children – migrant children*, Tübingen: Narr.

Austen, J. (1993), *Persuasion*, Ware: Wordsworth.

Baron, B. (2005), *Egypt as a woman: Nationalism, gender, and politics*, Berkeley, CA: University of California Press.

Bassiouney, R. (2003a), 'Theories of code switching in the light of empirical data from Egypt', in D. Parkinson and S. Farwaneh (eds), *Perspectives on Arabic Linguistics* xv: 19–39.

— (2003b), 'Linguistics', lemma in *Encyclopaedia of women in Islamic cultures (EWIC)*, Leiden: Brill.

— (2006), *Functions of code switching in Egypt: Evidence from monologues*, Leiden: Brill.

— (2009), 'The variety of housewives and cockroaches', in E. Al-Wer (ed.), *Arabic Dialectology*, Leiden: Brill.

Bastos, L. C. and M. Oliveira (2006), 'Identity and personal/institutional relations: people and tragedy in a health insurance customer service', in A. De Fina, D. Schiffrin and M. Bamberg (eds), *Discourse and identity*, Cambridge: Cambridge University Press, 188–212.

Bateson, M. C. (1967), *Arabic language handbook*, Washington, DC: Center for Applied Linguistics.

Bean, J. M. and B. Johnstone (2004), 'Gender, identity, and "strong language" in a professional woman's talk', in M. Bucholtz (ed.), *Language and woman's place: Text and commentaries*, Oxford: Oxford University Press, 237–43.

Behnstedt, P. and M. Woidich (1985–8), *Die ägyptisch-arabischen Dialekte*, Wiesbaden: Reichert.

Belal, A. and A. Agourram (1970), 'L'économie marocaine depuis l'indépendance', in C. Debasch (ed.), *Les économies maghrébines*, Paris: CNRS, 141–64.

Belazi, H., E. J. Rubin and A. J. Toribio (1994), 'Code switching and *x*-bar theory: The functional head constraint', *Linguistic Inquiry* 25(2): 221–37.

Bell, A. (1984), 'Language style as audience design', *Language in Society* 13(2): 145–204.

— (2001), 'Back in style: Reworking audience design', in P. Eckert and J. Rickford (eds), *Style and sociolinguistic variation*, Cambridge: Cambridge University Press, 139–169.

Belnap, R. K. and B. Bishop (2003), 'Arabic personal correspondence: A window on change in progress', *International Journal of the Sociology of Language* 163: 9–25.

Benrabah, M. (2005), 'The language planning situation in Algeria', *Current Issues in Language Planning* 6(4): 379–502.

— (2007a), 'Language-in-education planning in Algeria: Historical development and current issues', *Language Policy* 6: 225–52.

— (2007b), 'The language planning situation in Algeria', in R. B. Kaplan and R. B. Baldauf (eds), *Language planning and policy in Africa. Vol. 2: Algeria, Côte d'Ivoire, Nigeria and Tunisia*, Clevedon: Multilingual Matters, 25–148.

— (2007c), 'Language maintenance and spread: French in Algeria', *International Journal of Francophone Studies* 10(1–2): 193–215.

Bensadoun, M. (2007), 'The (re)fashioning of Moroccan national identity', in B. Maddy-Weitzman and D. Zisenwine (eds), *The Maghrib in the new century: Identity, religion, politics*, Gainesville: University Press of Florida, 15–35.

Bentahila, A. (1983), *Language attitudes among Arabic–French bilinguals in Morocco*, Clevedon: Multilingual Matters.

Bentahila, A. and E. E. Davies (1983), 'The syntax of Arabic–French code switching', *Lingua* 59: 301–30.

Berger, A.-E. (2002), *Algeria in others' languages*, Ithaca, NY: Cornell University Press.

Berk-Seligson, S. (1986), 'Linguistic constraints on intra-sentential code switching: A study of Spanish–Hebrew bilingualism', *Language in Society* 15: 313–48.

Bhat, D. N. S. (1978), 'A general study of palatization', in J. Greenberg, C. Ferguson and E.

Moravcsik (eds), *Universals of human language. Vol. 2: Phonology*, Stanford, CA: Stanford University Press, 47–91.

Bishai, W. B. (1964), 'Coptic lexical influence on Egyptian Arabic', *Journal of Near Eastern Studies* 23(1): 39–47.

Blanc, H. (1953), *Studies in North Palestinian Arabic: Linguistic inquiries among the Druzes of Western Galilee and Mt. Carmel*, Jerusalem: Israel Oriental Society.

— (1960), 'Style variations in Arabic: A sample of interdialectal conversation', in C. A. Ferguson (ed.), *Contributions to Arabic linguistics*, Cambridge, MA: Harvard University Press, 81–156.

— (1964), *Communal dialects of Baghdad*, Cambridge, MA: Harvard University Press.

— (1974), 'The *nekteb-nektebu* imperfect in a variety of Cairene Arabic', *Israel Oriental Studies* 4: 206–26.

Blau, J. (1977), *The beginnings of the Arabic diglossia: A study of the origins of Neoarabic*, Malibu: Undena.

Blom, J.-P. and J. J. Gumperz (1972), 'Social meaning in linguistic structure: Code-switching in Norway', in J. J. Gumperz (ed.), *Directions in sociolinguistics: The ethnography of communication*, New York: Holt, Rinehart and Winston, 407–34.

Bogaers, I. E. (1998), 'Gender in job interviews: Some implications of verbal interactions of women and men', *International Journal of the Sociology of Language* 129: 35–58.

Bohas, G., J.-P. Guillaume and D. Kouloughli (2006), *The Arabic linguistic tradition*, Washington, DC: Georgetown University Press.

Bolonyai, A. (1996), 'Turning it over: L2 dominance in Hungarian/English acquisition', unpublished paper, Second Language Research Forum (SLRF), University of Arizona.

— (2005), '"Who was the best?": Power, knowledge and rationality in bilingual girls' code choices', *Journal of Sociolinguistics* 9(1): 3–27.

Borg, A. and G. M. Kressel (2001), 'Bedouin personal names in the Negev and Sinai', *Zeitschrift für arabische Linguistik* 40: 32–70.

Boucherit, A. (1986), 'Contact et différenciation dialectale à Alger', *MAS-GELLAS* 2: 13–55.

— (2002), *L'arabe parlé à Alger: Aspects sociolinguistiques et énonciatifs*, Paris and Louvain: Peeters.

Boumans, L. (1996), 'Embedding verbs and collocations in Moroccan Arabic/Dutch code-switching', *Perspectives on Arabic Linguistics* ix: 45–65.

— (1998), *The syntax of codeswitching: Analysing Moroccan Arabic/Dutch conversation*, Tilburg: Tilburg University Press.

— (2002), 'Repetition phenomena in insertional codeswitching', in A. Rouchdy (ed.), *Language contact and language conflict in Arabic: Variations on a sociolinguistic theme*, London: RoutledgeCurzon, 297–316.

Bourdieu, P. (2001), 'Uniting to better dominate', *Items and Issues* 2(3–4): 1–6.

Boussofara-Omar, N. (1999), 'Arabic diglossic switching in Tunisia: An application of Myers-Scotton's MLF model', PhD thesis, University of Texas at Austin.

— (2003), 'Revisiting Arabic diglossic switching in light of the MLF model and its sub-models: The 4-M model and the Abstract Level model', *Bilingualism: Language and Cognition* 6(1): 33–46.

— (2006a), 'Diglossia', lemma in K. Versteegh, M. Eid, A. Elgibali, M. Woidich and A. Zaborski (eds), *Encyclopedia of Arabic language and linguistics*, Leiden: Brill, i: 629–37.

— (2006b), 'Neither third language nor middle varieties but diglossic switching', *Zeitschrift für arabische Linguistik* 45: 55–80.

Boxer, D. and E. Gritsenko (2005), 'Women and surnames across cultures: Reconstituting identity in marriage', *Women and Language* 28(2): 1–11.

Britto, F. (1986), *Diglossia: A study of the theory with application to Tamil*, Washington, DC: Georgetown University.

Brown, P. (1980), 'How and why are women more polite: Some evidence from a Mayan community', in S. McConnell-Ginet, R. Borker and N. Furman (eds), *Women and language in literature and society*, New York: Praeger, 111–36.

Brown, P. and A. Gilman (2003 [1987]), 'The pronouns of power and solidarity', in C. Paulston and R. Tucker (eds), *Sociolinguistics: The essential readings*, Oxford: Blackwell, 156–76.

Brown, P. and S. C. Levinson (1987), *Politeness: some universals in language usage*, Cambridge: Cambridge University Press.

— (1999), 'Politeness: Some universals in language usage', in A. Jaworski and N. Coupland (eds), *The discourse reader*, London: Routledge, 321–35.

Bucholtz, M. (ed.) (2004), *Language and woman's place: Text and commentaries*, Oxford: Oxford University Press.

Cameron, D. (1992), *Feminism and linguistic theory*, New York: St Martin's Press.

— (2003a), 'Gender issues in language change', *Annual Review of Applied Linguistics* 23: 187–201.

— (2003b), 'Gender and language ideologies', in J. Holmes and M. Meyerhoff (eds), *The handbook of language and gender*, Oxford: Blackwell, 447–67.

— (2005), 'Language, gender and sexuality: Current issues and new directions', *Applied Linguistics* 26(4): 482–502.

— (2006), *On language and sexual politics*, London: Routledge.

— (2008), *The myth of Mars and Venus: Do men and women really speak different languages?*, Oxford: Oxford University Press.

Caubet, D. (1998), 'Etude linguistique des traits préhilaliens dans un dialecte en voie d'urbanisation', in J. Aguadé, P. Cressier and A. Vicente (eds), *Peuplement et arabisation au Maghreb occidental*, Madrid: Casa de Velázquez, 165–75.

Chambers, J. K., P. Trudgill and N. Schilling-Estes (eds) (2002), *The handbook of language variation and change*, Oxford: Blackwell.

Cheng, W. (2003), *Intercultural conversation: A study of Hong Kong Chinese*, Amsterdam: Benjamins.

Cherfaoui, Z. (2004), 'Réforme de l'école et enseignement du français: Recrutement de 2000 diplômés, *El Watan* (7 June), 1–2.

Cheshire, J. (1982), 'Linguistic variation and social function', in S. Romaine (ed.), *Sociolinguistic variation in speech communities*, London: Arnold, 153–66.

Chomsky, N. (1993), *Lectures on government and binding: The Pisa lectures*, 7th edn, Berlin and New York: Mouton.

Chumbow, B. S. and A. S. Bobda (1996), 'The life-cycle of post-imperial English in Cameroon', in J. A. Fishman, A. Rubal-Lopez and A. W. Conrad (eds), *Post-imperial English*, Berlin: Mouton de Gruyter, 401–30.

Clark, L. (2008), 'Re-examining vocalic variation in Scottish Gaelic: A cognitive grammar approach', *Language Variation and Change* 20: 255–73.

Cleveland, R. L. (1963), 'A classification for the Arabic dialects of Jordan', *Bulletin of the American Schools of Oriental Research* 167: 56–63.

Clyne, M. G. (1982), *Multilingual Australia*, Melbourne: Hawthorne Press.

— (1987), 'Constraints on code switching: How universal are they?', *Linguistics* 25: 739–64.

— (ed.) (1992), *Pluricentric languages: Differing norms in different nations*, Berlin: Mouton.

Clyne, M. G. and S. Kipp (1999), *Pluricentric languages in an immigrant context: Spanish, Arabic and Chinese*, Berlin: Mouton.

Coates, J. (1993), *Women, men, and language*, London: Longman.

— (ed.) (1998), *Language and gender: A reader*, Oxford: Blackwell.

Cohen, J., K. McAlister, K. Rolstad and J. MacSwan (eds) (2005), *Proceedings of the Fourth International Symposium on Bilingualism*, Somerville, MA: Cascadilla Press.
Connor, W. (1978), 'A nation is a nation, is a state, is an ethnic group, is . . .', *Ethnic and Racial Studies* 1: 377–400.
Coulmas, F. (ed.) (1997), *The handbook of sociolinguistics*, Oxford: Blackwell.
Crystal, D. (1987), *The Cambridge encyclopedia of language*, Cambridge: Cambridge University Press.
— (2001), *A dictionary of language*, Chicago: Chicago University Press.
Daher, J. (1998), 'Gender in linguistic variation: The variable (q) in Damascus Arabic', *Perspectives on Arabic Linguistics* xi: 183–205.
— (1999), '(θ) and (ð) as ternary and binary variables in Damascene Arabic', *Perspectives on Arabic Linguistics* xii: 163–202.
Daoud, M. (2002), 'Language policy and planning in Tunisia: Accommodating language rivalry', http://www.miis.edu/docs/langpolicy/ch14.pdf, accessed 10 June 2006.
— (2007), 'The language situation in Tunisia', in R. B. Kaplan and R. B. Baldauf (eds), *Language planning and policy in Africa. Vol. 2: Algeria, Côte d'Ivoire, Nigeria and Tunisia*, Clevedon: Multilingual Matters, 256–307.
Davies, E. E. and Bentahila, A. (2006), 'Ethnicity and language', lemma in K. Versteegh, M. Eid, A. Elgibali, M. Woidich and A. Zaborski (eds), *Encyclopedia of Arabic language and linguistics*, Leiden: Brill, ii: 58–65.
De Fina, A. (2007), 'Code-switching and the construction of ethnic identity in a community of practice', *Language in Society* 36(3): 371–92.
De Fina, A., D. Schiffrin and M. Bamberg (eds) (2006), *Discourse and identity*, Cambridge: Cambridge University Press.
Dendane, Z. (1994), 'Sociolinguistic variation in an Arabic speech community: Tlemcen', *Cahiers de Dialectologie et de Linguistique Contrastive* 4: 62–77.
Deuchar, M. (1989), 'A pragmatic account of women's use of standard speech', in J. Coates and D. Cameron (eds), *Women in their speech communities: New perspectives on language and sex*, London: Longman, 27–32.
Deutch, Y. (2005), 'Language law in Israel', *Language Policy* 4: 261–85.
DiSciullo, A. M., P. Muysken and R. Singh (1986), 'Government and code mixing', *Journal of Linguistics* 22: 1–24.
Djité, P. G. (1992), 'The Arabization of Algeria: Linguistic and sociopolitical motivations', *International Journal of the Sociology of Language* 98: 15–28.
Dorian, N. (1973), 'Grammatical change in a dying dialect', *Language* 49: 413–38.
— (1981), *Language death: The life cycle of a Scottish Gaelic dialect*, Philadelphia: University of Pennsylvania Press.
Douglas, D. (1986), 'From school to university: Language policy and performance at the University of Khartum', *International Journal of the Sociology of Language* 61: 89–112.
Dubois, B. and I. Crouch (1975), 'The question of tag questions in women's speech: They really don't use more of them', *Language in Society* 4: 289–94.
Eckert, P. (1998), 'Gender and sociolinguistic variation', in J. Coates (ed.), *Language and gender: A reader*, Oxford: Blackwell, 64–75.
— (2002), 'Constructing meaning in sociolinguistic variation', unpublished paper presented at the annual meeting of the American Anthropological Association, New Orleans, http://www.stanford.edu/~eckert/AAA02.pdf, accessed 18 November 2008.
— (2003), 'Language and gender in adolescence', in J. Holmes and M. Meyerhoff (eds), *The handbook of language and gender*, Oxford: Blackwell, 381–400.
— (2005), 'Variation, convention, and social meaning', unpublished paper presented at the annual meeting of the Linguistic Society of America, Oakland, CA, 7 January 2005.

Eckert, P. and S. McConnell-Ginet (1995), 'Constructing meaning, constructing selves: Snapshots of language, gender and class from Belten High', in K. Hall and M. Bucholtz (eds), *Gender articulated: Language and the socially constructed self*, New York: Routledge, 469–508.

— (2003), *Language and gender*, Cambridge: Cambridge University Press.

— (2004), 'The good woman', in M. Bucholtz (ed.), *Language and woman's place: Text and commentaries*, Oxford: Oxford University Press, 165–77.

Eckert, P. and J. R. Rickford (eds) (2001), *Style and sociolinguistic variation*, Cambridge: Cambridge University Press.

Edelsky, C. and K. Adams (1990), 'Creating inequality: Breaking the rules in debates', *Journal of Language and Social Psychology* 9(3): 171–90.

Edwards, J. R. (1979), 'Social class differences and the identification of sex in children's speech', *Journal of Child Language* 6(1): 121–7.

— (1985), *Language, society, and identity*, Oxford: Blackwell.

Eid, M. (1982), 'The non-randomness of diglossic variation in Arabic', *Glossa* 16(1): 54–84.

— (1988), 'Principles of code switching between standard and Egyptian Arabic', *Al-Arabiyya* 21: 51–79.

— (2002a), *The world of obituaries: Gender across cultures and over time*, Detroit: Wayne State University Press.

— (2002b), 'Language is a choice: Variation in Egyptian women's written discourse', in A. Rouchdy (ed.), *Language contact and language conflict in Arabic: Variations on a sociolinguistic theme*, London: RoutledgeCurzon, 203–32.

— (2007), 'Arabic on the media: Hybridity and styles', in E. Ditters and H. Motzki (eds), *Approaches to Arabic linguistics: Presented to Kees Versteegh on the occasion of his sixtieth birthday*, Leiden: Brill, 403–34.

Eisele, J. C. (2002), 'Approaching diglossia: Authorities, values, and representations', in A. Rouchdy (ed.), *Language contact and language conflict in Arabic: Variations on a sociolinguistic theme*, London: RoutledgeCurzon, 3–23.

Eisikovits, E. (1987), 'Sex differences in the inter-group and intra-group interaction among adolescents', in A. Pauwels (ed.), *Women and language in Australian and New Zealand society*, Sydney: Australian Professional Publications, 45–58.

El-Hassan, S. (1977), 'Educated spoken Arabic in Egypt and the Levant: A critical review of diglossia and related concepts', *Archivum Linguisticum* 8(2): 112–32.

— (1980), 'Variation in the demonstrative system in educated spoken Arabic', *Archivum Linguisticum* 9(1): 32–57.

El-Kholy, H. (2002), *Defiance and compliance: Negotiating gender in low-income Cairo*, New York: Berghahn Books.

Ennaji, M. (1997), 'The sociology of Berber: Change and continuity', *International Journal of the Sociology of Language* 123: 23–40.

— (2002), 'Language contact, Arabization policy and education in Morocco', in A. Rouchdy (ed.), *Language contact and language conflict in Arabic: Variations on a sociolinguistic theme*, London: RoutledgeCurzon, 70–88.

Errihani, M. (2006), 'Language policy in Morocco: Problems and prospects of teaching Tamazight', *Journal of North African Studies* 11(2): 143–54.

Faiq, S. (1999), 'The status of Berber: A permanent challenge to language policy in Morocco', in Y. Suleiman (ed.), *Language and society in the Middle East and North Africa: Studies in variation and identity*, Richmond: Curzon, 37–53.

Fakhsh, M. A. (1980), 'The consequences of the introduction and spread of modern education: Education and national integration in Egypt', in E. Kedourie and S. G. Haim (eds), *Modern Egypt: Studies in politics and society*, London: Cass, 42–55.

Fasold, R. (1995), *The sociolinguistics of society*, Oxford: Blackwell.
Ferguson, C. A. (1971), *Language structure and language use: essays*, Stanford, CA: Stanford University Press.
— (1972 [1959]), 'Diglossia', *Word* 15: 325–40. Reprinted in P. P. Giglioli (ed.), *Language and social context*, Harmondsworth: Penguin, 232–51.
— (1990), 'Come forth with a Surah like it: Arabic as a measure of Arab society', *Perspectives on Arabic Linguistics* i: 39–51.
— (1996 [1991]), 'Diglossia revisited', in A. Elgibali (ed.), *Understanding Arabic: Essays in contemporary Arabic linguistics in honour of El-Said Badawi*, Cairo: AUC Press, 49–67.
Ferguson, C. A., R. K. Belnap and N. Haeri (1997), *Structuralist studies in Arabic linguistics: Charles A. Ferguson's papers, 1954–1994*, Leiden and New York: Brill.
Findlow, S. (2001), 'Global and local tensions in an Arab Gulf state: Conflicting values in UAE higher education', paper presented at the International Conference 'Travelling policy/ local space: Globalization, identities, and education policy in Europe', Keele University, 27–9 June.
Fischer, W. (2006), 'Classical Arabic', in K. Versteegh, M. Eid, A. Elgibali, M. Woidich and A. Zaborski (eds), *Encyclopedia of Arabic language and linguistics*, Leiden: Brill, i: 397–405.
Fishman, J. A. (1967), 'Bilingualism with and without diglossia, diglossia with and without bilingualism', *Journal of Social Issues* 23: 29–38.
— (1977), 'Language and ethnicity', in H. Giles (ed.), *Language, ethnicity, and intergroup relations*, London: Academic Press, 15–57.
— (1997), 'Maintaining languages: What works and what doesn't', in G. Cantoni (ed.), *Stabilizing Indigenous Languages*, Flagstaff, AZ: Northern Arizona University. 186–98.
— (2002), 'Endangered minority languages: Prospects for sociolinguistic research', *International Journal on Multicultural Societies* 4(2): 1–9.
Fishman, J. A., R. L. Cooper and A. W. Conrad (1977), *The spread of English: The sociology of English as an additional language*, Rowley, MA: Newbury House.
Fishman, J. A., C. A. Ferguson and J. Das Gupta (eds) (1968), *Language problems of developing nations*, New York: Wiley.
Fishman, P. A. (1980), 'Conversational insecurity', in H. Giles, P. Robinson and P. M. Smith (eds), *Language: Social psychological perspectives*, Oxford: Pergamon, 127–32.
— (1983), 'Interaction: The work women do', in B. Thorne, C. Kramarae and N. Henley (eds), *Language, gender, and society*, Rowley, MA: Newbury House, 89–101.
Fleisch, H. (1971), 'Imāla', in P. Bearman, T. Bianquis , C. E. Bosworth , E. van Donzel and W. P. Heinrichs (eds), *Encyclopaedia of Islam*, 2nd edn, Leiden: Brill, iii: 1162–3.
Fontaine, J. (2004), 'La population libyenne, un demi-siècle de mutations', in O. Pliez (ed.), *La nouvelle Libye: Sociétés, espaces et géopolitiques au lendemain de l'embargo*, Paris: Karthala, 159–75.
Fought, C. (ed.) (2004), *Sociolinguistic variation: Critical reflections*, Oxford: Oxford University Press.
Freed, A. F. (2003), 'Epilogue: Reflections on language and gender research', in J. Holmes and M. Meyerhoff (eds), *The handbook of language and gender*, Oxford: Blackwell, 699–721.
Gal, S. (1978a), 'Peasant men can't get wives: Language change and sex roles in a bilingual community', *Language in Society* 7: 1–16.
— (1978b), 'Variation and change in patterns of speaking: Language shift in Austria', in D. Sankoff (ed.), *Linguistic variation: Models and methods*, New York: Academic Press, 227–38.
Gallagher, C. F. (1964), 'North African problems and prospects: Language and identity', in J. A. Fishman, C. A. Ferguson and J. Das Gupta (eds), *Language problems of developing nations*, New York: Wiley, 129–50.

Gardener-Chloros, P. (1985), 'Language selection and switching among Strasbourg shoppers', *International Journal of the Sociology of Language* 54: 117–35.

— (1991), *Language selection and switching in Strasbourg*, Oxford: Oxford University Press.

Germanos, M. (2007), 'Greetings in Beirut: Social distribution and attitudes towards different formulae', in C. Miller, E. Al-Wer, D. Caubet and J. C. E. Watson (eds), *Arabic in the city: Issues in dialect contact and language variation*, London and New York: Routledge, 147–65.

Gernoble, L. and L. Whaley (eds) (1998), *Endangered languages: Language loss and community response*, Cambridge: Cambridge University Press.

Gibson, M. (2002), 'Dialect levelling in Tunisian Arabic: Towards a new spoken standard', in A. Rouchdy (ed.), *Language contact and language conflict in Arabic: Variations on a sociolinguistic theme*, London: RoutledgeCurzon, 24–40.

Giles, H., A. Mulac, J. Bradac and P. Johnson (1987), 'Speech accommodation theory: The first decade and beyond', in M. L. McLaughlin (ed.), *Communication yearbook 10*, Beverly Hills, CA: Sage, 13–48.

Gill, H. (1999), 'Language choice, language policy and the tradition–modernity debate in culturally mixed postcolonial communities: France and the francophone Maghreb as a case study', in Y. Suleiman (ed.), *Language and society in the Middle East and North Africa*, Richmond: Curzon, 122–36.

Glassé, C. (ed.) (1989), *A concise encyclopedia of Islam*, San Francisco: Harper and Row.

Goffman, E. (1981), *Forms of talk*, Philadelphia: University of Pennsylvania Press.

Goodwin, M. H. (2003), 'The relevance of ethnicity, class, and gender in children's peer negotiations', in J. Holmes and M. Meyerhoff (eds), *The handbook of language and gender*, Oxford: Blackwell, 229–51.

Gordon, D. C. (1978), *The French language and national identity*, The Hague: Mouton.

Gordon, M. and J. Heath (1998), 'Sex, sound, symbolism and sociolinguistics', *Current Anthropology* 10(4): 421–49.

Grice, P. (1975), 'Logic and conversation', in P. Cole and J. Morgan (eds), *Syntax and semantics 3*, New York: Academic Press, 41–58.

Grin, F. (2005), 'Linguistic human rights as a source of policy guidelines: A critical assessment', *Journal of Sociolinguistics* 9(3): 448–60.

Grosby, S. (2005), *Nationalism: A very short introduction*, Oxford: Oxford University Press.

Guibernau, M. (2007), *The identity of nations*, Cambridge: Polity.

Gumperz, J. J. (1976), 'The sociolinguistic significance of conversational code switching', Papers on Language and Context (Working Paper 46), Berkeley: University of California, Language Behaviour Research Laboratory.

— (1982a), *Discourse strategies*, Cambridge: Cambridge University Press.

— (1982b), *Language and social identity*, Cambridge: Cambridge University Press.

Gumperz, J. J. and D. Hymes (eds) (1972), *Directions in sociolinguistics: The ethnography of communication*, New York: Holt, Rinehart and Winston.

Guy, G. R., C. Feagin, D. Schiffrin and J. Baugh (eds) (1996), *Towards a social science of language: Papers in honor of William Labov*, Amsterdam and Philadelphia: Benjamins.

Haag, M. (2003), *The timeline history of Egypt*, New York: Barnes & Noble.

Haak, M., R. De Jong and K. Versteegh (eds) (2004), *Approaches to Arabic dialects: A collection of articles presented to Manfred Woidich on the occasion of his sixtieth birthday*, Leiden: Brill.

Haas, W. (1982), *Standard languages, spoken and written*, Manchester: Manchester University Press.

Hachimi, A. (2001), 'Shifting sands: Language and gender in Moroccan Arabic', in M. Hellinger and H. Bussmann (eds), *Gender across languages: The linguistic representation of women and men*, Amsterdam: Benjamins, I: 27–51.

— (2007), 'Becoming Casablancan: Fessis in Casablanca as a case study', in C. Miller,

E. Al-Wer, D. Caubet and J. C. E. Watson (eds), *Arabic in the city: Issues in dialect contact and language variation*, London and New York: Routledge, 97–122.
Haeri, N. (1991), 'Sociolinguistic variation in Cairene Arabic: Palatalization and the qaf in the speech of men and women', PhD thesis, University of Philadelphia.
— (1992), 'Synchronic variation in Cairene Arabic: The case of palatization', *Perspectives on Arabic Linguistics* iv: 169–80.
— (1994), 'A linguistic innovation of women in Cairo', *Language Variation and Change* 6: 87–112.
— (1996a), *The sociolinguistic market of Cairo: Gender, class, and education*, London and New York: Kegan Paul International.
— (1996b), '"Why do women do this?": Sex and gender differences in speech', in G. R. Guy (ed.), *Towards a social science of language. Vol. I: Variation and change in language and society*, Amsterdam: Benjamins, 101–14.
— (1997), 'The reproduction of symbolic capital: Language, state, and class in Egypt', *World Journal of Human Sciences* 38(5): 795–816.
— (2000), 'Form and ideology: Arabic sociolinguistics and beyond', *Annual Review of Anthropology* 29: 61–87.
— (2003), *Sacred language, ordinary people: Dilemmas of culture and politics in Egypt*, New York and Basingstoke: Palgrave Macmillan.
— (2006), 'Culture and language', lemma in K. Versteegh, M. Eid, A. Elgibali, M. Woidich and A. Zaborski (eds), *Encyclopedia of Arabic language and linguistics*, Leiden: Brill, i: 527–36.
Hall, K. (2003), 'Exceptional speakers: Contested and problematized gender identities', in M. Meyerhoff and J. Holmes (eds), *Handbook of language and gender*, Oxford: Blackwell, 352–80.
Hammond, M. (2000), 'Subsuming the feminine other: Gender and narration in Idwar al-Kharrat's Ya Banat Iskandariyya', *Journal of Arabic Literature* 31: 38–58.
Harvey, P. (1994), 'The presence and absence of speech in the communication of gender', in P. Burton, K. Kushari Dyson and S. Ardener (eds), *Bilingual women*, Oxford: Berg, 44–64.
Hary, B. H. (1992), *Multiglossia in Judeo-Arabic: With an edition, translation and grammatical study of the Cairene Purim scroll*, Leiden and New York: Brill.
Havelova, A. (2000), 'Sociolinguistic description of Nazareth', in M. Mifsud (ed.), *Proceedings of the Third International Conference of AIDA*, Ḫal Lija: Association internationale de dialectologie arabe (AÏDA), 141–4.
Hayasi, T. (1998), 'Gender differences in modern Turkish discourse', *International Journal of the Sociology of Language* 129: 117–26.
Heath, J. (1989), *From code-switching to borrowing: Foreign and diglossic mixing in Moroccan Arabic*, London and New York: Kegan Paul International.
— (2008), *The veil: Women writers on its history, lore and politics*, Berkeley: University of California Press.
Heller, M. S. (1978), 'Bonjour, hello? Negotiations of language choice in Montreal', Working Papers in Sociolinguistics 49, Austin, TX: Southwest Educational Development Lab.
— (1982), 'Negotiations of language choice in Montreal', in J. J. Gumperz (ed.), *Languages and social identity*, Cambridge: Cambridge University Press, 108–18.
— (1988), *Code switching: Anthropological and sociological perspectives*, Berlin: Mouton.
Herbert, R. K. (2002), 'The political economy of language shift: Language and gendered ethnicity in a Thonga community', in R. Mesthrie (ed.), *Language in South Africa*, Cambridge: Cambridge University Press, 316–37.
Hill, J. H. (1987), 'Women's speech in Mexicano', in S. U. Philips, S. Steele and C. Tanz (eds), *Language, gender and sex in comparative perspective*, Cambridge: Cambridge University Press, 121–60.

Hill, J. H. and K. C. Hill (1986), *Speaking Mexicano: The dynamics of syncretic language in Central Mexico*, Tucson, AZ: University of Arizona Press.

Hill, J. and B. Mannheim (1992), 'Language and world view', *Annual Review of Anthropology* 21: 381–406.

Hobbs, P. (2004), 'In their own voices: Codeswitching and code choice in the print and online versions of an African-American women's magazine', *Women and Language* 27(1): 1–12.

Hoffmann, C. (1995), 'Monolingualism, bilingualism, cultural pluralism and national identity: 20 years of language planning in contemporary Spain', *Current Issues in Language and Society* 1(3): 59–90.

Hoffman, K. (2006), 'Berber language ideologies, maintenance, and contraction: Gendered variation in the indigenous margins of Morocco', *Language and Communication* 26: 144–67.

Holes, C. (1983a), 'Bahraini dialects: Sectarian differences and the sedentary/nomadic split', *Zeitschrift für arabische Linguistik* 10: 7–38.

— (1983b), 'Patterns of communal language in Bahrain', *Language in Society* 12(4): 433–57.

— (1984), 'Bahraini dialects: Sectarian differences exemplified through texts', *Zeitschrift für arabische Linguistik* 13: 27–67.

— (1986), 'The social motivation for phonological convergence in three Arabic dialects', *International Journal of the Sociology of Language* 61: 33–51.

— (1993), 'The uses of variation: A study of the political speeches of Gamal Abd al-Nasir', *Perspectives on Arabic Linguistics* v: 13–45.

— (1995), 'Community, dialect, and urbanization in the Arabic-speaking Middle East', *Bulletin of the School of Oriental and African Studies* 58(2): 270–87.

— (1996), 'The Arabic dialects of South Eastern Arabia in a socio-historical perspective', *Zeitschrift für arabische Linguistik* 31: 34–56.

— (2004), *Modern Arabic: Structures, functions, and varieties*, Washington, DC: Georgetown University Press.

— (2005), 'Dialect and national identity: The cultural politics of self-representation in Bahraini musalsalaat', in P. Dresch and J. Piscatori (eds), *Monarchies and nations: Globalization and identity in the Arab states of the Gulf*, Reading: Tauris, 52–72.

— (2006a), 'Bahraini Arabic', lemma in K. Versteegh, M. Eid, A. Elgibali, M. Woidich and A. Zaborski (eds), *Encyclopedia of Arabic language and linguistics*, Leiden: Brill, i: 241–55.

— (2006b), 'Gulf States', lemma in K. Versteegh, M. Eid, A. Elgibali, M. Woidich and A. Zaborski (eds), *Encyclopedia of Arabic language and linguistics*, Leiden: Brill, ii: 210–16.

— (2007), '"Hello, I say, and welcome! Where from, these riding men?" Arabic popular poetry and political satire: A study in intertextuality from Jordan', in E. Ditters and H. Motzki (eds), *Approaches to Arabic linguistics: Presented to Kees Versteeth on the occasion of his sixtieth birthday*, Leiden: Brill, 543–63.

Holmes, J. (1992), *An introduction to sociolinguistics*, London: Longman.

— (1995), *Women, men and politeness*, London: Longman.

— (1998), 'Women's talk: The question of sociolinguistic universals', in J. Coates (ed.), *Language and gender: A reader*, Oxford: Blackwell, 461–83.

— (2004), 'Power, *lady*, and linguistic politeness in *Language and woman's place*', in M. Bucholtz (ed.), *Language and woman's place: Text and commentaries*, Oxford: Oxford University Press, 151–7.

Holmes, J. and M. Meyerhoff (eds) (2003a), *The handbook of language and gender*, Oxford: Blackwell.

— (2003b), 'Different voices, different views: An introduction to current research in language and gender', in J. Holmes and M. Meyerhoff (eds), *The handbook of language and gender*, Oxford: Blackwell, 1–17.

Holmes, J. and M. Stubbe (2003), '"Feminine" workplaces: Stereotype and reality', in J.

Holmes and M. Meyerhoff (eds), *The handbook of language and gender*, Oxford: Blackwell, 573–99.

Holmquist, J. C. (1985), 'Social correlates of a linguistic variable: A study in a Spanish village', *Language in Society* 14(2): 191–203.

Holt, M. (1994), 'Algeria: Language, nation, and state', in Y. Suleiman (ed.), *Arabic sociolinguistics: Issues and perspectives*, Richmond: Curzon, 25–41.

Houis, M. (1971), *Anthropologie linguistique de l'Afrique noire*, Paris: PUF.

Houtsma, M. T., T. W. Arnold, R. Basset and R. Hartmann (eds) (1913–36), *The Encyclopaedia of Islam: A dictionary of the geography, ethnography and biography of the Muhammadan peoples*, Leiden: Brill.

Hurreiz, S. H. (1978), 'Social stratification and linguistic variation in Khartoum and its vicinity', in R. Thelwall (ed.), *Aspects of language in the Sudan*, Ulster: New University of Ulster, 41–9.

Hymes, D. (2003), 'Models of the interaction of language and social life', in C. Paulston and R. Tucker (eds), *Sociolinguistics: The essential readings*, Oxford: Blackwell, 30–47.

Ibrahim, M. H. (1986), 'Standard and prestige language: A problem in Arabic sociolinguistics', *Anthropological Linguistics* 28(1): 115–26.

Iraqui-Sinaceur, Z. (1998), 'Le dialecte de Tanger', in J. Aguadé, P. Cressier and A. Vicente (eds), *Peuplement et arabisation au Maghreb occidental*, Madrid: Casa de Velázquez, 131–40.

Isaksson, B. (1999), 'The non-standard first person singular pronoun in the modern Arabic dialects', *Zeitschrift für arabische Linguistik* 37: 54–83.

Ismail, H. (2007), 'The urban and suburban modes: Patterns of linguistic variation and change in Damascus', in C. Miller, E. Al-Wer, D. Caubet and J. C. E. Watson (eds), *Arabic in the city: Issues in dialect contact and language variation*, London and New York: Routledge, 188–212.

Jabeur, M. (1987), 'A sociolinguistic study in Tunisia: Rhades', PhD Thesis, University of Reading.

— (1996), 'Women, social change, and linguistic variation in the urban dialect of Tunis', in C. Holes (ed.), *Proceedings of the 2nd conference of AIDA, held at Cambridge, 10–14 September 1995*, Cambridge: University Publications Centre, 85–94.

Jaffe, A. (2007), 'Codeswitching and stance: Issues in interpretation', *Journal of Language, Identity, and Education* 6(1): 53–77.

Jakobson, R. (1978 [1957]), 'Mufaxxama: The "emphatic" phonemes of Arabic', in S. Al-Ani (ed.), *Readings in Arabic linguistics*, Indiana: Indiana University Linguistics Club, 269–81.

James, D. and S. Clarke (1993), 'Women, men and interruptions: A critical review', in D. Tannen (ed.), *Gender and conversational interaction*, Oxford: Oxford University Press, 231–68.

James, D. and J. Drakich (1993), 'Understanding gender differences in amount of talk: A critical review of research', in D. Tannen (ed.), *Gender and conversational interaction*, Oxford: Oxford University Press, 281–312.

Jassem, Z. A. (1994), *Lectures in English and Arabic sociolinguistics*, Kuala Lumpur: Pustaka Antara.

Jastrow, O. (1978), *Die mesopotamisch-arabischen qəltu-Dialekte*, Wiesbaden: Franz Steiner.

— (2004), 'Jüdisches, christliches and muslimisches Arabisch in Mossul', in M. Haak, R. De Jong and K. Versteegh (eds), *Approaches to Arabic dialects: A collection of articles presented to Manfred Woidich on the occasion of his sixtieth birthday*, Leiden: Brill, 135–50.

Jernudd, B. H., M. H. Ibrahim and J. A. Fishman (1986), *Aspects of Arabic sociolinguistics*, Berlin: Mouton.

Johnstone, B. (1996), *The linguistic individual: Self-expression in language and linguistics*, Oxford: Oxford University Press.

Johnstone, B. and J. M. Bean (1997), 'Self-expression and linguistic variation', *Language in Society* 26(2): 221–46.
Kahlouche, R. (2004), 'Le berbère dans la politique linguistique algérienne', *Revue d'Aménagement Linguistique* 107(Winter): 103–32.
Kamhawi, D. L. W. (2001), 'Code-switching: A social phenomenon in Jordanian society', Master's dissertation, University of Edinburgh
Kanakri, A. (1984), 'Linguistic variation in the Jordanian Arabic dialect of males and females', Master's dissertation, Wayne State University.
Kapchan, D. (1996), *Gender on the market: Moroccan women and the revoicing of tradition*, Philadelphia: University of Pennsylvania Press.
Kaplan, R. B. and R. B. Baldauf (eds) (2007), *Language planning and policy in Africa. Vol. 2: Algeria, Côte d'Ivoire, Nigeria and Tunisia*, Clevedon: Multilingual Matters.
Keating, E. (1998), 'Honor and stratification in Pohnpei, Micronesia', *American Ethnologist* 25(3): 399–411.
Keddad, S. (1986), 'An analysis of French–Arabic code-switching in Algiers', PhD thesis, University of London.
Kedar, M. (1999), '"Arabness" in the Syrian media: Political messages conveyed by linguistic means', *International Journal of the Sociology of Language* 137: 141–6.
Keenan, E. (1974), 'Norm-makers, norm-breakers: Uses of speech by men and women in a Malagasy community', in R. Baumann and J. Sherzer (eds), *Explorations in the ethnography of speaking*, Cambridge: Cambridge University Press, 125–43.
Kendall, S. (2004), 'Mother's place in "Language and woman's place"', in M. Bucholtz (ed.), *Language and woman's place: Text and commentaries*, Oxford: Oxford University Press, 202–8.
Kenny, K. D. (2002), 'Code-switch fluency and language attrition in an Arab immigrant community', in A. Rouchdy (ed.), *Language contact and language conflict in Arabic: Variations on a sociolinguistic theme*, London: RoutledgeCurzon, 331–52.
Kiesling, S. F. (2003), 'Prestige, cultural models, and other ways of talking about underlying norms and gender', in J. Holmes and M. Meyerhoff (eds), *The handbook of language and gender*, Oxford: Blackwell, 509–27.
Khan, G. (1997), 'The Arabic dialect of the Karaite Jews of Hīt', *Zeitschrift für arabische Linguistik* 34: 53–102.
Kharraki, A. (2001), 'Moroccan sex-based linguistic difference in bargaining', *Discourse and Society* 12: 615–32.
Kroch, A. (1996), 'Dialect and style in the speech of upper class Philadelphia', in G. R. Guy, C. Feagin, D. Schiffrin and J. Baugh (eds), *Towards a social science of language. Vol. 1: Variation and change in language and society*, Amsterdam: Benjamins, 23–45.
Kuntjara, E. (2005), 'Gender and assertiveness: Bargaining in the traditional market in East Java', *Women and Language* 28(1): 54–61.
Labov, W. (1966), *The social stratification of English in New York City*, Washington, DC: Center for Applied Linguistics.
— (1971), 'The notion of "system" in creole studies', in D. Hymes (ed.), *Pidginization and creolization of languages*, Cambridge: Cambridge University Press, 447–72.
— (1972a), *Sociolinguistic patterns*, Philadelphia: University of Pennsylvania Press.
— (1972b), *Language in the inner city: Studies in the Black English vernacular*, Philadelphia: University of Pennsylvania Press.
— (1982), 'Building on empirical foundations', in W. Lehmann and Y. Malkiel (eds), *Perspectives on historical linguistics*, Amsterdam: Benjamins, 17–82.
— (1990), 'The intersection of sex and social class in the course of linguistic change', *Language Variation and Change* 2(2): 205–54.

— (2003 [1969]), 'Some sociolinguistic principles', in C. Paulston and R. G. Tucker (eds), *Sociolinguistics: The essential readings*, Oxford: Blackwell, 234–50.

Lahlou, M. (1991), 'A morpho-syntactic study of code switching between Moroccan Arabic and French', PhD thesis, University of Texas at Austin.

Lake, J. L. and C. Myers-Scotton (2002), 'Second generation shifts in sociopragmatic orientation and codeswitching patterns', in A. Rouchdy (ed.), *Language contact and language conflict in Arabic: Variations on a sociolinguistic theme*, London: RoutledgeCurzon, 317–30.

Lakoff, R. (2003a [1975]), 'Selections from "Language and woman's place"', in C. B. Paulston and R. G. Tucker (eds), *Sociolinguistics: The essential readings*, Oxford: Blackwell, 203–7.

— (2003b), 'Language, gender, and politics: Putting "women" and "power" in the same sentence', in J. Holmes and M. Meyerhoff (eds), *The handbook of language and gender*, Oxford: Blackwell, 159–78.

— (2006), 'Identity a la carte: You are what you eat', in A. De Fina, D. Schiffrin and M. Bamberg (eds), *Discourse and identity*, Cambridge: Cambridge University Press, 142–65.

Lambert, R. D. (1999), 'A scaffolding for language policy', *International Journal of the Sociology of Language* 137: 3–25.

Larson, K. (1982), 'Role playing and the real thing: Socialization and standard speech in Norway', *Journal of Anthropological Research* 38: 401–10.

Lawson-Sako, S. (2001), 'Assellema, ça va? Aspects of ethnolinguistic vitality, language attitudes and behaviour in Tunisia', PhD thesis, University of London.

Lawson-Sako, S. and I. Sachdev (1996), 'Ethnolinguistic communication in Tunisian streets', in Y. Suleiman (ed.), *Language and ethnic identity in the Middle East and North Africa*, Richmond: Curzon, 61–79.

Lawson-Sako, S. and I. Sachdev (2000), 'Codeswitching in Tunisia: Attitudinal and behavioural dimensions', *Journal of Pragmatics* 32(9): 1343–61.

Leet-Pellegrini, H. M. (1980), 'Conversational dominance as a function of gender and expertise', in H. Giles, P. Robinson and P. M. Smith (eds), *Language: Social psychological perspectives*, Oxford: Pergamon, 97–104.

Lentin, J. (1981) 'Remarques sociolinguistiques sur l'arabe parlé à Damas', Professorial thesis, University of Paris III, Sorbonne Nouvelle.

Lesch, A. M. (1998), *Sudan: Contested national identities*, Bloominton: Indiana University Press.

Lewis, J. E. (2004), 'Freedom of speech – in any language', *Middle East Quarterly* 11(3): 1–10.

Lipski, J. (1977), 'Code-switching and the problem of bilingual competence', in M. Paradis (ed.), *Aspects of bilingualism*, Columbia, SC: Hornbeam Press, 250–63.

Luke, A., C. Luke and P. W. Graham (2007), 'Globalization, corporatism, and critical language education', *International Multilingual Research Journal* 1(1): 1–13.

MacSwan, J. (2005), 'Codeswitching and generative grammar: A critique of the MLF model and some remarks on "modified minimalism"', *Bilingualism: Language and Cognition* 8(1): 1–22.

Maddy-Weitzmann, B. and D. Zisenwine (eds) (2007), *The Maghrib in the new century: Identity, religion and politics*, Gainesville, FL: University of Florida Press.

Mahé , A. (2001), *Histoire de la grande Kabylie (XIXe–XXe siècles): Anthropologie historique du lien social dans les communautés villageoises*, Paris: Editions Bouchène.

Mahfouz, N. (2001), *The Cairo trilogy*, London: Everyman.

Mahmud, U. A. (1979), 'Variation and change in the aspectual system of Juba Arabic', PhD thesis, Georgetown University.

Maïz, M. and A. Rouadjia (2005). 'Quelles langues pour l'enseignement des sciences? Arabe, français ou anglais?', *El Watan* (28 December), 13.

Maltz, D. and R. Borker (1982), 'A cultural approach to male–female miscommunication', in

J. Gumperz (ed.), *Language and social identity*, Cambridge: Cambridge University Press, 196–216

Mansfield, P. (2003), *A history of the Middle East*, 2nd edn, New York: Penguin.

Marley, D. (2000), 'Interactions between French and Islamic cultures in the Maghreb', http://www.surrey.ac.uk/LIS/MNP/may2000/Marley.html, accessed 21 October 2008.

— (2004), 'Language attitudes in Morocco following recent changes in language policy', *Language Policy* 3: 25–46.

Mar-Molinero, C. and P. Stevenson (eds) (2006), *Language ideologies, policies and practices: Language and the future of Europe*, Basingstoke: Palgrave Macmillan.

Mazraani, N. (1997), *Aspects of language variation in Arabic political speech-making*, Richmond: Curzon.

McCarus, E. N. (2007), 'Modern standard Arabic', lemma in K. Versteegh, M. Eid, A. Elgibali, M. Woidich and A. Zaborski (eds), *Encyclopedia of Arabic language and linguistics*, Leiden: Brill, iii: 238–62.

McConnell-Ginet, S. (2003), '"What's in a name?" Social labelling and gender practices', in J. Holmes and M. Meyerhoff (eds), *The handbook of language and gender*, Oxford: Blackwell, 69–97.

— (2004), 'Positioning ideas and gendered subjects: "Women's language" revisited', in M. Bucholtz (ed.), *Language and woman's place: Text and commentaries*, Oxford: Oxford University Press, 136–42.

McElhinny, B. (2003), 'Theorizing gender in sociolinguistics and linguistic anthropology', in J. Holmes and M. Meyerhoff (eds), *The handbook of language and gender*, Oxford: Blackwell, 21–42.

McFerren, M. (1984), *Arabization in the Maghreb*, Washington, DC: Center for Applied Linguistics.

McOmber, M. L. (1996), 'Phonemic pharyngalization', *Perspectives on Arabic Linguistics* viii: 233–58.

Meiseles, G. (1980), 'Educated spoken Arabic and the Arabic language continuum', *Archivum Linguisticum* 11(2): 118–48.

Mejdell, G. (1996), 'Some sociolinguistic concepts of style and stylistic variation in spoken Arabic, with reference to Nagib Mahfuz talking about his life', in J. R. Smart (ed.), *Tradition and modernity in Arabic language and literature*, Richmond: Curzon, 316–26.

— (1999), 'Switching, mixing – code interaction in spoken Arabic', in B. Brendemoen, E. Lanza and E. Ryen (eds), *Language encounters across time and space*, Oslo: Novus, 225–41.

— (2006), *Mixed styles in spoken Arabic in Egypt*, Leiden: Brill.

Messaoudi, L. (2001), 'Urbanisation linguistique et dynamique langagière dans la ville de Rabat', in T. Bulot, C. Bauvois and P. Blanchet (eds), *Sociolinguistique urbaine: Variations linguistiques, images urbaines et sociales*, Rennes: Presses de l'Université de Rennes, 87–98.

— (2002), 'Le parler ancien de Rabat face a l'urbanisation linguistique', in A. Youssi (ed.), *Proceedings of the 4th International Conference of AIDA, held at Marrakesh, 1–4 April 2000*, Rabat: Amapatril, 223–33.

Miller, C. (1997), 'Pour une étude du contact dialectal en zone urbaine', in B. Cameron (ed.), *Proceedings of the 16th International Conference of Linguistics*, Oxford: Pergamon, no. 0106.

— (2002), 'Jeux de langues: Humour and codeswitching in the Maghreb', in A. Rouchdy (ed.), *Language contact and language conflict in Arabic: Variations on a sociolinguistic theme*, London: RoutledgeCurzon, 233–55.

— (2003), 'Linguistic policies and the issue of ethno-linguistic minorities in the Middle East', in A. Usuki and H. Kato (eds), *Islam in the Middle Eastern studies: Muslims and minorities*, Osaka: Japan Center for Area Studies, 149–74.

— (2004), 'Variation and change in Arabic urban vernaculars', in M. Haak, R. De Jong and

K. Versteegh (eds), *Approaches to Arabic dialects: A collection of articles presented to Manfred Woidich on the occasion of his sixtieth birthday*, Leiden: Brill, 177–206.

— (2007), 'Arabic urban vernaculars: Development and change', in C. Miller, E. Al-Wer, D. Caubet and J. C. E. Watson (eds), *Arabic in the city: Issues in dialect contact and language variation*, London and New York: Routledge, 1–31.

Miller, C. and A. Abu-Manga (1992), *Language change and national integration: The Sudan*, Khartoum: Khartoum University Press.

Miller, C., E. Al-Wer, D. Caubet and J. C. E. Watson (eds) (2007), *Arabic in the city: Issues in dialect contact and language variation*, London and New York: Routledge.

Mills, S. (2004), 'Class, gender and politeness', *Multilingua* 23: 171–90.

— (2005), 'Gender and impoliteness', *Journal of Politeness Research* 1: 263–80.

Milroy, L. (1987), *Language and social networks*, Oxford: Blackwell.

Milroy, L. and M. Gordon (2003), *Sociolinguistics: Method and interpretation*, Oxford: Blackwell.

Minai, N. (1981), *Women in Islam: Tradition and transition in the Middle East*, New York: Seaview Books.

Mitchell, T. F. (1986), 'What is educated spoken Arabic?', *International Journal of the Sociology of Language* 61: 7–32.

Morsly, D. (1984), 'L'enseignement du français et de l'arabe en Algérie pendant la période coloniale', in C. Achour (ed.), *Réflexions sur la culture*, Algiers: Office des Publications Universitaires, 33–43.

Mortimer, R. (2007), 'Algerian identity and memory', in B. Maddy-Weitzmann and D. Zisenwine (eds), *The Maghrib in the new century: Identity, religion and politics*, Gainesville, FL: University of Florida Press, 36–49.

Moseley, C. and R.E. Asher (eds) (1994), *Atlas of the world's languages*, London: Routledge.

Mostari, H. (2004), 'A sociolinguistic perspective on Arabisation and language use in Algeria', *Language Problems and Language Planning* 28(1): 25–44.

Mugaddam, A. H. (2006), 'Language maintenance and shift in Sudan: The case of migrant ethnic groups in Khartoum', *International Journal of the Sociology of Language* 181: 123–36.

Myers-Scotton, C. (1986), 'Diglossia and code switching', in J. A. Fishman, A. Tabouret-Keller, M. Clyne, B. Krishnamurti and M. Abdulaziz (eds), *The Fergusonian impact*, Berlin: Mouton, 403–15.

— (1993), *Social motivations for code switching: Evidence from Africa*, Oxford: Oxford University Press.

— (1997), *Duelling languages*, Oxford: Clarendon Press.

— (1998a), 'A way to dusty death: The matrix language turnover hypothesis', in L. Gernoble and L. Whaley (eds), *Endangered languages: Language loss and community response*, Cambridge: Cambridge University Press, 289–316.

— (ed.) (1998b), *Codes and consequences: Choosing linguistic varieties*, Oxford: Oxford University Press.

— (2004a), 'Precision tuning of the Matrix Language Frame (MLF) model of codeswitching', *Sociolinguistica* 18: 106–17.

— (2004b), 'Research note and erratum', *Bilingualism: Language and Cognition* 7(1): 89–90.

— (2006), *Multiple voices: An introduction to bilingualism*, Malden, MA: Blackwell.

Nait M'barek, M. and D. Sankoff (1988), 'Le discours mixte arabe/français: Emprunts ou alternances de langue', *Canadian Journal of Linguistics* 33(2): 143–54.

Nevo, M. (1999), 'Notes on the Judaeo-Arabic dialect of Siverek', *Zeitschrift für arabische Linguistik* 36: 66–84.

Nichols, P. (1983), 'Linguistic options and choices for Black women in the rural South', in B. Thorne, N. Henley and C. Kramarae (eds), *Language, gender and society*, Newbury, MA: Newbury House, 54–68.

Niehoff-Panagiotidis, J. (1994), *Koine und Diglossie*, Wiesbaden: Harrassowitz.

Nielsen, H. L. (1996), 'How to teach Arabic communicatively: Toward a theoretical framework for TAFL', in A. Elgibali (ed.), *Understanding Arabic*, Cairo: AUC Press, 211–39.

Nordberg, B. and E. Sundgren (1998), *On observing language change: A Swedish case study*, Uppsala: Institutionen för nordiska språk.

O'Barr, W. M. and B. K. Atkins (1980), '"Women's Language" or "powerless language"?', in S. McConnell-Ginet, R. Borker and N. Furman (eds), *Women and languages in literature and society*, New York: Praeger, 93–110.

Ochs, E. (1991), 'Indexing gender', in A. Duranti and C. Goodwin (eds), *Rethinking context: Language as an interactive phenomenon*, Cambridge: Cambridge University Press, 335–58.

Omoniyi, T. and G. White (2006), *The sociolinguistics of identity*, London: Continuum.

Owens, J. (1995), 'Minority languages and urban norms: A case study', *Linguistics* 33: 305–58.

— (2000), *Arabic as a minority language*, Berlin and New York: Mouton.

— (2001), 'Arabic sociolinguistics', *Arabica* 48: 419–69.

— (2007), 'Close encounters of a different kind: Two types of insertion in Nigerian Arabic codeswitching', in C. Miller, E. Al-Wer, D. Caubet and J. C. E. Watson (eds), *Arabic in the city: Issues in dialect contact and language variation*, London and New York: Routledge, 249–74.

Owens, J. and R. Bani-Yasin (1987), 'The lexical basis of variation in Jordanian Arabic', *Linguistics* 25(4): 705–38.

Palesterian National Authority, Ministry of Education (1998), http://www.pcdc.edu.ps/Arabic/secondary_education_plan.pdf, last accessed 17 October 2008.

Palva, H. (1969), *Notes on classicization in modern colloquial Arabic*, Helsinki: Snallmanink.

— (1982), 'Patterns of koineization in modern colloquial Arabic', *Acta Orientalia* 43: 13–32.

— (2006), 'Dialects: Classification', lemma in K. Versteegh, M. Eid, A. Elgibali, M. Woidich and A. Zaborski (eds), *Encyclopedia of Arabic language and linguistics*, Leiden: Brill, i: 604–13.

Parkinson, D. B. (1985), *Constructing the social context of communication: Terms of address in Egyptian Arabic*, Berlin: Mouton.

— (2003), 'Verbal features in oral fusha in Cairo', *International Journal of the Sociology of Language* 163: 27–41.

Paulston, C. B. (1994), *Linguistic minorities in multilingual settings*, Amsterdam: Benjamins.

Paulston, C. B. and R. G. Tucker (eds) (2003), *Sociolinguistics: The essential readings*, Oxford: Blackwell.

Pereira, C. (2007), 'Urbanization and dialect change: The Arabic dialect of Tripoli (Libya)', in C. Miller, E. Al-Wer, D. Caubet and J. C. E. Watson (eds), *Arabic in the city: Issues in dialect contact and language variation*, London and New York: Routledge, 77–96.

Philips, S. U. (2003), 'The power of gender ideologies in discourse', in J. Holmes and M. Meyerhoff (eds), *The handbook of language and gender*, Oxford: Blackwell, 252–76.

Preisler, B. (1986), *Linguistic sex roles in conversation*, Berlin: Mouton.

Ricento, T. (2006), 'Americanization, language ideologies and the construction of European identities', in C. Mar-Molinero and P. Stevenson (eds), *Language ideologies, policies and practices: Language and the future of Europe*, Basingstoke: Palgrave Macmillan, 44–57.

Rizq, S. (2007), 'The language of Cairo's young university students', in C. Miller, E. Al-Wer, D. Caubet and J. C. E. Watson (eds), *Arabic in the city: Issues in dialect contact and language variation*, London and New York: Routledge, 291–308.

Roberts, I. (1997), *Comparative syntax*, London: Arnold.

Romaine, S. (ed.) (1982), *Sociolinguistic variation in speech communities*, London: Edward Arnold.

— (1995), *Bilingualism*, Oxford: Blackwell.

— (1998), 'Why women are supposed to talk like ladies: The glamour of grammar', in N. Warner, J. Ahlers, L. Bilmes, M. Oliver, S. Wertheim and M. Chen (eds), *Gender and belief systems: Proceedings of the third Berkeley Women and Language Conference*, Berkeley, CA: Berkeley Women and Language Group.

— (2003), 'Variation in language and gender', in J. Holmes and M. Meyerhoff (eds), *The handbook of language and gender*, Oxford: Blackwell, 98–118.

Rosenbaum, G. M. (2000), '"Fushammiyya": Alternating style in Egyptian prose', *Zeitschrift für arabische Linguistik* 38: 68–87.

Rosenhouse, J. (2001), 'A comparative analysis of stories narrated by Bedouin and sedentary male and female speakers', *Zeitschrift für arabische Linguistik* 39: 64–83.

Rouchdy, A. (ed.) (1992), *The Arabic language in America*, Detroit: Wayne State University Press.

— (2002), *Language contact and language conflict in Arabic: Variations on a sociolinguistic theme*, London: RoutledgeCurzon.

Roux, A. (1952), 'Quelques mots sur le langage des musulmanes marocaines', *Orbis* 1: 376–84.

Royal, A. M. (1985), 'Male/female pharyngalization patterns in Cairo Arabic: A sociolinguistic study of two neighbourhoods', PhD thesis, University of Texas.

Russell, M. (1994), *Cultural reproduction in Egypt's private university*, PhD thesis, University of Kentucky.

Ryding, K. C. (2005), *A reference grammar of Modern Standard Arabic*, Cambridge and New York: Cambridge University Press.

Saad, Z. (1992), 'Language planning and policy attitudes: A case study of Arabization in Algeria', PdD thesis, Columbia University.

Sadiqi, F. (1991), 'The spread of English in Morocco', *International Journal of the Sociology of Language* 87: 99–114.

— (1995), 'The language of women in the city of Fès, Morocco', *International Journal of the Sociology of Language* 112: 63–79.

— (1997), 'The place of Berber in Morocco', *International Journal of the Sociology of Language* 123: 7–21.

— (2002), 'The language of introduction in the city of Fès: The gender–identity interaction', in A. Rouchdy (ed.), *Language contact and language conflict in Arabic: Variations on a sociolinguistic theme*, London: RoutledgeCurzon, 116–48.

— (2003a), *Women, gender and language in Morocco*, Leiden: Brill.

— (2003b), 'Women and linguistic space in Morocco', *Women and Language* 26(1): 35–43.

— (2006), 'Language and gender', lemma in K. Versteegh, M. Eid, A. Elgibali, M. Woidich and A. Zaborski (eds), *Encyclopedia of Arabic language and linguistics*, Leiden: Brill, ii: 642–50.

Safi, S. (1992), 'Functions of code switching: Saudi Arabic in the United States', in A. Rouchdy (ed.), *The Arabic language in America*, Detroit: Wayne State University Press, 72–80.

Salami, L. O. (1991), 'Diffusing and focussing: Phonological variation and social networks in Ife-Ife, Nigeria', *Language in Society* 20(2): 217–45.

Sallo, I. K. (1994), 'Code-switching at the university: A sociolinguistic study', in R. de Beaugrande, A. Shunnaq and M. H. Heliel (eds), *Language, discourse and translation in the West and Middle East*, Amsterdam: Benjamins, 115–32.

Sankoff, D. and S. Poplack (1981), 'A formal grammar for code switching', *Papers in Linguistics* 14: 3–45.

Sankoff, D., S. Poplack and S. Vanniarajan (1990), 'The case of the nonce loan in Tamil', *Language Variation and Change* 2: 71–101.

Sawaie, M. (1986), 'Arabic language academies as language planners', in N. Schweda-Nicholson (ed.), *Languages in the international perspective*, Norwood, NJ: Ablex, 56–65.

— (2006), 'Language academies', lemma in K. Versteegh, M. Eid, A. Elgibali, M. Woidich and A. Zaborski (eds), *Encyclopedia of Arabic language and linguistics*, Leiden: Brill, ii: 634–42.

Schaub, M. (2000), 'English in the Arab Republic of Egypt', *World Englishes* 19(2): 225–38.
Schick-Case, S. (1988), 'Cultural differences, not deficiencies: An analysis of managerial women's language', in S. Rose and L. Larwood (eds), *Women's careers: Pathways and pitfalls*, New York: Praeger, 41–63.
Schieffelin, B. B., K. A. Woolard and Paul V. Kroskrity (eds) (1998), *Language ideologies: Practice and theory*, Oxford: Oxford University Press.
Schiffman, H. R. (1996), *Linguistic culture and language policy*, London: Routledge.
Schmidt, R. W. (1974), 'Sociostylistic variation in spoken Egyptian Arabic: A re-examination of the concept of diglossia', PhD thesis, Brown University.
Schulz, D. E. (1981), 'Diglossia and variation in formal spoken Arabic in Egypt', PhD thesis, University of Wisconsin-Madison.
Scotton, C. M. and W. Ury (1977), 'Bilingual strategies: The social functions of code switching', *Linguistics* 193: 5–20.
Sellam, A. (1990), 'Aspects of the communicative approach to language teaching', *Revue de la Faculté des Lettres* 1(1): 81–93.
Shaaban, K. (2006), 'Language policies and language planning', lemma in K. Versteegh, M. Eid, A. Elgibali, M. Woidich and A. Zaborski (eds), *Encyclopedia of Arabic language and linguistics*, Leiden: Brill, ii: 694–707.
Shaaban, K. and G. Ghaith (1999), 'Lebanon's language-in-education policies: From bilingualism to trilingualism', *Language Problems and Language Planning* 23(1): 1–16.
— (2002), 'University students' perceptions of the ethnolinguistic vitality of Arabic, French and English in Lebanon', *Journal of Sociolinguistics* 6(4): 557–74.
Sharkey, H. J. (2008), 'Arab identity and ideology in the Sudan: The politics of language, ethnicity, and race', *African Affairs* 107/426: 21–43.
S'hiri, S. (2002), 'Speak Arabic, please! Tunisian Arabic speakers' linguistic accommodation to Middle Easterners', in A. Rouchdy (ed.), *Language contact and language conflict in Arabic: Variations on a sociolinguistic theme*, London: RoutledgeCurzon, 149–74.
Shorrab, G. (1986), 'Bilingual patterns of an Arabic-English speech community', *International Journal of the Sociology of Language* 61: 79–88.
Shraybom-Shivtiel, S. (1999), 'Language and political change in modern Egypt', *International Journal of the Sociology of Language* 137: 131–40.
Shuy, R. W. (2003 [1990]), 'A brief history of American sociolinguistics', in C. B. Paulston and R. G. Tucker (eds), *Sociolinguistics: The essential readings*, Oxford: Blackwell, 4–16.
Sidnell, J. (2003), 'Constructing and managing male exclusivity in talk-in-interaction', in J. Holmes and M. Meyerhoff (eds), *The handbook of language and gender*, Oxford: Blackwell, 327–52.
Silverstein, M. (1996), 'Indexical order and the dialectics of sociolinguistic life', in R. Ide, R. Parker and Y. Sunaoshi (eds), *Salsa III: Proceedings of the Third Annual Symposium about Language and Society*, Austin: University of Texas, Department of Linguistics, 266–95
Silverstein, P. A. (2007), 'The Maghrib abroad: Immigrant transpolitics and cultural involution in France', in B. Maddy-Weitzmann and D. Zisenwine (eds), *The Maghrib in the new century: Identity, religion and politics*, Gainesville, FL: University of Florida Press, 237–66.
Sirles, C. A. (1985), 'An evaluative procedure for language planning: The case of Morocco', PhD thesis, Northwestern University.
— (1999), 'Politics and Arabization: The evolution of post-independence North Africa', *International Journal of the Sociology of Language* 137: 115–29.
Smith-Hefner, N. J. (1988), 'Women and politeness: The Javanese example', *Language in Society* 17(4): 535–54.
Sperber, D. and D. Wilson (1986), 'Loose talk', *Proceedings of the Aristotelian Society*, NS 6: 153–71.

Spolsky, B. (1994), 'The situation of Arabic in Israel', in Y. Suleiman (ed.), *Arabic sociolinguistics: Issues and perspectives*, Richmond: Curzon, 227–34.

— (2004), *Language policy*, Cambridge: Cambridge University Press.

Spolsky, B. and E. Shohamy (1999), *The languages of Israel: Policy, ideology, and practice*, Clevedon: Multilingual Matters.

Spolsky, B., H. Tushyeh, M. Amara and K. Bot (2000), *Languages in Bethlehem: The sociolinguistic transformation of a Palestinian town*, Amsterdam: Royal Tropical Institute.

Stapleton, K. (2003), 'Gender and swearing: A community practice', *Women and Language* 26(2): 23–33.

Stevenson, P. (2005), '"National" languages in transnational contexts: Language, migration and citizenship in Europe', in C. Mar-Molinero and P. Stevenson (eds), *Language ideologies, policies and practices: Language and the future of Europe*, Basingstoke: Palgrave, 147–61.

Stillman, N. A. and Y. K. Stillman (1978), 'The art of a Moroccan folk poetess', *Zeitschrift der deutschen Morgenländischen Gesellschaft* 128: 65–89.

Stokoe, E. H. (2005), 'Analysing language and gender', *Journal of Sociolinguistics* 9(1): 118–33.

Stokoe, E. H. and J. Smithson (2001), 'Making gender relevant: Conversation analysis and gender categories in inderaction', *Discourse and Society* 12(2): 217–44.

Stora, B. (2001), *Algeria 1830–2000: A short history*, Ithaca, NY: Cornell University Press.

Stroomer, H. (2004), 'The Arabic dialect of women in Meknès (Morocco): Gender linked sound changes?', in M. Haak, R. De Jong and K. Versteegh (eds), *Approaches to Arabic dialects: A collection of articles presented to Manfred Woidich on the occasion of his sixtieth birthday*, Leiden: Brill, 291–307.

Suleiman, S. M. K. (1985), *Jordanian Arabic between diglossia and bilingualism: Linguistic analysis*, Amsterdam and Philadelphia: Benjamins.

Suleiman, Y. (1994), *Arabic sociolinguistics: Issues and perspectives*, Richmond: Curzon.

— (ed.) (1999), *Language and society in the Middle East and North Africa: Studies in variation and identity*, Richmond: Curzon.

— (2003), *The Arabic language and national identity: A study in ideology*, Edinburgh: Edinburgh University Press.

— (2004), *A war of words: Language and conflict in the Middle East*, Cambridge: Cambridge University Press.

— (2006a), 'The betweenness of identity: Language in trans-national literature', in Z. S. Salhi and I. R. Netton (eds), *The Arab diaspora: Voices of an anguished scream*, London: Routledge, 11–25.

— (2006b), 'Charting the nation: Arabic and the politics of identity', *Annual Review of Applied Linguistics* 26: 125–48.

Syria, Ministry of Education (2008), http://syrianeducation.org.sy/nstyle/index.php?op=articulos&task=verart&aid=394, last accessed 17 October 2008.

Taine-Cheikh, C. (2007), 'The (r)urbanization of Mauritania: Historical context and contemporary developments, in C. Miller, E. Al-Wer, D. Caubet and J. C. E. Watson (eds), *Arabic in the city: Issues in dialect contact and language variation*, London and New York: Routledge, 35–54.

Talbot, M. (2003), 'Gender stereotypes: Reproduction and challenge', in J. Holmes and M. Meyerhoff (eds), *The handbook of language and gender*, Oxford: Blackwell, 468–86.

Talmoudi, F. (1984), *The diglossic situation in North Africa: A study of classical Arabic/dialectal Arabic diglossia with sample text in 'mixed Arabic'*, Göteborg: Acta Universitatis Gothoburgensis.

Tannen, D. (1990), *You just don't understand: Women and men in conversation*, New York: William Morrow.

— (ed.) (1993), *Gender and conversational interaction*, Oxford: Oxford University Press.

— (1994), *Gender and discourse*, Oxford: Oxford University Press.

— (1998), 'The relativity of linguistic strategies: Rethinking power and solidarity in gender and dominance', in D. Cameron (ed.), *The feminist critique of language: A reader*, London: Routledge, 261–79.

— (2004), 'Cultural patterning in "Language and woman's place"', in M. Bucholtz (ed.), *Language and woman's place: Text and commentaries*, Oxford: Oxford University Press, 158–64.

Temim, D. (2006), 'Politiques scholaire et linguistique: quelle(s) perspective(s) pour l'Algérie?', *Le Français Aujourd'hui* 154: 19–24.

Thakerar, J., H. Giles and J. Cheshire (1982), 'Psychological and linguistic parameters of speech accommodation theory', in C. Fraser and K. R. Scherer (eds), *Advances in the social psychology of language*, Cambridge: Cambridge University Press, 205–55.

Thimm, C., S. C. Koch and S. Schey (2003), 'Communicating gendered professional identity: Competence, cooperation, and conflict in the workplace', in J. Holmes and M. Meyerhoff (eds), *The handbook of language and gender*, Oxford: Blackwell, 528–49.

Thomason, S. G. (2001), *Language contact: An introduction*, Washington, DC: Georgetown University Press.

Thorne, B. and N. Henley (1975), *Language and sex: Difference and dominance*, Rowley, MA: Newbury House.

Tigrizi, N. (2004), 'Les langues dans les constitutions algériennes', *Cahiers de l'ILSL* 17: 289–99.

Tocqueville, A. de (2001), *Writings on empire and slavery*, ed. and trans. J. Pitts, Baltimore: Johns Hopkins University Press.

Tomiche, N. (1968), 'La situation linguistique en Egypte', in A. Martinet (ed.), *Le language*, Paris: Encyclopédie de la Pléiade, 1173–87.

Trabelsi, C. (1988), 'Les usages linguistiques des femmes de Tunis', Professorial thesis, University of Paris III.

Trudgill, P. (1972), 'Sex, covert prestige, and linguistic change in the urban British English of Norwich', *Language in Society* 1: 215–46.

— (1974), *The social differentiation of English in Norwich*, Cambridge: Cambridge University Press.

— (1983), *On dialect: Social and geographical perspectives*, Oxford: Blackwell.

— (1986), *Dialects in contact*, Oxford: Blackwell.

Unesco (2007), *World data on education*, 6th edn, http://www.ibe.unesco.org/Countries/WDE/2006/index.html, last accessed 20 October 2008.

Versteegh, K. (1984), *Pidginization and creolization: The case of Arabic*, Amsterdam: Benjamins.

— (1993), 'Levelling in the Sudan: From Arabic creole to Arabic dialect', *International Journal of the Sociology of Language* 99: 65–79.

— (2001), *The Arabic language*, Edinburgh: Edinburgh University Press.

— (2004), 'Pidginization and creolization revisited: The case of Arabic', in M. Haak, R. de Jong and K. Versteegh (eds), *Approaches to Arabic dialects: A collection of articles presented to Manfred Woidich on the occasion of his sixtieth birthday*, Leiden: Brill, 343–57.

Versteegh, K., M. Eid, A. Elgibali, M. Woidich and A. Zabroski (eds) (2006–7), *Encyclopedia of Arabic language and linguistics*, Leiden: Brill.

Walters, K. (1988), 'Dialectology', in F. J. Newmeyer (ed.), *Linguistics: The Cambridge survey*, Cambridge: Cambridge University Press, iv: 119–39.

— (1991), 'Women, men, and linguistic variation in the Arab world', *Perspectives on Arabic Linguistics* iii: 199–229.

— (1996a), 'Diglossia, linguistic variation, and language change in Arabic', *Perspectives on Arabic Linguistics* viii: 157–97.

— (1996b), 'Gender, identity, and the political economy of language: Anglophone wives in Tunisia', *Language in Society* 25(4): 515–55.
— (2003), 'Fergie's prescience: The changing nature of diglossia in Tunisia', *International Journal of the Sociology of Language* 163: 77–109.
— (2006a), 'Communal dialects', lemma in K. Versteegh, M. Eid, A. Elgibali, M. Woidich and A. Zaborski (eds), *Encyclopedia of Arabic language and linguistics*, Leiden: Brill, i: 442–8.
— (2006b), 'Language attitudes', lemma in K. Versteegh, M. Eid, A. Elgibali, M. Woidich and A. Zaborski (eds), *Encyclopedia of Arabic language and linguistics*, Leiden: Brill, ii: 650–64 .
Watson, J. (2003), 'Insiders, outsiders, and language development in San'a', in I. Ferrando and J. J. Sánchez Sandoval (eds), *AIDA: 5th conference proceedings: Cádiz, September 2002*, Cadiz: Universidad de Cádiz, 561–70.
— (2007), 'Linguistic leveling in Sanՙani Arabic as reflected in a popular radio serial', in C. Miller, E. Al-Wer, D. Caubet and J. C. E. Watson (eds), *Arabic in the city: Issues in dialect contact and language variation*, London and New York: Routledge, 166–87.
Weinreich, U. (1953), *Languages in contact: Findings and problems*, New York: Linguistic Circle of New York.
Wernberg-Moller, A. (1999), 'Sociolinguistic meaning in code-switching: The case of Moroccans in Edinburgh', in Y. Suleiman (ed.), *Language and society in the Middle East and North Africa: Studies in variation and identity*, Richmond: Curzon, 234–58.
Whiteley, W. (1969), *Swahili: The rise of a national language*, London: Methuen.
Wodak, R. (2003), 'Multiple identities: The roles of female parliamentarians in the EU parliament', in J. Holmes and M. Meyerhoff (eds), *The handbook of language and gender*, Oxford: Blackwell, 671–98.
Woidich, M. (1994), 'Cairo Arabic and the Egyptian dialects', in D. Caubet and M. Vanhove (eds), *Actes des Premières Journées Internationales de Dialectologie Arabe de Paris: Colloque international tenu à Paris du 27 au 30 janvier 1993*, Paris: Langues'O, 493–507.
Woolard, K. A. (2004), 'Codeswitching', in A. Duranti (ed.), *Companion to linguistic anthropology*, Oxford: Blackwell, 73–94.
Wright, S. (2004), *Language policy and language planning: From nationalism to globalisation*, New York: Palgrave Macmillan.
Yokwe, E. M. (1984), 'Arabicization and language policy in the Sudan', *Studies in the Linguistic Sciences* 14(2): 157–70.
Ziamari, K. (2007), 'Development and linguistic change in Moroccan Arabic–French codeswitching', in C. Miller, E. Al-Wer, D. Caubet and J. C. E. Watson (eds), *Arabic in the city: Issues in dialect contact and language variation*, London and New York: Routledge, 275–90.
Zuhur, S. (2005), *The Middle East: Politics, history and neonationalism*, [s.l.]: Institute of Middle Eastern, Islamic, and Diasporic Studies.

Index

CPSIA information can be obtained
at www.ICGtesting.com
Printed in the USA
LVOW13s0923110318
568755LV00025B/97/P

9 781589 015739